Dawn of Darkness

Daeva: Book One

Daniel A. Kaine

DEDICATION

To Vic. You are an incredible person, deserving of so much happiness. I hope all your dreams come true, and that you succeed in saving the world. And at the risk of sounding sappy and ripping off Avatar... I see you.

ACKNOWLEDGMENTS

I'd like to say a big thanks to Amy Marshall. I can't believe how much time has passed already since we started trading chapters on the NaNoWriMo forums. I honestly believe that without you, and your encouragement, that I might have quit early. You believed in me, and for that I am eternally grateful. Keep at the writing, because you are fantastic, and the world needs to know who you are.

To Patricia Lynne, and MaryBeth Mulhall. You guys are awesome. You've kept my head up, made me laugh and smile, through the drudgery that is editing and formatting. I wish you guys all the success in the world with your own ventures.

And to Michael. I love you, always. P.S. Write your damn book already! I'm still waiting to read it.

Chapter 1

"I'm not taking no for an answer."

I opened my eyes to see my room-mate leaning against the off-white wall next to my bed. I groaned and rolled over, facing away from him. There was a sharp prod in my side, and then another.

"I'll stop if you say yes," he said, poking me over and over again. I tried to slap his hand away, becoming increasingly annoyed with him, but he caught my wrist in one hand and continued his assault with the other. "Come on, it'll be fun."

"Dammit, Ash! I'm not going, so just leave me alone."

He dropped my wrist and let out a dejected sigh. Ash had been pestering me for several hours to join him and the rest of our squad in celebration of our last night as cadets. I didn't care much for socialising, least of all when it involved alcohol. The thought of having my inhibitions lowered did not appeal to me in the slightest. Not to mention being hung over the next morning.

Still, Ash was nothing, if not persistent, and I could hardly kick him out of his own room. Not that I would have been able to manage if I tried. At six foot, Ash towered over the bed. His blond hair was cut short and spiked, complimenting his olive complexion and crystal blue eyes. A black tank-top stretched across his chest and abs, showing off his rather athletic build.

"Please, Mik?"

"I'm tired, okay? The General made me spend all evening washing the transports for that comment I made earlier."

"He never did have much of a sense of humour." Ash laughed, and then his smile dropped. "Please come celebrate with us. It wouldn't be right without the whole squad there."

"No."

"Mikhail, I will drag you out if I have to," he said, his arms folded across his chest. I rolled over again and tried to ignore him. I closed my eyes and heard footsteps moving away from me. Just when I thought he had given up, his hands locked around my ankles. I gave a surprised yelp as he began pulling me towards the bottom of the bed. My hands grasped at the bed, desperate for something to hold onto. They found only the covers, which slipped through my fingers.

"Okay, fine! Fine." Ash stopped. I sat up and groaned. I glared at him, my brown eyes locked in mental combat with his. The edges of his mouth crept upwards, and he gave a quick snigger as he made his way into the adjoining bathroom.

I stood, opened the nearby wardrobe and reached for a black jumper. I pulled it on over my t-shirt before ruffling my hair until it looked presentable. Whereas Ash's hair was always neat, mine was a mess of black waves. Almost being dragged off the bed hadn't helped.

Meanwhile, Ash had emerged from the bathroom. He squeezed past me, through the gap between the wardrobe and my bed, and picked up some deodorant from the bedside table. I jumped, feeling a firm pinch on my backside, and smacked the hand away. He flashed me a toothy grin.

"Bastard," I muttered under my breath. I'm sure he heard me, not that it would ever deter him. Ash was openly bisexual and had a bit of a reputation for getting around the block. I may only have known Ash for a year, but I knew what people said about him, and that was he never kept a partner for longer than one night. As for myself, well, I never thought about that kind of stuff. Sex is only another way to get attached to people, and when that happens you're setting yourself up to be hurt. People always leave you. It's inevitable. The best way – the only way – to avoid the heartbreak is to just not care. And this was something I had been good at, until Ash was forced into my life.

It was only a year ago when I entered the Military Academy and was assigned to Ash's squad. I ended up sharing a room with him too, which I had not been pleased about. He and the other members of our squad, the Third Sunreaver Cadets, were at the academy for two years prior to my arrival. An unfortunate accident left their fifth member paraplegic, and so I was fast-tracked to the final year on account of my supposed compatibility with the group. You see, the five of us were gifted. And when I say gifted, I mean we had abilities that most people don't – Daeva, they call us.

The Daeva were a relatively new phenomenon, and most 'normal' humans feared us. As a result, most of us ended up in the military, who had no qualms about hiring us. It was the only choice available to us, but it wasn't a bad deal – we were given food, accommodation, clothing, and a decent pay. In return the army got itself a nifty superhuman soldier.

"Cheer up. Tonight is supposed to be a celebration." I turned to see Ash looking out of the small window. He didn't need to look at me to tell what I was feeling. Ash was an empath, and a powerful one at that. Besides his empathy, he could also create ice from thin air. He was watching snowflakes fall gently from the night sky, the moon illuminating each and every one of them. "It's New Year's Eve, and our last night as cadets! Aren't you the least bit excited?"

Truth be told, I was excited, but not because it was New Year's Eve. I never understood what all the fuss was about. Every year people get wasted and make promises to themselves for the coming year that they invariably break. I was excited because from that point on, we would be fully-fledged members of the Silver Dawn Battalion. Finally, after all the training drills and simulations we would be given real missions; a chance to let loose and show everyone what we were made of.

"A bit," I replied, "but you know I hate this kinda stuff."

"You don't hate it. You hate that a part of you enjoys it." Well, that was news to me. Ash moved to stand at my side and his hands gripped my shoulders, turning me to face him. His eyes gazed into mine, searching for something deep inside of me. "What is it you're so afraid of?"

"Nothing," I snapped and shrugged him off, feeling a little annoyed that he had tried to read my innermost emotions. That was a boundary we agreed long ago was off-limits. The physical contact strengthened his reception. Fortunately for me I had a psychic ability of my own, allowing me to mentally shield myself. He was more powerful than I. He could have forced his way past my shields and peered down into my soul. But he didn't. Point for Ash. "Can we get going now?"

"Yeah, sure." The serious look on his face melted back into his trademark smile, his lips twisting upwards slightly and flashing a small amount of teeth. It was something I always liked about Ash, and made me able to tolerate him. He could let things go and get on with life rather than trying to force an issue.

We grabbed our jackets from their hooks on the back of the door and Ash led out into the corridor.

"We're meeting Katiya over at her dorm first."

My mood worsened at the mere mention of Katiya, causing me to pull the door shut a little harder than I should have on the way out.

*****

4

Katiya's dormitory was part of a separate building, a short walk from our own. We made our way across the square and past the stone statue of the Prophet Jules, to a small three-story apartment block used by the female members of the army. A few of the windows in the smaller building remained lit, and as we passed them we could hear the sounds of giggling and laughter; the sound of drunken females entertaining themselves until the New Year countdown. At one window, a young cadet leaned out and tried to tempt us into joining her and some friends, for what I could only imagine would turn into an alcohol-fueled competition for Ash's attention.

"Maybe another night," he smiled and winked at her. He laughed quietly as we moved out of earshot of the girl, who remained hanging out of the window, probably to enjoy the view. "Looks like you got an admirer."

"What makes you think she's not another of your fan-girls?" I asked. I had a reputation for being cold and uninviting, and I was fine with that, especially if it meant not having to put up with hordes of swooning admirers, as was commonplace with Ash. At least he enjoyed the attention.

"Because I just know. I mean, yeah, she probably wouldn't mind a piece of me, but when she looked at *you*... didn't you see the way she froze?"

"That doesn't mean anything."

Ash sighed. "You're hopeless. Trust me, I felt her desire hit me like a brick. She wants you. So, what do you say? I could go back and get her name for you. Maybe fix you up on a date or something."

I looked back in time to see her blow me a quick kiss before retreating inside. A shudder ran up my spine, and I was sure it wasn't from the cold. "Not interested."

Ash's brow furrowed. "You know, I don't think I've ever seen you show the slightest bit of interest in anyone... female or male."

I stopped walking and turned to face him. "What about you? You haven't shown interest in anyone beyond that of a quick fuck."

Ash's teeth ground together. "You know what, Mik? Just... forget it."

I didn't have to be an empath to know I'd unintentionally hit a sore nerve. But how was I supposed to know? With anyone else he would have laughed it off and made a joke about the other person being jealous. Perhaps, it was because I was one of the few who didn't judge his lifestyle that made my comment all the more hurtful. My only goal was to deflect the conversation away from my personal life. That was something I didn't talk about. How could anyone understand I had no desire to be that close to anyone? Ash especially, I thought wouldn't understand.

He turned and started to walk away from me. Seeing his reaction created a pit in the bottom of my stomach, an awful hollow feeling that I was unfamiliar with. Each step he took made the feeling grow, and so I did something I hadn't done since I was very young.

"I'm sorry."

Ash froze. I saw the tension in his shoulders, manifesting itself as a subtle twitch. I don't know whether it was the fact that I apologised – and meant it – or if he could feel how awful I felt, but he came back to me and wrapped his arms around me.

He was two or three inches taller than me, his breath scalding against the shell of my ear as he spoke. "I'm sorry too. I guess we both have some issues to work out."

Issues. I had plenty of those, but none I wanted to share. I didn't want people to pity or feel sorry for me. Or worse still, I didn't want them trying to 'fix' me. I pulled away from the embrace, feeling more than a little uncomfortable by the display of emotion. It felt good, and that was the problem.

*****

We continued on to Katiya's room. It was on the third floor of the building, room fifty-four I noted. It was my first time there. Unlike a certain someone I never had any reason to visit the female dorms.

6

Ash knocked twice.

"One minute," Katiya called to us.

We stood, for what seemed like an eternity, with Ash drumming his fingers on the door frame, and I tapping my foot. The door opened to reveal Katiya clad in a long, white bathrobe. Her chestnut hair fell in waves and curls to her shoulders, framing her healthy-pink skin and matching brown eyes. She looked almost a different person. During training she always tied her hair back into a tight ponytail, and was definitely one of the lads. I guess she had to be in a squad with four guys. Now she looked feminine and softer, though I knew not to judge this particular book by its cover.

"I was just doing my hair," she said as we made our way into the room. It was a single bedroom, painted white like all the others. A small bed with light-blue sheets, a wardrobe, a desk cluttered with make-up and mirrors, and a metal stool were the only furniture.

"Typical woman," Ash said. "Never ready on time." He made himself comfortable on the edge of the bed. I chose to stand, leaning back on the desk.

"I figured you of all people would understand a gal needs to look good for a night out," she said.

"Sure, but couldn't you start getting ready earlier?" It was a good point, I thought. Katiya dismissed it with a huff as she turned to her wardrobe. She lifted a low-cut white sweater and black jeans from their hangers on the wardrobe door, and carried them into the bathroom with her.

"I won't be long," she said, peering from behind the door before closing it to.

Ash let out a long breath and laid back across the bed, his arms stretching up over his head. He turned to face me. "I'm sorry I snapped at you back there. I... well, some things happened in my past I wish I could forget about."

I nodded gently, knowing only too well what he meant. I was born an orphan. My mother died during childbirth, and even to her my father was unknown, or so I've been told. As soon as I could leave the hospital I was sent to an orphanage where the kindly old lady who ran the place looked after me. At the age of six, I lost her too. I remember waking one night after a nightmare, and in a panic I ran to her room. It wasn't until the morning when I realised why she hadn't woke when I climbed into her bed.

The new owner had no love for any of us. I was shipped off to several foster families, only to be returned when they realised they were unable to deal with me. Even that stopped eventually. No-one wanted to adopt an angry teen. Abandonment issues – who, me?

"You know you can talk to me, right?" Ash said. "Whatever is eating you up from inside, maybe you just need to let it out."

"I'd rather not remember, either."

I sometimes wondered, would I be more like Ash if I could forget my past? If the pain of being abandoned could be erased, would I be able to be happy?

"Maybe you need to get laid then. It might help take your mind off things." Ash rolled onto his side, propping himself up on his elbow. Sex was his answer to pretty much everything.

At that moment Katiya exited the bathroom. "I agree," she said, planting herself on the bed and forcing Ash to sit up. She reached underneath to pull out a pair of black, high-heeled boots. "Sorry, did I interrupt your man-talk?" she asked, observing the silence that had settled over the room.

"Yes, now can we get going?" I said, pushing myself off the desk.

"Gee, sorry for making your highness a couple of minutes late." Katiya stood and scowled at me.

*****

The bar was only a ten minute walk from the dorms, located outside of the military compound. As we approached the entrance a long, thick arm barred our path.

"I'm gonna need to see some I.D."

The owner of the offending arm gave us a hard look. He was over six foot, well-built and dressed entirely in black. I'm sure to most people he would have seemed imposing, but being a Daeva puts regular humans at a severe disadvantage. Ash reached into his pocket and pulled out a small military I.D. card. The bouncer looked at it for a few seconds then threw it to the ground.

"Looks fake to me," he said. Of course, he knew it wasn't. Another bigot trying to get in the way of anyone who was different. A lot of people were afraid of us, but not this guy. That didn't make him brave, just stupid.

"You might wanna rethink that." Ash stepped forward, until only an inch remained between him and the bouncer, who was almost twice his size. I sighed. Tonight was going to be one of those nights.

Katiya was watching intently. She loved a good fight, especially when she could watch her crush in action. It was well known she had a thing for Ash, though the feelings appeared to be one-sided.

The bouncer grinned. "I'll teach you a lesson in respect, freak."

"You could try." Ash grinned back. He took a few steps back onto the pavement. The bouncer started to follow but froze when a hand landed on his shoulder.

"What seems to be the problem here?" the man asked. The bouncer looked back at him. "No problem, boss. These kids were trying to start a fight when I asked for I.D., but they're leaving now."

The older man narrowed his eyes at us. "Well, what are you waiting for? Clear off! If you're looking to start fights then you'll find no service here."

Ash picked up his I.D. and we moved away from the bar to wait for the last two members of our group. He glared at the bouncer from a distance, muttering about how he wished he could wipe the smug look off his face. If there was one thing I'd learned about Ash, it was that you did not want to get in a fight with him. Ice manipulation is a terrifying ability to go up against. You can stand still and end up rooted to the spot by his ice, or try and keep moving, only to find yourself on an ice slick. Either way, you lose. The bouncer wouldn't have stood a chance, I thought.

I was pulled from my thoughts when Katiya spotted Brad coming around the street corner. He was easy to spot amidst the crowd of party-goers, standing at six foot five and being built like a brick wall. His skin was dark, almost brown, but not quite, and you could never tell whether his eyes were green or brown depending on the light. His dark t-shirt threatened to burst at the seams with every movement. A crew cut, crooked nose and square jaw completed his 'bad ass' ensemble. Lucas, who looked tiny in comparison, was walking alongside him. He had long, blond hair, dark enough that you could almost call it brown, and deep blue eyes set against his pale skin.

"You could've waited inside," Lucas said as they approached us. Katiya had her arms folded and was rubbing her hands up and down them. Of course, she hadn't planned on being outside for too long. Ash explained to them what had happened, and with the barracks bar being closed in preparation for graduation day, we decided to head back to the dorms and have a party of our own.

*****

When we reached the common room of Lucas and Brad's dormitory, it appeared we weren't the only ones to have had that idea. Still, we found enough free seats and set ourselves up at one side of the room, with some drinks bought from the nearby twenty-four hour store. While the others were on lager and spirits, I was content with my ginger beer. Katiya watched me open a bottle and shook her head.

"You should have a real drink once in a while," she said. "You never know, it might help dislodge that giant pole from your rear."

"Leave him alone, Kat." This was from Brad. "He'll open up when he's ready."

"I'm just trying to encourage him to have some fun for once in his life."

Katiya and I had never really gotten along. She thought I was an

10

emotionally-stunted asshole, and I saw her as a condescending bitch. Put us both in the same room and we would usually butt heads. That night was no different.

"Well maybe if you removed whatever crawled up your ass years ago and died, you'd be able to say something nice for once," I said.

The look on Katiya's face was priceless. It was a mixture of disbelief, embarrassment and anger. She opened her mouth, and then shut it again. Her cheeks flushed red. The others laughed, and Ash gave me a pat on the back.

We ended up playing a drinking game that involved blowing a deck of cards off the top of a can, until none remained. If you were unlucky enough to be the one who blew off the last card, then you downed a shot. I tried to back out at first, being the only one not drinking, but they insisted I should still join in.

Several rounds later, and Brad was pegged as the clear loser. We moved onto Truth or Dare, at Katiya's suggestion, much to my dismay. Again I tried to excuse myself, but to no avail. I sighed and watched as Lucas was dared to return wearing a bra belonging to one of the girls in the room. He tried Katiya first but was shot down with a hard glare and her middle finger. A couple of minutes later he came back wearing a lacy black bra over his shirt.

Ash, not to be outdone, also opted for a dare. He ended up on the nearby pool table, where he dropped his pants. There were some cheers from around the room, and a couple of groans. I looked away, feeling embarrassed for him, and dreading what was to come next. Ash returned to the group and their eyes fixed on me.

I picked truth, hoping it would be an easy question, or one I could lie about. There was silence from the group as they thought over what they could ask. I didn't even want to imagine what Katiya and Ash were thinking up. It was Brad who spoke up first and asked about how I was outed as a Daeva. This was something I had never shared with them. To be honest, I never told them anything of my past. They waited for me to answer, but I was torn between what to say. Did I want to share that part of my life with them? Not if I could help it.

"I'll tell you what," said Lucas. "We'll tell you how it happened with us, then you can tell us your story. Okay?"

I shrugged. I had never thought to ask them about their pasts.

"Well," he said, taking my shrug to mean yes. "I got caught breaking into the General's office. It was a set up, of course. I mean, I never get caught. Anyway, I was offered a clean slate if I joined the army, so here I am."

Lucas had 'worked' – and I use the term loosely – as a thief before he ended up in the military. At one point he claimed to be the most wanted man in the city, though no-one knew what he looked like. It was his ability that made this possible. Lucas could move at high-speed without making a single sound. Now he was our recon guy, sniper and technology enthusiast.

Brad went next. "I was walking home one night when a bunch of youths jumped me with a knife. They must've stabbed me a dozen times before they were interrupted and took off with my things. I was half unconscious, but I remember a young couple calling for help. By the time the medics got there, wasn't a scratch on me. Confused the hell out of them it did."

Spontaneous healing was Brad's ability, though to what extent he could survive was unknown. He sometimes joked that one day he'd test to see whether he could survive a grenade blast. I wasn't convinced he could heal it – all of our powers had their limits and drawbacks.

"I was in a grocery store when it happened," said Katiya. "Some guy almost knocked me over and didn't even bother to apologise. I was pissed, and as I went to confront him the fruit around me started exploding. I turned that place into a fruit salad."

Her power was to create explosions. She said it was to do with increasing the kinetic energy of an object, or something. I hadn't paid much attention when she explained it at our first meeting.

I looked at Ash who was sat next to me. He cast his gaze down at the table, hesitating. I guessed it had something to do with the painful memories he mentioned earlier. For a lot of Daeva, being outed wasn't a pleasant experience. And for those who lost control, it was usually their last.

"My empathy started when I was twelve," he said. "Back then I didn't have a clue what was happening, and I ended up being diagnosed as schizophrenic. Then at nineteen I got into a fight and accidentally froze someone's leg. They lost all feeling in one foot."

I got the impression he wasn't telling me the whole story, but I understood. Everyone's eyes were on me and I had to come up with something or, as per the rules of the game, I'd have to take the dare. I decided to follow Ash's example, and give them half of the story.

"I made someone so angry that he almost killed two kids. I didn't realise I was causing it."

"Damn, are the kids okay now?" Brad asked.

"I haven't seen them since I left the orphanage, but I heard one of them is engaged now."

"You never mentioned you were an orphan," said Ash. He rested a hand on my shoulder.

"I don't like talking about it," I said, wishing I hadn't let that piece of information slip. All through school I was singled out and given extra attention because I had no parents, as if it made me disabled or mentally retarded in some way. The other kids resented me for my special treatment. All I ever wanted was to be treated the same as anyone else. Coming to the realisation that I had the ability to project emotions onto others hadn't helped.

"It's okay. We understand." The hand on my shoulder gave a light squeeze.

Together we formed the Third Sunreaver squad, the academy's first squad of Daeva to graduate together. It was an exciting time for the army, though I couldn't say everyone in the city was happy about it. Despite the backing of the Silver Dawn – our government and spiritual leaders – who had declared us 'safe', there were many who wanted us gone. I couldn't blame them. After all, the last time humans consorted with supernatural creatures, it had almost ended the human race.

Chapter 2

I awoke the next morning at six-thirty. Our usual wake-up call was nowhere to be heard. The bells in the middle of the square would sound every morning, but not today. New Year's Day was one of the few when we were allowed to sleep in. I rolled over to see Ash, still asleep, curled on his side with the blankets tucked tight around him. No doubt he would be praying for a quiet morning after the events of last night. He would get no sympathy from me.

I lay there for a while, hoping to drift off again, until I got restless. Since I was awake, I decided to head for the shower. I closed the door behind me and left my shorts in the laundry bag that hung from the hook on the back of the door. I turned the shower on and let the water warm up, before I stepped in and pulled the curtain across. The hot water beat against my skin, turning it a deep shade of pink. Just the way I like it. I let the water wash over me until I felt my skin begin to tingle and there was a knock at the door.

"If you're gonna use all the hot water, you could at least give me a reason to need a cold shower," Ash shouted over the running water.

"You always need a cold shower."

"Yeah, well, if you're not out soon I'll be joining you in there."

I let out a long sigh. Ash did not make idle threats. It was times like these I wished they had installed locks on the bathroom doors. Hell, I should have been grateful he didn't barge in to begin with, but I wasn't. I was annoyed that my sanctuary had been disturbed. I don't know why hot showers make me feel so peaceful. They just do. Ash knew that, but he also knew that left to my own devices, there would never be any hot water left for him. It wasn't my fault though. I possessed a secret ability to warp time in the shower. It's true! How else could you explain that what felt like only five to ten minutes for me, was in actual fact over half an hour? Yeah, no-one else believed me either.

I finished washing and reached for a towel from the nearby rack. When I was dried off, I wrapped it around my waist and went back into the main room. Ash looked over at me as I exited. He was sprawled out across his bed, wearing only a pair of black joggers.

"What do you do in there that takes so long?" he asked.

"Nothing." I moved to the wardrobe and picked out some fresh clothes.

"Must be a whole lot of nothing then." Ash laughed. He sat, stretching his arms upwards and outwards, and yawned. His hair was wild and dishevelled from tossing and turning in his sleep, as he often did after a few drinks. "I'll have mine black," he said, and made his way into the bathroom.

I nodded and finished dressing, before heading out into the corridor and to the shared kitchen. The hallway was usually a hub of activity at this time of morning, but today it was empty. Silent. Everybody was taking advantage of their morning off, no doubt. For once, I was able to make the coffee in peace. Ash and I had an agreement; whoever showered first, made the coffee. He liked his milky and sweet, but hangovers called for something a little stronger. Mine was black, no sugar.

I took the coffees back into the bedroom, placing Ash's on the bedside table, and then sat on the edge of my bed to drink mine. The first sip of coffee in the morning was always a jolt to my system. I couldn't function properly without it. Some called it grumpy. I called it caffeine-deprived.

Now my brain was awake, I began making sure everything was ready for the graduation ceremony. My boots were cleaned and polished. We still needed to collect our uniforms, but the collection office wouldn't be open for another hour or so. There was more than enough time left before we needed to be at the parade ground.

Ash was out of the bathroom before I was even half-finished with my coffee, his damp hair lying flat on his head. How anyone could spend so little time in the shower was a mystery to me. We decided to hit the gym, to kill some time before picking up our uniforms. For us, the gym wasn't just a way to keep in shape – we had more than enough drills for that – it was a way to pass the time, and if needed, vent some frustration. We kept the workout light. It was enough to get our blood pumping, and bring some of the colour back to Ash's cheeks, but still conserve our energy for the day ahead.

Next we went to the collection office where a middle-aged woman sat reading. She took our names and squad, and then retreated into a jungle of uniforms. She returned soon after with two hangers, each with a neatly pressed uniform on, and handed one each to us. Having never been to a graduation ceremony before meant it was my first time seeing the uniform. The jacket was black with gold trim and bright brass buttons. More gold adorned the shoulders in the form of tassels, and the sleeve bore a single white stripe, indicating we were fresh out of the academy. A pair of matching trousers were folded over the hanger, along with a black belt.

I turned to begin my way back to our room when something landed on my head. I reached up with my free hand to remove the offending object.

"You forgot your hat," Ash said. I looked back to see him grinning and adjusting his hat. It was a white army hat with a black visor and a brass emblem on the front – our squad's insignia, a Fleur-de-Lys superimposed over a rising sun. "What do you think?"

"You look like an idiot no matter what you wear."

"Ouch." Ash pouted, feigning hurt.

"You'll get over it," I said, and knocked his hat to the ground.

We headed back across the complex to our room, and Ash went about making some bacon sandwiches. When it came to cooking, even something simple, I was useless. Back at the orphanage, I was never given the chance to try my hand at it. Now that duty was left to Ash, who seemed to enjoy it.

Having had nothing to eat that morning made the smell coming from the kitchen torturous. My stomach grumbled and groaned in anticipation. I was on the edge of my bed when Ash came back carrying two plates. He handed one to me, and then perched himself on the desk near the window. I lifted the top slice of bread, as I always did, to check it was made exactly how I liked it. There was no rind, only a splash of ketchup, and the bacon cooked until it was almost crispy. As always, it was done perfectly. I lifted the first slice to my mouth, and then paused, spotting someone in our doorway.

"Well, well, boys. Looks like the women beat you at getting ready today," Katiya said. She was already dressed in her uniform, which was identical to ours, save for the knee-length skirt. I almost felt sorry for her, having to wear that in the middle of winter. Almost.

"I hope you made some for me," she said, and stopped in front of me.

"Here," Ash said, handing her half of his sandwich. "Uniform looks good on you."

"Thanks." She smiled, her cheeks beginning to flush. "So, are you two planning on getting ready anytime soon?"

"Just about to," I replied.

"Yeah, well I'd like to get to the parade ground *before* the rush starts, so hurry up."

"Don't worry, Kat," Ash said. "Unlike you women, it only takes us a minute to get ready."

I laughed, if you could call the noise that came out through the mouthful of bacon a laugh. Snorted would be a more accurate term.

Katiya looked at me as though she could will me into choking on my food. Luckily, that wasn't her ability, though I wasn't sure the alternative of having my head explode was preferable.

With my sandwich finished, I set my plate down on the bedside table and picked up my uniform by the tip of the hanger, being careful not to touch it with my greasy fingers. I hung it on the back of the bathroom door, and washed my hands and face before getting changed. The choker collar certainly lived up to its name, I thought, treading the fine line between being tight and air-restricting. I exited the bathroom, still fidgeting with the collar. The dirty plates were gone, and Katiya had taken up Ash's perch on the desk, her short legs unable to reach the floor.

"Hey, not bad," she said. I chose not to respond, instead rummaging under the bed for my boots. Ash returned while I was fiddling with the lace on one shoe that had managed to get itself knotted.

"I'll be out in two secs," he said, grabbing his uniform and taking it into the bathroom with him. He must have sensed something in the air, because as the door shut behind him he added, "Play nice you two."

When I looked up from tying my boots, I realised Katiya was leaning against the wardrobe in front of me.

"What's your problem?" she asked.

"You... always drooling over him."

"I never had you pegged as the jealous type."

"I'm not jealous," I said, standing up to meet her face-to-face. "I just think it's pathetic."

Katiya gave me a hard glare. She opened her mouth to speak when Ash strode out of the bathroom, his jacket only half-fastened. He sat on the edge of the bed, hunched over. His fingers rubbed against his temples.

"God, you guys are gonna give me a migraine," he said. Having to deal with the emotions of everyone around you would give anyone a headache. Add to that a slight hangover, two people butting heads in the same room as you, and the excitement of graduation day, and you get one grumpy empath.

It was a minute or so before Ash sat up straight. "Sorry, I guess I'm a little nervous, and excited. Stuff like that can throw off my shielding," he said, forcing a smile. He pulled on his boots and fastened his jacket the rest of the way. "Shall we get going then? Don't wanna get caught in the rush."

Katiya's face lit up, happy to see Ash looking more like his usual carefree self. They say 'love is blind', but Katiya could sometimes take it to a whole new level. Oblivious was more like it. She led the way, a slight bounce in her step as she left the room. I went to follow when a hand caught my shoulder.

Ash's smile had vanished. His brows furrowed as he leaned in to whisper, "Whatever that was between you and Kat, just drop it. Please, for me. I can't be dealing with the two of you as well today."

I nodded and he said thanks, though I thought he should have been talking to Katiya instead. Maybe it was childish to blame her for the tension between us. If anything, a large part of the blame was on Ash's shoulders. I couldn't see why he kept stringing her along, never accepting her advances, and yet never denying them either. Did he hope one day she'd get bored and move on, without him having to let her down? All I knew was Katiya wanted more from Ash than he was willing to give. If I could see that, then surely she could too. Since I agreed to let it slide, I pushed the matter to the back of my mind and focused on the day ahead. I closed the door behind us, and we set off for the graduation ceremony.

*****

It was a ten minute walk to the parade ground, situated at the main entrance to the military complex. Tall, white walls and an iron gate separated us from the rest of the city. Behind the gate we could see the crowds already gathered and cheering, waiting for the first event of the day, the graduation march. It was a big day for everyone in the city, not just ourselves. The citizens would be celebrating the graduation of their newest protectors.

We got to talking as the rest of the graduates and the volunteer helpers showed up. Ash was looking forward to seeing his younger brother. His parents refused to support a 'freak of nature', and his father doubly so after learning of Ash's sexuality. Katiya said her Dad and older brother would be in the audience too, her only remaining family. I, on the other hand, would have no-one waiting to congratulate me at the end of the ceremony.

To my surprise, it was Katiya who looked over her shoulder at me and said, "You don't have any family left, do you?"

I didn't answer, letting the silence hang uneasily in the air around us. I had no memories of my biological parents, not even a photo. Any fond memories I had had of Mrs. Rousseau were long since marred by the feeling that she abandoned me, leaving me with the evil witch of a woman who took over the place. To me, it wasn't as though my family was all gone. It was more like I never had one to begin with.

"You have us now," Ash said. He wrapped one arm around me, the other around Katiya, and pulled us in close. "We're one big dysfunctional family."

Just what I need, I thought.

"I hope you're not forgetting about me," Lucas said, appearing behind Katiya. She jumped and drew in a sharp breath.

"Jesus, don't sneak up on people like that!" She took a couple of deep breaths, glaring at myself and Ash as we laughed. Brad appeared soon after, his hat clearly visible above the sea of cadets.

It didn't take long before the place was filled up. Family members were directed to the rows of seats set in front of a small raised stage in the centre of the parade ground. The ceremony co-ordinators ran to and fro, making sure everyone was in line, ready for our grand entrance. The five of us were at the back of the parade, with only a single float behind us. It was an elaborate diorama, depicting a vampire succumbing to the power of the dawn.

We had been standing for what seemed like forever in the biting cold, when finally the bells began to sound. As the last bell rang, the drums started. Following soon after was the myriad of brass and wind instruments, and then we were off.

The march took us out of the gates and past hordes of cheering citizens, kept back by small, temporary, iron fences that looked like they could topple over at any moment. More than once I heard a few angry shouts rise above the clamour. 'Freaks,' they shouted, or 'Demons'. I tried my hardest to ignore the heckling, and kept my eyes facing forward. My fists clenched. Once or twice I found myself glancing into the audience, looking for the source of the animosity, but it was hard to pick anyone out in the crowd.

We reached the heart of the city, and circled once around the large, white church of the Silver Dawn. This building was the cornerstone of our city, the last ray of hope humanity clung to. While religion wasn't a mandatory part of our lives, the majority of people believed, at least to some extent, in God. Without the Silver Dawn's protection, the human race may not have survived at all, and so it seemed only natural to believe in them and their teachings. I was still on the fence about the whole God debate. A higher power I could believe in, but not this all-knowing, all-loving God. Where was he during the apocalypse? What kind of God could let a child be born into this world with no family? If this God existed, I figured he stopped caring a long time ago.

Past the church was the old marketplace. The various stalls were still open, trying to cash in on the annual event as we marched proudly past them. Beyond that were the suburbs, the factory district, and then the towering white walls of the academy loomed once more.

The gates shut behind us with a loud clang. The marching band and floats detoured to one side of the parade ground, leaving us graduates to continue down the centre. We came to a stop in front of the raised stage, where General Marsten stood to one side. He stepped up to his podium, and the quiet murmur of voices stopped abruptly. The General was a middle-aged man, dressed in a uniform similar to our own, though his was all white, with black and gold trim, and bore many decorations across his chest. A neatly trimmed handlebar moustache adorned his slim, angular face.

"Ladies and Gentleman, I welcome you to the fifty-seventh annual graduation ceremony." He paused while the audience applauded. "Today we celebrate not only the graduation of these fine cadets, but also our persistence as a species pushed to the brink of extinction. Almost a century ago, vampires walked among us as friends."

I sighed, shifting on my feet. We had all heard this speech before, in one form of another; when we joined the academy, at church, or during History lessons at school. Our predecessors legalised vampirism, befriending the undead, despite the warnings of the church. The most prominent of those against the legislation was the Silver Dawn, who warned that consorting with vampires would bring about the end – the apocalypse. Unfortunately, they were right. A plague swept across the Earth, systematically infecting the human race. It was only a matter of weeks before it had spread across the entire globe.

"It was in this very city that the Prophet Jules delivered a message from Heaven. A message of hope, of a cure."

People from all over the world flocked to the churches, desperate to receive the blessing that would save them from certain doom. For most, however, it was too late.

"For those who survived, it was merely the beginning of the ordeal. Many loved ones were lost. Homes, communities, and entire cities were lost. Our way of life was taken from us!"

The remaining survivors banded together, to form a new city centred around the Silver Dawn's church. Rachat, the barrier city, so called because of the protective wards that surrounded it, and prevented any advance from the vampires, was built upon the remains of what was once Bourges in France. As far as we knew, Rachat was the only such city in France, and maybe even in the entire world.

"Yet we stand here today, despite all of this. We persist in this world because of our faith, courage, strength, resilience and unity. All of these are qualities you will find in each and every one of our graduates today. They represent not only our will to survive, but also hope. Hope for a better future, where our children and our children's children will be able to walk free, outside of the barriers, without fear of attack from vampires, werewolves, or whatever else may spawn from the deepest pits of Hell. They are our salvation, and our protectors. They are the graduates of 2105!"

The audience stood, clapping and cheering louder than before.

"Finally," Lucas muttered beneath his breath. "I thought he would go on forever."

"You and me both," I replied.

"Now, I'd like to invite Principal Wilkes to begin the presentations." General Marsten stepped down and moved to the opposite side of the stage.

Principal Wilkes, formerly Colonel Wilkes, until he retired from active duty on account of the loss of his left leg, hobbled over to the podium with his walking stick in-hand. His uniform was identical to the General's, only with less badges on show. He spoke with a rough, deep voice; the kind you would expect from someone who looked as he did, with his square jaw, busted nose, and short-cropped hair. He held a piece of paper in his hands, and began to read out the list of names.

Each squad marched in turn onto the stage as their names were called out. The audience clapped after each name, and General Marsten shook their hands before they exited the stage and rejoined the back of the line, which crept forward with every squad that was called.

We made it to the front of the queue and waited for our names. To our surprise, Principal Wilkes stepped back, allowing the General to come forward once more. It appeared we would be getting a special introduction.

"Before we bring our final graduates onto the stage, I would like to say a few words. This last decade has proven to be a joyous one indeed. Each year, our scientists and engineers are rediscovering lost technology, and inventing new ones, such as the eco-domes, allowing us to grow fruit and vegetables all year round that would otherwise not survive in our climate."

He went on to give more examples, rambling on about the recent advances in medicine and weaponry, which allowed us to fight back against the monsters roaming outside the city walls. I started to tune it out, when a nudge from my right caught my attention.

"There's something wrong," Ash whispered. I raised an eyebrow in question. "I've been trying to block everything out, but there's this one feeling I can't shake. It's not good. Something bad is gonna happen. I can feel it."

"First time a full squad of Daeva has graduated together," said Lucas. "They made a pretty big deal out of it too. There's bound to be some people not happy about that."

"What do we do?" I asked.

"Give me a sec," Ash said, closing his eyes. I understood he was concentrating on the invisible waves of emotion around him. His hand twitched, as though it were grasping at something. When his eyes opened, he looked to his right, into the audience. "Back row, third or fourth from the left."

I glanced over at the people in question. "Bald guy?"

Ash nodded. "Either him or the brunette. There's too much interference here to tell."

"I'll pass the word on to keep an eye out," said Lucas.

Everything went silent. General Marsten eyed us before continuing. "It was eight years ago, when a miracle happened within the walls of our great city. A woman by the name of Elaine created fire with her bare hands."

What the General failed to mention was Elaine lost control of her ability, killing five and wounding several others, before someone took an axe to her head. And that was only the first of many.

"That same year, a young boy named Michael found he could levitate."

Shot twice in the head and branded a demon-child.

"These people, Daeva as they have come to be known, have been given gifts from God himself. Long have we had the disadvantage in this war, but no more! Today, we present to you five such extraordinary people, who have faced much adversity to be here."

General Marsten stepped back, and Principal Wilkes retook the podium.

"The Third Sunreaver squad."

We began our march up onto the stage, led by Brad, who paused to whisper something in the Principal's ear, presumably about Ash's warning. Wilkes nodded before continuing.

"Bradley Mitchell." Brad strode across the stage and shook hands with the General. Again, he stopped to whisper. From where I stood, I had a good view of the suspicious couple. The man was tall, wearing a dark jacket, his arms folded across his broad chest. Next to him sat the woman. She was much shorter and frail looking, her body trembling from the cold wind that blew about us. My money was on Baldie.

"Katiya Alexandros," said the Principal, and Katiya walked over to complete the hand shake.

"Lucas Quinn." Baldie was looking agitated by now, shuffling in his seat. I tried to convince myself that it was only because the seats were uncomfortable.

"Mikhail Hart." I walked forward, trying not to stare at Baldie, whose eyes were fixed on the stage.

General Marsten took my hand in his firm grip. "Congratulations, Son."

I nodded and said thanks. It took all my self-control not to run off the stage.

"Ashley White," Wilkes announced. Seconds later we were all back in formation at the rear of the line. I wanted to punch Ash for making us worry over nothing.

With the final round of applause dying down, General Marsten spoke up. "It is now time for the oath-taking. Please raise your right hand and repeat after me."

The oath was well known to us all by now. It went, "I do solemnly and sincerely swear, before God and the people of Rachat, that I will fulfil my duties to the best of my abilities; that I will support and defend the city and its people against all enemies, foreign or domestic; that I take this oath of my own free will and without any reservation, so help me God."

"Congratulations, graduates of 2105 and welcome to the army." The crowd stood, applauding. Many of the hats were thrown into the air. It was too much fuss for my liking. They would only have to chase down the hats to return them at the end of the day. "Thank you all for attending. I'd like to invite all of you to join us in the main lobby, located through the double doors behind the stage, where there will be refreshments, and a chance to talk to the graduates. Dismissed."

The marching band that had sat quietly to one side chimed in as the crowd began to disappear. Many of them went straight for the hall, though I spotted a few heading towards the gates.

I turned and gave Ash a quick jab to his left arm. "What was that all about?"

"I dunno. Must be the excitement getting to me."

"You guys coming?" Brad called to us.

Everyone was going to meet their families. There was nothing for me in that hall.

"Come on, I'll introduce you to my brother." Ash threw an arm over my shoulder, and dragged me along with him.

Chapter 3

I let Ash lead me into the lobby, which by now was overflowing with people. To our left stood a line of tables, filled with plastic cups of orange juice, and a stack of Styrofoam cups next to a hot water tank, which I could only assume was filled with coffee. Feeling a little chilled from standing out in the cold, I decided to make myself one. Ash passed on the hot drink and stood near the door, his eyes scanning the room.

When I returned with my drink, I noticed Ash was talking to a younger man, who *had* to be his brother. The family resemblance was plain to see. He was taller than Ash by an inch or so, and slimmer. The hair was the same blond, though longer and shaggier, and his eyes held the same unmistakable sapphire sparkle.

"You must be Mik," he said, extending his hand to me. We shook briefly. "I'm Graeme. Ash has told me a lot about you."

"Oh, has he?" I looked to Ash, wondering what exactly he had been saying.

"You can alter what people are feeling, right?"

I nodded and took a cautious sip of my coffee, making sure it wouldn't scald my tongue and throat. The warmth was a welcome relief.

"That's so cool. So you could walk up to a chick and make her feel horny?" he asked.

If I had had coffee in my mouth, it would have ended up all over Ash and his brother. "I guess the resemblance is more than physical," I said, unsure of what else to say. That was one feeling I had never tried to manipulate, nor would I ever want to try.

"What can I say? I have an awesome big bro. He taught me everything I need to know. Now look at him, all grown up and in the army."

"So, how are things at home?" Ash asked, sounding rather reluctant.

"Oh, you know, same as always. Dad's not happy unless he's making someone's life miserable, and Mom's leg has been playing up again. She misses you."

"Yeah, well, she made it clear she wanted nothing more to do with me. They both did." Ash cast his eyes down for a moment, and then looked at me. "Can you give us a moment alone?"

"Sure," I replied.

Ash and Graeme retreated into the corner of the room. From what I could see, Ash was getting worked up over something, and Graeme was trying to calm him down. Deciding that it was none of my business, I turned away. In doing so, I bumped shoulders with someone. A bit of coffee sloshed over the edge of my cup, landing on the arm of their jacket.

"Sorry," I mumbled, and turned to walk away. A large hand caught my elbow. I turned back to the man, to see that the hand belonged to Baldie, who looked down his nose at me.

"You're one of 'em, aren't you?"

I didn't answer, instead opting to stare right back at him.

"I'm looking for Ashley White."

The mere mention of Ash's name was enough to make me glance in his direction. Baldie's eyes followed mine. He smiled, pushing me away, rather than letting go. He turned his back to me, thrusting his hands inside his jacket pockets. It struck me as odd, that Ash would have picked him out of the crowd as suspicious if he had known him. I started to follow, wondering what he was up to, when I saw the glinting metal being withdrawn from his right pocket.

My initial thought was to shout 'knife' and alert everyone to the danger, but there were too many innocent people around. The last thing I wanted was to cause a hostage situation. I thought maybe I could use my ability on him, and make him so afraid he wouldn't go through with whatever he was planning. But then I couldn't be sure how he'd react, so I improvised. I tapped him on the shoulder. He spun around, and I threw my drink in his face. His hands went up to cover his eyes, but it was too late. He let out a low, guttural scream as the hot coffee hit. The knife was in plain sight now. People around us gasped and backed away from him as he rubbed at his face.

"You bastard," he yelled. His skin glowed a deep red, matching the bloodshot whites of his eyes. He swung the knife at me, missing by some margin. There was a scream from the crowd, and for a split second my attention was elsewhere. It was enough for Baldie to grab hold of my jacket with one hand, the other raised to strike again. Time appeared to slow as the knife came down.

Without warning, Baldie gave a sudden yelp and dropped the knife to the floor. He let go of me, and clutched his right hand, blood beginning to drip through his fingers. The knife clattered against the tiled floor, before coming to rest. Its hilt was coated in a thick layer of icy spikes, their tips coated red. I took the opportunity to push myself away from him.

The crowd backed further away, leaving the two of us in the centre of the ever-expanding clearing. Ash was at one edge, walking towards us with a satisfied smirk on his face. Sometimes, I cursed my lack of a physical ability and small size. This was one of those times.

Baldie set his sights on Ash, who stood there, confident, as the large brute strode over to him, still clutching his bleeding hand. A loud bang came out of nowhere, eliciting more than a few shrieks from the onlookers. Baldie fell to the ground, his knee giving way in an eruption of blood.

General Marsten walked over to the collapsed heap on the floor, his gum aimed directly at him. He looked over at myself and Ash. "You two are not to go anywhere." Pointing at one of the other graduates, he said, "You there, report this to the infirmary. I want some medics and a stretcher here ASAP to sedate this man and take him in. And bring a mop back with you." The young man saluted and pushed his way through the crowd.

The General raised his voice to speak to the whole room. "I apologise for the inconvenience, but I need this area vacated. If you could all please head through the double doors at the back of the room, and we will relocate to the library. I would also advise that no-one leaves until we are sure of what happened here."

Everyone began to filter out through the doors. Principal Wilkes was one of the few who remained. "Get a team together," the General told him. "Have them find any witnesses and question them." Wilkes nodded, and hobbled to catch up with the crowd.

Two medics rushed through the side door not long after, carrying a stretcher between them, followed by the mop-wielding graduate. Baldie writhed in agony on the floor as they tried to sedate him. It took one of them to hold down his arm, while the other injected him.

"He should have been here," he grumbled as he drifted off. The medics managed to roll him onto the stretcher.

"I want him cuffed to a bed and kept sedated until I say otherwise. Understood?"

"Yes Sir," they replied, and Baldie was carried off. That left the unfortunate graduate to clean up the mess his knee had made.

The General finally looked back at us. To say he looked pissed was an understatement. "Both of you in my office. Now!"

We walked in silence, out of the lobby and up to the third floor, with General Marsten trailing behind us. His office was the third on the left. Ash went inside first, while I waited outside. From the other side of the door, I could hear their voices, but not what was being said. It was some minutes before Ash exited the room, indicating with a tilt of his head that I should go in.

The office was a large room with deep green walls, lined with neatly stacked bookshelves and filing cabinets. At the far end, the General sat behind his ordered desk, his hands clasped. I closed the door, and then stood to attention in front of the desk.

"At ease," he said. I relaxed my stance. "I want you to tell me exactly what happened."

I did just that, starting with Ash's suspicions during the presentations, to our meeting in the lobby, and finally the confrontation that resulted in Baldie's knee being shot out. He nodded every now and then as I talked. When I finished explaining, he brought Ash back in, who stood at my side.

"Your friend informs me that this man was looking specifically for you," he said, his eyes focused on Ash. "Any idea why that might be?"

"No, Sir. Never seen him before."

"I'll be questioning this man myself. I hope for your sake you're telling the truth."

There was a knock at the door and the General answered, "Come in." It was one of the graduates, who reported on the information gathered from the witnesses downstairs.

"Okay, it appears your stories check out." I let out a breath I hadn't realised I was holding. "I want to see written reports on my desk by tomorrow morning. You are dismissed. Go enjoy the rest of your graduation." We saluted and turned on our heels.

"Have you really never seen him before?" I asked as we retraced our steps back downstairs.

"If I have, I don't remember him."

I wanted to believe him, but the attack wasn't random. Baldie had set out looking for Ash. I supposed it was possible he could have been hired, or maybe a relative of someone who held a grudge against Ash, however, the whole ordeal seemed very personal.

"Thanks for the help," I said. If it hadn't been for Ash making him drop the weapon, things could have ended very differently. I had let myself get distracted by my surroundings – a mistake that could have cost me my life. Alone, it would have been a different story; I wouldn't have had to worry about his reaction to my ability. I chuckled to myself at the mental image of Baldie trembling in fear at the sight of someone half his size.

"Don't mention it. Besides, I should be thanking you. Who knows what would have happened if you hadn't spotted the knife?"

He gave me a quick pat on the back and smiled as we traversed the lobby. The library was packed with people, though it was clear the crowd had thinned somewhat since we last saw it. There was a short silence as the doors opened, and people turned to observe us. A few wandered up to us, asking if we were all right. One nearby elderly woman scoffed at us, saying we deserved to be put down. I glared at her until she huffed and turned her back on us.

We looked around the room and managed to spot Lucas and Graeme, who were getting acquainted in our absence. They asked about what happened, and we found ourselves retelling the events once more.

Lucas asked Graeme if he had thought about following in his brother's footsteps and joining the army. He shrugged. Graeme was studying mechanics at the Engineer's Guild. They were working on designing and implementing a form of public transport that would run on rails above the rooftops of Rachat. It would certainly make getting around the city easier. As it was, transport vehicles were limited to military operations outside of the city, on account of the city streets being too narrow.

Ash yawned, and for the first time that day I noticed how tired he looked, his shoulders drooping a little, and his eyes not quite fully open.

"You look beat, Bro. Rough night?"

Ash shook his head. "I've been trying to shield myself all day, which is exhausting enough on its own. Then I had to freeze that knife, which might not have looked like much, but it takes a lot more energy to do it that quickly. The hangover this morning didn't exactly help either." He laughed.

"Well, I should head back home. Mom and Dad are probably freaking out by now."

"They'll be pissed that you came anyway. You should stay a few more hours," Ash said. "I hardly get to see you these days."

"Nah, I got things to take care of for tomorrow." Graeme put an arm around Ash and gave him a few taps to the back. "I'll tell Mom you said 'hi'. She'll be glad to know you're doing okay."

"Yeah, whatever," Ash grumbled.

"It was nice meeting you guys. Take care of my big bro, okay?" We shook hands again and he left, waving as he passed out of sight.

Ash left soon after, saying he needed a nap, leaving Lucas and I to head to the cafeteria for lunch. I hadn't realised how hungry I was until Lucas mentioned food. We parted ways afterwards, and I went back to the dorms, stopping along the way to pick up two copies of the incident report form, in case Ash had forgotten. He was already fast asleep, so I changed out of my uniform and sat down at the desk to fill out my report. Ash stirred a couple of times, mumbling something I couldn't quite make out. Sleep-talking was common after exhausting ourselves through the use of our abilities, especially for Ash. It was as though he reacted to the emotions around him even in sleep. I felt tired myself, so I decided on having a quick power nap, and laid down on my bed, looking up at the ceiling.

*****

When I awoke, I noticed Ash was up and nowhere to be seen. Only the faint glow of the street lamps illuminated the room. So much for a power nap, I thought. The sound of the door opening and closing caught my attention.

"Look who's finally up," Ash said. I sat up and wiped the gunk from the corners of my eyes. Ash was out of breath and I saw the sweat beading on his forehead. "I went for a jog to clear my head," he said. "You up for a bit of sparring? I need a chance to really vent."

I was a little frustrated too after the day's events, so I nodded and we gathered up our things to head to the gym. There were only a few others using the facilities when we arrived. We secured our items in the locker room, and went out into the open hall. After doing some stretches and a couple of laps around the place, we grabbed some head guards from the storeroom. The sparring started off light, but we quickly got into it. Ash had been kick-boxing since he joined the academy. It had become more of a way to relieve stress than an actual hobby. My interest in the sport only begun after meeting Ash a little over a year ago. Since then, he had taught me everything he knew.

"That all you got?" he taunted me, dodging another blow to the head. I replied with a front kick, catching him off-guard. He let out a gratifying grunt. His feet continued to dance every which way, keeping me on my toes, but he was tiring. I could hear it in his shallow breaths, and see it in his sluggish movements. He was slowing down. I wasn't in much better condition. My heart beat against my rib cage, and sweat poured from my brow and everywhere else imaginable. Every muscle was beginning to ache, begging me to stop, but my first victory was just within reach. A little more and I would finally beat him.

I willed myself to keep going, barely blocking the flurry of punches aimed at my head. I focused on his movements, biding my time as he wore himself down, and waiting for an opening. I blocked a kick to my side, and seeing my chance, lifted my right leg into a front kick. Ash moved back out of reach, as I hoped he would. At the last moment I faked out and moved into a roundhouse kick with my back leg, aiming for his unprotected flank.

For a short while, time slowed almost to a halt. I could see him grinning as he dropped to the floor, his leg sweeping mine out from under me. Then I was falling and time resumed. I landed with a thud on the mats, gasping for breath as the wind was knocked out of me.

"Man, I'm exhausted." Ash was at my side, hunched over, fists resting on his knees as he caught his breath. He ripped the Velcro strap open and threw his head-guard to one side. As I lay there, all I could think of was how close I was to beating him. In the year we had been training together, I had never been as close as I was then. And I blew it. I gritted my teeth in frustration. Next time would be different.

"You ready to hit the showers?" Ash asked. He stood over me, one hand held out.

"Whatever," I grumbled as I reached out and was pulled to my feet.

We made our way back to the locker room, discarding our protective gear into the basket on the way out. I decided not to shower at the gym, instead choosing to head back to the dorms for a real shower. I pulled on my jacket and gathered the rest of my belongings into my gym bag.

"I'm heading back for a long, hot shower," I called out over the noise of the running water.

"Okay, I'll see you back there."

Outside was cold and pitch black, save for the soft glow emanating from the windows of the nearby buildings and an occasional street lamp. The sky was overcast, the moon hid behind a blanket of silver-lined clouds. I walked on autopilot, down the dimly lit short-cut to the dorms, planning the rest of my evening. I would shower, grab something to eat, and then settle down with a book until I felt ready to sleep.

It was as I approached the end of the alleyway that a dark figure ran around the corner into me, dropping the papers he was carrying. He apologised and I mumbled under my breath that he should watch where he was going. Regardless, I bent down to help gather the loose sheets. A quick glance at one of the papers told me they were blood reports, most likely from the research department.

The man was about my size, though better built. He wore a navy jacket, the hood pulled close around his head. Strands of what I could only describe as silver hair spilled out of the hood, falling over his downcast eyes. I handed him the few sheets I had collected and he thanked me, keeping his head down the whole time, as if trying to avoid eye contact. With that he raced off into the night, to complete whatever errand it was he was on. Strange guy, I thought. I shrugged it off and continued on my way.

Chapter 4

Six days passed since graduation, and not a single mission came up. Or rather, there were none they deemed worthy enough of their newest superhuman squad. Ash was called back to General Marsten's office twice during that time. He wouldn't say much about it, only that they needed to debrief him on why someone had wanted to kill him.

We gathered at our usual spot, in one of the small meeting rooms on the ground floor of the main building, where Sergeant Locke was waiting for us, his hands clasped firmly behind his back. He raised himself onto his tiptoes, and back down again repeatedly as he waited for the last of us to fall into line.

"Okay. I know the five of you have been itching for some action," he said, "but there's been little activity outside the city. As a result, very few missions have been approved by the council. However, I managed to snag one of the lower priority missions, so you can get some experience out in the field."

I don't think any of us cared what priority the mission was given. This wouldn't just be our first mission, but also our first time outside the city walls. When I was younger, I often tried to climb the ramparts surrounding Rachat, to steal a quick look at the world outside. Unfortunately, they were too high for a mere runt such as myself, and a guard always found me before I managed to make any significant progress. I gave up on that pursuit eventually. Everything we had seen of the outside world came from books, and now we would be able to go beyond the walls and see it for ourselves. The excitement amongst the group was palpable.

"Your mission is to survey the ruins west of Rachat." Sergeant Locke pointed to a map on the wall. "The council has deemed it necessary to expand the city, so you'll be going to make sure it's safe before the techs can go in to set up the barriers."

The barriers in question were what enabled us to live safely within the city. They were eerie, black-metal structures that rose from the dirt like giant tentacles, and kept the vampires from crossing their perimeter. No-one knew exactly how they worked, though there were many theories. Some said they emitted an invisible light that was harmful to vampires, in the same way sunlight was. Then there were the wilder theories, like voodoo priests imbuing them with blood magic. God only knows where you'd find a voodoo priest in this day and age.

"White, you'll be in charge of this mission."

"Yes, Sir." Ash saluted.

"I want your team geared up and at the garage in twenty minutes. We'll go over intel in the Wisent. Dismissed." Sergeant Locke turned and walked briskly through the far door, leaving us to prepare. The silence was broken as soon as the door snapped shut.

"All right! Time for some action," Brad cheered.

"I wonder if we'll run into the enemy," said Katiya. "I've been itching to let off some steam."

"You're always itching to blow shit up," said Lucas. "Must be frustrated cause you're not getting any."

"Ha! Ironic coming from you."

"Okay, guys, listen up." Ash moved to stand in front of the group.

We turned our attention to him. "This might be a low-ranked mission, but it's also our first. So let's get it done smoothly, and show the rest of them how the Sunreavers do things."

Ash held his hand out in front of him, and one-by-one the others put their hand in too. They looked over at me expectantly. Sighing, I humoured them. Each of them let out a strange, but apparently traditional, battle-cry, which I imitated. It sounded something like 'hoo-aah'. They laughed at my pitiful effort. So much for morale boosting. Now I just felt like an idiot.

With our new-found ritual out of the way, we headed to the locker room to gear up. Our combat gear consisted of a black armoured vest and pants. It resembled something you'd expect to see on a spy rather than a soldier, but when you're dealing with creatures that could tear through bulletproof armour with ease... well, it was better to keep it light and flexible. Taking into account the cold weather, we added a long-sleeved thermal top to our outfits, which we wore beneath the vests. Sometimes, your worst enemy isn't living or undead, it's nature herself.

Last on our shopping list was weapons. I opted for a handgun and assault rifle, both with silver bullets, of course. A pair of silver knives completed my equipment, in case anything decided to get up close and personal. Lucas was the master of knives. With his ability he could slice open an opponent before they knew what hit them. How he would fare against a vampire's speed was still up for debate since we had never met one yet. Lucas was also our sharpshooter, packing his modified sniper. Katiya and Brad preferred their shotguns, whereas Ash went for a more all-round approach like me.

With our gear on, we jogged over to the garage, located at the edge of the city, and at the back of the military base. Sergeant Locke was waiting for us. He checked his watch as we reached him, looking pleased with our response time. The Wisent was a long, armoured vehicle, with enough space in the back to carry two full squads. Next to it, three large supply trucks were being loaded with the strange black-metal tendrils, and what I supposed was the heavy machinery needed to securely plant them into the ground.

We climbed into the back of the Wisent, with Sergeant Locke joining us and closing the doors behind him. He gave two sharp taps on the glass panel that separated us from the cab, and the engine flared to life.

"Okay, as you know, you'll be sweeping the ruins of Marmagne for any threats, so we can safely erect the barriers. Once that's done, demolition'll be going in to clean up the mess, and then the building can start. We've had scouts keeping an eye on this place for some time. Intel suggests the place is clean, but we've had reports of minor activity nearby, so we need to be damn sure. The last thing we need is to find out there's some hidden tunnels beneath the ruins, crawling with vampires."

Sergeant Locke took a roll of laminated paper out from a compartment under his seat, and laid it out across the raised structure between the two rows of inward-facing seats. It was a map of the areas surrounding Rachat. The area we were heading to was circled in black ink. He pointed to it, making sure we all took notice.

"This is Marmagne. We'll be arriving here," he said, pointing again, "by what's left of the main road. Marmagne was the site of a large-scale battle some forty years ago, back when I was still learning to crawl. The centre of the town was spared, mostly, but any buildings still standing may be in the process of collapsing, so caution is advised should you need to go inside. Also, our scouts have marked some of the structures as priority targets." He pointed to several small crosses on the map. "If the enemy is present, this is where they'll most likely be hiding, as these buildings are mostly intact. Any questions?"

We all responded with a, "No, Sir."

"Good. When we arrive, I'll be handing over command to Captain White. Since this is your first time out in the field, I'll be evaluating your performance out there. I'll be staying with the Wisent to monitor your progress via the radio, and to await the supply convoy's arrival."

Sergeant Locke handed a headset to each of us, and we put them on. We took it in turn to check they were working, by pressing the small button next to the ear piece and reporting in.

It wasn't long before the Wisent lurched to a stop, and a voice from the cab told us we had arrived. We hopped out and were greeted by the sight of jagged hills of copper dirt, and the haunting remains of what was once a small community. Houses lay in ruin, some of them recognisable only by the house-shaped stumps of white stone and wood. A church stood defiantly amidst the graves of its neighbours. Long-dead trees scattered the landscape, rising like ghosts from the dried, cracked earth, with their withered bark and out-stretched limbs. The wind whistled through the ruins, carrying with it a chill that penetrated me to the core.

A tap on my shoulder snapped me back into reality. The others were huddled around the back of the Wisent, studying the map and waiting for Ash to give our orders.

"Lucas, I want you to head through the centre of town. See if you can get to the top of the church steeple and watch for any movement. Kat and Mik, head towards the old mill on the north side of town, then swing round and check out these buildings." He pointed to the map, showing our intended route. "Brad and I will go south to the farmhouses, and we'll meet up with you guys on the far side. After that, we'll fan out and head back through to check all these ruins."

We nodded in agreement, and I silently cursed Ash for pairing me up with Katiya, though I understood his reasoning. He and I were the only two of the group with a psychic ability. That alone meant we'd be in separate groups. Brad didn't have an offensive ability, and so Katiya was the only choice remaining. I understood, but that didn't mean I had to like it.

"We're not expecting any contact, but stay alert and let's get back safe. Move out!"

Katiya and I began our trek through the deserted town, checking each of the crumbling ruins for any signs of life, or un-life. Luckily, most of the buildings had only a single floor remaining, and with half of their walls missing, there wasn't much place to hide anything.

"This sucks," Katiya moaned as we checked yet another empty house. "All clear... again."

It felt like an eternity passed before we came to the end of the street. So much for an exciting first time outside the city, I thought. I was expecting more than some old ruins and a dead landscape. A large, barren field lay before us, with our destination on the other side. A narrow path ran down the side of the field, dotted with potholes and craters, filled with muddy water.

"I'm in position," Lucas' voice crackled over the radio. There was silence for a minute before he said, "I can see the happy couple approaching the mill now."

"Can you see this too?" Katiya said, turning in the direction of the church and giving Lucas the finger. He laughed, but said nothing.

The mill was a large, wooden building with a gabled roof, or what was left of one. The windows were boarded up, and the walls damp and rotting. A waterwheel that had long since broken away from the mill, found itself stranded downstream, caught on a fallen tree and covered in a blanket of moss.

"I'll take the back," I said, and Katiya nodded.

The wooden steps leading to the back door creaked and groaned under my weight. I stepped carefully, not wanting to put a foot through them. Once at the top, I peered inside. Sensing no immediate threat I opened the door and went in. The smell that hit me then was horrid. It was a damp, musty smell that threatened to bring up the contents of my stomach. And there was a sharp, metallic smell, almost acidic, that lingered in the air and caught on the back of my throat. I tried breathing through my mouth, but the air was so thick it left a taste on my tongue, which only made things worse. I backed outside to take a few deep breaths and regain my composure.

There was no way to avoid the smell, so I took one last breath before charging back in. With my gun aimed, I scanned the corners of the room. There were two exits, one straight ahead and the other to my left. I chose left. The smaller room was empty, just like the last. I turned to check the other exit, when I saw something flash past the second doorway, out of the corner of my eye. I ducked back behind the wall, praying that whatever it was hadn't seen me.

"Katiya, where are you?" I whispered into the radio.

"Basement," came the reply. "This place stinks."

I crept forward, hoping to avoid any creaky floorboards, until I reached the doorway, and pressed my back against the wall. From where I stood, I could see the staircase at one end of the hall. The movement had looked like it was heading the other way. I stepped out into the hallway, gun held directly in front of me. It was a dead end, save for one last door.

I positioned myself against the wall, as I had done before, and took short, shallow breaths, trying to steady myself while avoiding the stench that pervaded the air. A ruffling noise came from inside the room. My heart beat wildly against my chest. I spun around the door frame, my eyes scanning the room for any movement. At one side of the room a crow sat on an old dresser. It cocked its head at me and squawked.

"Shit," I muttered, and gave a nervous laugh. Then I saw the 'body'. I use the term loosely because calling it a body implies it was shaped like one, with all the necessary parts. Skeletal remains was more like it, and I doubted it was a complete set at that. The stained bones lay strewn across the floor, snapped and broken in so many places. Were it not for the fractured skull staring blankly back at me, I probably wouldn't have recognised them as human.

The crow continued to watch me with its beady black eyes. It gave another squawk and fluttered away through one of the holes in the ceiling. My heart leaped into my mouth when a hand landed on my shoulder. I span around and backed up, gun aimed at Katiya, whose eyes widened, as though I would actually shoot her. The thought had crossed my mind a few times in the past.

"Jesus... fuck! Don't do that." I could hear the blood racing through my skull.

She laughed. "Oh man, that was priceless." Reaching up to her headset she said, "All clear at the mill, but we're gonna need a change of underwear for Mik."

There were some laughs from Brad and Lucas.

"Not funny," I growled, making sure to knock shoulders with her as I stormed out of the room.

"Oh, come on. It was kinda funny." Katiya chased after me.

"You startled me. I could have shot you." Tempting as it was at times, I had no desire to be put through a series of investigations and disciplinaries because of one annoying female.

"Okay, okay. I'm sorry. I shouldn't have snuck up on you. Happy now?"

"Not really."

Katiya sighed. "Didn't think so."

We walked in silence to the next row of houses. The radio crackled, "Farmhouses are clear. We're gonna work our way towards you guys now."

"Roger that," Katiya replied. "You take that side." She pointed to the left side of the street, and I nodded.

The houses here were in better condition than the first lot. Still, there wasn't a lot to check. Sergeant Locke had mentioned there had been a battle here. I wondered what all the fighting had been over. Nothing about this town seemed terribly important. We found nothing in the houses. About half an hour later, we met up with Ash and Brad on the far side of the ruins.

"How's things looking up there, Lucas?" Ash asked.

"Just peachy, if you don't mind staring at lifeless ruins all day. Techs have arrived. They're starting to unload now."

"Okay, we'll fan out from here and make our way back to the Wisent. Brad, you'll take the southern-most block. Mik, you're on the north block. Kat and I will cover the square in the centre. Let's get this finished up so we can head home."

Finally, I could get away from Katiya. My section had only a small number of houses, though they were mostly intact and larger than the previous ones. Old cars littered the street, blackened and rusting, stripped down to their bare frames. Sighing, I made my way to the first house.

The door still hung from one of its hinges, laid across the dirt and gravel, the wood warped and splintered from years of abuse at the hands of the elements. Inside was as bare as outside. A few pieces of broken furniture lay here and there; a table smashed in half; wooden chairs with broken legs and backs; a rotten bed reduced to nothing more than tatters and springs. No sign of anything living.

I stepped back outside, and the radio buzzed to life. "I got movement. North quarter," Lucas said. "I can't get a clean view from here."

"I'm on it," I replied. "Point me in the right direction."

"Okay, I see you. The house in front of you and to the right. It was in the downstairs window."

"Got it." I ran towards the house, flattening myself against the outside wall.

"I'm on my way over to you, Mik. Don't do anything stupid," Ash told me. "Kat, you keep the search going."

The front room was clear. It seemed unlikely they went upstairs, since they would have had to pass the front door to do so. Footsteps. I turned towards the source, handgun drawn. The figure dashed past a doorway. I fired a single shot and it grazed the door frame. Missed. I was in pursuit. He ran out into a small courtyard. No cover out there, I thought. Stupid man.

I fired again, aiming for the ground beneath his feet. "Don't move," I yelled. He froze, his hands raised in the air as he turned to me. "What are you?" I asked. He wasn't a vampire, not outside in the middle of the day.

"What do you mean?"

"*What* are you?" I repeated.

He laughed, as though the answer were obvious. "I'm like you... human."

"How do I know you're not a shifter?"

"My left hand." He tilted his head towards it. It was bleeding, though the cut wasn't deep. Any shifter would have healed a cut that shallow in seconds.

"Then you're one of their minions."

Again with the laugh. "Minions? Boy, they sure have you brainwashed in that little sanctuary of yours."

"Ironic, coming from you. You've probably been mind-fucked by a vampire."

"Is that what you think? I chose this life of my own free will."

"Then you're nothing but a traitor." I spat the word at him, disgusted that anyone could turn against their own kind. Anyone who could do that had to be scum.

"I'm a traitor? You're the one holding a gun to a fellow human."

He had a point. If I was right and he was under a vampire's spell, then it wasn't his fault. He could be innocent, and maybe he could lead us to the real enemy.

"Mik," the voice in my ear called. "Where are you?"

"Courtyard, behind the houses on the north side," I replied. "Target is a middle-aged male, human, no visible weapons."

"Understood. I'll be there in a minute."

I edged towards the man, gun still aimed at his chest. He stared back at me. I didn't want to kill him, not if there was a way to save him. There had to be a way to break a vampire's spell. Maybe if we killed the vampire, he would return to normal. Keeping him alive was the best option, and I kept telling myself this.

He groaned in pain, doubling over and clutching his stomach. He hadn't seemed wounded or in pain before. Then he lunged at me. I fired without thinking. Three shots hit him square in the chest, just as I had been trained. He fell to his knees. His hands brushed over the bullet wounds and came away smeared in blood. I saw his eyes widen as he took in the sight of his blood-soaked hands. Then his eyelids fell and so did his body, landing on the flagstones with a thud.

"Mik, thank God you're okay." Ash ran to my side. He looked down at the body, and rolled him over with his foot. "I heard the gunshots."

"He was a human," I said. Just a human. Another victim in this endless war, except this time it was a human spilling human blood.

"Yeah, I know you can take care of yourself," he said. "Doesn't stop me worrying about you though. Come on, let's get the rest of this mission finished." He kneeled next the body to check for a pulse, and with his free hand activated his headset. "Enemy is down. Continue as planned."

Chapter 5

The rest of the mission went by without a hitch. By all means it was a successful mission. There were no casualties on our side, the area was now cleared of any enemies, and the perimeter was set. I guess most people would have been ready to celebrate, but not me. My mind flashed back to the moment I pulled the trigger and shot another human being. I watched the life drain from his eyes, unable to look away. All of the physical and emotional training I received over the last year meant nothing when faced with the reality of death. Nothing could have prepared me.

I kept reminding myself he was a traitor to the human race, a servant to vampires, in the hope it would make things easier. It didn't. He was the enemy, but still, he was human. One of us.

I wandered the halls of the dormitories, my hands tucked into the pockets of my faded blue jeans, barely registering people as they passed me by. My head hung, I could feel an unbearable weight pressing down on me, enveloping me in its foul warmth. Before long I found myself outside. The sky looked as gloomy as I felt. Only a few stars were visible behind the bleak carpet of clouds. An icy wind blew over me, stinging against my skin as the fine hairs on my arms stood to attention. The black t-shirt I wore offered little protection. My feet carried me in no particular direction, away from the noise and commotion of the dormitories and into the dark silence. I rounded a corner, a small figure stumbling into me.

"Watch where you're fucking going," I spat the words at him, continuing my slow walk to anywhere and nowhere.

"Mikhail?" the voice came from behind me. I paused briefly and looked over my shoulder to see Lucas. "You okay?"

"I'm fine," I replied, hoping he wouldn't start to follow me, which he did. The last thing I needed was anyone pestering me and feeling sorry for me.

"You sure? You look pretty pissed off to me."

"I'm fine. I just want to be *left alone.*" I made sure to grind out those last two words. He stopped following.

"Are you drunk?"

"No." But maybe I should be, I added silently. People always talk about drowning their sorrows in alcohol, and finding solace at the bottom of a pint glass, so there had to be something to it. Perhaps I could drown my misery. And best of all, no-one would think to look for me at a bar. Perpetually sober Mik drinking? Katiya would probably die of laughter.

I turned the next corner and waited a moment, then peered out to see Lucas heading in the opposite direction. No doubt he'd be running off to find Ash. A sharp drop of cold water landed on my nose. I looked up to see more following, illuminated in the glow of a nearby lantern. They fell slowly at first but were soon picking up their pace. I took off in the direction of the barracks bar, hoping to make it there before the skies opened up.

*****

The rain was forgiving, holding back until I reached the bar. The warmth inside stung my damp, cold skin. I went to the bar, taking up a stool at the far end. As I hoped, the place was almost empty. A few small groups of friends sat at some of the round tables, their voices barely audible over the sound of music from the speakers placed around the room.

Hans was working behind the bar, as always, his back turned to me while he wiped down an already sparkling clean worktop. I guess keeping busy helped to pass the time. From the back I could see his wiry, grey hair was starting to thin, leaving a small bald patch on top of his head. His eyes caught mine in the mirror behind the rows of spirits and liquors. Most of the human race had been obliterated a century ago, but humanity would be damned if it didn't reinvent a vast range of alcohol during that time. It certainly wouldn't have been one of my priorities.

"Well, if it ain't Mikhail. Ya all alone tonight?" His eyes scanned the room, probably looking for the rest of my squad.

"Just me," I replied.

"What can I get ya?" A good question. Having never drank alcohol before, I was unsure what would be good.

"A pint of this," I said, pointing to the nearest of the large pump handles.

"Bad day?" Hans asked as he poured the drink. "Don't think I ever saw ya drink anythin' but ginger ale before." He placed the glass in front of me. The clear, golden liquid sloshed against the sides, underneath the white foam that decorated it. A small trickle meandered down the side of the glass, pooling at the bottom.

"Yeah, something like that." I gave Hans my payment and lifted the glass to my mouth, sipping at the sweet liquid, my throat tingling with a surprising warmth. It was a far more pleasant experience than I imagined it would be. I lifted the glass further, indulging in bigger mouthfuls until I had to stop and gasp for air.

"So, what's troublin' ya, lad?" I looked up to meet his eyes, set in a rounded mass of defined wrinkles and bristly grey-black whiskers. "Ya graduated not long ago, didn't ya? Trouble on ya first mission?" I had to hand it to him. His mind was sharper than I would have guessed. Perhaps, that came from working around people all the time.

"I killed someone," I answered before going back to my drink.

"Ah, say no more." Hans turned to pick up a shot glass. He reached up to the top shelf and picked off a brown glass bottle, from which he poured a dark-brown liquid. He set the glass in front of me and I looked at him, confused. "On the house."

I lifted the glass to my lips, intending to sip it at first.

"Ya're gonna wanna knock that back quickly. Trust me."

The smell alone was enough to make me feel light-headed. It smelled of pure alcohol, and something I couldn't quite put my finger on. I swallowed it in one gulp, figuring I may as well do as Hans suggested. I coughed, the bitter, spicy shot coating my throat in a layer of fire. That was more like what I expected alcohol to be. I downed some more of the pint in an attempt to douse the flames at the back of my throat, though it only calmed them.

Hans looked down at my empty glass. "Another?"

I nodded and handed him the glass.

"Look, ya ain't the first, nor will ya be the last guy ta come here and try ta forget the fact that ya killed someone," he said, his hand pulling back the pump once more. "But let me tell ya somethin'. Gettin' wasted might help tonight, but it won't solve anythin' in the long run."

"Maybe not," I said, handing him some more coins. I'd worry about that part when I got to it. Right then, I just wanted to forget.

I could feel my cheeks starting to radiate as I continued with the second pint. When I started on the third, it felt as though there was a haze blanketing my brain, and the air around me was somehow less thick. Starting to work, I thought, my mind beginning to wander elsewhere, and the troubles washed away with the flow of alcohol.

"You asshole." I set my drink down and looked to my left, to see Ash walking towards me, his fists clenched. I smiled, though I'm not sure why. "I've been worried sick looking for you." He sat on the stool next to me and motioned for Hans. "I'll have whatever he's having."

Hans nodded and finished drying the glass in his hand, before pouring another pint.

"How many has he had?"

"That there's his third."

Ash turned on his stool to face me. "So what was your plan? You come here without telling anyone, get pissed, and then what?" I continued drinking, though it appeared this was one problem I couldn't make disappear by drowning it in alcohol. "Come on, Mik. Talk to me. I can't help you if I don't know what the problem is."

"Maybe you can't help me," I growled, slamming my half-empty glass onto the bar. "How could *you* understand? You didn't kill someone today."

"That's what this is all about?" Ash sighed. "I should have guessed. Still, do I have to remind you that if I wanted, I could feel exactly what you're feeling?"

"Just because you can feel it doesn't mean you understand."

"I understand better than you could imagine." Ash took a few large mouthfuls of his drink. "You're not the only one who has killed before."

I looked at him in disbelief. Surely he was only saying it to make me feel better.

"The day I found out I could do this..." He lifted his free hand from where it rested on his knee. The water in the air above his hand began to condense, then freeze, creating a small sphere of ice. "There were two casualties, a young girl and her... boyfriend." His fist clenched, crushing the ice. "I couldn't stop it. He froze to death."

"How is that the same? You had no choice. You couldn't control it."

"And what choice did you have? Let him kill you? This is the army, Mik. When we're out there, it's kill or be killed."

"I know, I know. I thought it would be easier because they're the enemy, but it's not. I feel like I've done something awful."

"I hear you, man. But sometimes, there's nothing you can do about it. You did what you had to... to survive. And if it makes you feel any better, I'm glad you did."

We sat in silence for the next few minutes, while I pondered over Ash's words. It was true it was either me or the enemy, and I had no desire to die anytime soon. When it was put as simple as that, it seemed to make a sad sort of sense. I really didn't have a choice. Still, that didn't mean I had to feel good about it, but at least I could stop blaming myself. That man forced my hand when he lunged for me. He made his choice, and died for it.

"Feeling better?" Ash asked. Not that he had to ask.

"A little."

"Lemme give ya kids some advice," Hans said. He lined three shot glasses out on the bar, and filled them with the same dark liquid he had given me earlier. He handed one each to us both and took the last for himself. "Ya didn't want to kill him. Ya have a good heart. Be thankful for that and pray ya don't lose it along the way. Now, bottoms up."

We downed our shots together. Hans let out a quick 'Ahh", as though it weren't liquid fire he had swallowed. Ash screwed up his face a little, but didn't seem overly affected by it. I coughed and spluttered, which the others found hilarious. I scowled at Ash, who held up his hands as if to say, 'Hey, not my fault'.

Hans cleared up the empty glasses and moved them to the sink at the far end of the bar, where another customer waited.

Now we had some privacy, I asked, "Did you want to kill him?"

Ash looked away from me. For a moment he stayed silent, staring into the bottom of his glass. "Yes," he whispered. "I was so angry, so confused... there was a moment when I wanted him to die." I watched as Ash downed the rest of his drink, the pain clearly written across his face. "But then I heard his screams. He died slowly and painfully. I wanted to take it all back, to make it stop, but I couldn't. I wished for his death, and it came true. If I hadn't blacked out from the stress, I probably would've killed the girl too."

"Sorry, I shouldn't have–"

"It's okay," he interrupted. "It's in the past. I just wanna forget." Ash picked up his empty glass and raised it to Hans, who was walking back to us. "Something a little stronger please, Hans."

Hans paused, observing the look on Ash's face. He said nothing, instead doing as he was asked and filling a small tumbler with something clear and brown. He sat the glass in front of Ash, who handed him a note and took a mouthful.

We spent the next hour or so, talking about anything we could think of that didn't involve death, in an attempt to forget about the lives we had taken. We talked about our first views of the outside world, and the latest rumours, which Hans was happy to fill us in on. Katiya would not be pleased when she found out who she had supposedly slept with. I felt sorry for whoever started that rumour.

As I finished my last drink, I didn't feel as drunk as I hoped I would be. That is, until I stood up and almost fell. Ash was there to catch me, and I laughed off my lack of balance. We left the bar, waving bye to Hans on the way out as he wiped down the tables.

*****

The walk back to our room was excruciatingly slow. My left arm was draped over Ash's shoulders, and his right arm around my waist. By then the streets were quiet, as were the dormitory corridors, meaning few people saw me in my sorry state. Ash fumbled with the lock to our door and carried me inside, throwing me onto my bed. The room appeared to spin, making me feel nauseous. I pushed myself up onto my elbows and the room steadied. Ash kneeled down in front of me and began removing my shoes. I giggled as he pulled off my socks, his cold hands brushing against the soles of my feet.

"Arms up," he said, gripping my t-shirt and beginning to pull it up. I lifted my arms up and a hand brushed past my nipple, still hard from the cold wind and rain. I gasped and Ash paused. A second later, the t-shirt was pulled over my head and thrown to the floor.

Ash sat beside me on the bed, one hand brushing through my hair, and the other circling my left nipple. A long finger began to flick over it. I sucked in a breath and Ash smirked, pleased with the reaction he was getting. The hand on my chest pressed against me, forcing me onto my back. Ash's head lowered to meet mine, his lips pressing gently against my own. His tongue traced the line of my jaw, and then my neck. My skin tingled in its wake as he made his way down past my shoulders. I lifted my head to watch him, and his eyes fixed on mine.

Like a cobra, his lips clamped over my nipple. He sucked hard, his tongue flicking across the tip. It was an intense mix of pleasure and pain that arched my back and made me cry out. I felt him chuckle against me. My hands gripped the back of his short hair, torn between pressing him into me and pulling him off.

My heart beat wild against my chest and my breath was ragged. The pleasure washed over my mind, blocking out any coherent thoughts. He stopped, giving the sensitive skin a quick kiss before he sat up to pull off his sweater, and tossed it carelessly to one side. The haze in my head lifted ever so slightly, enough to notice from where I lay that Ash was very excited. And in that brief moment, I realised I was too.

Before I could protest, his lips descended once more, heading straight for the untouched nipple. As the sensation took over me once more, I felt a few sharp tugs at my waist, then warmth, his hand sliding down into my boxers to take hold of me. I inhaled sharply. The hand began to move, slowly at first, but picking up speed, jerking against the cloth that seemed to grow tighter with every stroke. All the while, his mouth continued its relentless assault.

I opened my eyes when the hand retreated, unable to remember when I had closed them. His lips gave one last touch to the sore skin they had worked on so meticulously. Ash stood and moved to the bottom of the bed, his hands gripping the waist of my jeans. I lifted my hips as he pulled them down over my legs. He reached up once more, tugging at the thin material that covered my erection, exposing me completely.

I watched as he started to unfasten his belt, then a button. He looked up, caught me staring and smiled. The zip came down ever so slowly, teasing me. He wiggled his hips gently, letting the jeans fall of their own accord. One hand played over the line of his abs, following a thin trail of golden hair. It disappeared beneath his waistband, grasping and stroking as he watched me watch him.

He dropped the boxers in one swift movement and crawled onto the bed, parting my legs so he could kneel between them. His erection was in plain view above my own. I had the sudden urge to reach out and touch it. Ash gave a surprised look when my hand wrapped around him. I moved my hand down to the base, feeling the soft skin slide over him, and back up again, fascinated by the slight curve as he let out a deep moan. I repeated the movement again, and again. His hands played along the inside of my thighs as his hips began to rock impatiently.

Without warning, his lips crashed down onto mine. His tongue pressed inside me, snaking around my own. I could feel his body begin to tremble as he pulled back. His hand gripped mine, prying it from him.

"Not yet," he whispered to me. Ash stalked backwards, until his head was above my waist. As he crouched down, his tongue swept across the tip of my erection. My whole body shuddered with anticipation. "I love virgins," he said. "They're always so responsive."

I felt the heat creep up into my cheeks, and opened my mouth to say something. The words were cut off, and all thought lost as the warmth of his mouth enveloped me. I threw my head back and cried out. With each bob of his head, the tension in my lower gut grew and grew, his tongue working in time with every stroke. I clawed at the edges of the mattress, desperate for something to hold onto. Each second the urgency, the need for release, became stronger. I began to thrust my hips upward, diving deeper into his mouth, faster and faster. I could feel *it* coming. Just below the surface it was waiting, gaining strength with every lunge.

Ash's hands latched onto my hips, restricting my movement. I looked down to see his eyes focused on mine. He moved slowly up and down, and it wasn't enough. I thrashed wildly against him, trying to find my release, but his grip held me firm, prolonging the torture.

I whimpered softly when he lifted his head and climbed back into position, kneeling over me. His arousal brushed against mine and he took them both in one hand. The salty taste of his lips was thrust into me, his tongue exploring deeper than before. I mimicked its movements as I pressed into the kiss, and it was back again.

It started in one leg, a small twitch. My fingers dug into Ash's shoulders and he grunted, the sound mixing into my pants and groans. Then out of nowhere, I felt it hit me. My body writhed and convulsed under him. I screamed my pleasure into his mouth as he fought to keep the kiss going. It racked through my body until it spilled over, a warm, wet feeling landing on my chest and stomach. Ash began to shudder above me, his strokes losing their rhythm. He broke the kiss, gasping for air. I felt the length of him, still pressed against me in his hand, begin to spasm as he let out a chorus of moans. The wet feeling hit me again, mixing with my own release.

Ash gave a long sigh and collapsed on top of me, his face buried in the pillow. My chest heaved against Ash as we panted to regain our breath. It was a few minutes before Ash pushed himself up onto his elbows. He looked down at me and smiled.

"I guess you're not so asexual after all." He laughed. I tried to frown, to think of something to say, but nothing came. My mind was blank, still awash with the afterglow. A feeling of relaxation spread through my entire body, turning my limbs to jelly. "I'll go get a towel," he said, bringing my attention to the stickiness that joined us together.

It was then the realisation started to sink in. I had had sex with Ash, my best friend and room-mate. Not full intercourse though. Thank God. However, I definitely needed to rethink my self-proclaimed asexuality. Or was it too far-fetched to blame it on the alcohol?

Ash was stood in the doorway, wiping himself down with a blue towel. "God, you look so hot like that," he said, walking towards the bed. He climbed over me, dropping the towel on my chest. A quick look down as I wiped away the evidence of our drunken adventure told me he was ready to go again. The sight of it was enough to hitch my breath and my lower regions responded to him.

"Wanna go again?" he whispered in my ear.

"Fuck you," I said, pushing him off to one side. There, I was sobering up already.

"That could be arranged." I didn't need to see his face to know he was smirking behind me. He spooned against my back, trapping his hard length between us. One arm draped across my chest. Somehow, I hadn't pictured Ash as the type to cuddle after sex. But I couldn't have imagined I would end up having sex with him either, so my judgements could hardly be trusted. And then there were the other thoughts plaguing my mind. What did this mean for me, and for us?

"Don't think about it too hard," Ash said. "Just take it for what it is and don't try to complicate things."

I asked, "How do you do that?" It was as if he knew what I was thinking, though that was beyond the limits of his ability.

"What? Read your mind?" He laughed. "I can't, but I've known you for a year now, so I can take a pretty good guess. Plus, you're broadcasting your emotions clearly tonight."

I hadn't even thought about keeping up my psychic shields. Shit!

"Don't bother. Alcohol messes with your shielding," he said. I wish I had known that before drinking myself stupid. "You're confused and scared. Why?"

"Because... I don't know what this means."

"It was just sex. It doesn't have to mean anything. Nothing has to change because we had a bit of fun."

I thought about it for a minute. Could sex be nothing more than a bit of fun? I had never thought of it as anything other than pointless intimacy, designed to create attachments and ultimately end with pain. I couldn't deny that it felt good. Scratch that, it felt amazing. Maybe it was as Ash had said, and I should accept it for what it was, a bit of drunken fun.

Ash's fingers danced lightly over my skin, his warm breath caressing the back of my neck. I sighed, and his arm wrapped around me tighter, pulling me deeper into the embrace. His lips pressed against my cheek and I could feel his smile widen.

"What are you afraid of?" he asked. "You could have this and so much more if you let yourself." When I didn't answer, he said, "Okay, let me tell you a story then. Once upon a time, there was a boy named Ash. He fell in love with the most beautiful girl in the world, Lisa Albridge. But Ash wasn't like the other boys and girls. He had a secret."

"Why are you telling me this?"

His hand reached up, and he pressed a single finger to my lips. "Just listen. For a while he didn't tell Lisa, but he hated keeping it from her and lying to her. So one day, he told her. Lisa was scared and angry. She ran all the way home and refused to speak to him. Ash was so upset that he locked himself in his room and wouldn't come out. Then later that day, Lisa called and asked to see him. He was so happy to see her, but she had another boy with her. A new boyfriend."

Ash's arms began to twitch. His head buried into the nape of my neck, and I felt the slightest trickle run across my skin. "She wanted to show me how little I meant to her. She wanted to watch as her new boyfriend beat me up. They called me a freak, and a monster. He started hitting me and I let him. That's when the ice came."

The trickle turned into a steady stream. I rolled over to face him and meet his eyes, their sparkle hidden behind a veil of tears. God, I'd been so selfish and stupid. All those times he tried to get me to open up and help me with my pain, and I denied him. All the times I saw his pain surface, and I did nothing, thinking only of myself and my desire to keep a distance between us. I was a horrible friend.

"They were right," he sobbed. I lifted a hand to his cheek, wiping away the tears with my thumb. It hurt inside, like a knife twisting deep within me, to see Ash like that. He was supposed to be happy and carefree. Not *this*.

"You're not a monster," I said. "You are *anything*, but a monster. You're a good person and they didn't deserve you. I don't deserve you."

"Don't say that."

"Why not? It's true. All I've ever done is wallow in my self-pity. I saw you were hurting deep down, and I ignored it. A good friend would have done anything to try and make it better."

"But you have done something." He gave me a weak smile. "This. Right here. You're the only person I've told willingly about what I did. You're here for me now, and that means a lot to me."

"What else can I do?"

"Trust me," he said. "Tell me what bothers you so much, so I can help you."

I sighed and looked away from him, turning to face the ceiling. Whether it was the alcohol or a sense of duty to Ash that made me open up, I don't know. "Everybody leaves me. My parents, Mrs. Rousseau, the kids at the orphanage, foster parents... everyone. There's something wrong with me, and it makes everyone leave me. I don't know if I could go through that again."

"I get it now. You're scared to get close to anyone, because you think they'll leave you."

I nodded. "It scares me, you know, how close I've gotten to you without realising it. I tried to push you away at first, but you kept coming back. Truth is, deep down I was happy that someone wanted to be my friend." Now it was my turn with the tears, my eyes starting to fill up. "But I'm scared I'll wake up one day, and you'll be gone too. I don't know what I'd do if you were gone."

Without Ash, I honestly believed I would have nothing. Lucas, Brad, Katiya... I considered them friends, but not in the way Ash was my friend. They didn't understand me like Ash did. He was my only real close-friend. He got me in a way that no-one else did, and now I understood why. Ash had been through his own hell, and had his own pain to show for it. The thought of him being gone was too much to even think about.

"Shh, it's all right," he said, one hand running through my hair. "I'm not going anywhere." He leaned in to plant a kiss on my forehead. "Do you want me to sleep with you tonight?"

I nodded and turned away from him. His chest moulded against the line of my back and his arm reached over to take my hand in his.

"I won't leave you," he whispered. "Not ever. You can count on it."

I lay there, afraid to move. I felt the rise and fall of Ash's chest, his breath ghosting over my skin. His heart beat against me, slowing as he drifted off. Nothing has to change, I thought, his words echoing in the back of my mind. I didn't believe him. Something had already changed, and I wasn't sure if we'd be able to turn back now. A sudden wave of fear washed over me. Ash's hand gripped mine tighter. It was as if he was trying to comfort me, even in sleep.

He's still here, I thought. And in that moment, it was enough.

Chapter 6

From the moment I opened my eyes the next morning, I knew something was wrong. For one thing, the light seemed brighter than usual, and it felt as though someone had used my skull as a drum. More worrying, was the fact that I couldn't move for the heavy arm wrapped tight around me, and said arm had a body attached to it. A very happy, naked body, for that matter.

I lay completely frozen, hoping not to wake Ash as I recalled the events of the previous night. A suffocating heat began to creep over my body. I had to get out. Fighting the wave of panic, I lifted the arm carefully and began shuffling to the edge of the bed. Ash moved suddenly and I froze. He withdrew his hand to scratch at his face, giving me the opportunity to escape.

Standing up quickly, however, was not a good idea. My stomach lurched into my mouth and I ran into the bathroom, tripping over the clothes that lay strewn across the floor. Upon reaching the toilet, I collapsed to my knees and lifted the seat, just in time as my stomach convulsed and the first wave of bitter vomit forced its way out. When one wave ended, another started, giving me no time to regain my breath. This continued until I was sure there was nothing left inside me, leaving me with an empty hollow feeling in my stomach.

"You okay in there?" Ash asked. I looked round to see him peering round the door frame.

"Just great."

"If you say so. Make sure you drink plenty of water."

I glared at Ash. Just because it was my first time drinking, didn't mean I knew nothing about hangovers. I mean, I had witnessed Ash's more than a few times. He shrugged and retreated back into the main room, presumably to crawl back into bed now he was sure I wasn't dying. I flushed the toilet and pulled myself up to the sink, where I drank from the tap, attempting to wash away the horrid taste that clung to my mouth and throat.

Content that the taste had subsided, and worried that drinking any more would make me feel sick again, I closed the bathroom door. It was only then it dawned on me, I was well and truly naked. The events of the previous night bombarded my mind again, the insufferable heat crawling over my skin. I stepped into the shower and the icy water blasted over me.

I slid to the floor, not bothering to adjust the temperature dial. What had I done? Surely there was some rule against sleeping with your best friend. And to top it off, it went against my own personal rules, designed to keep me from getting attached to anyone. Then there were the other implications. All my life, I had had no desire to be close to anyone, so what was different about last night? I could blame everything on the alcohol, but I knew that would be a lie. I was upset over killing someone, and that left me vulnerable. But was I ready to accuse my best and only real friend of taking advantage of me? No, it wasn't his fault. I was as much to blame for not saying no.

Our pain was drawing us to each other and soon we'd pass the point of no-return, if we hadn't passed it already. If we continued on, it would only make things worse in the end. I needed to distance myself from Ash. It was the only option.

I pulled myself to my feet and turned off the water. My whole body shivered as I wrapped a towel around me and dried off. Ash was asleep, as expected, though he had moved to his own bed now. Trying to make as little noise as possible, I opened the wardrobe and grabbed a white t-shirt and black joggers. I dressed, threw a change of clothes in my gym bag and left the room. I needed to work out some frustration. Alone.

*****

The gym was almost deserted, as you might expect early on a Sunday morning. I stored my bag in one of the lockers and grabbed a pair of boxing gloves from the storeroom. After a quick stretch, I started on the punching bag. Given my condition, it wasn't the greatest workout of all time, but it helped.

"Didn't expect to find you here," Katiya called out from the other side of the hall. I stopped punching for a moment and noticed she was walking straight towards me. She hesitated for a second as she got closer. "Man, you look pale. I mean, more so than usual. You feeling all right?"

"I was," I said, hoping she would take the hint. My wishful thinking appeared to be just that.

"Sure? You look really ill."

"I'll be fine."

"Suit yourself." Katiya started stretching at the edge of the mat. "So, where's Ash?"

I should have known she would ask sooner or later. Ash was all she really cared about. "Asleep... maybe. How should I know?"

"Well, the two of you normally come here together, and he spends nearly all his time with you."

"Jealous?" I took another swing at the bag.

"Maybe I am." For once, I had to give her credit for being honest. "Did you two have a fight?"

"No. Am I not allowed to spend some time alone without having had a fight with him? Is that what you think of me? That I'm some lost puppy who can't survive away from Ash?"

"Gee, I was just being concerned." Whether it was the anger or

65

the hangover, I don't know, but my head began to swim, and the dizziness made me nauseous. "Are you–?"

I ran straight to the locker room, not bothering to try and remove the gloves on the way. Fortunately I found a toilet with its seat up. My stomach retched, and at first I thought nothing would come. Then my throat began to burn. My mouth was filled with the vilest tasting substance I had ever known. It looked as bad as it tasted. Neon-yellow. I coughed, trying to rid myself of the sensation when the second wave hit.

I heard footsteps behind me. Katiya crouched down beside me and set to work on removing the gloves from my hands. I started to thank her, albeit reluctantly, when my stomach interrupted me. When I finished, she said, "I'm gonna take a wild guess here. Tell me if I'm wrong, but you're hung over, aren't you?"

I felt ashamed, like I was the biggest hypocrite in the world. All my preaching about how drinking alcohol was stupid, and there I was, praying to the porcelain God. I turned my head, avoiding her gaze. "Go ahead. Mock me. I know you're dying to."

Katiya sighed. "I remember my first time. It was my eighteenth birthday. My brother took me out to a bar. I woke up the next morning in a pile of my own vomit, feeling like I was dying. You see, I'm in no position to make fun of you."

I gagged and coughed as my stomach convulsed once more, but nothing came. Katiya walked out into the locker room and returned soon after with a bottle of water, which she handed to me. Normally, I would have been disinclined to accept anything from her, but the burning in my throat and the bitter taste weren't going anywhere, and right then, that was more important than my pride. I screwed off the lid, dropping it in the process, and drank as much as I could before I needed to breathe.

"So," Katiya started. "You got drunk last night. I'm assuming Ash was there, and now the two of you have had a falling out?"

"It's none of your business," I snapped.

"Well, you're not denying it at least. But whatever happened between the two of you could affect the whole squad, so yes, it is my business."

"It's nothing. I just want to do things on my own."

"Whatever. You don't have to tell me. I know you don't like me."

"No, I don't dislike you. I..." I wasn't sure how to finish my sentence. There was just something about her that annoyed me.

"I'm the one who's trying to steal your best friend from you," she said.

"Something like that."

"And you're the best friend I have to compete with for his attention. We're rivals."

Rivals. That wasn't a bad way of putting it. It was a game of tug-of-war, with Ash as the rope. I had to choke back a laugh because, in a way, Katiya had already lost. The question was, would I accept my victory or pass on it? My mind screamed at me, urging... no, telling me to get out while I still could. But deep down there was a small part of me that wanted it. It was a part of me I hadn't realised existed until the night before, a part that recognised how happy I had felt. Then there was the doubt at the back of my mind, trying to convince me I was making a mountain out of nothing. Ash said it was just sex, nothing more. What if he was right and I was making a fool out of myself?

I jumped from my skin when I heard my name being called. It was Ash. Without thinking I pulled my shields around me, stopping him from sensing me. It's difficult to describe what shielding is like to someone without a psychic ability. The analogy Ash used was that of a long cloak, long enough to wrap around my entire body, covering me completely.

Katiya glanced at me. "You owe me," she said and walked out of the toilets.

"Hey, Kat. Have you seen Mik?"

"Yeah, he was here not long ago. He wasn't feeling too good so he left."

"Oh. Do you know where he went? I need to talk to him."

"No, sorry. Did you two have a fight or something?"

"Or something," he replied. There was a loud crash. "Fuck! I'm so stupid."

"Hey, come on now. I'm sure whatever it is he just needs some time alone to think. Look, why don't I grab my things and we can go back to your room, make some breakfast, and you can tell me all about it."

"Yeah, maybe. Thanks, Kat."

The mention of food made me realise again how empty my stomach felt. It groaned in protest. When the coast was clear I exited from the toilets and changed into the spare clothes I had brought with me. With my things packed I headed to the cafeteria. I really did owe Katiya for helping me escape.

*****

I had intended on ordering a fried breakfast, but the smell alone was enough to make me feel queasy. Instead, I settled for some pink grapefruit, toast and a coffee. Black, of course. I sat down in one corner of the large hall and looked out of the far window. The sun was starting to peek over the rooftops of Rachat, and people were now trickling into the cafeteria. Sipping at my coffee, I noticed someone had stopped beside me, and there was a moment of dread when I thought it might have been Ash. It was a relief to hear Lucas' voice.

"Hey man, how are you feeling?" He sat down opposite me with his breakfast packed full of fat and grease. Understandably, given his ability, he had an abnormally high metabolism. I looked away as his knife cut into a sausage, the juices oozing out with every stroke.

"I've felt better," I replied, trying to concentrate on my own food.

"Don't worry. The great thing about being a Daeva is we recover faster than regular humans. You'll be feeling right as rain in no time."

"Is it that obvious?"

"Yes, and I saw you and Ash at the bar last night. It looked like things were getting pretty heavy, so I left you two to it."

I sighed. Heavy didn't even begin to cover it. I hadn't really processed the knowledge that Ash had killed someone. Knowing his past didn't change anything. Still, I couldn't begin to imagine the burden he carried. Having someone's death on your conscience, and hearing the person you loved call you a monster. It was unbearable just thinking about it.

"I assume he told you then." My eyes widened. There was no way Lucas could be talking about the same thing. "About the night he killed someone."

"He said he'd never told anyone." I plunged my spoon into the grapefruit. Juice spurted out of the mutilated segments.

"Oh, he didn't tell me." Lucas leaned in to whisper. "I get my information through other means."

"You mean you've been snooping through classified files?"

"Shhh, keep your voice down. Yes."

"You could get into serious trouble, you know?"

"Please, I am Rachat's number one master thief."

"You got caught before," I reminded him.

"I told you, I was set up. Anyway, get this. The man with the knife at our graduation, he's the father of the guy Ash killed."

That would certainly explain why he had been looking for Ash.

"That's not all." Lucas paused as a group of cadets walked past us. They sat a couple of tables down from us. "They have files on civilians flagged as potential Daeva."

"So? We all know they've been scouting for more Daeva to join the army. Makes sense they'd keep an eye on any potentials."

"It's more than that. Some of these files were for newborn children, and you know as well as I do there's no genetic link. Becoming a Daeva... it just seems to happen at random."

"Then they've cracked it."

Lucas nodded. "Possibly."

This new information didn't bode well with me. If they figured out what made us different, then it would only be a matter of time before they managed to recreate it. General Marsten called our abilities 'gifts from God'. If that were the case, then we should never be able to unravel their secrets. It seemed humanity was destined to jump from one sin to the next.

"So, are you feeling better yet?"

"Much, thanks," I replied. The food and coffee helped quiet my stomach, which just left the splitting headache. Having something to think about besides Ash helped as well. With our food finished, we carried our trays over to the counter where they were taken from us.

Lucas asked what I had planned for the rest of the day, and mentioned he and Brad were going to watch a hockey game that afternoon. He invited me along and I accepted, welcoming the distraction with open arms. We agreed to meet at his dorm at noon, and parted ways as we left the cafeteria. I spent the next few hours hidden away at the back of the library, catching up on my reading. It was scarce to come across many paperbacks, with most of them being lost to the wear and tear of the last century – the majority of what we read was stored on the city's electronic archives. However, I managed to find a well-preserved copy of 'The Hobbit' amidst the clutter of books, and I sat down to learn all about the adventures of Mr. Bilbo Baggins.

Reading fantasy was something I enjoyed a lot as a kid. They were an escape from the misery and suffering in my own life. I could visit all manner of magical worlds with their unique and wonderful races, and monsters, and forget all about my own problems. But in the end, it was only fantasy, and the time always came that I had to put the book down and face real life once more. I checked the book out of the library, and took it with me.

*****

I left my things in Lucas' room, and the three of us started on our long walk across the city to the stadium. It made me wonder when the public transport Graeme mentioned might be operational. Once there, we ordered drinks and began our search for some free seats.

Hockey was one of the few sports I enjoyed playing at school. I wasn't much of a spectator though. It seemed boring to watch other people play, but I resigned myself to at least try and enjoy the match, if only to prove I could without Ash being there.

As the game wore on, I got more and more into it, and before I knew it the match was over. Once more, I was faced with the reality that I couldn't avoid Ash forever. We stopped off at a sandwich shop on the way back and I found my appetite had returned. I bought a garlic chicken sandwich, my favourite filling, and devoured it as we walked. I spent most of the walk thinking about Ash. I missed him. Him and his carefree attitude and goofy grin.

I picked up my things from Lucas' room, and said goodbye to him and Brad, before heading back to my room. I hesitated outside the door, half-expecting Ash to pounce on me with a feral look in his eyes, but in the end I was greeted only by the silence of an empty room. For a while I lay on my bed reading, until my eyelids grew heavy and I drifted off.

*****

The first thing I noted when I slipped back into the conscious world, was that I wasn't alone. I felt the weight of someone sat on the edge of my bed, and I didn't need to open my eyes to know who it was.

"Hey," he said as I opened my eyes. Ash didn't look annoyed as I expected. If anything he looked nervous, his smile faltering.

"How long have you been there?" I asked, wiping my eyes.

He looked over the clock on the desk. "About fifteen minutes. I couldn't decide whether to wake you or not."

"So..." I sat up, waiting for Ash to say something.

"So..." He replied. "Awkward."

"Yup."

"Look, I know you're probably angry at me and I understand, but I'm sorry."

"I'm not angry at you," I said, wondering where he might have gotten that idea from.

"Then what is it? Why have you been avoiding me all day? I've been worried that you might hate me or something."

I looked away from him, hesitating.

"Come on, you can talk to me." Ash put an arm around my shoulder. I shrugged it off.

"I'm scared, okay? The way things are... I don't know what to think anymore. It just seemed to happen out of nowhere, and now I'm scared things are gonna change and we might end up losing our friendship. I don't want that to happen. I thought I could fix things if I kept my distance for a while."

Ash sighed. "I don't think this is something we can just 'fix'. Are you that worried we could end up as something more than friends?"

"No," I replied. "I'm scared that a part of me wants it." It wasn't just about the sex. It was about the parts that came before and after it. That night in his arms I felt something I couldn't remember ever feeling before. It felt like I belonged somewhere, and I wasn't alone.

"I'm scared too," he said. "Ever since Lisa, I've been running away, trying to use my past as an excuse. But now, it scares me to think of a future where I didn't take this chance. I'm tired of running. Aren't you?"

"I want to stop, but I don't know if I can do it."

"You can. I believe in you. I know you have it in you."

"How can you be so sure?"

"Because, you made me feel human again. I didn't think a monster like me deserved love, not after what I've done. But last night..." His voice trailed off.

Love. Was that what I was feeling? The strongest bond between two people, and the most painful if it was to be severed. It scared the hell out of me. I tried to imagine my life without Ash, and I couldn't. I was already in too deep to pull out. There was no more running.

"I don't know if I can, but I want to try."

I reached out to take hold of his hand, and he smiled. Really smiled. If anyone had thought his smiles were stunning, then they were wrong, because they paled in comparison to the one I saw then. Or perhaps, I was seeing it through a different set of eyes.

Ash pressed his lips hard against mine. I melted into the kiss as he leaned into me, forcing me onto my back. His tongue dived into my mouth. His hips ground against mine and I could feel my self-control begin to crumble around me.

He pulled back, his lips pressed together and brow furrowed. "Are you sure this is what you want?"

"Yes," I whispered.

I saw Ash's face transform. His smile was replaced by a smirk, and his eyes filled with a lustful need. His mouth locked onto my neck, sucking and nipping as his hands found their way underneath my clothing, wandering over my chest.

"Wait," I moaned, struggling to catch my breath. I knew sex would be something Ash wanted, but right now? Without the alcohol my inhibitions were screaming at me. I wasn't ready.

"Too fast?"

I nodded. Ash sat, pulling me up with him. He wrapped his arms around me.

"How about this?" he asked.

"I could get used to it." I sighed, my cheek brushing against his.

"Oh," he said, poking the side of my neck. "That's gonna leave a mark."

I gritted my teeth. My face flushed with anger. Everyone would see the mark and know about us. I wasn't sure yet what we were going to tell everyone. "I'm gonna kill you."

Ash laughed. "I'm kidding. There's barely even a mark left."

"What are we going to tell everyone?" I asked. Lucas and Brad would be delighted, I was sure. Katiya, on the other hand, wouldn't be too thrilled.

"I don't wanna hide this from them, but if you're not comfortable telling them, then we can wait a bit."

I didn't mind so much if a few people knew, it was more that I was unsure of how I'd answer the inevitable questions. Did this make me gay? Bi? Were we serious? All these questions and more, I didn't have the answers to. It was overwhelming. I pulled away from the embrace, feeling the sudden urge to run.

"Let's wait. I have some things I want to figure out first."

"Like what?"

"It's embarrassing."

"Mik, if we're gonna do this, then you need to share these things with me. Let me help you find the answers." Ash reached up to stroke the back of my head.

I turned to face him. "Am I gay?"

"Why does it matter what you are?" he replied. "Maybe in time you'll figure it out, but all you need to know for now, is that you're with me."

"People are going to ask. What do I tell them?"

"Say you're Ashexual."

"I'm being serious," I said, giving him a quick jab to the arm.

"So was I." He grinned. "Okay, maybe not completely serious, but I haven't seen you show any sexual interest in either gender before. Maybe you're attracted to individuals, and right now, that person happens to be me."

I couldn't help but chuckle. It made a weird kind of sense. And I knew that the events of the previous night wouldn't have happened with anyone else. It had to be Ash. He was the only one who could break through my defences, and make me realise that deep down I didn't want to be alone anymore.

That evening we discussed how things were going to work between us. We decided against pushing the beds together, until I was ready to tell people about our 'thing'. I wasn't even sure what to call it yet. But Ash did get me to agree to sharing a bed, under the condition he didn't sleep completely naked. There would be no contact outside of what was normal for two friends when we were in public. And in private, Ash agreed, albeit reluctantly, to only kissing and cuddling until I felt ready.

It all felt so strange, discussing those things with the person I considered to be my best friend. But even I couldn't deny he was more than that to me now, and maybe he had been for some time.

We had an early start the next day, so we climbed into bed

together. Ash lay on his back, his arm around me and my head resting on his chest. His heart thudded in my ear. It was strangely hypnotic and relaxing. Still, there was a nagging at the back of my mind, telling me that one day he would be gone, and all that would remain is heartbreak and despair.

"Don't leave me," I whispered.

"I won't ever abandon you. Promise." Ash leaned down to kiss my forehead.

I closed my eyes and the sound of his heartbeat was all that was left. There was no worry, no pain, just that sound drowning out everything else. Ba-dum. Ba-dum.

Chapter 7

The clanging of bells from across the square jerked me from my sleep. Ash groaned and stretched his limbs, almost rolling me off the bed. My bed, I might add.

"Morning," he mumbled.

"Morning." I smiled, and started to get out of bed. Ash grabbed hold of me and pulled me back down. He rolled over me, onto his hands and knees, trapping me. His head lowered to meet mine and he gave me a quick kiss on the lips.

"I don't wanna get out of bed," he moaned.

"Tough, you know what happens if we're late."

"Maybe you could help me wake up then." He grinned, rubbing against me and revealing that he was already very much awake.

I glared at him. "Let me up. I need to shower."

"Can I join you?"

"No," I replied without pause to think about it. Ash pouted and rolled to one side, letting me off the bed. "You could use a cold shower anyway," I told him.

Once we were showered, dressed, and drank our coffee, we

headed over to our usual meeting spot. As always, Sergeant Locke was waiting for us. The rest of the squad were already there, dressed in the same navy-blue joggers and matching t-shirt. Sergeant Locke gave us a stern look. We were only just on time.

"Okay soldiers, listen up. A few hours ago, the council approved a top priority mission. The five of you are to complete this mission under my supervision."

The air around us buzzed with excitement and tension.

"Yesterday, the Fifth Covenant squad was investigating an abandoned bunker north of Rachat, after scouts reported movement in that area. At approximately nineteen-hundred hours, things started to get a little weird." There was a long pause. "What little communication was made with them after that, indicates that something spooked them. It spooked them so bad they completely lost it."

There was an audible gulp to my left. Katiya shifted uneasily on her feet.

"By twenty-one hundred hours, all communication with the squad was lost. We have reason to believe they may have encountered an 'M-type' vampire, and that it is still in there. We're not sure what its ability is, but the most likely scenario is the vampire can trigger hallucinations."

The 'M' stood for mental. This was our way of classifying vampires with a psychic ability. The other type was 'P' for physical. M-types are considered to be the most dangerous by far. You can't dodge or parry their attacks. The only way to defend yourself against an M-type is to be able to shield yourself, and only those with a psychic ability of their own could do that. Of the twelve Daeva enlisted in the army, there were only three of us with a psychic power, myself and Ash being two of them. That was probably why our squad was chosen for the mission.

"Reports also indicate a dozen or so Renfields. White and Hart, you will be focusing on the vampire. The rest of you are tasked with eliminating the Renfields."

'Renfield' was the codename we gave to humans who served vampires. It was believed many of them were traitors, choosing to side with the vampires in exchange for the promise of power and immortality. Then there were those afflicted by a vampire's compulsion. I would have preferred to save the latter, but there was no way of telling the difference. Army policy was to shoot on sight, unless it was believed they held valuable information.

The rest of the briefing was general information, about the area we would be investigating, or rather, the lack of information. The bunker only recently surfaced outside of Montargis, another of France's many ghost towns. We prepared as we always did, changing into our combat gear and selecting our weapons.

*****

The Wisent was waiting for us at the garage, and we began our long journey. I watched the scenery pass us by through the small bulletproof window for most of the trip. Our first venture into the outside world was disappointing to say the least, and for the first half hour of our trip, I saw nothing I hadn't seen already. Barren wastelands and ruined towns stretched as far as the eye could see. Then, slowly, there was a change.

It started with a patch of green here and there. Then there were fields of grass, dotted with red and white flowers, and giant trees. To my amazement we even passed a small herd of wild grey horses, drinking from a small river. We had horses in Rachat, but there was something of an ethereal beauty about seeing them in the wild. Our journey followed the river north for a while, but eventually our paths diverged, and the colour began to fade from the landscape, being replaced once more by the cracked earth and deserted towns.

I sighed, my mind returning to the mission. If the reports were right, which I was sure they were, then we would be encountering our first vampire. Everything we knew about them came from books, or stories told by retired army veterans. I recalled some of the anecdotes. They told of vampires with the ability to cause tremors, produce deafening screeches, and even one that could create darkness and fill an entire room with it. It made me wonder what type of ability we would be going up against.

Something about the way Sergeant Locke described the events had me on edge. I gripped the edge of my seat. My palms were damp and butterflies fluttered in my stomach. Ash, who was sat in the seat next to me, had been silent for most of the trip. He covered my hand with his.

"You scared?" he asked.

"Yeah."

"Me too," Ash said.

Lucas was sat opposite us. He lifted his head and gave me a knowing grin. I pulled my hand free of Ash's. I didn't think Lucas would say anything, but I was still angry at Ash for having broken our rule about public contact. But deep down, I wanted him to put his arms around me and tell me everything was going to be fine, that we'd kill the vampire and all get home safe. I wanted to feel anything but the cold fear.

"So you should be," said Sergeant Locke. "A vampire could tear you limb from limb in seconds if you let it. The worst mistake you can ever make, is to not be afraid. You get cocky, and it's over."

"Have you ever killed one?" Brad asked.

"I've met more than my fair share. Only killed a handful of them though. The scariest thing about a vampire isn't their strength, their speed, or their abilities. It's their lack of humanity."

I could see Sergeant Locke's face tense up. Sweat was beginning to form on his brow.

"Seventeen years ago, my squad and I were assigned to locate a group of scouts operating near what we call the Dead Pass, who went missing after a bad storm. We found a series of caves, figuring they might have taken shelter from the storm and were unable to report in because of it. What we found at the back of those caves was something straight out of a nightmare."

Sergeant Locke paused again. There was an eerie silence in the air, despite the noise of the Wisent's engine humming and groaning.

"We found corpses... so many corpses. They were nailed to the walls of the cave with iron spikes. Their eyes and mouths were sewn shut. Their bodies were naked and shaved. We couldn't see the cave walls for them. Even the ceiling was covered."

I shuddered at the thought. The unease in the vehicle hung around us like a heavy shroud. Looking outside, I noticed the sky had turned grey and it was starting to snow.

"Some of the corpses were nothing more than husks, tattered flesh and bones. Then there were those that were only partly decomposed. But the worst were the fresh ones. I still see their faces sometimes. We never did identify most of them."

"My God, that's awful," said Katiya.

"Did you find the vamp?" Lucas asked.

"He found us. Took out one of our men and wounded another before we got him. We found the scouts alive, locked in tiny wooden cages, bound and stripped. All except one. They never returned to active duty after that. Every day, I pray to God you kids never have to witness anything like what we saw that day."

I hoped so too.

"Why are you telling us this now?" asked Ash.

"Because, I want you to be afraid. I want you to know what they are capable of, so that when the time comes, you do not hesitate to kill them. If you do, then you'd better pray they kill you, because they can do so much worse than just take your life."

We sat mostly in silence for the remainder of the journey, contemplating the Sergeant's words. Fear. It's a natural response to the unknown, an innate safety mechanism meant to help keep you alive. But it can also paralyse you, and if that happens, you've already lost.

*****

We arrived after two hours of driving. The Wisent was parked amidst a cluster of rolling hills, blanketed in a layer of snow, where the ruins of Montargis sat ominously in the distance.

"Beyond this hill is the entrance to the bunker. Remember, the vampire will sense you coming. It may already know we're here. Your first task will be to locate the enemy," Sergeant Locke told us. "Good luck, and I'll be praying for your safety."

The snow crunched beneath our boots. From the top of the hill we could see for miles around us. There wasn't a whole lot of life. There were no trees, no bushes, just endless plains of white and crumbling ruins. Sure enough, we found the bunker's entrance protruding from the other side of the hill. The doors were jammed shut, half buried beneath the dirt. Fortunately, there was a hole in what little was visible of the wall, large enough for us to fit through.

Inside was pitch black, save for the light that spilled through the hole. An incessant dripping could be heard in the distance. We activated the flashlights on our helmets, and awaited our orders.

Ash was crouched, his eyes closed, head tilting every now and then as he reached out with his mind, listening to things the rest of us could neither see nor hear. We waited patiently, keeping an eye out for any enemies, with our lights penetrating the darkness. The path before us sloped down, heading deeper into the dark underground. Nothing came.

"That's weird," Ash said. "There's like a dead zone, or something."

"What do you mean?" Katiya asked.

"It's like there's something there, but it's empty... devoid of any emotion. Hang on, I'll see if I can–" Ash's body flew backwards, slamming into the wall behind him, as though he were thrown by some invisible force. He fell to the floor, landing on his hands and knees. Katiya and Brad, who were closest to him, rushed to his side.

"I'm fine," he said, waving them off and reaching for his headset. "We've got maybe a dozen Renfields on one side of the bunker. The vampire is near the centre with a single human, possibly Fifth Covenant judging by his emotions."

"Good work," Sergeant Locke's voice crackled over the radio. "Hart and White, you know what you have to do. The rest of you, eliminate those Renfields and make sure they don't reach the vampire."

"You heard the man," Ash said, picking himself up off the floor. "We'll head down together, and I'll point you in the right direction."

We began our descent into the darkness with Ash taking point. Occasionally, he would stop to sense the direction of the enemy, and we followed blindly, trusting his ability. Katiya stopped in front of me, causing me to bump into the back of her. She shrieked.

"It's just me," I mocked her. She was looking around wide-eyed. "Ash, something's wrong."

He took hold of Katiya's shoulders and shook her, but she backed away into the nearest wall.

"We need to get out of here," said Brad. He was visibly trembling.

Ash took a deep breath and closed his eyes. "Are you projecting fear?" he asked.

"No."

"Are you sure? Because this feels exactly like your ability."

"It's not me," I snapped. "Can't you trace it?"

"Yeah, give me a sec."

"Can't you hear the voices?" said Lucas. "They're everywhere... in the walls, in the air. They're coming for us."

"Shit. It's the vampire. We need to get these guys out of here before they lose it. Think you can counter it long enough?"

I nodded and dropped my shields. Even lowering them a little, I could feel the vampire's magic drifting through the air like a cold breeze. I reached out with my magic, letting it flow over the others. It's hard to describe how my ability works, but it feels like a wind emanating from my skin. When the wind touched the others, they began to settle down, the fear chased out of them. But the vampire wasn't going to give up easily. I felt its power breathe through the passageway like a dam had been opened. I staggered as the first wave hit me, buckling my knees. Slowly, but surely, the vampire was going to undo my magic and regain control.

"I can't hold it."

"Okay, let's get going," Ash said, grabbing hold of Katiya and pulling her to her feet. As we reached the bottom of the ramp I felt the power subside, like stepping out of a pool of water.

Ash reported the situation to Sergeant Locke over the radio.

"Did you sense any movement from the Renfields?"

"No, Sir."

"Good, then the vampire is probably cocky enough to feel he doesn't need them. You and Hart will have to go in and destroy the vampire first, so the rest of the squad can join up with you."

"Understood, Sir." Ash looked at me and I nodded, letting him know I was ready to go.

We descended once more, taking a different path to the heart of the bunker. The vampire's power still lingered in the air, though it wasn't quite as thick as before. I thought about what Ash had said, that it felt exactly like my ability. The thought raised a lot of questions. Did I have a vampire's ability? How did I get it? Was it the same for the other Daeva? I couldn't answer any of these questions, so I pushed them to the back of my mind. I needed to focus on staying alive and completing the mission. Questions could come later.

Up ahead we spotted a flickering light, dancing across the walls from around a corner. Ash turned his flashlight off, and clicked the safety off his handgun. I followed suit. We approached the corner and Ash peered round.

"Well, don't keep me waiting," a voice called from the room. "I do very much despise being kept waiting."

Ash charged into the room, and I followed close behind. A large fire sat in the centre of the room, crackling away. Behind it stood a tall, skinny man with short brown hair. He could have passed for a human, were it not for the ghostly pale skin and two long fangs on display. Before him kneeled one of the Fifth Covenant squad, bloody and bruised, barely conscious.

The vampire smiled as we entered, taking the soldier's head into his hands. "Too late." He laughed manically. A loud snap echoed off the walls and the body slumped to the floor. We both fired, but in a blur the vampire was gone.

"You know, I was getting tired of feeding from that worthless bunch of ingrates I call servants," the voice came from above. He was standing upside-down on the ceiling, watching us with a bemused look. "But then five tasty snacks walked right into my new abode." We fired again, and he disappeared faster than our eyes could follow.

"And now it seems dessert has arrived too." He was kneeling by the corpse this time.

Ash whispered to me, "He's toying with us. Keep him talking and buy me some time."

"Please, give me some credit. I am a vampire, after all," he wearied. "I suppose you're wondering why I haven't killed you yet."

"I was wondering when you might shut up," I replied.

"Feisty. I like it." The vampire licked his lips. "You both smell so delicious. You're not quite human, are you?"

"I don't know what you mean."

"Of course you do. So tell me, which of you was it who was able to push back my magic?" He looked over at Ash, who was circling around the fire.

"Me," I said, hoping to draw his attention back to me. I swallowed hard, a lump forming in my throat. "It was me."

"Then that would make your friend here the empath." He waved a hand, seemingly disregarding Ash. His eyes were focused entirely on me now. Whether or not this was part of Ash's plan, I wished he would hurry up. "I could teach you so much more about your power. You could be so much more than you are now."

"I don't care about any of that." That was only a half-truth. I wanted to know about my ability, and more specifically, where it came from. Were humans more related to vampires than we knew? Why were these abilities only showing themselves in humans now? There were so many questions, but as I looked at the vampire, I knew he had no intention to answer them. We were prey, something to toy with. Nothing more.

The vampire sighed. "A shame that such power must go to waste, but I shall enjoy sucking you both dry. And then I'll drain your friends too."

"You won't get the chance," said Ash.

The vampire snorted. "And what makes you think you can stop me, Empath?"

Ash smirked. "It's like the Sergeant said. You get cocky, and it's over. Well, you got cocky."

The vampire threw his head back and laughed. "Cocky? I think it is you who is cocky. Did you hope you could distract me and sneak around to shoot me in the back? Tch. Perhaps, I'll save you until last, so you can watch as your friends die."

"I never planned on shooting you."

The vampire's eyes widened and he looked to the ground, letting out a blood-curdling shriek as he realised what was happening. Ice snapped at his feet, encasing them and rooting him to the ground, steadily rising up to capture his legs.

"You stopped seeing me as a threat the second you learned I was an empath. Big mistake."

The ice grew upwards, and I could see the strain on Ash's face, the way he gritted his teeth and his eyebrows furrowed. The vampire smashed frantically at the ice in an attempt to free himself.

"Too late," I said, firing three shots into his chest. His eyes grew wider still as the bullets hit. A second later there were more shots. The vampire's head exploded in an eruption of blood and bone where the bullets exited his skull, and he fell lifeless to the floor.

I walked over to the body, keeping my gun aimed at him, just in case. The body was still twitching. I fired the rest of my clip into his head, leaving nothing but a bloody mess.

"Target is down," I reported to the rest of the group.

"Good work," Sergeant Locke replied. "Any sign of the Fifth Covenant?"

"We have one corpse," Ash said. "No sign of the others yet."

"Okay, I want you to scout the rest of the bunker, clear out those Renfields, and check for survivors. We'll bring the Wisent round to the entrance. Once the place is clear, you are to bring our soldiers out with you, dead or alive."

"Yes, Sir." The radio cut off.

"What do you think the vampire meant about my power?" I asked.

"Nothing. He was probably lying to confuse you."

"But you said his ability felt exactly like mine. How is that even possible?"

"I'm sure it's just a coincidence." Ash waved his hand, dismissing it.

"But–" Static from the radio interrupted me. There were gunshots, followed by screaming.

"We've made contact with the Renfields," said Lucas. "They're rushing the entrance. I'm guessing they sensed their master's death."

"How many?" Ash asked.

"Eight." More shots. "Nine."

I looked around the room we were stood in. There was only one other exit. A wide flight of stairs led even further underground. I turned my flashlight on to get a better look. Another corridor.

"I'm still picking up two or three signals near your location."

"There's another level below us," I said. Ash acknowledged this with a quick nod.

"You guys start sweeping this floor. Mik and I will check out the lower level."

The air seemed to grow colder as we went down the stairs. I could feel my heart speeding up, a sense of foreboding bearing down on me. The corridor opened out in front of us. Ash pointed me in one direction and he went in the other. There was another dripping sound, similar to the one I heard at the entrance. Drip. I told myself it was probably just water from above dripping through a leak in the ceiling, and tried to ignore it. Drip, drip.

A quick scan with my light revealed three large, metal sliding doors on my side. I went to the first and pulled at the handle. It didn't budge. I pulled harder and it groaned and shrieked, stiff from lack of use. It finally opened with a loud clang. The room housed what appeared to be an old, rusty generator, its pipes running up through the cracked ceiling. Water trickled down one of the pipes, dripping to form a small puddle on the floor below. Drip, drip, drip.

As my flashlight passed over the puddle, I spotted a black boot. I recognised it as one of our standard issue footwear. The leg attached to it disappeared behind the generator, clothed in the same attire as I was. I reached the corner, searching with my light for his face. At first, my mind refused to accept what it saw. Red. White. Black. I stared at it, unblinking, trying to make sense of the image. Muscle. Bone. No skin. There was no skin. Where the nose should have been was only a bloody arch of bone and sinew. Teeth exposed, stained with blood, where there should have been lips. Bloodshot eyes, wide with terror, stared back at me, with no eyelids to shield them from the horror. Instead of hair there was only glistening bone, spattered red. Where the ears once were, only two holes remained.

It became hard to breathe. My windpipe started to close up on me. Choking. I turned away to regain my breath. It took a minute before I could work up the courage to turn back around. The tormented soul lay there, unmoving, his eyes seemingly locked onto me. His jacket was torn open, revealing the blood-soaked flesh beneath. From his neck up the skin had been flayed. No, it had been torn off. There were patches of bone where the muscle had come away with the skin. The neck was a bloody mess, like an animal had taken a chunk out of it.

I couldn't bear to look at it anymore, and so I left the room as quickly as I could, and reached up to activate the radio. "Ash, you're gonna wanna see this." I turned to look in his direction and could see his flashlight emerging from one of the rooms on his side.

"What did you find?" he asked.

"One of the Fifth Covenant. He's dead and it's not pretty." Understatement of the century right there.

When Ash reached me he put a hand on my shoulder and gave a

quick squeeze. I pointed him in the direction of the body. He walked up to it, and for a few seconds his entire body went stiff. He stared right at it, and then bolted out of the room in a flash, doubled over and coughing.

"Jesus Christ! You could have warned me," he said.

"I told you it wasn't pretty."

Ash glared at me. "If that's your idea of 'not pretty', then I'd hate to see what you think counts as horrifying." He took a deep breath and stood up to report the details to the rest of the group.

While Ash was occupied on the radio, I decided to check out the second door. Unlike the first, it opened with ease. Inside was a bunch of broken, rotted wooden boxes. Whatever was stored in them was long gone. Behind the boxes I found two more sets of legs. I took a deep breath through my mouth, and shone my light towards their heads. I turned away quickly.

"I've got another two members of the Fifth Covenant here, same condition as the other," I reported. "Moving on to the last room now."

The last door was bolted shut. I pulled at the bolt and slid the door open. In the middle of the empty room lay the last body. Unlike the others his face was still intact, save for a gash down one side, the blood already dried. I let out a sigh of relief and kneeled down next to him. His chest was moving.

"We've got a survivor," I said. His eyes flew open. A hand grabbed at me, attempting to pull me to the floor. I pulled away, losing my balance and ended up on my backside. The survivor crouched, ready to strike when I clicked the safety off my gun – a sound I'm sure he was all too familiar with.

"You're not one of them," he said.

"Mikhail Hart. Third Sunreavers." I stood and dusted myself off before offering him a hand. He took it and pulled himself to his feet.

"Thanks. I'm Liam Duntz. Fifth Covenant. Did you find the rest of my men?"

Even knowing that he couldn't see my face clearly, with the

flashlight pointing straight at him, I had to look away. How was I supposed to tell a man his four comrades were dead? Especially given the mutilations that had occurred to three of them. My silence spoke louder than any words could have.

"It's okay," he said. "You don't have to say it. I guess I kinda already knew."

"Are you hurt?" Ash asked from the doorway.

"No."

"Okay, come with me. We'll get you escorted out of here."

Liam nodded and let himself be led to the room at the top of the stairs. He paused in front of the body, then fell to his knees, howling and bellowing. From the screams, I managed to deduce that the man whose neck had been snapped was called Xander. Liam seemed so calm about their deaths at first, I thought. I guessed there was a difference between coming to the conclusion your friends are dead, and actually seeing it first-hand. Seeing the body adds a certain finality to the whole thing. Once you see it for yourself, there is no more denying it. No more hope.

Ash instructed the others to meet up with us, so we could get to work on hauling the bodies out. Lucas arrived first, and after some gentle coaxing, was able to lead Liam back out of the bunker. The worst was yet to come for him. I wondered if he would even recognise the rest of his squad with their facial features removed. It was bad enough to see a stranger end up like that.

Katiya and Brad joined us not long after. There were four of us, and four bodies to be carried out. To my dismay, and I'm sure Ash and Brad weren't happy about this either, Katiya took the lightest of the bodies, which happened to be Xander. Brad was able to carry one of the bodies easily over his shoulders, paying special attention to make sure the head was behind him, and not dangling in front where his flashlight would illuminate the grotesque face. Ash had a little more trouble with his body, but finally managed by draping its arms over his shoulders and leaving the feet to trail along behind.

I, on the other hand, was smaller than the body I would be

carrying. The body was still limp, so I tried lifting it over my shoulder at first, but found it to be too off-balancing. I eventually settled on pulling it along by the hands, with the heels dragging along the floor. When I reached the final corner at the bottom of the ramp, my corpse snagged on something. I sighed, dropped the hands, and was about to search for the problem when something took hold of me. It grabbed at my ankle, pulling it out from under me. I landed on my back, stunned.

There was a scream not far away, and I felt something moving at my feet. The corpse was alive, or undead I should say. I went for my handgun, only to find it had been knocked out of reach when I fell. The corpse continued to climb over me and was eyeing my neck. Thanks to the absence of its lips, I saw the fangs starting to slide out from the gums. I grasped at one of my knives and shoved it into the underside of the corpse's jaw. It let out a gargled scream, rearing its head into the air as it tried to remove the knife. There was a bang, and something thick and wet splattered across my face. The corpse collapsed on top of me. Our faces met. I panicked and threw the body to one side, before scooting over to the wall as far away from the monster as possible.

"You okay?" Brad asked.

"I'll live," I replied, scraping away some of the coagulated blood and tiny chunks of flesh from my face. Disgusting.

I looked up towards the entrance where the rest of the squad was standing. Ash was clutching at his shoulder, gritting his teeth. The others seemed unscathed. I retrieved my knife and Brad offered to carry my body the rest of the way. I followed behind, the corpse staring defiantly back at me.

"Is it bad?" I asked Ash. He lifted his hand enough for me to see. There was a fair amount of blood, and two large, ragged holes where the fangs had torn into his skin.

"Just a flesh wound," he said. "Stings like a bitch though."

Sergeant Locke jumped down into the bunker. He went to Ash first. "Let's have a look at it." He pulled out a small flashlight and examined the wound. "We've got a first aid kit in the Wisent. We'll get the wound cleaned up and dressed, but you're to report to the infirmary as soon as we arrive home. You're probably gonna need a few stitches. Understood?"

"Yes, Sir." Ash saluted with his left hand. I could have sworn he was smiling.

"What are you so happy about?" I asked.

"This could be my first battle scar," he said. "I think it'll add character."

"Idiot." I didn't want him to be scarred. Every scar would be a reminder of a time when he had been hurt. They would be reminders of his mortality. It was minor this time, but the next time he might not be so lucky.

Ash raised an eyebrow at me, but said nothing. With a hand from Brad and Sergeant Locke, he was able to climb out of the bunker, leaving the rest of us to deal with the bodies. Getting them into the Wisent without them going up in flames from the sunlight was going to be a pain.

Lucas jumped out of the bunker to find something to cover the bodies with. He returned with some blankets, meant for warming soldiers who had been out in the cold for too long. We managed to wrap them up individually, and Brad passed them out to the rest of us. There was nowhere else to put them, so we placed them on the floor of the Wisent. I was not happy about the thought of sharing the journey home, in an enclosed space, with four corpses. But at least their faces were covered, and the deaths were recent enough that there wasn't much of a smell.

Liam was asleep, strapped into one of the seats. He had had to be sedated using some of the emergency medical supplies, Lucas told me. Ash was sat outside on a small rock. His armoured vest had been removed and the thermals torn, exposing the wound completely. I could see his jaw clenched, his hands gripping the edge of the rock as Sergeant Locke disinfected the bite with a hip flask of whiskey. The blood was wiped away, and a temporary bandage placed over it.

With Ash's wound dressed and everything packed up, we started back home. Most of the journey was in silence. Ash spent much of his time wincing as the strap of his seatbelt rubbed against his shoulder. I tried as hard as I could to ignore the bodies lying at our feet. My mind flashed back to the sight of those skinless faces. I tried to shake off the images, but being so close to the bodies with nothing to occupy my mind wasn't helping.

That drive was possibly the longest two hours of my life.

Chapter 8

Ash went straight to the infirmary upon our arrival, while the rest of us changed out of our gear. Looking in the mirror, I noticed my face was still spattered with dried blood. I scrubbed it as clean as I could get, without scouring off my own skin. Before I left the locker room, I grabbed a plastic bag and put Ash's clothes in it.

Katiya and I went over to the infirmary to check on him. The nurse was finishing his stitches. She wound a bandage around him, explaining the things he shouldn't do for the next few days, and telling him to come for a check-up the next day. Given our increased rate of healing, which varied from Daeva to Daeva, he would be healed in a couple of days.

We had the rest of the day off, but Ash was feeling tired so we said goodbye to Katiya and retreated to the safety of our room. I hadn't eaten since breakfast, but the thought of food made my stomach churn. Ash took off his t-shirt and made himself comfortable on my bed, inviting me to join him. It felt good to be up against a warm body, after getting too close for comfort with a dead one. Ash was asleep before long. Whether it was the long ride or the adrenaline wearing off, my eyes started to feel heavy, and I followed him soon after.

*****

I found myself standing in the centre of a large room, with a burning torch in one hand. There was no light, other than the crackling flames. Darkness surrounded me. A rotten scent permeated through the air, clinging to the back of my throat. I started to walk in no particular direction.

I don't know how long I walked for, but I never found any walls. The room appeared to go on forever. I thought, perhaps, I had been going in circles, which was entirely possible as there was no way of judging what direction I was walking in. And then I thought that maybe it wasn't a room at all. There was no ceiling that I could see, but there was no moon or stars above either. There was no breeze, just darkness, and that smell.

I began to wander some more, wondering if I would ever find anything. The smell was getting stronger, and it being the only thing I could sense, I tried to track down the source. Then I heard footsteps. I listened, trying to judge the direction of the noise. They were straight ahead and I ran towards them, until I saw the outline of a person in the flame's light. The figure turned to me as I approached it.

My heart stopped, and then began to race. Pounding. Its entire body was skinned. I thought for a moment it was trying to say something, but what came out was nothing more than blood-choked gargles. My knees shook. I turned and ran, until the groaning was inaudible. I struggled to catch my breath, blood thundering through past my ears. The groaning and footsteps started again, slowly getting louder. Closer. I started to run again, but it was gaining on me.

No. I was running towards it. Up ahead I could see the figure coming into view. I turned and fled once more, but whichever way I ran, I found myself running into one of the horrors. Surrounded. The footsteps drew closer and closer, the padding and squishing a cacophony of percussion, accompanied by their tormented cries. I spun on the spot, watching as their net drew tighter around me. Trapped. They were upon me.

I tried to beat them back with the torch, but their skinless hands grabbed at me, tearing away my clothes. The torch fell to the floor, its light dancing across their hideous faces. Nails dug into my skin. It was a dull pain. Then there a wet ripping sound, and my body was engulfed in searing agony. I screamed.

"Mik," a voice called to me.

My eyes opened to see Ash leaning over me, shaking me. My chest rose and fell to the same urgency that my heart pounded against my ribs. The pain was gone, but the memory of it was still there. My whole body felt cold and damp, drenched in sweat. I jumped up, wrapping my arms around Ash. He let out a small grunt when I knocked his wound, but said nothing. I buried my face into his uninjured shoulder, my body still shaking.

"Hey, it's okay," he whispered, his hand resting on the back of my head. "It was just a dream."

"I know," I replied, still trying to slow my breathing. "But it felt so real."

"Do you wanna tell me about it?"

I shook my head.

"Okay, how about a nice hot shower then?"

I nodded.

"You go do that, and I'll make us something to eat. I was thinking sausage pasta. Sound good?"

"No meat," I replied.

"Veggie pasta it is then." He planted a quick kiss on my lips as he stood. "I'll give you a shout when it's ready. Now, go shower. You're getting kinda sticky."

I couldn't help but laugh. Ash left the room, and I picked myself up off the bed. I went into the bathroom and peeled off my sweat-drenched clothes, leaving them in a small pile in the corner. The hot water from the shower was comforting. Inside the cubicle there was nothing but warmth and the sound of running water. There was no pain, no fear, and no skinless zombie creatures from Hell. I let the hot water wash over me, as though it were burning away the memory of my nightmare.

"Food's almost ready," Ash called. I turned off the shower and let out a weary sigh. I dried myself off, and pulled on some clean clothes. By the time I got to the kitchen, Ash was dishing out of the pasta, still naked from the waist up.

"Just in time," he said, handing me my bowl and a fork. I got a glass of water, and we ate in our room. Ash didn't once ask about my dream, which I was thankful for. With food out of the way, we took our dirty clothes to the laundry room, then stopped by the admin office to pick up some copies of the mission report form.

We spent at least an hour filling in our reports. Recalling the discovery of the bodies that day was the last thing I wanted to be doing, but it had to be done, whether I liked it or not. Ash finished first and sat on my bed. He picked up my book from the bedside table and began to flick through it. I joined him when I finished my report, cuddling up to his bare chest as he read to me. He stopped every few minutes to ask questions; Who is Smaug? What's a hobbit?

As he read, I let my hands wander over him. Every now and then I felt Ash's body tense up, and he would pause briefly. At first, I wondered why he kept stopping and looked up at him, urging him to continue. Soon, I realised it was due to my hands wandering lower on his body. It became a new game for me, teasing him. I let my hand go lower, until I was brushing past the waistband of his joggers. When I felt him tense, I moved my hand away. Each time I did this, I noted that Ash was getting more and more excited.

"If you keep doing that, then I might not be able to hold back," he warned me with a grin on his face. One of our agreements was that it would be me who initiated any sex, at least to begin with. Knowing Ash, I knew how hard he was trying to stick to that. I felt bad for denying him, as though I was asking him to give up a part of himself. And why? I wanted it too. The urge to slip my hand beneath the waistband was overwhelming, but it also scared me, because I had never felt anything like it before. Don't get me wrong, I had always had a sex drive. Even I had times when I needed to relieve myself, but this was the first time my drive had ever been directed at another person.

Ash took my silence as a sign to continue reading. Throwing caution to the wind, I slid my hand down and took hold of him. Ash gasped as I started to stroke him. He lowered himself down on the bed, pulled the waist of his trousers down and laid back, with his hands behind his head. I raised an eyebrow at him.

"What? The nurse said I should relax and not exert myself."

I laughed. I loved that he could make me laugh, even when I was nervous. Focusing on the task at hand – no pun intended – I began stroking again. I started slow, and then built up speed, trying different things. I found that playing with the tip would make him moan and writhe. Long, slow strokes made his hips rock. There was an innocence to the whole thing, like playing with a new piece of equipment and working out what each of the buttons does.

Remembering our drunken adventure two nights ago, I began to kiss his chest, working my way towards a nipple. I flicked my tongue across one, and when Ash let out a deep breath I took it into my mouth and sucked. The moans grew louder, and Ash's back arched. I felt his chest rise and fall beneath me, his breath getting faster and shallower.

I released the nipple, and moved up to the line between his neck and shoulder. I bit down gently and Ash groaned, followed shortly after by the sound of his release. He sighed and panted. His hand cupped my face, guiding me up to his lips. We kissed long and hard, our tongues dancing between us as he went limp in my hand.

When we finally broke the kiss, Ash smiled at me. "What did I do to deserve that?"

"N-nothing. I dunno," I stuttered.

"Well, it was nice. Thank you." Ash gave me one last kiss before

I rolled onto my back. "So, biting, huh? I always figured you'd have some kinda kink."

"It's not... I just–"

Ash laughed. "I'm kidding. And you know, I kinda like it. Maybe you wanna try something else now?"

I glared at him. "Don't push your luck."

"Worth a try." Ash shrugged and went to the bathroom to clean himself up. When he came back he asked, "So what do you wanna do for the rest of the evening?"

"I dunno. What do you wanna do?"

Ash lay back down on the bed, resting his head on my chest. "Nothing really."

We lay in silence for a while. My mind started to wander back to the vampire and what he said to me.

"I still think the vampire knew something about my power."

Ash groaned. "You're not still thinking about that, are you?"

"He had the same ability as me. That has to mean something!"

"Look, there's hundreds, maybe thousands of vampires out there. Don't you think there's a chance that one of them could end up with the same ability as you, without it being some big conspiracy?"

"I guess so." It made sense. After all, there were only so many different abilities a vampire could possess, so sooner or later, one of them would coincide with ours. It was still a massive coincidence though, and one I couldn't believe was just that.

We talked a bit about the other events of the day, and Ash was starting to yawn a lot. It was making me tired too, so we settled down into bed. I tried to close my eyes, but found I didn't want to. The memory of the nightmare was still too fresh.

"I don't wanna sleep," I said.

"The nightmare?"

I nodded and began to tell Ash all about it. He lay silent, listening to every word.

"Do you trust me?" he asked.

"Yes," I replied, confused as to where the question had come from.

"Then trust that I'll protect you." He snuggled even closer to me. "Nothing is gonna hurt you as long as I'm here."

That night, there were no more dreams of the grotesque creatures or the darkness. I had a guardian angel there to watch over and protect me. I was safe in his arms, his smile brighter than any sun, beating back the darkness.

Chapter 9

Wednesday morning. Another six-thirty start. Ash was still out of action. Or rather, he was ordered not to participate, because he was more than ready to join in. Our squad was relegated to basic training drills for the first half of the day, while Ash sat on the sidelines looking like a kicked puppy. We started with the obstacle course, and then moved onto laps around the compound. I hated drills. Lunch break could not come soon enough.

I was hunched over, my hands resting on my knees. Sweat covered my body, despite the freezing cold wind.

"Here," Ash said, handing me a bottle of water.

"Thanks." I took it, and must have drank half the bottle before I felt dizzy from lack of air.

"So what do you wanna do for lunch?"

"I was gonna go to the library. I wanted to see if I could find anything about my ability."

Ash shook his head. "Not this again. Besides, I know you've already searched for information on this last year and found nothing."

"But back then I didn't think to check the stuff on vampire abilities."

"You thinking your power is related to that vamp's somehow?" Lucas butted in. "Interesting theory."

Ash groaned. "Don't encourage him. This kinda stuff never ends well."

"I'm doing it anyway."

"Okay, fine. Let's go grab something from the cafeteria, and then we can go get this nonsense out of your head."

"I'll tag along if you don't mind," said Lucas.

"The more the merrier," said Ash. "Hey Kat, you coming with us?"

Katiya smiled and shook her head. "Actually, I've got plans. I'll see you guys after lunch." She turned and jogged off to the locker rooms.

The three of us went to the cafeteria together, and bought some sandwiches to take with us. Brad stayed behind to eat with some other friends, saying that libraries weren't his thing. We set up at an empty table, near the back of the library, and began looking through the bookshelves. Ash went straight to one of the archives terminals and browsed through some electronic articles.

Not surprisingly, there were a lot of books on vampires, most printed in the last fifty years. I scanned the titles, hoping to find something of use. *'101 Ways to Kill a Vampire'*. Interesting, but not what I was looking for. *'Supernatural Encyclopedia'*. Sounds promising, I thought, and picked it off the shelf. I picked up another two books and took them back to our table, where Lucas was already getting stuck into a rather hefty-looking book.

Most of what I found in those books was general information about vampires. There was nothing on specific abilities. I groaned and slammed the book shut.

"No luck?" Lucas asked.

I shook my head.

"Maybe you're looking in the wrong place for answers." He

closed his book, and placed it back on the table. "So, I've been meaning to ask you how you've been since *that* night."

"Fine, I guess. There's just a lot been happening recently."

Lucas raised an eyebrow. "Just fine? I dunno. It feels like something more. There's been something different about you these last couple of days."

I opened my mouth to speak, but was interrupted by Ash calling me over. I stood and excused myself from the conversation.

"What is it?" I asked.

"Well," he started, pointing to an article on the screen. "I found this in the missions archive. Last year, the Second Sunreaver squad went up against a vampire. It says here that the vampire's ability was short-range teleportation."

"But that's–"

"Jansen's ability. Right, and this was his report. But..." He pressed the screen and flicked to another report. "Same mission, but this is Dom's report. He encountered a vampire with the exact same appearance, only this vampire could manipulate the wind."

"Like Dom."

"Exactly."

"So, what? Two different vampires?"

Ash shook his head. "I don't think so. The reports all seem to indicate there was only one vampire. They reckon he could mimic the abilities of others. And here's the thing. He got away."

I knew what Ash was implying, but there was no way it was the same vampire we encountered. Sure, the physical descriptions were similar, but there was one thing still bugging me. "Okay, so let's say the vampire was mimicking my ability. How do you explain what freaked out the Fifth Covenant? None of them had any ability to copy."

Ash shrugged. "I dunno, but you heard Sergeant Locke's story. Sometimes a vampire doesn't need an ability to scare the crap out of you."

"What about Liam's report?"

"Hasn't been filed yet. Mik, the guy's squad was mutilated beyond recognition. I doubt he's gonna be up to retelling that tale for a while. Look, I know you're searching for answers, but what if there aren't any to be found? Sometimes things just happen."

"No, something is wrong here. I mean, what if we're not entirely human?"

"Okay, now you're just talking crazy. Last I checked, both my parents are human and totally ordinary. And their parents too."

"Then there must be something else. Our powers must have come from somewhere." I started tapping on the screen, searching for anything I could find on the Daeva.

"Mik, stop." Ash grabbed my wrists and turned me away from the terminal. "Stop, and think about this for a moment. Even if this were some big conspiracy, do you really think they'd leave evidence lying around?"

"No. But I can't shake this feeling. Has Lucas told you about the files he found? They have newborn children marked as potential Daeva. They're not telling us something."

"Did the files actually say potential Daeva?

"Ummm, yeah, I think that's what he said."

"Then they're not even sure." Ash sighed. "I think I know what this is all about."

"You do?"

"Yeah. A lot has happened this last week. I mean, first there was graduation, then killing that guy, us, the vampire and the Fifth Covenant. Anyone in your position would be feeling a little overwhelmed."

"I'm not–"

"Mik, trust me, I get it. There was a time when I was starting to realise I was bi. I was so confused. I couldn't figure out who I was supposed to be, and it scared me. I wouldn't blame you if you're going through something similar."

Perhaps Ash was right, and I was avoiding the real problem by making others to distract myself with. A lot had changed. I had changed, and I still wasn't sure whether my new-found sexuality was limited to Ash, or if there was something more to it.

"Maybe you're right. But... I dunno. Something just feels wrong."

"Okay, how about we make a deal? For the next week I want you to forget about all this nonsense and relax. Let yourself adjust. If you're still feeling uneasy after that, then I'll back you."

"Okay." I sighed. "One week."

Ash smiled. "Great. Starting now, you are not allowed to mention anything conspiracy-related, and I'm gonna keep you occupied so you don't even have time to think about it."

I began to wonder what I had gotten myself into, trying to imagine how Ash intended on keeping me busy for a whole week. Knowing Ash, it would likely involve a lot of bedroom activities, which I had to admit, I was feeling less adverse to after my venture the previous night. In fact, a part of me was looking forward to it.

"Come on," Ash said. "Let's go tell Lucas we're done here. Maybe we can go shoot some hoops til Sergeant Locke is expecting us back."

Ash took hold of my hand and started to pull me along with him. I paused, thinking back to how I had ran from Lucas' questions. "I think Lucas knows about us."

"Then I can do this," Ash whispered, leaning in to kiss me. Heat raced up my neck and face in a mix of anger and embarrassment. And then there was also a hint of frustration and desire. Okay, maybe a lot more than a hint. I wanted to grab hold of him and devour him right then and there. But at the same time I wasn't sure I was ready to reveal to the whole world the nature of our relationship.

"Bastard," I muttered. "Do you think he saw?"

Ash grinned. "Oh yeah. He saw."

I pulled my hand free of Ash's and stormed back to the table, trying to avoid eye contact with Lucas.

"So, you and Ash," he said.

I didn't answer, instead choosing to start piling up the books on the desk.

"Well, I can't say I'm surprised. I mean, you two are nearly always together, and there's some kinda spark between the two of you. I think Kat sees it too, and that's why she gives you so much stick."

"I don't wanna talk about it."

"Don't mind him," Ash said. His hand ruffled my hair. "He's just shy because it's all new to him."

"What are you gonna tell Kat?" Lucas asked.

Ash's hand froze. "We haven't figured that out yet."

"Well, don't worry. I definitely won't be telling her. She seems like the type to shoot the messenger." Lucas scratched his chin. "Oh, I have an idea. Why don't we fix her up with someone?"

"Who though?" Ash asked. "And how would we get them together?"

Lucas smirked. "You find a guy, and I'll get them to meet."

"Are you two done plotting?" I said wearily.

"Sure, let's get out of here," Ash said. He explained the situation to Lucas, who simply shrugged and smiled. We left the library and were heading back to the cafeteria to see if Brad was still there when we spotted a familiar face.

"Graeme," Ash yelled. He turned to wave and stopped to let us catch up to him. "What are you doing here?"

"Been showing some new schematics to the General," he said. He patted the bag he was carrying over his shoulder, which was filled with rolls of paper. "New weapon and vehicle designs. That kinda stuff."

"So I know this chick who would love to meet you," Lucas blurted out.

Ash's jaw dropped. "No. Just, no."

"Think about it," Lucas said. "Who better than a younger version of you?"

"He has a point," I added.

"Sorry." Graeme smiled. "I've actually got my eyes on someone. In fact, I was about to go meet her for lunch."

"Oh. Nice one," Ash cheered, giving his brother a pat on the back. "Now remember, make sure she pays her half."

"I got it, Bro. Don't worry." Graeme glanced at his watch. "Well, I'd love to stay, but I'm already running a little late. I'll try and catch up with you sometime soon."

"No worries. You go and enjoy yourself."

"Good luck," I said, waving as he jogged off to his lunch date.

"If he's anything like Ash, I doubt he'll need any luck," said Lucas.

Ash smiled. "Yeah, he'll be fine."

We continued on to the cafeteria and met up with Brad, who was just about ready to leave. There was still plenty of time until we were expected back, so we picked up a basketball from the storeroom and went out onto the courts. Ash, of course, picked me for his team, despite my lack of skill in that particular sport. The match ended in a narrow defeat for us.

The rest of the day was spent revising basic military tactics, so Ash could join in. I never did like the theory part of our training, but Sergeant Locke insisted it was essential, especially since I had missed the first two years of my military education.

*****

That evening, Ash stayed true to his word and kept me busy. We went out of the military base for dinner, which was a rare occasion for us both. I guess you could call it our first date. We sat on the frozen grass in the middle of the park, wrapped up nice and warm, eating battered sausage and chips. Not exactly first date material, but it was peaceful, and the sky was clear and dotted with stars. For a while we sat in each other's arms and Ash pointed out some of the constellations he knew; the Big Dipper, Orion and Ursa Major. I tried to follow, but had difficulty picturing some of the shapes he was describing.

The evening drew on, getting colder with each passing minute. Our breaths formed a dense mist in front of us and we retreated back to the warmth of our room, where Ash suggested giving me a massage. I agreed and he helped strip me of my clothes, leaving my upper half bare. Lying down on my stomach, I let his hands rub and knead the muscles in my back. It was so relaxing that I started drifting off to sleep, until I felt Ash's warm tongue against my lower back. He moved upwards, tracing the line of my spine. My whole body shuddered. I groaned as Ash nibbled at my earlobe, and rolled onto my back to meet his eyes. He pressed his body against mine, rocking his hips as we kissed, and soon we were giving each other a massage of a different kind.

Less than a week ago, if anyone had told me I would be doing this kind of thing near enough every night with my best friend, I would have called them insane. Yet, there I was, panting and moaning, exploring a side of me I never thought existed. Maybe I was the crazy one. Everything had happened so fast. In the space of three days, I had gone from asexual to definitely sexual. I still wasn't sure how it happened, but for the first time in my life that I could remember, I was happy. I guess that should have been my first warning.

Chapter 10

Friday the thirteenth, unlucky for some. I, however, have never believed in superstition. I've walked under plenty of ladders, broken my fair share of mirrors, and even crossed paths with a couple of black cats. Yet, I never experienced any of the bad luck that was supposed to follow. My life had been far from perfect, that was for sure, but I never considered it to be the product of ill-fortune. Bad choices, perhaps, but not luck. If anything, at that moment in time, I would have said things were looking up.

Things with Ash were going smoothly. No, better than that. Things were going great. Everything was great. Even Katiya seemed to be in a good mood.

That morning, Ash surprised me by sneaking up on me in the shower. At first I was angry, but as I had come to realise, I couldn't stay mad at him for long, especially when faced with a pouting lip and puppy-dog eyes. Needless to say, but we were left with very little time for breakfast.

We arrived at our meeting spot just on time. There was a grim look on Sergeant Locke's face, and it was soon clear why. General

Marsten strode into the room, fully geared for combat.

"Listen up, soldiers," he said. "Early this morning, the barriers at Marmagne came under attack from what we believe to be a small band of insurgents. Our scouts have tracked them to several locations. The five of you will be heading to Boursac, a small area of ruins, several miles north of Marmagne to locate any insurgents. Sergeant Locke will fill in the details for you on the way there."

"You heard the man," said Sergeant Locke. "Gear up and meet at the garage on the double. Dismissed."

We marched out of the room, leaving our superiors to discuss something in private.

"Been a while since I saw the General go out on an actual mission," Brad said when we reached the locker room.

"Maybe he got bored of sitting behind a desk and ordering people about," Ash said.

Once upon a time, I had thought of leading an ordinary, boring life with a desk job. Now I couldn't imagine it. I liked the adrenaline rush, and the idea of doing something worthwhile for the human race, even if it did scare the shit out of me at times.

The garage was packed full of people. I could see at least two other squads, including the Second Sunreavers, our Daeva predecessors. It seemed General Marsten would be accompanying our group, as he climbed into the cab of the Wisent that Sergeant Locke was stood next to, waiting for our arrival.

We climbed into the back and strapped ourselves in. Sergeant Locke pulled the doors shut, and gave two taps on the cab window. General Marsten peered through at us, and I felt his eyes settle on me for a moment. Then the engine sputtered to life and we were off. From the small window, I saw one other vehicle trailing us. It was another transport vehicle, a mobile jail cell. They were intending on taking prisoners.

Sergeant Locke began passing out some unfamiliar handguns. "These are the new B-28 tranquilliser guns," he said. "The council wishes to capture members of the insurgency for questioning. These guns have not yet been field tested, so we're not sure if they'll have any effects on vampires. Therefore, your orders are to capture any human insurgents. If you do encounter a vampire, it should be dealt with as normal. Any questions?"

"What about shifters?" Lucas asked.

"Capture them if you can. Just be warned, they're gonna take a few darts before they go down."

"What's General Marsten going to be doing?" This was from Lucas again.

"I thought someone might ask that. The General has received orders from the council to personally oversee and take part in this mission. That alone should tell you how important this mission is. If you fuck up, you'll be answering directly to the General, so I expect you all to bring your A-game today. Now, if there's no more questions..." He paused. There was only silence from the group. "Good."

Sergeant Locke picked up the map from its compartment and unrolled it. He pointed to the area labelled 'Boursac'. "This is where we are headed. The other two squads you saw in the garage will be scouting the ruins of Allogny." He pointed again, to a much larger town a few miles north-east of our destination. "Once we arrive, General Marsten will be giving each of you your assignments."

*****

It was about twenty minutes later when the Wisent came to a halt. We stepped outside and were surrounded by a dense woodland, overgrown with no-one to keep it in check. Except for the road we came through, the ruins were contained by a wall of trees with needle-like leaves, dusted with snow. Beneath us, the ground was covered in a blanket of moss and weeds. The wind whistled through the trees, carrying with it the sound of birds chirping.

I wondered how many places on Earth were like this, where nature had been left to run amok for a century. Inside the city we were safe from attacks, but the people living within the walls of Rachat would never see anything like this for themselves.

"Sightseeing's over," General Marsten called out. We snapped out of our daydreaming and gathered round, ready for our orders. "Starting from this point we will fan out and meet up over the other side." He gave us each a direction to travel in. The General would take the far north-east path, with me taking the next path to the south. To my dismay, Ash was assigned to the southern-most route, along with Lucas. That left Brad and Katiya covering the middle of town.

"Report any successful captures via the radio, and Sergeant Locke will send out two of our lucky cadets to retrieve the body. Are we all clear?"

"Yes, Sir," we said in unison.

The mobile containment vehicle pulled up behind us. Four young cadets poured out, carrying stretchers with them. There was something about the way the General had said 'lucky cadets' that made me think they were anything but lucky. Perhaps, they were being disciplined for something or other, but I had never seen body retrieval as a method of punishment before. It made me wonder what they were missing out on to be here. Or maybe, I was reading into something that wasn't there.

"All right then," General Marsten said, standing up straight and gripping the rifle that hung lazily from its shoulder strap. "Let's move out."

We split up, each heading along our designated routes. My path was littered with stone bungalows, blanketed in creeping vines and moss. The first house I approached still had its door attached. I pushed at the door, but it was stuck fast, probably swollen from the damp and held in place by the snaking vines. I gave it a swift kick, and still it refused to budge. Fortunately the windows were large enough for me to climb in through, and the glass was long since removed.

I peered inside, activating my flashlight There was a strong smell of damp, though it was more of a sweet smell, and not rotten like in Marmagne. With everything clear, I climbed inside. Surrounded by the musky darkness, I closed my eyes and took a deep breath. The memories of the skinned corpses were beginning to resurface.

"I can do this," I told myself. "There's no corpses here." I hoped.

With my back against the wall, I peeked out into the hallway. Nothing but more plant-covered walls. I moved to the next room, scanning each corner with my light. There was a squawk. My heart jumped into my mouth. A large, brown bird spread its wings, flying from its nest. I laughed quietly, hoping this thing with birds wasn't going to become a recurring theme with me. At least Katiya wasn't there to creep up on me. I turned quickly, just in case, and let out a sigh of relief when I found nothing. I'm sure I would have looked a fool, jumping at shadows, if anyone had been watching me.

I ventured deeper into the house, but found nothing more than old furnishings, destroyed by the damp and wildlife. I retraced my steps through the house, exiting out of the same window I climbed in through.

Not surprisingly, the next few houses I checked were in the same condition. There was no sign of life, other than the odd animal and the plants, which threatened to consume everything. The radio crackled and I heard Katiya announce that she had managed to sedate a young male. Sergeant Locke replied that he was sending out the cadets to retrieve the prisoner.

I continued on with my patrol, going from house to house. Nothing. A nest of rodents. More nothing. I glanced down the road, noting I wasn't even halfway done and sighed. Searching for the enemy was quickly becoming my least favourite mission objective. Not that I would have preferred to be fighting vampires all the time, but at least then there was the excitement and the adrenaline.

The next house was bigger than the rest, with a second floor to it. The downstairs was clear, and so, stepping over a pile of rubble, I headed up the flight of stairs. As expected, the place was empty, save for a large spider that scuttled off into the darkness when my flashlight passed over it. I was about to descend the stairs when a deafening screech exploded in my ear, threatening to split my skull in two. I ripped the radio from my ear, holding it at a safe distance as the feedback continued. Finally, it stopped and was replaced with static, accompanied by an incessant ringing in my ear.

"Can anyone hear me?" I asked. The only reply was more static. "Stupid thing," I cursed, giving the radio a couple of taps before trying it again. There was no change.

Standard operating procedures dictated that I should head for the designated rendezvous point. In this case, that would be base camp, where the vehicles were parked. I gave the radio one last try, before starting back to Sergeant Locke to explain my predicament.

As I walked down the street, the temperature began to drop. I looked up and saw masses of deep grey clouds rolling across the sky, blotting out the sun and darkening the world below. I sighed, dismayed at the thought of having to continue the mission in bad weather. Even through the thermals, I felt the hairs on my arms begin to stand on end. I hoped there were no more radios left, and the mission would be aborted because of it. Not likely, given the apparent importance of our objective, but one can dream. Movement from my left yanked me from my thoughts. I turned, my gun aimed.

"It's me, Hart," the voice said. I recognised General Marsten's voice before he stepped out from behind the building.

"Sir, my radio is down. I'm getting nothing but static."

The General nodded. "Mine too. Either something has happened back at the Wisent, or our signal is being jammed." He paused for a moment, resting his chin in one hand. "Okay, come with me."

"Sir?" I replied, wondering why he was heading in the opposite direction. "Shouldn't we be heading back to the others?"

General Marsten continued walking away and I hurried to catch up with him. "If there's a problem back at base then the others will deal with it. But if someone is jamming our signal, then we need to find them, and stop it. This mission is far too important to give up on because of a jammed radio."

If it were any other commanding officer, I might have argued it would have been better to meet up with the others first, and then seek out the source of the problem together. But I had to trust he knew what he was doing. After all, you don't get to be the General for nothing. Besides, he had a short temper when it came to questioning his orders, and the last thing I wanted was another evening of scrubbing the garage and vehicles.

We reached the edge of the ruins and General Marsten kept walking, pushing his way through the overgrown wilderness. He held his radio close to his ear in one hand, listening to the static. In his other hand was his rifle, held firm as he used it to push aside leaves and branches. I followed reluctantly, the undergrowth becoming thicker and harder to traverse, until we reached a small clearing. The edge of the clearing was lined with dead trees, and in the centre was a large pit. At various points around the crater were headstones, cracked and weathered with the passage of time. I looked down, standing at the edge of the slope, only to find a pool of mud.

"What is this place?" I asked.

The General stopped to answer. "It's a mass grave," he replied, his voice sounding more serious than usual. "The victims of the plague would have been thrown in here and burned."

"Must have been a lot of people," I said, judging by the size of it.

"This is one of the smaller ones. Boursac probably had a couple of thousand inhabitants at the most. The bigger cities would have had entire landfill sites overflowing with the dead, in an attempt to contain the plague."

I shuddered at the thought of so many people sharing a grave. It didn't seem right to me. The wind groaned and shrieked as it passed through the woods, sounding out the agony and pain of the grave's residents.

"Let's keep moving," General Marsten said.

Something about the situation caused a knot in my stomach and a nagging at the back of my mind. Maybe it was seeing the mass grave that put me on edge, even though I hadn't actually seen any of the bodies. Or maybe, it was because we were heading further from

Boursac and the rest of the squad, with no means of contacting them if we ran into trouble.

We were going slowly uphill now, as if level ground wasn't enough trouble in this place. The General stopped, listening again to the static.

"We're getting close," he said, pointing deeper into the woods. "This way."

"Sir, I really don't know about this. I–"

"You what?" He turned to face me, his lips curled. His voice was a low growl. "Unless you want to be spending the next few days scrubbing boots with a toothbrush, I suggest you get a hold of yourself, and do as I say without question. Do I make myself clear, soldier?"

"Sir," I replied, my eyes cast downwards. "Yes, Sir."

General Marsten turned and continued up the hill. I clenched my fists and followed after him. We came upon a small cave, set into the side of the hill, filled with stalactites and stalagmites. The entrance reminded me of a large, open mouth, complete with rows of pointy teeth.

"In here," General Marsten said, motioning for me to take point.

I pulled out my handgun and stepped inside, flattening myself against the wall as I came to a corner. There was a muffled bang, and at first, I couldn't figure out where it had come from. Then there was a sharp pain in my arm, and I grasped at the source of the pain, finding a small dart. I dropped to my knees, feeling my heartbeat begin to slow. My breaths grew longer and deeper. General Marsten crouched down next to me, removing my radio and pushing me to the ground. He crushed the radio under his boot, twisting his foot, to make sure it was well and truly destroyed.

"Why?" I whispered, willing my eyes to stay open. I kept telling myself to fight it, feeling the energy sapped from my body.

"You've been poking your nose into things that should stay hidden," he replied. "We can't have you finding out our secrets now, can we?"

With my last ounce of strength, I dug my nails into the palms of my hands, hoping the pain would help me fight the effects of the drug. So this was why the General was assigned to the mission, to remove me. And for what? All this, for the sake of a secret.

"I didn't want to do this," he said, shaking his head, "but the secrets of the Daeva must never be uncovered. It is for the good of humanity."

He stood over me, shooting another dart into my chest. At least, that's where I think he shot me. Everything was numb, and my eyelids closed of their own accord. As the last drip of consciousness left me, I smiled. Ash wouldn't leave me. He'd find me, even if it took all day and night.

Chapter 11

I opened my eyes slowly, shielding them from the piercing rays that shone down on me. I looked around, squinting, and noted I was in an old stone building. My mouth was dry, and my body ached. My arms were sore and cramped. I tried to stretch them, only to find they were restrained behind my back. Panic hit me, forcing me to awaken fully.

Where am I? How long was I out? Why am I tied up? Had everyone left me? Who found me? Where was Ash? So many questions. I struggled against the restraints, trying to pull my hands free, but it was no use. All I managed to accomplish was chafing my wrists against the rope.

I gave up struggling, lacking the energy to continue. I took a few deep breaths to calm myself and took in my surroundings. From what I could see out of the window, I was no longer in the woods. The room I was in was empty. I let out a long sigh, slumping against the pillar I was tied to. My neck was especially sore, feeling as though I had bruised it, and maybe I had when I fell to the ground.

Time passed by. I don't know how long I waited, but no-one

came. I tried more than once to free myself of the ropes, only to give up when it felt like they were sawing through my wrists. I was starting to think I hadn't been found at all, and I was brought here to die alone. As I entertained this thought, I heard the sound of laughter in the distance. My first instinct was to call out, but my throat was so dry that only a hoarse whisper escaped my lips. The voices came closer, and I could hear footsteps now.

I shuffled uncomfortably, straining against the ropes. The logical part of my brain kicked in, reminding me that these people were more than likely the ones who tied me up. I had to get myself free. Straining my neck, I managed to look over my shoulder and realised the pillar was square. Perhaps, I could fray the rope on the corners. I pulled the rope tight against the stone and began working it up and down over the edge.

I don't know how far I got, but I stopped when a silhouette paused in the doorway. I couldn't make out any of his features for the blinding light that shone from behind him, but it was a definitely a man.

"Hey, look who's awake," he said. "You thirsty?" The man held out a bottle of water. I glared at him, wondering if he was genuinely offering me a drink, or if it were merely a way to torment me. Without waiting for me to answer, he pressed the opening of the bottle to my lips and tilted it. At first I kept my mouth shut, letting the water dribble down my chin. The cold water against my cracked lips reminded me of how parched I was, so I opened up, drinking as much as the man would allow me.

I gasped for air as he withdrew the bottle, screwed the lid back on, and put it down beside me. My captor sat down against one of the other pillars, no longer with the light behind him. His face was slim and tanned, covered in a small amount of dark stubble, which he scratched at. He looked familiar, though I couldn't have seen him before. His shoulder-length hair looked grey at first, though he was much too young for grey hair, wasn't he? He couldn't have been much older than thirty.

"What're you staring at?" he asked, and began to crawl across the floor on his hands and feet with a surreal grace that no human should have been able to achieve, putting his face close to mine. As he passed the door, the sun spilled over his face, revealing that his hair was in fact a mix of silver-white with dark undertones. But the strangest thing was his eyes. His eyes were a green-yellow hue, and it finally dawned on me why he seemed so familiar. This was the man I had bumped into the night of our graduation, the man who was carrying the reports.

"Y-you're..." I started. He smiled at me, flashing what I can only describe as a pearly set of half-fangs. They were human teeth, but each was a little longer and more pointed than they should have been.

"So, you've remembered. The name's Daniel. I'd shake your hand, but it seems they're a bit tied up at the moment." He laughed, and then sniffed the air around me.

Werewolf. It was the only explanation. My body tensed as his nose brushed past my cheek. The significance wasn't lost on me. I had seen plenty of dogs do this, but the action seemed wrong when it was a human doing it.

"What are you going to do to me?" I asked.

"That's up to Violet to decide," he said, sitting himself back down. "Until then, I'm your new best friend."

He sat with his arms folded over his bent knees, forehead resting on his arms. There was so much I wanted to ask him, but I thought it better to stay quiet, and concentrate on escaping whatever fate they had in store for me. For now, it seemed my life was in no immediate danger, so I waited.

Daniel dozed off after a short while, an occasional snore filling the room. As quietly as I could, I continued fraying the rope that bound me. I felt the rope start to give when two more shadows blocked the doorway.

"Daniel," the first said. That one word was enough to wake the werewolf. "You call this keeping watch?"

"Yeah, what's your problem?" Daniel snarled.

"He's almost through the rope," said the second, kneeling down to inspect it. He was smaller than the first, with deep auburn hair.

Good to know, I thought. I had to take the chance before they could reinforce the ropes. I reached down inside myself, calling on my magic and drawing it out into the room. It emanated from me like a cold breeze, filling the space between us. Their eyes grew wide as it touched them. Daniel was the first to go, curling up into a ball and trembling.

I worked quickly, trying to finish off the rest of the rope, which was harder now I needed to focus on my magic as well. I pulled harder, gritting my teeth as it dug into my already sore wrists. A hand gripped my shoulder. I turned my head to see it belonged to the redhead.

"Bad move," I said, knowing from Ash that physical contact makes a psychic ability much more powerful. My magic lashed out at him, and the redhead released his hold on me, back-pedalling into the corner on his hands and feet. The third man collapsed to his knees in the doorway. He appeared to have the strongest will of the three.

"Violet!" he called out.

Seconds later, a tall woman appeared at the door, wearing a long, hooded cloak. She walked over to me, grabbing hold of my chin and forcing me to meet her gaze. Even touching me, she didn't flinch.

"Call off your song, Siren," she said. More questions added to my hoard. Why was she immune to my ability? What did she mean by 'my song'? Why did she call me 'Siren'? Questions could be answered later, but first I had to survive. I focused on her, redirecting every ounce of my magic to her.

She took hold of my right hand, twisting it at a painful angle. "We are not your enemy," she said. "But I will not hesitate to start breaking bones if you do not cease this."

My arm was twisted further, until I felt it was about to snap. A broken arm would do me no good for escaping, so I closed my eyes and took a deep breath, halting the flow of magic from within me. The residual energy in the air began to dissipate. I would have to come up with a new plan of escape now. Daniel leaped to his hands and feet, his back arched. He growled and snarled at me, inching closer.

"Control yourself, Daniel," said Violet. The werewolf froze, bowing his head. If he had had a tail in human form, I'm sure it would have been curled between his legs.

Violet released her grip on my arm. She pulled a small knife from a sheath at her waistband. I flinched as it passed me, wondering what she intended to do. The ropes went slack. I shook them off, and the first thing I did was to examine my wrists, which were bruised and angry. Violet stood, offering me a hand.

"Are you sure this is wise?" the redhead asked.

"He will not run," Violet said. She fixed her gaze on me. "No doubt you have questions. I will try and answer them for you."

I pushed myself to my feet, refusing her hand. My legs were wobbly beneath me, but they soon steadied. Violet motioned for me to leave the room and I obliged. I could see a line of trees near the edge of the ruins. I guessed we must have been on the other side of the woods General Marsten had led me through.

Violet walked up to me and held out the bottle of water. I accepted it and she began to walk around the back of the building. I started to follow, and when we were out of sight of the others, I turned down an alleyway and ran. I stumbled over small rocks and cracks in the pavement, pushing my legs as hard as they would go. The trees were only metres away, urging me forward with their promise of cover, when Violet stepped out from behind a building. I stopped and turned. A pair of arms wrapped around me. I kicked and thrashed against her, finding myself caught in an iron grip.

"Do I need to go find some more rope?" she asked.

I shook my head and stopped struggling. Violet set me down on the ground and pushed me forward, one hand gripping the back of my armoured vest. We walked until we reached a small yard, a campfire sat in the middle with several long sticks resting over it, each with what appeared to be chunks of meat skewered on them. The smell hit me, and my stomach began to rumble.

"Are you hungry?" Violet asked, laughing as my stomach answered for me. She led me over to a small rock at the edge of the fire and sat me down, before pulling back her hood to reveal long, black hair, framing her pale skin and deep green eyes. She picked up one of the sticks and twirled it around before handing it to me. I poked the chunk of meat, finding it wasn't too hot to eat and lifted it to my mouth, taking a small bite. It tasted a lot like beef, but with a slight tang to it. Violet was inspecting the rest of the meat, but I felt her eyes on me, watching in case I should make another break for it.

"Ask anything you like," Violet prompted me, sitting down opposite me. "I will answer as best I can."

"What is this?" I asked, taking a larger bite. "It's good." I washed the meat down with some water.

"Deer. Daniel and Nate were out hunting for it when they found you," she replied, stifling a laugh. "Honestly, of all the questions you could ask first, and you ask *that*."

I shrugged. I wasn't sure what to think, a voice at the back of my mind whispering to me, and telling me I couldn't trust these people. There was no guarantee my questions would be answered truthfully. Then another part of my brain began to kick in, reminding me that so far they had given me food and water, and I needed answers. Maybe they didn't want to hurt me, I thought. Or maybe they're making sure you're in good health for their master, another thought replied.

"What happened after I was knocked out?" I asked. As long as the offer for answers stood, I may as well take it. It would be some hours before the sun set, so there was still time to make another attempt at escaping. My fingers brushed past the holster on the side of my leg. It didn't surprise me to find my gun and knife gone. If I was going to escape, then it had to be before nightfall and the vampires came out to play.

"They spotted you and the older man..." She paused.

"General Marsten."

"Forgive me," Violet said. "I haven't even asked your name yet."

"Mikhail," I said, and then wondered if I should have given a false name. No point, I thought. What was a name outside of the city anyway?

"Mikhail," she repeated. "I am Violet, as you're probably already aware. Anyway, they spotted you walking through the woods while they were out hunting and decided to follow. I don't know what your General was planning to do with you, but something startled him and he left in a hurry. Nate insisted on bringing you back here."

I jumped when something warm and furry brushed past me. A large wolf, probably twice the size of a normal wolf – I couldn't be sure, having never seen one outside of a book before – nudged at my leg. I was so wrapped up in wanting to find my answers that I hadn't heard the wolf approach, which was saying something, considering its size. It looked at my food with those green-yellow eyes I recognised as Daniel's. He licked his lips, a few drops of saliva hitting the ground. In wolf form, his fur was the same colour as his hair, silvery-grey and black.

"Here, Daniel," Violet said, removing one of the larger chunks of meat from its skewer. His tail wagged as he gripped it in his teeth and lay down at my feet. He ripped at the meat, holding it as best he could between his front paws and swallowing it in huge pieces.

"He enjoys spending time in that form," said Violet. "As a result he retains certain features even in human form. Is there anything else you wish to ask?"

"What are you?" I asked, wondering how it was Violet was unaffected by my ability. Daniel displayed no resistance, so that ruled out werewolf. My first guess would have been vampire, if it weren't for the sun still being out. She certainly didn't show any signs of bursting into flames. Maybe a psychic human? That would have made her able to shield against me.

"I'm a vampire," she said bluntly.

I stopped chewing for a moment, raising an eyebrow in disbelief.

"Do you think I'm stupid?" I said. What little trust she had earned was gone, replaced with anger. Daniel paused eating for a moment and looked up at me. He whined, and then went back to eating.

Violet smiled, my eyes locked onto her mouth as I saw two long, sharp fangs begin to extend from her gums. I gulped, my stomach hollowing out in dread. It wasn't possible. She was out in broad daylight. She should have been burning up by now. That was the first thing we were taught about vampires.

"I come from the Daywalker bloodline," she added. "Sunlight weakens me, but it does not kill me, as with other vampires. I guess they neglected to teach you about our existence, of which they are very much aware. That I can assure you. You're probably wondering what else they forgot to tell you, or lied about."

"No," I said. Yes, I thought. My mind flashed back to General Marsten, and what little I could piece together from the moments before I slipped into unconsciousness. I remembered him saying something about secrets, and the uneasy feeling I had since my encounter with the vampire was back again. I knew something was up. I knew they were hiding things from us.

My thoughts returned to the vampire sat in front of me. What could she possibly want with me? Not death. She could easily have killed me already. Water, food, even trusting me enough that I almost escaped into the woods. That wasn't something you did to a person you were going to kill. Unless maybe it was all a plan to gain my trust, in the hopes I would spill information on the Silver Dawn. But she could have just mind-raped me into telling her everything I knew. Sergeant Locke's words still echoed at the back of my mind, reminding me that a quick death was sometimes the better option.

"I know it will be hard for you to trust me," she said, her voice filled with sincerity. "But I promise you, we are not your enemies."

Daniel, who had finished eating his slab of meat, pushed himself up and rested his muzzle on my lap. He let out a soft whine, eyeing the rest of my meat. My stomach churned with unease, and so I picked what was left of the meat off the skewer and held it in the palm of my hand, praying he wouldn't take my hand with it. He picked up the meat, chewed it a few times, and then threw his head back to swallow it.

"Deer is his favourite," Violet said, smiling.

What was happening? Nothing seemed real. Vampires were evil, blood-sucking creatures. They weren't supposed to smile and talk about others as though they were dear friends, or family. They weren't supposed to be kind to their captives. And they certainly weren't supposed to be out in the middle of the day.

Daniel's tongue lolled out of the side of his mouth, dripping with saliva. I reached out to scratch him behind the ear. He tilted his head to one side, his eyes closed and tail wagging. This wasn't the werewolf I was brought up to know – a savage beast that would not hesitate to rip the meat from my bones. Daniel whimpered again.

"Behave yourself, Daniel," Violet scalded him. "He's such a baby when it comes to food."

The urge to escape still nagged at my mind. I wanted nothing more than to be back in my room, with Ash's arms around me. And yet, there were questions I needed to ask. There were answers I needed, and I had no idea whether this opportunity would arise again.

"Why did you call me Siren back there?" I asked. "And what did you mean by 'my song'?"

"You don't know? Sirens are another of the vampire bloodlines."

"So Sirens were actually vampires?" I asked, and Violet nodded. "But I thought they lured people to them. What does that have to do with my ability?"

"Sirens can manipulate the emotions of those around them. In the past they would prey on travellers, luring them to their deaths with feelings of love and safety. That is how the mythological Siren you know was born."

"And the song?"

"Your ability. Those who fall under its spell, sometimes report hearing a song. I think it's their way of interpreting the magic in a form they can understand."

"I see."

Had the Silver Dawn known all this and chose not to tell me? If so, then what did it all mean? Why would they lie to us about such a thing? Why all the secrecy?

"Now let me ask you something. Why did your General want rid of you?"

"I had suspicions about the Daeva, and where we got our abilities from. He said the secrets of the Daeva should remain hidden, and it was for the good of humanity."

Footsteps approached me from behind. The two men from earlier sat down at the fire, each taking a skewer from the slowly dying fire. Daniel finally moved his head from my knee and plodded over to them, whimpering and giving them his puppy-dog eyes.

"I had the same suspicions," said the redhead, who began to tear into his food. "That's why they kicked me out." He looked to be around my age, maybe a little older. His fiery, auburn hair was a little longer, falling in subtle waves that reached his grey-blue eyes. Body-wise he was about the same height and build as me.

"Kicked you out?" I asked.

He smiled and held out his hand towards the fire. A stream of flames spouted from his hand, causing the fire to spark to life, and startling me. "I'm like you," he said. "I'm Nathaniel, by the way, but you can call me Nate."

"Mik," I replied.

"And this is Sebastian," said Violet, motioning to the other man who sat beside her. He gave a quick nod and continued eating. Sebastian was, I assumed, the oldest of the group, possibly barring Violet. He appeared to be in his early forties, with short-cropped brown hair and matching brown eyes. He was taller than the others – though not quite as tall as Brad was – and well built, but not particularly muscled.

My mind was torn. I still couldn't quite believe everything I had heard. But then there was Nate, a Daeva like myself, who had had the same suspicions about his powers. How many other times had the Silver Dawn tried to cover their tracks by removing people?

"So do you all live here?" I asked, wondering what they were doing in the ruined village. And I thought that, perhaps, if I could casually get some information from them, then I could learn what their motives where.

"No," Nate replied, his hand running through Daniel's fur. "We go where we're ordered, gathering infor–"

"Stop," Sebastian interrupted him. "We don't know if we can trust him yet."

"It's okay, dear." Violet stood and walked behind Sebastian. She reached down, putting her arms around him. "I trust he is no longer one of them."

"Have you thought about what you're going to do now?" Nate asked. "I mean, I assume you realise you can't go back to Rachat now."

What was I going to do now? Was going back even an option? After all I had just learned, I wasn't so sure. The tiny thread of hope I was holding onto, that Ash would find me and we'd go back to the city together, slipped fast through my fingers. I thought, maybe we could expose the General for what he did to me, and learn what was so important it had been deemed necessary to leave me unconscious in the middle of enemy territory. But the more I thought about it, the more I realised how foolish it was.

I had no idea how many people were in on the secret, and I doubted the General would leave anything to chance. If I tried to re-enter the city, I'd probably be killed on sight as a traitor. And who would believe me over the Silver Dawn's highest ranking officer? Ash would. Lucas might. Brad and Katiya, I wasn't so sure about, but I would have liked to believe they would have. Four people; that was hardly enough to make a difference. More than likely, even if I did make it to Rachat, they'd say I was delusional.

A wave of panic washed over me, the reality of the situation setting in. I found it difficult to breathe. There was no going back for me. Just when I had found a true friend, and lover. The realisation that I might never see Ash again was like a crushing weight on my chest.

"Fuck," I screamed, running my hands through my hair and clutching fiercely at it. I doubled over, fighting back the tears that threatened to spill over. This couldn't be happening. Not now. A cold, wet nose nudged my cheek.

"Come on, Daniel. Let's go do our rounds," said Violet. She whispered something to Nate and Sebastian that I didn't quite catch, before leading Daniel away. Sebastian followed soon after.

Nate sat next to me, his hand resting on my back. "It's okay," he said. "Just let it all out."

I brushed his hand off and stood, beginning to pace back and forth. I kicked at the gravel, and then fell to my hands and knees, letting out a ragged scream of anguish, and slamming my fists against the ground. Nate caught my fist and I looked up to glare at him.

"I know what you're going through," he said, releasing my hand. "I wanted to go back too. I had friends. I had a family. And because of some dumb secret I had to leave them all behind. But it gets easier with time, you know?"

His words were no comfort. I didn't want it to get easier, because I didn't want it to be real. I wished I would wake up to the sounds of the morning bells, with Ash's arm draped over me. He would kiss me, and I'd realise it was all an awful dream. Deep down in my heart, I knew that would never happen.

I raised my fist again, noting the blood decorating my knuckles, and began punching the floor once more. Nate grabbed hold of my arms. I thrashed against him, screaming as he wrapped his arms around me and held me. "Hey, stop that. Hurting yourself isn't gonna do any good."

I resorted to beating my fists against his chest, until the anger seemed to subside and all that was left was tears. I slumped against him, my head resting on his shoulders until even the tears stopped.

It was their fault, I thought. The Silver Dawn. They used me and dumped me like a broken toy. I wanted them to pay. My blood boiled with hatred towards them.

"You want to get back at them, don't you?" Nate whispered in my ear. My head shot up, looking him right in the eye. "I know, because I do too."

"How?" I asked. The idea should have seemed unbelievable. How could I hope to get back at them? They were locked away safely in Rachat. Out of reach.

"Violet and the others are part of a group, known as The Twilight Resistance." Nate gripped my shoulders and stared straight at me. "Join us. We can get our revenge together, for what they did to us. Forcing us to leave everyone behind."

I opened my mouth to speak, the word 'yes' lingering on the tip of my tongue. But then I thought of Ash. That stopped my voice, quieting the rage and thoughts of revenge against those who wronged me. Was he still out there looking for me? Before I could even think of revenge, I had to find him.

"It's okay. You don't have to say anything. Why don't you get some rest and think it about it more in the morning?"

I nodded. After everything that had happened, my energy was drained. Nate led me into one of the ruined buildings and up a crumbling flight of stairs. The windows were mostly boarded up, the evening sun slipping in through the cracks. Nate took a bottle of water, and some cotton wool from a backpack, and began to clean the blood and dirt from my hands. And then he motioned for me to take off the armoured vest and slip into one of the sleeping bags that was laid out on the floor.

"You can take this one," he said. "It belongs to Violet, but I'm sure she'll understand. It's not like she actually needs to sleep anyway."

I pulled off my boots and climbed in, not having the energy to argue.

Nate crouched down next to me. "You've got a lot to learn about life outside the city, Mik. But trust me, it has its good points."

I nodded, feeling my eyelids grow heavy. The sleeping bag provided little comfort against the hard, wooden floor. It didn't matter. I needed rest, and my body was already drifting off.

"Sleep well," Nate said. I heard his footsteps going down the stairs. Now that I was alone, a few tears began to flow again. It seemed stupid, after having cried in his arms, but I allowed myself that moment in private as sleep took me under.

Chapter 12

It was light outside when I finally awoke. I was the only one in the small room. The other sleeping bags were already rolled up and packed away at the side of the room. Everything felt surreal, like a dream I hadn't quite awoken from. My first real thought was I needed a hot shower. A fresh change of clothes and a coffee wouldn't hurt either. I climbed out of the sleeping bag and stretched my arms. Every muscle in my body ached from sleeping on the hard floor. I hobbled downstairs, squinting as I stepped through the door and the light hit my eyes.

"Morning, Sleepy," a voice startled me. Daniel stood leaning against the wall, his arms folded.

"Where is everyone?" I asked.

"Away on an assignment. They made me stay behind to watch you," he grumbled. I got the feeling he didn't much like babysitting duty.

"Is there somewhere I can get cleaned up?"

"Follow me," he said, pushing himself away from the wall. He picked up a small bag sat at his feet and handed it to me. "There's a change of clothes and a towel in there. You're about the same size as Nate, so they should fit."

We reached the edge of the ruins and Daniel led me into the woods to a large river. "You can wash here," he said.

I glared at Daniel. He sighed and turned around. It didn't feel right washing outdoors. I undressed anyway, and tested the water with my toes. The icy water sent a shiver up my spine and through my entire body, goosebumps raising on my arms.

"Oh, just get it over with. The water's not gonna get any warmer," Daniel moaned. I turned my head to make sure he was still looking away. He was sitting down, his legs crossed, and was whittling away at a long stick.

I marched into the river, deciding Daniel was right, and not wanting to prolong the experience. A couple of steps in, and the water was already past my knees. I took another step, and then I was falling, going under. I flailed about wildly, breaking the surface and gasping for air, half out of surprise, and half shock from the biting cold.

"By the way," Daniel shouted, "there's a steep drop."

"Gee, thanks for telling me," I shouted back, my teeth beginning to chatter.

"You're welcome."

I washed as quickly as possible, my whole body shivering. I swam to the edge and picked up the towel, drying myself off before I froze to death. From the bag, I pulled out a pair of blue jeans with a tear in one knee, a red sweater and a black padded vest. I kept my thermals on underneath, as a precaution against the cold weather. Lastly, I attempted to make my hair presentable by running my fingers through it.

"I'm done," I said. Daniel jumped to his feet and spun round, throwing a long stick at me. I caught it in one hand, stumbling back as it threatened to smack me in the face. One of the ends had been sharpened to a point.

"Let's go catch some lunch, and I'll show you the ropes," he said, leading me further up the river to a shallow stream that branched off from the main body of water. Daniel stood at the edge, staring at the water. I stood next to him, searching for what he was looking at. At first I saw nothing, until I spotted movement beneath the surface. I raised an eyebrow at him.

"You're gonna try and spear a fish?" I laughed.

"Uh-huh," he replied, biting his bottom lip. His arm extended in a flash, thrusting the makeshift spear into the water. I shook my head, thinking it an impossible task. To my surprise, he lifted the stick into the air, revealing a fish wiggling helplessly on the end. "See? Now you try."

Daniel made it look so easy with his supernatural speed. I tried over and over, getting more and more frustrated that I couldn't manage to catch something as simple as a fish. After many tries the novelty wore off, and all that was left was frustration and anger. Daniel showed me how to remove the scales from the fish with the blunt edge of a knife, and left that task to me while he went about catching some more. The first fish came out a little mangled, but I soon got the hang of it.

While I was busy scaling the fish, my mind began to wander. I wondered how far we were from the ruins of Boursac. We couldn't have been too far, if Daniel and Nate were hunting for deer when they spotted me. I had the sudden urge to make a run for it. Violet wasn't there to stop me now. I could escape and make it back to Rachat. Then the rational part of my brain chimed in again, reminding me I didn't know which direction to head, or if Ash would even be there searching for me. General Marsten went to such lengths to isolate me that it seemed unlikely he would let them look. He probably told them I was dead. Besides, there was no chance of me being able to return to the city, not with what I knew now. My best hope of survival was to stick with Violet and the others, join the so-called resistance and hope to get revenge. Maybe they'd help me find Ash, if I explained it to them. And maybe Ash would join me.

"What's wrong?" Daniel asked.

"Nothing," I said, trying to keep my focus on the fish. But whatever I did, I couldn't escape the unease of not knowing. That was worse than anything else. What if he was in the ruins right now, searching for me? My finger slipped and a sharp pain shot through my hand, the knife slicing into my thumb. "Shit," I muttered. Blood welled to the surface.

Daniel sighed. "Let me see," he said, taking hold of my hand. "It's not too deep. Go wash it in the river. I'll finish up here."

I did as I was told, dipping my bleeding thumb into the cold water.

"So are you gonna tell me what's wrong?"

"I've got things on my mind, okay?"

"Like what?"

My thumb was already starting to feel numb. I pulled it out of the water and examined the cut. Daniel held out a tissue for me and I wrapped it around tight. "I'm wondering about what the General told everyone, about how I disappeared. I don't wanna believe they're not out there looking for me. God, I can't even begin to imagine what Ash is going through right now. Does he think I'm still alive, or..."

"This Ash... was he your best friend, or something?"

I nodded, and for reasons I can't explain, began telling Daniel everything about Ash, from how we first met at the academy, and how I tried to push him away, to the recent developments in our relationship. I chose to omit certain details, such as our drunken adventure, and other late-night activities.

"Sounds like you guys were pretty close," Daniel said, gutting the last of the fish and placing it in a plastic bag with the rest.

"Yeah. It all happened so fast, and now..." I paused, leaving the rest of the sentence unspoken. "What if I could get him to join us?" I blurted out. "He's powerful, and he'd be useful." I know it sounded desperate, but more than anything right then I needed Ash to be there for me. I needed him to comfort me, to tell me everything was all right, and that we'd get through it together.

Daniel let out a long breath, his gaze drifting down, and then back to me. "It's not that easy. He probably has friends and family in the city, right?"

I nodded and hung my head. I understood exactly what Daniel meant. If it was this hard for me to leave one person behind, then I couldn't even imagine how hard it would be for someone like Ash to leave everyone. I didn't doubt he had strong feelings towards me, but were they strong enough for him to sacrifice everything, to leave the city, for me? Somehow, I doubted it.

"Look, I probably shouldn't be doing this, but... the place where we found you isn't far from here. If you want, we could go take a look. At least then you can know for sure if they're searching for you or not."

I looked up at him. Was it that simple? Could Ash and I really be reunited so soon?

"One condition though. If I sense any danger, then we leave immediately. Understood?"

"Fine," I said, following him across the stream. If there was a chance, then I had to take it, no matter how small.

"Hope you can keep up." Daniel grinned, launching into a full-out sprint. I ran after him, stumbling over tree roots and catching myself on the foliage, whereas Daniel seemed to slip through the plants and trees, as though they moved out of the way for him. No doubt that was one of the perks of being a werewolf.

I reached the top of the hill, panting and wheezing. Daniel waited for me, the bag of fish slung casually over his shoulder and a pleased grin on his face. From the peak of the ridge I could see the ruins in the distance. They certainly looked empty, but I needed to be sure.

On the way down to Boursac, we stopped at the cave. Daniel sniffed at the air and said, "There's only four scents here. Me, Nate, you, and that other dude." Of course, the chances Ash would have found the place were slim at best. The woods completely encircled Boursac, and it would be easy enough to lose your way once you were in them. We passed the giant crater. The pool of mud was shallower now, revealing partially buried bones.

"One hundred years, and the stench of death still lingers," Daniel said, covering his nose. Having an ultra-sensitive nose must have been a real pain.

When we reached the inner edge of the woods, Daniel crouched to the floor, tilting his head to one side. Next he sniffed. "Seems empty to me," he said. We went a little way in, but Daniel was unable to sense that anyone had been there since the day before, and there was certainly no-one there but us. I was expecting it, but that didn't help squash the feeling of disappointment that washed over me. And then there was the anger. General Marsten. What had he said or done to keep them away? I can't imagine them having given in easily.

We walked back to the camp, mostly in silence. Daniel tried a few times to start a conversation, only to hit a dead end when I didn't reply. The others still weren't back, so Daniel began teaching me about the world outside Rachat, in an attempt to distract me from my moping and seething.

"First thing you need to know, is the Silver Dawn lied to you about a lot of stuff, but they're also right on the money about other things."

"Like what?" I asked, my curiosity piqued. I was eager to learn exactly how much of what I had been taught was a lie.

"Well, for starters, not all vampires are blood-sucking monsters."

I nodded in agreement. So far, Violet seemed almost human. She was nothing at all like the vampire I encountered only a few days ago. She, and her friends, had given me food, water, clothing, and emotional support. What had the other vampire proposed to me? A quick death as he sucked my veins dry. Yes, Violet was a far cry from what I assumed all vampires to be like.

"However, most of the vamps out in the wild will rip your throat out and drain you without asking questions. It's all about survival out here. And with the Silver Dawn's scouts running around during the day, it's doubly important we remain unnoticed, which brings me onto my next point."

Again I nodded, acknowledging what was being said.

"Staying undetected. We only light fires for cooking or if it gets really cold. Last thing we need is a smoke trail bringing in some wild vamps. And if we hunt, we gut and skin the meat away from camp, to avoid attracting predators and scavengers. We don't leave any waste. When we leave a camp, it's as if we were never there."

There were other rules too, like not wandering outside of the camp unless absolutely necessary. Common sense, really.

"Anything you wanna ask?"

I shrugged, then remembered the way Violet held Sebastian the previous night. "Are Violet and Sebastian together?"

"Fifteen years now, I think," Daniel replied.

"They must love each other," I said, thinking over what Sergeant Locke told us, that vampires have no humanity left in them. "I was taught vampires don't have emotions. Not like we do."

"Some don't. They just keep on living, while everyone around them ages and dies. They grow apart from the world, and eventually forget what it was like to be human. Others just turn off their emotions. They give in to the hunger and becomes the monsters they believe themselves to be, because it's easier than facing reality."

I had never thought of vampires like that before, as humans struggling with what they had become. It must have been a lonely existence, watching everyone around you die while you, immortal, remain the same forever.

"Of course, then you get the ones that enjoy it. The power. The immortality. To them, killing is a small price to pay." Daniel looked up into the sky, using a hand to shield his eyes from the sun. "The others should be back soon. How good are you at cooking?"

"Awful."

"Well, ol' Daniel here's gonna teach you how to set up a fry rock," he said standing and placing his hands on his hips.

"What's a fry rock?" I asked.

"You'll see soon enough. I want you to go find a thin, flat slab of rock and bring it to the spot where we ate yesterday. It needs to be about this wide–" Daniel demonstrated with his hands, "–and this long. Think you can do that?"

"Sure."

I thought it would be an easy task to find a piece of rock. After all, we were surrounded by crumbling stone buildings, but they were all too thick, or uneven. Having no luck in the ruins, I ventured out into the woods. It didn't take long to find a suitable slab of rock. I lifted it up. There was something on the underside of the rock, and when it moved I yelped and dropped the rock on my foot, swearing and cursing. My heart pounded against my chest. I had never seen anything like it before. The thing was long and thin, with hundreds of legs, patterned in black and yellow stripes. I laughed at how pathetic I was being. I was a trained soldier with supernatural powers, who fought and killed a vampire, and yet there I was, jumping out of my skin at the sight of a strange bug. It was probably harmless.

Regaining my courage, I used my foot to flip the stone over. The bug was still there, and still crawling about. How it had not died from the impact of hitting the ground with a rock on top of it was a mystery to me. Using a small twig from a nearby tree, I managed to brush the bug off the rock, along with the rest of the dirt, and I returned to Daniel with the slab.

Daniel, in my absence, had set up two larger stones, about two feet apart with an unlit fire between them.

"Let's have a look," he said, holding out his hands. I placed the stone in them. "Not bad." He positioned it on top of the two rocks, across where the fire would be. "This should do nicely."

He cleaned the rock using some water and an old rag, then placed two small stones under the slab so it titled slightly towards the ground. "This way the grease runs off as the food cooks," he said, and began working on the fire.

I watched as he struck a piece of flint against a chunk of metal, trying to catch the spark on some cloth. Several strikes later and the cloth began to glow, the fire quickly spreading to the dry leaves, and finally the wood. Daniel poked at the fire with a stick, making sure it spread evenly under the slab.

"The trick is to keep the fire small and contained. Remember, we want to heat the rock, not incinerate it." He stood, handing me the stick and a bottle of water. "Keep an eye on it for me, and let me know when it's ready. Just drip a tiny bit of water on the rock. If it sizzles, then we're ready to start cooking," he said, walking away. "I'm gonna watch out for the others."

"Okay," I said, poking the stick half-heartedly at the burning embers. I wasn't sure how to tend a fire, but luckily Daniel was back within a few minutes, announcing that he had spotted them in the distance. He sighed, snatched the stick from me, and began to fix the mess I had made.

"Can I ask you something?" I asked hesitantly.

"Sure."

"What's it like... being a werewolf?"

"Why? Do you wanna become one?" he grinned, flashing his pointy teeth.

"Just curious," I replied. "You're the first one I've seen."

"Hmmm, well, it's painful. The changing, I mean. Every bone in my body has to break and reform. It's indescribable."

"So, what's the upside?" There had to be a massive incentive, I thought, for a person to put themselves through that much pain.

"The pain is over pretty quick. Maybe thirty seconds and it's done. But once it's over, it's the most liberating experience ever. With animals, everything is simple. It's all about food, survival, sex..."

Did he–? I cringed at the thought. It must have shown on my face because Daniel paused to laugh.

"Okay, forget that last part." Daniel grinned, dismissing it with a wave of his hand. "It's like being in a dream. I'm completely aware, but it doesn't feel real, if that makes sense. I have control, but I don't think the same way as when I'm in this form."

I had to admit, it did sound intriguing. Humans definitely over-complicated things a lot. I could see how someone would enjoy the freedom of giving themselves over to their primal instincts.

"Anything else?"

"There is one thing. What were you doing in Rachat?"

"I wondered when you might ask that," he said. "Those files I was carrying when you bumped into me... well, you had a blood test when you entered the academy, right? Those were the results of the tests done on all the Daeva."

"And? What did they say?" I asked hurriedly.

Daniel shrugged. "Don't look at me. I'm no scientist."

I let out a dejected sigh.

"Hey, cheer up. After we're finished our job here, we'll be able to get the files to someone who can decipher them. You're gonna come with us, right?"

"I'm not sure yet. There's still–"

"Ash," Daniel interrupted me. I nodded. "Look, I won't lie to you. The chances of you getting him alone outside the city are slim to none. Chances of him joining us are probably even worse."

"I know, but I have to try."

"Just don't get your hopes up, kid."

I heard footsteps behind us. "We're back," Nate called out. He paused, looking blankly at the fire. "Man, where's the food? I'm starved. I hope you two didn't eat it all."

Daniel laughed. "Keep your pants on. The rock's just heating up." He held out his hand to me. I stared back at him, wondering what he was doing. It took a few seconds, before I realised he was after the water I was absently holding in one hand. I had forgotten all about it. Daniel poured a couple of drops onto the rock and it hissed, evaporating straight away.

"Hand over the fish," he said. "Time to start cooking."

Nate and Sebastian went to clean themselves up. Violet sat with us, filling Daniel in on their progress. She explained to me that they were sent to gather information on the exposed barriers at Marmagne, but thanks to the recent attack they couldn't get anywhere close without being spotted.

"Back to the drawing board then." Daniel sighed. "So what do we do now?"

"We move tonight. I've already told the others. Mik, you're welcome to join us, of course."

I thanked her, agreeing to stay with them for the time being, at least until I figured out what I was going to do. Realistically though, what choice did I have? I had lived in the city all my life. Chances were I wouldn't survive more than a few days on my own, if that.

Nate and Sebastian returned and soon the fish was cooked. The others, minus Violet for obvious reasons, picked up their fish and started cutting into them, removing the bones from the meat. I sat staring at mine, not sure what to do with it. It was Nate who finally looked over at me and offered to demonstrate. I watched carefully as he made several cuts and slid his knife under the flesh. Then he opened the fish up, pulling out the backbone and chopped off the head and tail. At the end, I was still none the wiser.

"You'll get it soon enough," he said.

"Took him forever to get the hang of it," Daniel said. "Now look at him, showing off."

"Go lick yourself clean, dog-breath," Nate replied. Daniel laughed, and Sebastian sputtered, almost choking on a mouthful of fish, which made them laugh even more.

I had to suppress a slight smile, feeling bad that I could even think about laughing, given the circumstances. But what else could I do in my situation? I was alive, and that had to count for something. And as long as I survived, I'd get my chance for revenge and to see Ash again.

Chapter 13

After the sun set, we began our trek to find a new camp. We stuck to the edges of the woods for a while, remaining under the cover of the trees, before venturing out into the open, following the path of a small stream. I looked up at the sky and noticed how much brighter the stars were, now that I was away from the lights of the city. I wondered what Ash was doing at that moment in time. Was he also watching the stars, as he often did, thinking of me? Was he still sleeping in my bed, alone? I was so wrapped up in my thoughts that I hadn't noticed Violet walking beside me.

"Daniel told me about your friend," she said.

"Oh."

"I understand why you want to search for him..." Violet paused.

"But?"

"Try to think of this from his perspective. You'd be asking him to give up everything for you; his friends, his family, and his way of life. It might hurt now, but at least he'll be safe in the city."

I froze, my fists clenching. "I am thinking of him," I snapped, raising my voice loud enough that the others heard me. "He doesn't know where I am. He doesn't know if I'm okay, or being tortured by the enemy, or even if I'm still alive. If I can find him, then at least I can explain, and he can make his own choice. He won't have to go on living, never knowing what happened to me." My throat felt as though it was beginning to close up. "I can't leave him like that. I just can't."

"Okay," Violet said, resting a hand on my shoulder. "Then we will do our best to help you, but you have to understand there are no guarantees. You might never get your chance to explain."

"I have to try."

Violet nodded and put her arm around me as we started walking again. "He must really be something," she said. "My heart feels for you. It really does. I don't know what I'd do if I lost Sebastian."

I opened my mouth to ask a question, but seeing the downcast look in her eyes, I chose not to say anything. I was thinking about what Daniel had said, about vampires having to watch their loved ones die. What would she do when Sebastian grew old? Would she turn him before then, or choose to die with him?

Violet looked like she was about to say something when Daniel came racing back to us. "Vampires," he said. "They're approaching fast."

Nate and Sebastian were already running towards the nearest cover; an abandoned gas station. Violet grabbed hold of my arm, pulling me along so fast that I'm not sure if my feet ever touched the ground. She pulled me inside the building, put her hand over my mouth and whispered, "Do not make a sound. Don't even breathe if you can help it."

I nodded and her hand fell to her side. From our hiding place, crouched behind an old display stand, I saw them whizz past us. One. Two. Three. They were a blur. The fourth paused in the front of the building. He looked around, as though he was unsure if he heard something, and then sped off in the direction of his pack.

We stayed crouching, unmoving, waiting until we were sure they were far enough away. Daniel was the first to stand. "Whew, that was a close one," he said, wiping his brow.

"No shit," Nate said.

"What would we have done if they spotted us?" I asked Nate as we continued walking.

"Fight, usually. We've met a couple who stopped to talk, but most vampires out here don't care about anyone outside of their group. Food is scarce out here, so they'll kill other vampires just to claim humans as their own." He paused, and began fumbling with something at his belt, then held out a small leather sheath. "Here, you should probably take this. I don't need a weapon anyway."

"Thanks," I said, giving him a weak smile and fastening it to my waist.

"No problem."

"How long has it been?" I asked. "I mean, since you left the city."

He scratched his head. "Probably a little over a year now."

"How come I've never heard of you?" It was something that had bugged me when I first heard he was from Rachat. There weren't many Daeva, so when one was discovered it always stirred up a commotion.

"What do you think happens to Daeva who refuse to join the army?"

"I don't know," I replied. "I've never heard of anyone declining before." What else were we to do? It's not like anyone else would have hired us.

"You remember the story of Shannon, right?"

"Yeah, it wasn't long before my ability manifested. She could manipulate electricity, but she lost control and killed a group of civilians before someone killed her."

"No." Nate shook his head. "She refused, so they killed her and made up some bullshit cover story."

"Why would they do that?"

"Fear. It's all about the fear. They wanted to keep the public afraid of us, so we had no choice, but to join them."

"And what does this have to do with you?"

"I refused."

"But you're not dead."

"No." Nate laughed. "I'm not. But think about it. If they killed everyone who refused, it would start to get out of hand. Too much fear and it would incite another witch hunt. So instead, they made us disappear."

"Like they did with me."

"Exactly. Who knows how many people they've exiled? We were lucky these guys found us, or we might have ended up as someone's main course."

"You almost did, Nate," Daniel said. "When we found Nate, he was busy fighting off three vamps. We tried to help, and he nearly roasted us alive."

"Well, what did you expect me to do? A giant wolf leaped out at me from nowhere. Of course I was gonna try to protect myself."

"Sorry. Animal instinct, and all that," Daniel said, grinning.

*****

Daniel and Nate began told me stories of their exploits since they had joined up with Violet. It didn't seem like long before we arrived at our next destination, their stories managing to distract me from my thoughts. Another set of ruins lay before us, similar to the ones we had left behind that night. They weren't too big, making them easy to patrol, but large enough to give us adequate cover, and situated right next to a convergence point for several small streams.

When we found a suitable place to set up camp, Violet began delegating. She chose Daniel to go with her, and scout the surrounding areas, while the rest of us stayed to unpack a few things. To my surprise, Daniel began stripping right in front of me, and no-one else seemed shocked by this. He caught sight of me and grinned.

"Sorry, but you're probably gonna wanna turn away for this," he said. "It freaks most people out."

I faced away, realising he was about to shift. What followed was a combination of sounds; popping, snapping, tearing and groaning. Curiosity got the better of me. I stole a quick glance over my shoulder. His skin was wet and glistening. It seemed to ripple and vibrate as his skeleton reformed underneath. Bones moved about, poking out at odd angles, threatening to claw their way out of his skin. I felt slightly nauseous, and decided to focus on looking straight ahead at the wall, trying to ignore the way his screams slowly became snarls and growls.

"It's safe to look now," Violet said. I turned to see Daniel scratching behind one ear with his back paw, his head tilted. It was as if he hadn't gone through a small portion of Hell to change into that form. His eyes caught mine and his black lips appeared to curve upward, flashing his fangs at me. It was a very human expression, but on the face of a wolf it was just creepy.

"See if you can find anything to eat while you're out there," Nate said.

"Of course, young master. Shall I also polish your shoes when I get back?" Violet replied, as she left with Daniel, who gave a playful bark then bounded outside.

"You're always hungry," Sebastian muttered as he started unpacking the sleeping bags.

"I can't help it. I'm still growing." Nate smiled and took a bundle of clothes from his luggage, placing them into a small plastic bag. "I'm gonna go to the river and do some washing."

Sebastian laid down on top of his sleeping bag, his hands behind his head.

"Is there nothing else to do?" I asked.

"Not until Violet gets back," he replied. I let out a long sigh and sat down, drumming my fingers against the floor.

"Don't you get bored?"

"Sometimes, but it's not always like this. We're usually only away from home a week or two at a time."

"Home? Where's that?"

"We call it Aldar, the hidden city."

"City? You mean there are others out there?"

Sebastian laughed. "Of course. Rachat isn't the only city left on the continent, you know? There's at least two others, that we know of. The Silver Dawn doesn't know about them yet, and if they do, they don't know where to find them. Hopefully it'll stay that way."

"This city, Aldar. Vampires live there too?"

Sebastian nodded. "It's mostly humans, but there's a lot of vampires too."

"Wow," I said, beginning to feel a little light-headed. I shook my head. "All these years I've believed there was only one city left, that vampires were all evil..."

"You feeling all right? You look a little pale."

"It's just a lot to take in," I replied. "I'm gonna go walk down to the river. Clear my head."

The cold wind stung against my hands and face. My stomach turned and knotted. I thrust my hands into the warm pockets of the vest, and wandered off in the direction of the running water. As I approached the stream, I heard a voice muttering. I found Nate alone at the water's edge, seemingly talking to himself. He jumped as I moved closer to him, clutching his chest.

"Jesus, Mik. You scared the life out of me."

"Sorry," I said. "What were you doing? Sounded like you were talking to someone."

"Nothing." Nate scratched the back of his head. "I just think out loud sometimes."

I sighed, and sat down near the water's edge, leaning back on my elbows. How could there be a city where vampires and humans lived together, without us knowing? Surely, such a thing would be big news with the Silver Dawn, unless it was another fact they simply forgot to mention. Or maybe they really didn't know of its existence.

I began wondering what such a city must be like. Wouldn't it be scary, to live in the same city as the undead? What if one of them got hungry one night and went on a rampage? How would you tell the difference between a good vampire and a bad vampire? And what if it was all an elaborate ruse to build up a supply of fresh food? No, I told myself, that was the Silver Dawn talking. How could I trust anything they had taught me? How could I know what was the truth, and what was a lie? I guessed I'd have to see it with my own eyes. That would be the only way to know for sure, to find the truth for myself.

"Hello?" I heard Nate say. "Mik?"

I shook my head, realising I had spaced out. "Sorry, what?"

Nate was wringing out a t-shirt. "I asked how you were feeling."

"Oh. Still in shock, I guess. I'm not sure what to believe anymore."

"Yeah, I know what you mean. It takes some getting used to, after living under the thumb of the Silver Dawn for so long. Sometimes I'm still a little unsure, but I just have to have faith in what I do believe in."

"And what do you believe?"

"I believe that I'm gonna get my revenge, even if it kills me. I believe that us finding you wasn't by chance. It was meant to happen, you know? And I believe that you'll see your friend again."

"What makes you say that?"

"Call it intuition." Nate placed the last of his wet clothes into the bag. He started back to camp, giving me a quick nudge on the shoulder. "Come on. Violet will be back before long."

Back at camp, Nate set up a washing line using some wire and hydraulic hooks that fastened themselves into the walls of the building. He was mid-way through hanging the wet clothes over the line when Violet and Daniel returned.

"Oi, Nate. Catch," Violet said, throwing a small round object at him. She threw another to me, and handed a final one to Sebastian. They were oranges.

"Where'd you get these?" Nate asked.

"There's a couple of trees further downstream," she replied. "Not many fruit at this time of year though, and they're probably not at their best."

Nate shrugged, ripping the rind from his orange and shoving segment after segment into his mouth. I picked at mine, tearing the first piece away and lifting it to my mouth. The juice exploded onto my tongue as I bit down, causing me to screw up my face. It tasted more sour than sweet, but it was a welcome change after two days of fish and meat.

"Where's Daniel?" I asked, noting he wasn't in the room anymore.

"He caught his own meal," Violet said. "He knows not to bring his food inside."

My eyes widened. Had he actually killed an animal and brought it back to eat raw? I knew wolves did that, but Daniel wasn't a real wolf.

"Rabbit?" Nate asked.

"Hare, I believe."

The lack of surprise in their voices told me this wasn't the first time it had happened, and in all likeliness, was probably a common incident. He must have it so easy, I thought, being able to shift and eat anything he could catch, while the rest struggled by on a minimal diet. Still, I don't think I would have been able to stomach eating a raw animal, even as a werewolf.

It occurred to me that I had no idea how Violet was feeding. I glanced at Sebastian. There were no visible bite marks on his neck or wrists. I supposed it was possible for her to feed from less visible spots. The femoral artery, perhaps. I shuddered at the image, which was far too intimate for my liking.

Violet leaned out of the window. "Daniel, get your furry butt in here," she said. A minute or so later, Daniel strode into the room as a human, completely naked, I might add. His mouth was decorated with streaks of blood, as though he had tried to wipe it clean. It was clear his body now felt the cold without the layer of fur covering him. I'd rather not go into detail about how I could deduce that. He pulled on some thick clothes and sat back against the wall with a bottle of water.

"Okay, now the mutt has finished eating..." Violet narrowed her eyes at Daniel. He smiled back. "We need to come up with a plan. The barriers at Marmagne are still exposed. This is our best chance to gather information on them, and to figure out how they work."

"Unfortunately," Sebastian added, "thanks to the idiots who attacked them a couple of days ago, the Silver Dawn is on high alert. Getting past the patrols unseen is going to be difficult."

"What about a diversion?" Nate said. "If we can make them think they're under attack, maybe they'll leave an opening elsewhere."

"Too risky," Violet replied. "We're not going to risk someone's life for this." Her gaze settled on me. "You know how they operate. Any input?"

Everyone's eyes seemed to follow Violet's, landing on me. What were they expecting from me? Officially I had only been a member of the army for two weeks, and I was definitely no strategist. Ash and Lucas were usually the ones to handle that kind of stuff. I racked my brain, trying to think of anything useful to say.

"I got nothing," I admitted. There was a collective sigh from the group.

"Come on, we need to think of something," Violet said. "If we lose this chance, it could be another decade before another opportunity like this arises."

"I hate to say it, but I think Nate is right," said Daniel. "A diversion might be the only way."

"No, I won't allow it." Violet shook her head and folded her arms.

"Daniel is right, Dear," Sebastian said. "Getting information on those barriers could turn the tide of this war. You said it yourself, this is the best chance we've had in a long time. We need to take it now, before those walls are erected."

"Then what would you suggest, Nate?"

"Well, not to blow my own horn or anything, but if you want a big, flashy diversion..." Nate paused and held out one hand, lighting up the room for a split second with a jet of fire that disappeared, leaving only a blackened mark on the ceiling, and spots in my vision. "I think I could handle that."

Violet rolled her eyes.

"Plus, we have a Siren," Nate said.

"Hmmm. Create a diversion to thin their numbers, and then have Mik lure any that remain into an ambush. It could work," Violet said.

"There's just one small problem," I said. "I don't know how to do that."

When I first learned about my ability, the only thing I could do with it was project my own emotions onto other people, which wasn't particularly useful, unless you wanted a room full of pissed off people. After Ash and I became room mates, he helped me train, until I could project an emotion without needing to feel it myself. His empathy was a massive help in my training. However, manipulating emotions to lure people to me was something I had never tried before. Hell, I hadn't even known it was possible until a couple of days ago. How would I even go about doing such a thing?

"Luring is one of the most basic Siren abilities," Sebastian said. "You should be able to manage it, if you try."

Violet agreed and insisted that I give it a try. She and Daniel led me into one of the old buildings away from camp, where we hid on the second floor. My task was simple; to draw Nate and Sebastian to me. Violet and Daniel were automatically disqualified from the experiment because of their supernatural senses. Not to mention the fact that my ability didn't work on Violet.

I sat down in the small room and took a deep breath. I focused on the rise and fall of my chest, and the beating of my heart. It was a technique I learned from Ash, one he often used when he needed to clear his mind. When I felt ready I inhaled one last time. As I exhaled I let go of my control, feeling my magic spill out into the ruins. I could sense Daniel was getting restless. Unfortunately, I had no way to direct my magic without being able to physically see my targets.

I tried focusing on sending out feelings of love and safety, as Violet had mentioned when she explained the nature of my ability. But to that, I added something else. I tried to draw them in. The cold wind fluttered, reaching outwards. Grasping. There was a clatter to one side of the room. My eyes flew open to see Daniel backing into a corner.

"What's wrong?" Violet asked.

I closed off my magic, giving Daniel time to recover.

"I could feel it in my head," he said, his voice trembling. "It was like it was trying to suck me in."

"You're trying too hard," Violet said. "You shouldn't be trying to mind-rape them into coming to you. Be more gentle."

I nodded, closing my eyes for the second attempt and letting the magic loose again. This time I concentrated on the same feelings, but without trying to draw them in. The room was quiet.

"Feel anything, Daniel?" Violet asked.

"It's there, but it's not drawing me to him."

I groaned and shut off my magic once more. "I don't get it. How can I be gentle and lure people to me at the same time?"

"You need to make them want to come to you. Give them something that will make them drop everything to find you," Violet said. "Think of a moment when you were truly happy, and you didn't ever want that moment to end. Feel it, and show it to them."

"Okay." I took another deep breath. I thought back to that night with Ash, as we lay in bed, our bodies melded together. I remembered the way his arm held me tight against him, his fingers playing along my skin, the warmth of his body, his smile, and the taste of his lips.

The wind came out from within, but this time it was different. It became something different, warmer and soothing. This had never happened before. In the past it always manifested as a cold breeze. Something brushed against me, and I opened one eye to find Daniel rubbing his cheek against my shoulder. His eyes looked up at me, filled with longing and need.

"What is that?" he whispered. "It feels so good."

"All right, enough of that," Violet said, keeping her voice low. She pulled Daniel away from me, pinning him to the ground with a hand over his mouth. Daniel was fighting tooth and nail to break free and come to me. Violet was struggling, with only one hand to pin his wrists, the other busy muffling his protests.

"Let him go," I said. "I can't concentrate with you two wrestling." Violet paused and looked at me for a second, but did as I asked. Daniel scurried across the floor to me, where he curled up in front of me, his cheek rubbing against my leg. A couple of times he would get uncomfortably close to my groin, but he always backed off before it became too awkward.

A minute later there were footsteps below us. Nate and Sebastian walked up the stairs, as though they were in a trance. Their eyes were fixed on me, and only me. I closed my eyes again and reigned in my magic.

Daniel froze, and then jumped up in surprise. "Okay, now that was freaky," he said.

"No," Sebastian said. "That was love."

Daniel snorted. "It was like a whisper in my head, telling me it loved me, and promising me we could be together, forever. God, it was like being hypnotised by a vampire. He could have told me to kill you all for him and I would have done it."

I stood up, bracing myself against the wall as my legs felt a little shaky. "What do you mean?" I asked.

"Don't worry yourself about it," Violet said. "The effect is only temporary."

I think I heard Violet say something else, but it was muffled, as though I was underwater. My vision grew dark, and the last thing I remember was falling. The floorboards drew closer and closer, as everything went black.

Chapter 14

"Hey, he's waking up."

"Get some water."

I opened my eyes, blinking. Everything was muffled and hazy. Where was I? What happened? I remembered falling, and then nothing. There were faces above me, barely visible in the dim moonlight. I could hear blood rushing through my head, pounding in my ears.

"Hey, are you okay?" Nate asked. "You blacked out."

"Here, have a drink," Daniel said, lifting me into a sitting position and pressing a bottle against my mouth.

"Back off and give him some breathing room," said Violet as she walked into the room. "Go see if Sebastian needs any help. I got this."

Daniel and Nate scampered outside, which I was thankful for. I needed time to process my thoughts, and not have people fussing over me.

"What happened?" I asked.

"You passed out a couple of hours ago, after we experimented with your ability. "

"I know overusing my ability can cause exhaustion, but I've never blacked out before. And I didn't even use it that much. At least, I don't think I did."

"It's okay. I have my own theory on what happened. Your ability is exactly like that of a Siren vampire, so we can assume it has similar drawbacks."

"What drawbacks?"

Violet sighed. "Did they teach you nothing about real vampires? When a vampire uses their ability, the need to feed increases. You haven't been eating as much as you're probably used to. That, combined with using your ability in a new form could have placed too much strain on your body."

"So, what now?"

"We're planning on heading to Marmagne this evening at full dark. You should sleep now. I'll send Daniel and Sebastian out to round up as much food as they can before then. You and Nate are going to need your energy."

I nodded, already feeling the pull of sleep. "What if it happens again?" I asked, lying back down on my side.

"I'll be with you the whole time. If anything happens, I'll get you out of there." Violet's footsteps grew quieter as she went downstairs. A few minutes later I heard someone coming up the stairs. They climbed into the sleeping bag behind me. Nate called my name a few times, but I didn't answer. I pretended to be asleep, and soon I actually was.

*****

I found myself surrounded by a familiar darkness. It started the same way as my last dream. I wandered, with no way of telling in which direction I was headed. There was nothing but the sound of my footsteps.

I kept wandering, my stomach beginning to feel jittery. My heart beat faster. With every step I expected to run into one of the flayed horrors, but I found nothing. It seemed to me I was alone in the darkness. Well and truly alone. Then I saw a figure in front of me. It was crouched down and hunched over, crying. I edged closer, waiting for it to turn and reveal its featureless face, but I soon realised it wasn't one of them. It had skin, and hair of the short, spiky blond variety.

"Ash," I yelled. There was no reaction. "Ash!" Nothing. I took another step and the crying stopped. He stood, but instead of turning to face me, he began to walk away. I cried out again. I tried to run after him, but he only got further and further away from me.

"Ash!" Why couldn't he hear me? His body began to fade into the darkness, until I could no longer see him. "Ash," I called out one last time, falling to my knees.

I felt a hand on my shoulder. "Mik."

The hand shook me and my eyes flew open. Nate was kneeling over me.

"You sounded like you were having a bad dream."

"It was nothing." I shrugged off his hand and turned away from him.

"You sure? It didn't sound like nothing. You were calling his name."

"It was just a dream."

Except, it wasn't just a dream. It was my subconscious telling me Ash was out of reach. Gone. Lost forever.

"You sure you don't wanna talk about it?"

I shook my head. There was nothing to talk about. I knew what my dream was telling me, and worst of all, I knew it was probably true. I closed my eyes and tried to go back to sleep, but to no avail. Soon, Daniel was shouting for us, telling us that our food was ready. I stood and pulled on the black vest that I had used as a pillow. Nate sat watching me silently. I could see the worry in his eyes, and it created a heaviness in my chest. Not because I made him worry, but because it was the same look Ash would have given me.

That day the sky was clear. The sun shone down on me, though it did little to abate the cold that came with the howling wind, biting at my ears and fingers. Sebastian handed me a plastic bowl, filled with meat, and what looked like wild mushrooms. We took the food inside to eat, seeking shelter from the harsh winds, for what little good it did.

Nate continued to pester me about my dream as we ate. I knew he was only trying to help, but seeing Ash's look in his eyes had set off an alarm bell in my head. I couldn't allow myself to start getting that close to anyone again. If I couldn't get Ash back, then there would be no replacement best friend. Only more pain would come of it.

*****

As darkness came, we finished off what was left of the stew, and Violet began to go over the plan.

"We will form two groups. Sebastian and Nate, you will be the diversion group. When I give the signal, I want you to do your thing. Make it as showy as you can. We want them to think they're under a massive attack. The more of their troops you can draw away, the better. However, the second it's done, you get out of there."

"Don't worry," said Nate. "I'll make them think Armageddon has come."

"Armageddon, huh?" Daniel laughed. "You're such a show-off."

"Well, we'll see who's laughing after tonight."

"I'm sure we will, Nate," Violet said, rolling her eyes. "Just try not to overdo it. Anyway. Mik, Daniel and I will be the second group. During the confusion, Mik will lure any remaining patrols into an ambush. Once it's clear, we'll only have a short amount of time to work with. We don't know what we're looking for, but we need some evidence as to how those barriers work. Any questions?"

"What do we do if we make contact with the soldiers?" I asked. Chances were, I knew some of these people, maybe even trained with them in the academy. If all hell broke loose, I wasn't sure I'd be able to fight them. After all, they were puppets, just like I was, deceived by the Silver Dawn's lies.

"Use as much force as you deem necessary, but remember, we want to avoid confrontation as much as possible."

157

It dawned on me then that Ash might be at Marmagne. If they were on high alert, then it made sense to bring out the big guns. Unless, of course, something more important had come up. I opened my mouth to speak, but Violet stopped me.

"The barriers come first," she said. "If your friend is there, then we will do what can to help, but you must understand how important this assignment is. The Silver Dawn is locked up in that city of theirs, and until we can find a way to enter it and take them down, they will continue to hunt us until they are all that remains."

I sighed, nodding. I should have known the mission would come first. There were no more questions, so we finished eating and prepared ourselves.

*****

When full darkness had set in, we began our hike. It was a long walk, which was to be expected. After all, setting up camp near Marmagne would have put us in too much danger of being spotted by the Silver Dawn.

We passed through woods, hills and open fields, following one of the smaller streams until we reached the edge of Marmagne. The wind grew stronger still, and colder, as the night drew on. We crouched in a small wooded area, on the edge of what appeared to be a circle of death. I remembered my first visit, noting that everything in and around the ruins was dead. From here on, there was no more cover.

Before we began, we set a rendezvous point and decided on an escape route. There was what remained of a small demolished building amidst the trees, its crumbling walls rising no more than three feet from the ground, which would serve as our meeting point. We wouldn't be able to escape across the open fields, not if there was a possibility of the Silver Dawn trying to follow us. Our only option was to cross the stream and head deeper into the woods. It would take us further away from camp, but it was better to be safe than sorry.

With everything set, Nate and Sebastian began to creep away to

158

the far side of Marmagne, where they could await the signal to begin the diversion. It occurred to me that Violet never mentioned what the signal would be, and no-one had thought to ask. I guessed they must have their own signal they were used to, but I asked anyway.

"It's when I say go," Violet replied, her eyes fixed in the distance.

"Telepathy," Daniel added. "Vampires can communicate mentally with humans they've bonded with."

"Oh," I said, thinking up a million more questions about vampires and their servants. Perhaps, servant wasn't the correct word in this case. Would Violet be offended if I referred to Sebastian as her servant? I made a mental note to ask Daniel or Nate later, in private.

Violet was studying the patrols of troops wandering around the barriers. Were it not for the flashlights attached to their weapons, I might not have been able to spot them in the dark. From what little I could see, the Silver Dawn had already begun to build the metal walls around Marmagne, encasing the black spikes within them. The side closest to us had a large gap, probably the result of the attack a few nights ago. That was our target; the exposed barrier spike. One more night, and they would be encased in the walls, lost to us. And with it, our chance to gain an upper hand against the Silver Dawn, and what was probably my best shot at getting revenge.

"Three patrols of two near the target," Violet said. "Another two groups either side. Two stationary guards at the wall."

"I'm betting those two won't budge," Daniel said. "And the four at the far side might stick to their patrol."

We waited some more, watching the paths of the patrols, until Violet said, "They're in position."

"Hope you're ready for this, Mik," said Daniel. I nodded, though in truth I was quite anxious. One year of training to fight the supernatural, and I was about to go up against regular humans with guns. Still, my job was easy. All I had to do was lure a few guards out. I could do that.

"Go," Violet whispered. I looked at her, wondering if she was talking to me or Sebastian. My question was answered when the sky was illuminated in flames. A wave of fire rose up from the earth, rushing towards Marmagne, clashing and roaring against the metal walls.

The guards closest panicked, and rushed off to find the cause of the problem. Another stream erupted, spurting upwards, and sending another of the patrols running. I was in awe. I hadn't realised until then how powerful Nate was.

"Mik." Violet nudged me. She nodded towards the remaining four soldiers. The diversion had worked better than expected.

I took a deep breath, and let the magic flow from within me. I concentrated on the same thoughts I used previously. This time it was different. The wind did not begin cold as it had always done, but instead it was warm from the start. It reached out of me, heading straight for the guards. At first, nothing happened, and I thought perhaps they were out of range. But then I saw their flashlights turn in our direction, one at a time. They drew closer. Daniel and Violet hid closer to the edge, behind some trees. When the guards approached, they jumped out from both sides, taking out one man each. The remaining two did not flinch, nor did they look back to see what befell their comrades. They kept walking towards me, their eyes blank and a smile on their faces. I was all they cared about. That is, until they fell down, unconscious.

They would have let their friends die, I thought. And all for a promise of love that didn't exist. The thought of how much my ability could affect others was frightening. In a sense, I was turning them into mindless lovesick zombies. No, not even zombies. Slaves. They would have done anything for me.

"Come on," Daniel shouted. "We don't have much time before they figure out it was a diversion." I didn't reply or move, until Daniel pulled me to my feet, shaking me from my stupor.

"How do you feel?" Violet asked. There was no shakiness in my legs like before. I didn't feel dizzy.

"I'm okay," I replied, leaving out the bit about how I was terrified of what my ability was capable of.

With the guards out of the way, we ran to the gap in the wall. I pulled out a flashlight I had been given, and shone it on the surface of the black metal spike. It must have been about fifteen feet tall, and it curved in towards the centre of the ruins as it narrowed to a point. By all accounts, it looked completely ordinary, if a little creepy. Daniel took out a knife, and began collecting shavings of the metal, which he caught in a small plastic bag and sealed.

Violet pressed her hand to the spike. She didn't flinch or recoil. Next she tried passing her hand between two of the spikes. Her hand froze, as though it had hit something solid. Daniel tried it, and found he could pass through the invisible wall without any problem.

"Must be some kind of spell," Violet muttered.

"Mik, shine the light down here," Daniel said. I stepped inside the wall and crouched next to him. He was examining something on the metal, close to the floor. I shone the light at the bottom of the spike, and found a strange symbol etched into the metal. There were two upside-down triangles, one smaller inside the other, both joined at the base. The sides of the larger triangle continued on past the apex, curving and overlapping what looked like a 'V'. At five points around the central shape were smaller etchings, resembling nails from the side.

"What is it?" Violet asked.

"Looks like some kinda glyph or rune," Daniel replied. "Give me a minute to memorise it."

"We do not have one minute, Daniel. Sebastian tells me some of the guards are already beginning to head back. They may already suspect it was a diversion."

Daniel was muttering to himself, probably trying to imprint the shapes onto his memory.

"Mik," Violet said. "Come on. We have to go."

I was torn between the two. On the one hand, Violet had a point. We needed to get going before the guards returned. But what if the symbol was the key they were looking for?

"Hand me the light," Daniel said, and I did as he asked. "Now, go."

"Daniel–"

"Go," he said, raising his voice. "I can run faster than you. I'll catch up."

I stepped outside the barrier, looking back at Daniel. My feet had barely touched the ground on the other side when Violet took hold of my arm.

"You had better," she said, before pulling me along with her. We were about halfway to the cover of the woods when I looked back to Marmagne. I saw the lights of the guards starting to appear once more as they headed back to their posts. In the distance, there were several small fires burning, but it looked like they were under control. There was no sign of Daniel. Probably still inspecting the barrier, I thought. It was as we reached the edge of the woods that we heard shots fire in the distance. Violet froze, her eyes searching the darkness.

"Come on, you stupid mutt," she mumbled to herself. Her fists clenched. The guards' lights were waving to and fro, searching in all directions. I prayed Daniel had gotten away unhurt. Those guns were using silver bullets, that was for sure. What if he had been hit?

"There. That's him," Violet said, her voice filled with relief. I looked in the direction she was pointing, to see a figure running in the distance. None of the flashlights were following him.

We retreated back into the woods and to our rendezvous point, where Nate and Sebastian were waiting for us.

"Where's Daniel?" Sebastian asked.

There were more shots. A sense of dread lingered in the air, until Daniel burst through the undergrowth, panting. He clutched at his shoulder, his hands stained red.

"I'm fine," he reassured us before anyone could point out the obvious. "Let's get out of here before they catch up."

We all agreed and started downstream, to a point where the water was narrow and shallow enough for us to get across without getting too wet. Once over the stream, we continued to follow it a little way.

It seemed our pursuers had turned back or gotten lost along the way, so we slowed our pace, adjusting our course to head back to camp. It hadn't been more than a few minutes after we stopped running, when there was a thud from behind. We turned to see Daniel collapsed on the floor.

"Shit," I said, rushing over to him. His breathing was fast and shallow. He writhed in pain, groaning, and clawing at his wound. "What's wrong with him?" I asked Violet, who was now knelt by him. She peeled back his blood-soaked clothes to get a better look. There was one neat hole where the bullet entered. Next she rolled him onto his side, examining the back of his shoulder.

"Idiot," she snapped. "The bullet didn't pass through. We have to get it out so he can heal."

Violet began handing out tasks to everyone. Nate heated a blade with his fire and handed it to her, then moved to help Sebastian and I with holding down Daniel's arms. Violet straddled his body, lowering the knife to his skin. He screamed as the blade bit into him, his arms lifting off the ground. It took all of my strength, and Nate's, our body weight combined, to hold down one arm. I watched in horror as Violet wiggled the blade about in the wound, digging at the skin to try and retrieve the bullet. There was blood everywhere. I honestly thought she might kill Daniel in her attempt to save him. He screamed louder, the knife going deeper. Violet pulled the knife out and poked her fingers into the hole. When she withdrew her fingers, she had hold of the silver bullet casing. She jumped off him quickly, as did Sebastian and Nate, who pulled me back with him.

Daniel's body began to jerk. I heard the sounds of bones cracking and looked away before I got a repeat performance of the other day. Still, I listened. I waited for his screams to become howls and snarls. There was more snapping, then popping, followed by the wet tearing. I let out a breath I hadn't realised I was holding when I heard a loud yip. His clothes lay ragged and torn on the floor beside him. Violet crouched down in front of him, inspecting his shoulder. She grabbed hold of him by the neck, lifting his front paws from the ground.

"You ever do anything stupid like that again, and I swear..." She left the sentence unfinished, the threat hanging in the air. Daniel whimpered, bowing his head when she released him.

*****

We managed to make it back to camp without any further incidents. Daniel changed back, now he had some spare clothes at hand, and was busying himself with a notepad and pencil. I watched over his shoulder as he sketched the strange symbol we had seen.

"There was another line here," I said, spotting a mistake and demonstrating it with my finger. He quickly corrected it. "Any idea what it is?"

"Not a clue." He showed it to the others who were equally as stumped by it.

Nate was fast asleep almost as soon as we arrived. I was surprised he could even stand after such a display of power. I saw Ash do something similar once, creating a giant wall of ice, but nothing close to what Nate had done.

Between all the walking and the use of my ability, I was starting to feel a little tired as well. Using the Luring Song, as I had come to call it, hadn't been nearly as draining as the first time I used it. Perhaps, Violet was right about the feeding, or it could have something to do with how the wind started off warm this time. I wondered what would happen if I tried to use my power as I had for the last year. Would it begin cold, or would it start warm then change? I looked over at Nate, who had his back to me, thinking it might be best to test it on someone who was asleep. I sent a small amount of my magic out to him. The wind was cold as it reached out and touched him. Nate shifted in his sleep and I withdrew my magic. Next I tried luring and the wind started warm again. I repeated this several times, fascinated with the change that had occurred to my magic. I laughed quietly to myself, because even knowing the results I had no idea what it meant. I could have guessed all I wanted, but in the end, it would have been speculation.

I began to wonder if I could call a sleeping person to me. The warm wind reached out, touching Nate. At first, nothing happened, but then Nate began to groan in his sleep. He rolled over, his hand reaching out for me. The second his hand touched me, he quieted again. I pulled in my magic and lifted Nate's hand off my knee, before climbing into the sleeping bag and settling down for a well-earned rest.

*****

I awoke with a start, feeling hands on my shoulders shaking me. Nate was hunched over me.

"Get up. We're leaving. Now!"

"What's happening?" I asked, jumping up and pulling on my boots. Nate was busy rolling up the sleeping bags and packing them into their holders. I started to help him.

"The Silver Dawn's onto us. Daniel sensed one of their vehicles while he was out patrolling. He's out there now with Violet, trying to find out what we're up against."

Before I could open my mouth, the others came running upstairs. "We got five or six foot soldiers at the most," Violet said.

"Does the Sunreaver squad mean anything to you?" Daniel asked, looking over at me.

The world appeared to come to a stop. A lump formed in my throat. "Sunreaver?"

"Yeah. That's what I overheard one of them say."

"Second or Third Sunreavers?"

Daniel shrugged. "Sorry, I didn't find out. Why?"

"The Sunreaver squads are made up entirely of Daeva. My squad was the Third Sunreavers. Ash was our captain."

"Shit," Nate cursed. "You think he's here?"

"It's possible."

"Look," said Violet. "If we stay here, they'll find us and we'll have no choice but to fight. I'm sure you don't want that. The weather's on our side with all this fog. If we leave now, they'll never know we were here."

"That's not entirely true," I said, shaking my head. "Ash is an empath. If he's there, he can track us."

"Double shit," Nate muttered.

"Then we need to go now," Violet said. "Grab the stuff and let's go. Mik, I'm sorry, but we need to retreat for now."

"And do what?" asked Nate. "If the empath is with them, they'll just follow us."

"Let me talk to him. If I can explain, I know he'll understand. Maybe he'll even come with us."

"Whoa, slow down," said Sebastian. "We don't even know for sure if he's with them. For now, let's get out of here."

"Sebastian's right," said Daniel. "We need to move somewhere safe, until we can figure out our next move."

Everyone else agreed, so, against what every fibre of my being was saying, I conceded. Nate put his hands on my shoulders and looked me in the eye. "You'll get your chance," he said. "But we need to know he's here for sure first."

"Okay." He was right. Safety had to come first, because what was the point in explaining if we all ended up captured or dead? We grabbed the luggage and headed outside, into a thick fog that lingered over the ruins, making it impossible to see more than a few metres in front of us. We trusted Daniel's nose and ears to lead us away from any potential danger. As we approached the edge of the ruins, the fog began to grow thicker, and colder. A violent shiver ran down my spine.

"Ice fog," said Sebastian.

It was then I knew Ash was there. "Ash can control ice too."

"And with all this water in the air..." Violet said.

"Two abilities?" Nate said. "Lucky git. So what now?"

The others were discussing what to do next, their eyes and ears focused on each other, and not on me. I took a step back, then another. The fog was beginning to obscure them from view when Violet's head shot up, her eyes fixing on me. She started to move when Nate's arm blocked her.

"Thank you," I mouthed, and he nodded. I turned and ran back into the ruins. This could be my only chance, I thought. This was something I had to do. What I had forgotten was that I could hardly see a thing. Finding Ash in the dense fog would be impossible. But then an idea came to me. Ash would be as blind as the rest of us, relying on his empathy to search for us.

With this in mind I chose one of the larger buildings and hid inside, near an open window on the second floor so I could watch the path below. I dropped my shields, praying with every ounce of my being it would be Ash who came looking. Lucas would be the worst possible match. I wouldn't even see him coming. As for the others, I could always paralyse them long enough to escape, and then we'd be back to square one.

It only took a minute before I saw someone walking slowly down the street towards my hiding place. Their gun was aimed, checking left and right. I could only see the outline, but I knew it was him. The body was too short to be Brad, and too large to be Lucas or Katiya. I pulled my shields tight around me and hid in the next room, waiting for him to come. The sound of footsteps drew closer, the floorboards of the stairs creaking underfoot, then further away as he moved to the spot where I stood only moments before.

"Ash." I stepped out from behind the door. His body froze. Before I could reach him he turned, throwing me up against the wall. His lips pressed forcefully into mine, teeth grazing my lips. I pushed back against him, my tongue searching for his. I tasted the salt on his lips, a few tears beginning to roll down his cheeks.

"Mik. I thought I'd never see you again."

"Me too." My eyes widened as he began to reach for his headset. "Don't!" I said, grabbing his hand.

"What? Why?" Ash said, startled. "We came to take you home."

"I can't go back there."

"What are you saying?" he asked, the confusion written clearly across his face.

"It was General Marsten. He led me away from Boursac so he

could get rid of me. He said something about protecting the secrets of the Daeva."

Ash was shaking his head.

"It's true," I said. "Think about it. I was starting to get suspicious, so he made sure I couldn't find out what the secret was, for good. He left me unconscious, probably hoping a vampire would find me."

"No. No," Ash muttered. He cupped my face in his hands. "General Marsten came back all bloodied and beaten up. He told us a group of Renfields ambushed you both and carried you off. A vampire must have brainwashed you. Come on, Mik. Think! What really happened?"

He was rationalising. I should have known it would be difficult for him to accept the truth, but I hoped he would believe me. Of all people, I thought he would.

"Let's go home," he said. "We can be together again. Don't you want that?"

"You know I do."

"Then come. We'll find the vampire and kill it. Then this'll all be over. You'll see."

"Ash, no. Listen to me. The Silver Dawn has been lying to us all the time. They've kept things from us, and they're trying to cover them up. I'm not the first person they've made disappear to keep their secrets hidden. If I go back, they'll kill me."

Ash was still shaking his head. "That's just what the vampire wants you to believe. I'd never let anyone hurt you. You know that, right?" I nodded. He reached out to take my hand in his. "So trust me. Everyone misses you. We just want you to come back home safe."

"No. You're not listening. They will kill me. I'm sorry, Ash. I can't go back. But there's another way, if you'll just trust me."

"And what way would that be?"

"Come with me. Leave Rachat and help me find out the truth. We could be together. We could–"

Ash dropped my hands. "What have they done to you, Mik?

You're asking me to betray everyone I know. My friends. My family. Can't you see? This isn't you talking."

"Yes, it is. I'm not the one that's been brainwashed here. You are! You and everyone else in the city. Ash, I'm not going back there, and that's final. Please, I want you to come with me. I need you."

For a moment, he said nothing. I thought maybe he was actually considering my proposal, until I felt the cold in my toes. I tried to lift my legs, but it was already too late.

"Ash, no!"

"I know this isn't your fault, Mik. That's why I want you to know I'm sorry. You're coming back with us. We'll fix you, somehow. I promise. And then we can go back to how things were."

"Don't do this." I pulled harder, trying to free myself from his icy clutches. There was a noise behind me, followed by the roaring of flames. They rushed across the floor, melting the ice that bound me. A wall of fire rose between us.

"He's not gonna listen," Nate said. "We need to go."

"No!" I pulled against him. "You said you'd never leave me," I shouted.

Ash collapsed to the ground, hunched over. His head shot up at hearing my words. "You're the one leaving, Mik, not me."

Ice began to creep across the walls and ceiling. The flames rose higher, cutting us off completely. Nate was still trying to drag me away when Daniel appeared.

"Grab him and let's go," Nate shouted over the blaze. Daniel lifted me up, carrying me under one arm. I began to scream Ash's name, until Daniel's hand was smothering my mouth. I kicked and wriggled, but his arm held me tight as he ran through the fog, with Nate following close behind. Eventually I gave up fighting, and all that was left was despair.

We caught up with Sebastian and Violet, who were waiting with the luggage. Violet opened her mouth, but Nate shook his head. Whatever questions she was about to ask stopped there. I sank to the floor, feeling the pressure start to build behind my eyes. Why did this always happen to me? No matter what happened, there was always one constant in my life. Everyone leaves me.

"We need to move now," said Nate. "I don't know how long my fires will hold the empath back."

I glared at Nate, remembering the sight of Ash surrounded by flames. If I ever found out Ash had been hurt, I wouldn't be held responsible for my actions. The anger helped fight back the tears, but now I felt drained. Lifeless.

Daniel carried me on his back as we set off once more. A few tears soaked into the rough fabric of his jacket. He whispered to me along the way, telling me everything would be all right in the end. I didn't believe him. I'd had my chance, and I blew it.

*****

I must have fallen asleep without realising, because the next thing I remember I was laid next to a small campfire, and the sun was beginning to set. My head rested on something soft, and it took a moment for me to realise it was Nate's lap. I sat up and he handed me a warm drink. I'm not sure what was in the cup because I never drank it. I sat there, absently holding the hot cup that made my fingers tingle. My body and mind felt numb, and I was glad of it. I couldn't bear to go through the pain of being abandoned again, and by the one person I believed would stay with me. Maybe it had been foolish of me to ever get my hopes up. I should have listened to my instincts from the start.

"What are you thinking?" Nate asked.

"That there's no point any more. I don't know why I even try. Maybe things would be better if I just–"

"Just what? I swear, if you're even thinking about what I think you are..." Nate paused, his hands gripping my shoulders. "Don't give up. There's still hope."

I looked blankly into his eyes. "No, there isn't."

"Yes, there is. All that's standing between the two of you is the Silver Dawn. Once we get rid of them, and have our revenge, you'll be free to be with him again. Do it for Ash, and me. We'll make them pay for using us."

In the darkness that was my soul at that point in time, there awoke a small flicker of light. No, not light. Fire. It burned within me, reigniting my purpose. The Silver Dawn was going down, even if I had to remove every last one of them myself.

Chapter 15

We set off for Aldar, the hidden city, later that evening. We passed through hills and woods, stopping only once when Daniel picked up on the scent of a herd of deer, and demanded we stop to eat. Who knows how long it might have been before we ran into any more? I volunteered to help with the hunting, partly because I wanted something to distract my mind, but also because I had questions I wouldn't feel comfortable asking around Violet and Sebastian. Daniel led me through the trees, which were dead for the winter in this part of the woods. He stopped to sniff the air several times along the way.

Eventually we came upon a group of deer, grazing on small patches of grass and weeds. Crouching low to the ground, we moved as close as possible without disturbing them. I was focused entirely on the deer, when I took another step forward. The snapping of a twig beneath my boot seemed almost deafening, and the deers' heads shot up, looking in my direction. Daniel grumbled something under his breath and leaped out at one of the larger females. The deer made a run for it, but with his speed he managed to catch it off guard and wrestle it to the ground. The animal bleated, its cries raking against my soul as Daniel pulled out a knife, and drew it across the throat. Blood poured out, gushing over the dried dirt and frozen leaves.

Daniel released his grip, letting his catch slump to the ground. He took the rope that was slung over his shoulder and secured it around the deer's hind legs before throwing the other end over what he deemed to be a sturdy enough branch. He pulled on the rope, hoisting the deer into the air, and with a little help, tied off the rope around the tree trunk.

With our meal hanging up-side down, Daniel rolled up his sleeves and began to work on skinning and gutting the poor, tasty creature. Unlike when he gutted the fish, I couldn't bear to watch. I heard the knife slicing deep into its stomach, and soon after a wet thud as its organs spilled out onto the floor. There was a horrid stench of blood and faeces that turned my stomach.

I figured this was as good a time as any for questions, so I asked him, "What did you mean when you said Violet and Sebastian are bonded?"

"So that's why you volunteered to help." He laughed. "Guess I can't blame you for being curious. It means they've drank each other's blood."

"Wouldn't that make him a vampire?" I asked, recalling one of the lessons I attended on vampires.

"It doesn't quite work like that," he said. There was more tearing and squelching. "To turn someone, you first gotta drain them almost completely. Then they have to ingest some of the vampire's blood. Violet and Sebastian only share a little at a time, just enough to maintain the bond."

"Then how does she feed?" I glanced over my shoulder. Daniel was still removing some of the skin, but it wasn't so bad to look at now. It looked less like an animal and more like a giant slab of meat. I just had to try and not let my eyes wander down to the pile of organs on the floor.

"She feeds from me. I heal faster, and that goes for blood loss too, not just the bite marks. Plus, werewolf blood is more potent than human blood, so she can go longer between feeding."

"Oh."

"Anything else you wanna ask?"

"There is one thing," I replied, unsure how he might react to the question.

"Fire away."

"How much of what they have is... real? And how much is the bond?"

"They loved each other long before they bonded. Sebastian wasn't forced into anything, if that's what you're asking," Daniel said, cutting into the deer's flank.

"You knew them back then?"

"Yup. I was sixteen when I first met Violet. The same night I snuck out of the orphanage. Almost died from a werewolf attack."

"Sorry. I shouldn't have pried." In a way it was comforting to know I wasn't the only orphan in the group. I had someone who shared a common past with me, though I didn't let Daniel know this.

"It's okay. I don't mind talking about it. You might have noticed but I'm comfortable with what I am." He smiled, flashing his pointy teeth at me. "Anyway, it was Violet who saved me. I owe her my life, because if she hadn't shown up, that werewolf would have killed me. She looked after me until I recovered. Even put in touch with another werewolf, who helped me deal with my new condition. After that, I just kinda stuck around. I guess she's kinda like my adoptive parent." He paused, and then chuckled to himself. "You know, she does seem to have a knack for picking up stray kids. First me, then Nate, and now you."

"And what about Sebastian?"

"Hmmm. It must've been a year or two after I started travelling with her. You can ask Violet if you wanna know the specifics, but they worked together for a while in Aldar. They just kinda fell for each other. Been together ever since."

"So it was only the three of you until you picked up Nate?"

Daniel stopped mid-cut. I saw his hand tremble on the hilt of his knife, clutching tight enough to make his knuckles go white. "No, there have been others. I'd rather not talk about that, if it's okay with you."

With a sudden downward stroke, Daniel severed a large slab of meat clean from the bone. He caught it in his hands and handed it to me.

"Take this back and I'll clean up here," he said. I noticed he avoided my eyes then. No doubt the topic was a rather sore one for him. I decided to leave it at that and carried the meat back to the others. The fire was lit, and the meat began to cook. Daniel joined us after some time, looking more subdued than usual. When he sat his shoulders slumped, his eyes staring absently into the fire.

After finishing our food, we set off again at a slow pace, heading northwards. With the sky threatening to rain down on us we found a small bunker and decided to get some rest.

*****

Everyone was still asleep when I awoke, even Violet, who was cuddled up to Sebastian. Unlike everyone else, her body didn't move at all. It was as if she was truly dead. I wondered how long it took Sebastian to get used to that. I know it would freak me out.

I felt restless, so I wandered outside for a bit to stretch my legs, making sure not to stray too far from camp. The rain had come and gone while I slept. Water dripped from the leafless branches, creating the illusion that it was still raining, although the sky was now clear. The sun would be setting again soon, and then our march across France would continue. I still had no real idea as to where we were headed, only that the city of Aldar would be there. The thought of a city full of vampires still scared the hell out of me.

I pulled myself up onto a low branch, and sat with my back against the trunk, thinking. Even if we were able to break past the barriers at Rachat, what then? Would the vampires all invade the city? How many innocent people would die, trying to protect their homes? What would happen to the city afterwards? There was so much I didn't have the answer to. I felt lost, confused, scared, hurt, and angry.

"You shouldn't wander off on your own," Violet said. I hadn't heard her approach. When I didn't reply, she said, "Are you okay?"

I looked away, letting out a deep sigh.

"What am I saying? Of course you're not okay." Violet jumped up onto the branch, landing with barely a sound, and walked over to me. She sat down at my feet, taking my hands in hers and squeezing them gently. "Talk to me," she said.

"I'm okay. Honest. I think I just need some time to absorb everything."

"Are you sure?"

I forced myself to smile and look Violet in the eye. "Yeah. I know what I have to do now." The smile dropped. "It just scares me a little because I have no idea how the future is going to play out, you know? Will Ash still be waiting for me? How will the city cope without the Silver Dawn?"

"No-one can know for sure what will happen, but I will tell you this. When the time comes it will be hard for people to accept the truth... Ash included. It may take some time, but I am sure he will come around in the end."

"You think so?"

"Yes, I do." Violet lifted a hand and placed it on my head, ruffling my hair. I scowled at her and she laughed before withdrawing her hand and placing it next the other on her lap. We were silent for a minute before Violet spoke up again.

"You wouldn't happen to know why Daniel has been withdrawn since the two of you went hunting, would you?"

I told her how I asked about how they met, and if it was just the three of them until they picked Nate up. Violet stopped me mid-sentence.

"Sarah. I should have guessed."

"Who's Sarah?"

"She was Daniel's mate. A werewolf like him. They were together for three years, and then one day, out of the blue, she asks to join us on our next assignment. Daniel begged her to stay at home, but she eventually managed to convince him."

"What happened?"

"We were sent to clear out a group of vampires that were disrupting the trade routes between Aldar and Felwood – one of the smaller human settlements out there. For days we tracked the vampires, hoping to find their base. Well, we found it. And so did the Silver Dawn. Sarah... didn't make it." Violet bowed her head. "That was two years ago, and he still blames himself."

I could hear the distress in her voice as she spoke. It must have been hard on her, to see him in pain and not be able to relieve it. Perhaps, she bore some of the blame herself.

"Why are vampires fighting each other?" I asked, trying to change the subject.

"The same reason humans have fought against each other since the beginning of time. They believe in different things. Those of us who live in the cities, alongside you humans, just want to be able to live without hiding ourselves... without having to scavenge our next meal. It's a mutually beneficial relationship, of course. We get fed, and the humans get protection."

"Was it like that before the plague too?"

"Not at all. Back then the only thing you humans needed protecting from was yourselves. When we came out of hiding we were a novelty. Businesses started popping up, and people would pay stupid amounts of money to meet a vampire. There'd be people lining up outside clubs, some of them wanting to see if we lived up to the legends, and others thinking they could seduce us – fang-bangers, they were called. There was no shortage of willing meals back then. They gave their blood freely. Then the Silver Dawn showed up." Violet sighed. "At first they had little support. People ruled them off as bigoted fear-mongers."

"Until the plague they predicted came true," I added.

"Exactly. After that, their numbers sky-rocketed. People began torching the clubs, and our homes. If anyone was suspected of being a sympathiser, they'd be beaten and often killed. It was horrifying. In order to try and redeem themselves, they would turn to killing others of their own kind. But by then it was much too late. Entire cities were infected. The world was in chaos."

"Were they right about why the plague came?"

"No-one can say for sure. But we do not believe we were the cause."

"Okay, so what about the other vampires? What do they believe in?"

"They believe we should not be making friends with our food. They see humans only as prey, and would rather we go back to skulking in the shadows."

There were footsteps from below. I spotted Nate walking up to us.

"There you two are. What you doing up there?"

Violet pushed herself from the branch, landing in front of Nate. "Just talking. Are the others up?"

"They were getting up when I left."

"Okay, well, be ready to move out soon. May as well get an early start." Violet went back to the bunker, leaving Nate stood below me, looking up.

"You hungry?" he asked, pulling two small foil-wrapped bars from his pocket.

"Starving,"I replied and jumped down with a smile. "What is it?"

"Some kinda energy bar. Honestly, they taste like shit, but it'll keep you full for a few hours. Just, uhhh, don't tell the others. I kinda snatched the last ones. Figured you might be needing one."

"Better than nothing," I said, taking one. "Thanks. I'll try to make it last."

"No problem."

I unwrapped the bar and took a bite. Nate's appraisal hadn't been entirely accurate. It tasted more of a bland mush than shit. Still, it felt good to get something into my stomach. I took another bite then wrapped the rest up and pushed it into my pocket.

"Do you ever wonder why we were left alive?" I asked.

"All the damn time. It was General Marsten that dumped me in the middle of nowhere too."

"He said to me he didn't want to do it, but he had to."

"Guilty conscience? Maybe he couldn't bring himself to kill us."

"Maybe," I said as we began walking up to the bunker.

Violet met us halfway, handing us each a backpack to carry. Daniel came out soon after, bounding towards us. He brushed past Violet's legs and nuzzled his head against her. She reached down and patted him on the head. His eyes caught mine, and for a second I thought I saw a flicker of pain, but then it was gone. He was running from the pain, I thought.

"Come on," Violet said. "We need to get moving again while the weather is still good." She turned and went back to the bunker where Sebastian was waiting. Nate followed. Daniel's eyes were fixed on me. He walked up to me, his nose brushing past my pocket as he sniffed at it. So much for keeping that a secret. He whimpered and nudged my leg.

"What? You get to eat rabbits and... stuff." I kneeled down in front of him, my hands stroking his ears. I began to wonder how much of the human Daniel was still in there.

"Must be so easy for you, being able to shift whenever you're hungry, or sad." Daniel tilted his head and whined. "It's their fault, you know? The Silver Dawn. They stole from us. Now we have to make them pay."

Daniel's tongue shot out, licking my cheek. He barked and ran off after Violet, his tail wagging. I shook my head, thinking about how stupid I must have seemed, talking to a wolf. But I think he understood. I hoped he did. He needed someone to blame other than himself.

As we walked I began asking the others about what the city of Aldar was like. Violet told me it was a preserved piece of history, one of the few cities that survived the ruin that came after the plague. She also said, I would have to wait and see, because she didn't want the surprise to be spoiled. This only served to fuel my curiosity, but everyone else sided with Violet and kept their mouths shut.

*****

We ventured out of the woods, and began traversing a barren wasteland, filled only with death and ruin. It seemed like hours passed as we navigated around the larger ruins, in case they were home to any wild vampires. We paused for a short while at a river to restock on water. I sat down on a small rock, taking in the scenery. Daniel laid next to me, his head resting on my lap. Across the river from us, sat on the horizon, jagged spires rose up into the sky, taller than any building in Rachat. The ruins seemed to stretch for miles across the landscape.

"What is that place?" I asked Violet.

"That was once the city of Orleans," she replied. "Now it is merely a nesting ground for wild vampires. Because of this, we have to detour through there." She pointed upstream, towards a set of hills, blanketed in trees.

"And after that?" I asked, wondering how much further we had to go. My feet were already beginning to feel the strain.

"North, around Paris, and to the port-town of Calais. At this rate it should only be another week or so before we reach Aldar."

"That far?" I sighed. I would be hundred of miles from Rachat. Hundreds of miles away from Ash.

"Don't worry. If this glyph from the barriers is the key we need, then we'll be heading back to Rachat before you know it."

"And if it isn't?"

"We'll cross that bridge when we come to it." Violet smiled, nudging my shoulder with her fist. Translation; it could be a long while before I got to see Ash again.

Chapter 16

Two days flew by since we passed Orleans. We stopped to rest at yet another small cluster of ruins, this time taking up camp in an old warehouse that stood defiantly against the test of time. Rotten boxes littered the place, adding a damp, musky smell to the place, but it was definitely preferable to sleeping in one of the more exposed buildings that offered little protection against the biting wind and snow.

I slept for a short while, on the floor of what was probably an office in its day. The wind whistled through the windows, boarded with sheets of metal and wood. Flakes of snow drifted in through the gaps. We were bunched together in the small room to conserve body heat, but Nate seemed to have edged closer to me since I had fallen asleep. It felt uncomfortable being that close. I told myself I was being stupid, and he had just rolled over in his sleep, seeking some warmth.

In the end, I crawled out of the sleeping bag, being careful not to wake anyone, and did some exercises. I had been slacking on my workouts since Boursac. The thought of it never crossed my mind until then. Still, I couldn't afford to slack, not if I wanted to stay alive against vampires, and who knows what else. I was doing some push-ups when Daniel walked into the room, stretching his arms and yawning.

"Can't sleep?"

"Just restless," I replied, panting and huffing. The exercise felt good. I would have killed for a sparring match against Ash right then.

"I've been meaning to talk to you about something," he said, sitting down in front of me. He pulled his jacket around him tighter as another gust of wind blew through the building.

"What about?" I started to push myself harder, hoping for more of an adrenaline rush.

"That thing you said to me... about revenge."

"Oh. So you do understand in that form."

"I know you want revenge for what they've done to you, but you can't let that be your reason for going after them. People become obsessed with revenge and it's not healthy."

"Don't tell me you don't want revenge." I stopped my exercises to look him in the eye. "They killed Sarah, and –"

"Don't you say her name!" Daniel snapped. He backed off, shaking his head. "Sorry. I'm sorry. I didn't mean to snap." His hands gripped his knees, fingernails digging into the flesh. "Of course I want revenge, but that's not all. They killed my parents too. My Dad went away on an assignment one day, and never came back. His team said they were ambushed by the Silver Dawn. Mom was so depressed she wouldn't eat or drink. She just kinda stopped living. The doctors told me she died of a broken heart."

"So, more revenge?"

"Shut up and listen," he scolded me. "I don't want any more kids to have to go through that. That's why I fight, to protect everyone, and their future. You should know what I'm on about."

"What do you mean?"

"Don't try and deny it. I saw that look in your eyes when I

mentioned I was an orphan. You've felt that pain too, haven't you?"

"I wasn't going to deny it," I said, looking away. "But it's different for me. I never knew my parents."

"Then you still know the pain of not having a family. Think how many people's lives are at stake because of this fucking war. Think how many children could end up without parents because of it."

"I know, but why does it matter why I fight? We fight to take down the Silver Dawn. At the end of the day, that's all that matters."

"It matters because revenge can make you do stupid things in pursuit of it. Trust me, I've been there." Daniel sighed, his fingers twitched against his knees, clutching tighter. "After they killed Sarah, I almost got myself killed trying to hunt the bastards down. I was reckless, and stupid. I was blind with rage, consumed by my revenge. But in the end, killing them didn't bring Sarah back. It just made me into a killer... a monster."

"What's that gotta do with me?"

"Well, what are you planning to do when we finally confront the Silver Dawn?"

"Kill them." The words passed my lips without so much as a thought.

"It's that simple, huh? You just remove them from the equation, and then you get to go back to the city to be with Ash?"

"Exactly. You guys are planning on killing them anyway. I just want in on it."

"And what will Ash think of you? If you become one of the monsters, will he want you back?"

My eyes widened as I absorbed his words. Ash would understand, wouldn't he? He would learn the truth and see it was something I had to do... for myself, and for us. Or would he only see the killer that took down the leaders of Rachat?

"If you want to be a part of this, then you need to think of a better reason than revenge." Daniel stood and turned to walk out of the room.

Didn't I already have another reason? So I could be with Ash again. But how far would I go to achieve my goal? Anger and rage bubbled up inside of me at the thought of everything they had done; lied to us; left myself and Nate for dead, exiled from the city to protect a secret; making Ash believe I was under some vampire's spell. It was true, I didn't want them dead so that I could be with Ash again. I wanted them dead because they needed to pay. I wanted them to feel a fraction of the pain they had caused to others.

No. I shook my head, trying to clear it of the images that bombarded me. Ash might never forgive me if I gave in to the emotions that threatened to bubble over. I had to be better than that, for Ash, and for everyone else in Rachat who might have wanted me back, which admittedly was only a handful of people. If the Silver Dawn were allowed to continue their reign, then how many people would they abandon to the outside world, left without friends or family? What if that next person was Ash?

"Wait," I called to Daniel.

He looked back over his shoulder at me. "Well? Have you thought of a reason?"

I nodded. "I want to save my friends, and everyone else in Rachat from those evil bastards. I want to make sure no-one else has to suffer what Nate and I have been through."

Daniel smiled. "Much better. I hope you'll keep that in mind when the time comes."

"I'll try. Thanks, Daniel."

"Don't mention it, kid. We orphans gotta stick together, right?" Daniel turned back to me and held out his fist in front of him. I recognised the gesture from my childhood, so I held out my fist and we bumped them together. I had seen children do it all the time at school, but never once had anyone done it with me. It filled me with a strange sense of happiness, realising once again I wasn't alone.

Daniel looked back towards the doorway and said, "Are you gonna come in, or stand there all day?"

Nate appeared from behind the door frame. Heat crept up to my cheeks and I looked away, wondering how much he heard of our conversation.

"Are you two finished bonding now?" Nate said. "Because, I dunno about you two, but I could do with something to eat."

Daniel grinned. "You guys would starve to death if it weren't for me."

"Don't remind me," Nate replied, smirking. "So, what's for lunch today, Mr. Chef?"

"Hmmm, I think I spotted some horses not far from here," Daniel said.

"Think you can manage to catch one, wolf-boy?"

"Maybe, but you two are gonna help, just in case."

"Why me?" I asked.

"Well, would you rather sit here doing nothing?"

"Fine," I grumbled. I was dying for a bit of action, though honestly, I wasn't sure how I was going to be of any help catching a horse, when they already had a werewolf and a powerful Daeva on their side.

I borrowed a pair of gloves from Sebastian, which were a little too big, and a hat from Daniel. We opened the large metal door of the warehouse and the wind rushed inside, carrying a wave of snow with it. I followed Daniel and Nate out to a small thicket nearby. The snow was travelling horizontally, blowing in my face and stinging my cheeks. I hadn't seen weather like this since I was in school, watching the snow fall from the window as the teachers told us we wouldn't be allowed outside during recess. We stumbled through the thicket, until we came across a small herd of horses. Some were huddled together, while others grazed on shrubs. We kept as much distance as possible while Daniel observed them. There were grey horses with black speckles, brown horses with black manes, and even some that were white with large brown patches.

"That one," Daniel said, pointing to one of the smaller grey horses.

"So, how are we gonna do this?" Nate asked.

"It'd be easier if we can get them out into the open, and try to manoeuvre the target to me with your ability," Daniel replied. "We'll need someone to startle them." Both of their eyes turned to me.

"No. Just no," I said. "I could get trampled."

"They'll run away from you. Trust me," Daniel said.

"Why can't you trap them with your fire now?"

"Because, plants, fire and wind don't exactly mix well," Nate said bluntly, mocking my apparent lack of common sense.

"Fine. Tell me what I need to do."

"Okay, you gotta sneak around behind them, and then jump out screaming and waving your arms." Daniel grinned.

"My eyebrow twitched and I glared at him. "I'm not doing that."

"You're no fun." Daniel pouted. "Just jump out from behind them then."

I crept around the horses, wondering what I was about to get myself into, and jumped out from behind a tree. The horse nearest to me leaped to its feet, letting out a shrill cry. As planned, the herd ran away from me and straight towards Daniel and Nate, who were waiting outside the thicket. I followed as quickly as I could. By the time I got there, they had managed to separate the young horse from the pack. Nate was using bursts of fire to try and control the horse's movement, and Daniel was attempting to tackle the horse. Figuring my job was done, I sat down on a fallen log under the shade of a tree, and laughed as Daniel threw himself at the horse, only to end up face down in the snow.

This went on for a few minutes. I began to wonder if my ability would work on horses, so I gave it a try. The horse began bounding straight for me, with Daniel screaming for us to stop it. And it did stop, right in front of me. Daniel caught up and blinked at the unmoving horse. He shook his head and withdrew his knife from its sheath, drawing it across the horse's throat. It cried out in pain, but soon collapsed to the floor, its legs giving way beneath it.

"Did you know you could do that?" Daniel asked.

"Nope."

"Good, because otherwise I'd have to kick your ass."

As always, Daniel took charge of skinning and gutting our catch, which was more difficult this time, given the size of the horse. I stood guard with Nate, trying not to catch a glimpse of all the guts and blood. When our meal was secured we dragged the horse back into the trees, and out of sight.

There was enough meat from the horse to last for two meals. Half of the meat was cooked, and we sat around a small fire eating. The rest was stored in plastic bags with some salt. After our stomachs settled, we packed up and got ready to head out into the snow. The wind was calmer and the blizzard had eased up somewhat. A crescent moon hung in the night sky, bathing the snow-covered land in its silvery light. Daniel was back in his wolf form again, after complaining that it was too cold to be a human. We hadn't even gone a hundred metres when I saw his ears prick. He scented the air and let out a low growl. His lips curled, flashing his razor sharp canines.

"Dammit," Violet cursed. "Back inside. Quick."

We ran back into our hideout, shutting the door quickly behind us. There were footsteps outside, the snow crunching beneath their feet. They stopped, and for a second I thought they might have passed by. The door flung open. A group of three men and one woman greeted our eyes. Vampires. I couldn't so much see it, as I could feel it in the air around them. They gave off a distinct aura of other-worldliness. My fingers twitched at the blade Nate had given me. I pulled it from the sheath, trying to keep the movement hidden.

"Well, well, look what we have here," said the first. He stood in front of the others, so I assumed him to be the leader.

"Looks like a feast to me," said the woman.

"I smell werewolf, human, and something else," said the second man. "The other two, they're human, but they have the smell of magic about them."

Violet moved to stand in front of Sebastian.

"Oh, don't worry, you can keep the human," their leader said. "But we'll be taking the other three." He smiled, the moonlight glinting off their fangs.

"I bet the two boys'll taste sweet," the woman added.

"You won't lay a finger on them," Violet snarled. "Leave **now**. This is your only warning."

"Or what?" the leader asked. "You think you and that pup of yours can protect them?"

"They don't need protecting," Violet said. "Why don't you show them, Nate?"

"Well? Let's see what you've got, *human.*" The leader taunted Nate, spitting out the last word as if it were something dirty. The rest of their group laughed.

"As you wish." Nate grinned, sweeping his hand out in front of him. Jets of fire erupted from the ground in an arc, forcing back the group of vampires and sending them scattering into the ruins.

"Keep your eyes open," Violet said. "They haven't gone far."

Daniel growled, his shoulders arching. There was a smashing noise from behind us. We turned to see the wood covering one of the windows smashed, the third male jumping through. Nate reacted instantly, his hand flying out in the direction of the vampire who retreated with a scream.

"Not bad," came the leader's voice from outside. "But how long can you keep it up?"

"All night long, baby," Nate shouted back.

A chorus of laughs sounded, echoing through the building.

"What's the plan?" I whispered to Violet.

"If we stay here, they'll try to wear Nate down, and they will outlast him," she said.

"Tch," Nate snorted. "Don't underestimate me."

"I'm not." Violet sighed. "You're just too cocky."

A crashing noise from upstairs caught our attention. Violet pointed to myself and Nate, and then nodded towards the stairs. Nate went first. I followed close behind, sticking to the wall with my knife in hand. Upstairs was another large room, like the one below. The moonlight flooded in through a hole in the ceiling. I couldn't see any sign of the vampires. A distraction? Then there was a blur in one corner of my eye. Nate must have seen it too because the room lit up as a stream of fire jumped from his hand. The vampire paused, jumping back to dodge the flames. It was the female. I sensed more movement to my left and swung around, slashing at the air. A deep laugh resonated through the room. There were two of them, at least. I heard noises from downstairs; clattering and barking.

Nate nudged my side. "Focus on our own opponents," he said. "Violet and Daniel can hold their own."

"Is that so?" the female vampire said, flicking her long, blonde hair over her shoulder. "Then we'll have to finish you two off quickly and go help."

"The redhead's mine, Cynthia," grunted the male. "I owe him for almost lighting me up."

"Fine by me," replied Cynthia, jumping up onto a roof beam as she dodged another wave of fire.

"Over here, Copperhead," the male taunted. More fire blazed in his direction.

"Stay close to me," Nate said.

"You can't fight both of them," I said.

"Your ability won't work on them."

"I can take care of myself. If you're that concerned, then finish off your guy quickly."

"Okay, go," he said. "But don't you dare die on me."

I stepped away from Nate and moved to the back of the room, where Cynthia sat watching from her beam. She jumped down, landing without a sound, and smiled at me.

"You're cute," she said, her voice a little higher pitched than it had been. "If you surrender, I promise to make it extremely pleasurable for you." She rolled the word pleasurable off her tongue, and twirled a strand of hair around one finger, avoiding looking me directly in the eye. I scoffed inwardly, having see this performance so many times with Ash's fan girls. I smiled, remembering some of Katiya's famous lines for turning down both her and Ash's admirers, and Cynthia smiled back, giggling.

"In your dreams, tramp."

Her eyes widened in shock, and she lunged forward, bearing her fangs at me. I swung the knife, feeling it bite into her skin as she tried to dodge it. She wasn't that fast, I thought. The vampire in the bunker at Montargis had been faster. My eyes could follow this one's movements. The question was, would my body be able to keep up?

"Is that all you got? One tiny prick?" Cynthia laughed, rushing at me again. I sidestepped and took another swing, missing her by an inch. From where I stood now I could see Nate wasn't having an easy time either. Flames lashed out in every direction, trying to catch the male, who was running circles around him. I looked back to Cynthia, in time to see her knee connect with my ribs. She rode me to the ground, pinning my wrists to the floor and straddling my waist.

"Don't fight it," she whispered. Her tongue darted out to lick the shell of my ear. I flinched at the cold, wet feeling. "You could be my new play thing. You'd like that, wouldn't you?"

"As if," I said.

Cynthia scowled and lowered her lips to mine. I tried turning my head away from her, but she followed, eventually managing to press our lips together. Acting on an impulse, I opened my mouth the tiniest little bit. Cynthia took it as an invitation and deepened the kiss. I bit down hard on her tongue, causing her to scream and pull away. The metallic taste of her blood filled my mouth. I spat the blood in her face and head butted her with as much force as I could muster. The pain echoed through my skull. Cynthia loosened her grip on my wrists as she reared back. I pulled my right hand free and drove the knife into her side. It slid easily between her ribs. With my other hand, I grabbed a handful of hair and pulled hard, hoping to yank her off me. She let out another scream, rolling off to one side and jumping to her feet. I rolled in the opposite direction and pushed myself up.

"Oh, I am so done with you," Cynthia growled, holding her side. The flesh steamed where the silver knife had penetrated her. "We could have had so much fun together. Now, I'll settle for ripping your fucking heart out."

She ran at me, though slower than before. The silver must have weakened her. I slashed, aiming for her throat. Cynthia managed to jump back, leaving the blade to whistle through the air. But then she froze, eyes going wide with confusion. She grasped at her throat, as blood began to pour out of it. Hacking and spluttering, she dropped to her hands and knees. I wasn't sure what was happening, but I took the opportunity to drive the knife into her back, piercing her heart. With a final cough, her body sagged to the floor, landing in a pool of blood.

"Cynthia," the male bellowed. A second later there was a rush of flames, and his body caught fire. He roared, dropping to the floor and rolling. It was a minute later when he stopped moving, the stench of burning flesh filling the room. He burned until all that was left was a blackened husk. Nate walked over to me. Just to be sure, he torched Cynthia's corpse too.

"Nice one," he said, patting me on the back. "How did you manage that?"

"I-I don't know," I replied. "I thought I missed." I could have sworn she dodged that last swing.

"Well, forget it for now. She's dead and that's all that matters. We should go check on the others."

We rushed downstairs to find Daniel sitting at the feet of a bloody, maimed corpse. Violet had the leader pinned against the wall by his throat. Daniel gave a loud yip when he saw us, wagging his tail.

"You two okay?" Sebastian asked.

"I'm good," Nate said.

Now the adrenaline was wearing off, I could feel my head and ribs throbbing. I lightly touched where it hurt and hissed when a sharp pain coursed through my chest.

"Sit down and let's take a look at it," Sebastian said. I did as I was told and lifted up my clothes. My chest was bruised an angry shade of purple. It looked a lot worse than it felt though. Sebastian pressed his fingers against the bones, eliciting some more hissing. "Doesn't feel broken. Any sharp pains when you breathe?"

"No. Only when you touch it."

"Looks like it's just bruised, but we'll bandage you up to be sure. The last thing we want is a fractured rib puncturing your lung."

Nate grabbed some bandages and other supplies from one of the bags. They placed strips of adhesive tape along the bruised ribs. Next an elastic bandage was wrapped around my chest, with some padding over the bruises. It was tight, but not so tight that I struggled to breathe.

"That should do it," Sebastian said. "Try to take deep breaths, even if it hurts, and don't sleep on that side for a few days."

I nodded and stood, wincing as the pain shot through me again. Violet was still interrogating the lead vampire. I pulled my clothes – or Nate's clothes, I should say – back on, and made my way over to them. Daniel was sat at her side, looking up at the vampire, his tail wagging.

"Are there any more of you out there?" Violet asked, her voice cold and emotionless.

"Like I'd tell you," the vampire answered. Violet took the blade in her hand and drew it across his face, the skin sizzling as it came into contact with the silver. "Fucking psycho bitch," he screamed. The knife was drawn across his chest.

"Answer the question," Violet said. She trailed the point of the knife down his chest, not breaking the skin, just touching, until she reached his groin.

"Fuck," the vampire gasped. "No. No, there's no more of us."

"You see how easy that was?" Violet said. "Now, what were you doing here?"

"We smelled food. That's all, I swear," he replied frantically. "Please, you have to believe me."

"Oh, I do believe you."

"Then you'll let me go?"

"No. There's still one last thing I need from you." Violet smiled.

"What? Anything!"

Violet grabbed a handful of hair and tilted the vampire's head to one side. She lunged for his neck, fangs extended, sucking and swallowing as the body in her arms struggled. His eyes stared at me, pleading with me, until his body went limp and his eyes closed. I stood there, watching, and not really believing what I was seeing. Did it count as cannibalism? Violet threw him to the ground and wiped the back of her hand across her mouth.

"Nate, burn the bodies. The rest of you, get ready to move out again," Violet ordered. Her head turned to me. I realised I was still staring. "I was going to kill him anyway," she said. "May as well get a meal out of it."

Violet turned and walked away, heading for the others. I shook my head, trying to shake off the image of the vampire dying in her arms. I had other concerns I needed to share.

"I killed one of them," I said, following after her.

"Good for you."

"But something happened, and I don't know how to explain it. I tried to slit her throat, and missed. At least, I think I missed, because she started bleeding and–"

"Then you didn't miss."

"It's that simple?" I asked. "After all the supernatural stuff you must have seen, and your answer is that I imagined it?"

"Yes. You said it yourself, you *think* you missed. But she definitely started bleeding, correct?"

"Well, yes, but–"

"No buts," she interrupted me. Violet turned to face me, gripping my shoulders and looking me in the eye. "Sometimes a snake is just a snake."

I raised an eyebrow, wondering what snakes had to do with anything. Violet sighed.

"It means that, sometimes, things are simply what they are, and nothing more. She bled, so you can't have missed. It's probably the stress getting to you."

"Yeah, you're probably right," I said. Violet smiled and thrust a backpack into my arms.

*****

Soon we were off again into the cold darkness. I plodded along, keeping my hands tucked inside the pockets of a jacket I borrowed from Daniel since he had no need for it. It was a little big, but it helped protect me from the biting wind that stung my cheeks and ears. Nate promised they would buy me some of my own stuff once we reached Aldar in a couple of day's time. The night drew on, and before long I could see a giant tower looming on the horizon.

"That's the Eiffel Tower," Nate told me.

"Used to be France's most well-known landmark," Violet said. "At night, it would be all lit up. It was beautiful. People would come from all over the world to see it. And now..."

"How old are you?" I asked. I figured she was at least a century old, from the way she talked about the world before the apocalypse. She glared at me.

Nate put an arm over my shoulders and whispered to me, "She might be a vampire, but she's still a woman." When Violet finally stopped shooting daggers at us with her eyes, Nate attempted to mouth something to me. It looked like he was trying to say three-hundred and twelve. A hand appeared out of nowhere, smacking Nate round the back of the head.

"You're not as silent as you think," Violet snapped. "And it's three-hundred and nine."

Sebastian laughed, but he was soon silenced when Violet turned to him. Three-hundred and twelve it was then. She must have seen so much over her life. Or should that be death? Over three centuries' worth of history, and three centuries' worth of death. There were so many questions I could ask her, but I didn't know where to start. It seemed all I was doing lately was asking questions, and yet, I still felt like I knew nothing.

Chapter 17

"Are we there yet?" Nate asked again.

"No," Sebastian replied, the irritation clear in his voice. We had only been walking for an hour or so that night, and if Nate's excited behaviour was anything to go by, we were definitely getting close to the hidden city of Aldar.

"How about now?"

"Nate," Daniel growled. "Shut up already. You know exactly where we are."

"Where are we?" I asked, looking around for some indication. There was nothing out of the ordinary; more ruins and overgrown fields. In fact, it looked identical to the landscape of the previous night.

"That set of ruins up there is Calais," Daniel said, pointing to a line of buildings on the horizon. After that, it's about five hours to Aldar."

"Finally." I let out a long, weary sigh. "My feet are killing me." The balls of my feet were throbbing. The clunky boots I was wearing felt as though they had shrunk in size.

"Yours and mine both," said Nate. "First thing I'm gonna do when we reach Aldar is have a nice long bath."

"Sounds good to me," Sebastian said.

"A hot shower, then a visit to the pub for me," said Daniel.

"And we'll finally be able to eat real food again," said Nate.

"What's wrong with my cooking?" Daniel asked.

"Dude, I love your cooking. You know that. But I need to eat something other than deer, fish, and that weird plant soup."

'Weird plant soup' summed it up perfectly. I was sceptical when Daniel showed up at camp holding an armful of leaves and yellow flowers. It wasn't bad, but Nate was right. My body was craving something more substantial. Maybe some chicken and potatoes, or a greasy, cheese pizza. My mouth watered at the thought of it.

*****

Calais was soon upon us, and as we rounded an old apartment block, I found myself stopping to take in the view. The ocean. Having lived in the city all my life, this was my first time seeing it outside of a book. I had always dreamed of being able to witness it for myself. The sliver of a moon reflected on the surface of the water, gently rippling. Waves crashed onto the beach, creating a white foam before the waterline retreated. I ran out onto the soft sand, kneeling to pick up a handful. The grains slipped through my fingers. I went further out to the water, dipping my fingers into it as an icy cold wave flowed over my fingertips. Violet appeared at my side, and I felt embarrassed for acting so child-like.

She smiled. "Nate did the exact same thing."

I looked out to the ocean, watching the moon's reflection glimmer and sway. It was so peaceful, and strangely hypnotic. My only regret was Ash wasn't there to see it with me. He would have loved it. Maybe after the war, I thought, then I could show it to him.

"Which way now?" I asked.

Violet pointed out to sea. "Aldar is across this body of water."

"Does this mean we get to ride a boat?" My heart raced at the thought of going out onto the water.

"No," she replied. My heart sank. "There's an old tunnel that goes underwater. But before we can use it, there's something I need to tell you."

"What's that?" I asked, a lump forming in my throat.

"The tunnel is protected by a powerful compulsion spell. Once you enter, you will be overcome by fear, compelling you to turn back. And the deeper you go, the worse it will get."

I swallowed hard. "So how do we get past it?"

"The rest of us have already been recognised by the spell. It will let us pass unhindered. You, on the other hand, will either have to face your fears, or go through unconscious. Your choice."

"What did Nate do?"

"What do you think?" Violet chuckled and shook her head. "He charged in and came out the other end crying like a baby."

"And the rest of you?"

Violet nodded. "We have all faced it too."

So, I could either take the easy way out and be carried through, making myself appear weak in front of the others, or tough it out and face whatever nightmares my mind could conjure up. Of course, I had to pick the brave choice. If everyone else had done it, then I wasn't about to be the first to chicken out. And what was the worst I could possibly face? The fear of never seeing Ash again? I had already met that fear several times already, and since then I found a new resolve, to remove the Silver Dawn. What else was there to fear? The skinless corpses from my nightmare, perhaps? As horrifying as they were, they weren't actually real.

"I'll face my fears," I said, figuring the spell couldn't conjure up anything worse than I had already faced. Besides, if it worked anything like my ability, then I should be able to shield against it. Wishful thinking? Maybe, but any hope is better than none.

"We should get going. If we hurry, we can make it to the other side with a few hours of darkness to spare, and I can talk to Marcus before he's dead to the world."

"Marcus is the leader of the resistance," Sebastian added. "He's a very old and wise vampire. If anyone can decipher the glyph we found, it'll be him."

"How old?" I asked.

"He lost count." Violet laughed. "But Marcus used to be a Viking warrior in life. That puts him around a thousand years old, at least."

"Wow," I said. I couldn't even imagine living that long. Marcus must have witnessed the rise and fall of entire civilisations, countless wars and battles, and the invention of so much technology, even things we took for granted.

"Oi!" Daniel shouted from back at the wall. "Are we gonna get going, or what?"

We rejoined them at the edge of the beach and set off again. The ruins of Calais weren't particularly ruined. It was more of a ghost town. The buildings were mostly intact, minus a window or a door here and there. As with Boursac, nature ran rampant. Vines scaled even the tallest buildings, rising up to eight stories high. Weeds sprouted out of every crack and crevice, in the pavement and on the walls. Soon after, we reached the start of the tunnel. There was just one small problem. Piles of rubble and debris blocked the entrance.

"I hope you have another entrance," I said, following Violet as she stepped over the metal tracks that disappeared into the sealed tunnel.

"That's the main tunnel," Daniel said. "We'll be using the service entrance."

I was led to a small grassy area on the far side of the tunnel. Sure enough, in the middle of the overgrown grass and weeds was a large metal hatch, which Violet crouched down to grasp the handle of. The hatch creaked and groaned as she pulled it open, ending with a loud clang of metal against stone.

I looked down into the dark hole and saw metal rungs embedded into the stone wall, going down as far as I could see, which wasn't far. Violet climbed down first, clutching a flashlight in her mouth. When she reached the bottom, she turned the light on and shone it at the ladders for the rest of us to see where we were going. Sebastian went next.

"Watch your step," Nate said as he kneeled at the edge. "The metal can sometimes get a bit damp, so make sure you hold on tight. Don't want you falling and cracking your head open now, do we?"

I went next, gripping the cold metal as I descended into the darkness, towards the small shaft of light that shone from below. Daniel came last, closing the hatch behind him. The sound of the hatch snapping shut echoed and reverberated off the walls, producing a soft ringing in my ears. I continued down, feeling for the next rung with my foot until I made it to the bottom.

Daniel pulled another flashlight from his pack and pointed it down into the tunnel. Damp moss blanketed the walls. The path sloped down to a large metal door. Broken light bulbs hung from the ceiling, long since shattered. The hallway was about wide enough for three people across. I walked at the back of the group with Nate, who had taken the torch from Violet.

As we approached the door, I heard a dripping noise. Drip, drip-drip. Drip, drip-drip. I shuddered, remembering the dripping noises in the bunker where I found the Fifth Covenant. I willed myself on, telling myself it was only water, and most likely just the spell trying to force me to turn back.

I must have muttered something out loud, because Nate laughed, startling me. "The spell doesn't affect this part of the tunnel," he said, putting an arm over my shoulders and dragging me along to catch up with the rest of the group.

Violet began working on unlocking the large door. She turned a giant wheel in its centre. The metal bars screeched as they slid out of their latches, allowing the door to be pulled open.

"Beyond this door is where your trial begins," Violet said. "We'll be with you the whole way, so keep moving forward as fast as you can."

"If it gets too bad we can still knock you out," Sebastian said. "Most new people come through that way."

"It won't come to that," I said, steeling myself for what lay ahead.

"That's good," Daniel said, patting me on the back. "Believe in yourself, that's the best advice I can give you."

Beyond the door, the tunnel continued to slope down. I took a deep breath and entered first. The air inside was heavier and staler. In the distance, I could see lights flickering on and off. I gulped, feeling a twinge of fear race up my spine.

'I can do this,' I repeated over and over in my mind. *'Focus on moving forward.'*

The tube lights in the ceiling buzzed as they wavered on and off. I wondered if the lighting was done intentionally, to add to the effect of the magic, or if it was a hallucination caused by the spell. Whatever it was, it was working. Spots filled my vision from the constant flashing of lights. I jumped, thinking I had seen something in the darkness, but when the next light came on, there was nothing. I took a deep breath and pulled my shields tight around me, like a solid iron wall. Whether it actually blocked out the magic, or I only thought it did, it helped.

Nate came up next to me, taking my hand in his. At first I was shocked, having not heard or seen him approach me. I wanted to pull my hand from his, but the contact was comforting. I held on tight as we delved deeper into the darkness. Unfortunately, the comfort didn't last long. A cold chill blew through the air, causing my whole body to shudder. What made it worse was the wind appeared to whisper in my ear. I couldn't understand what it said, but every bone in my body told me to turn and run.

'Just a spell,' I chanted.

Drip, drip-drip. There it was again, that same pattern of drips. Another illusion, perhaps?

"You're crushing my hand," Nate said.

"Oh, sorry." I released my grip and pulled away from Nate to walk in front of him.

The wind whispered to me again. "You're not real," I told it, forging on. The wind disagreed, whispering louder and more often, as if to prove its existence. "No, you're not."

The hairs on the back of my neck stood to attention as it whispered back, "Are you sure?"

"You're not real," I yelled. The beams of light from the torches that were bobbing along behind me came to a stop.

"Are you okay?" Violet asked.

I didn't reply for a second, listening for the voice. Nothing. "I am now."

"You're doing well," Sebastian said.

"Better than Nate did," Daniel added. Nate pouted and I laughed. It felt good to laugh. It helped erase some of the fear from my mind.

I continued on with my renewed sense of courage, the lights still blinking. This isn't so hard, I thought, wondering what Nate might have seen to have him crying by the end of it.

"Wouldn't you like to know?" the wind asked. My pulse sped up. I could feel it beating violently in my neck. "I can taste your fear, but this is only the beginning."

"What do you want?"

The wind brushed past my cheek. "I want to watch you pretend to be brave, when I know you are fucking terrified. I want to see you burst into tears like a child. And make no mistake, I will make you cry. And I will enjoy it. I want to see you tremble and shudder. I want to watch you die a slow and painful inner death."

I clenched my fists, walking faster than before. "Bring it on."

The wind blew stronger, laughing in my ear. "You think you have nothing more to fear, but I know you better than you know yourself. I know what you truly fear. Do you know why that is?"

"Why would I care? You're a figment of my imagination."

The wind laughed manically. "No. I am very real. I'm the part of your mind that tells you to fear the dark; the deepest abyss of your subconscious manifested. By the way, how did you like those dreams I sent you?"

I didn't reply, and kept walking forward as fast as I could. Maybe, if I ignored it, it would go away.

"Very well then. How about a reminder?"

The tunnel lights began to dim, until soon I couldn't see even my hand in front of me. There was no sign of the others behind me. I took a deep breath, telling myself it was just an illusion and everyone else was right behind me. They wouldn't leave me. Even if I couldn't see them, I knew they were still there. All I had to do was keep walking, and eventually the spell would pass. And that's what I did. I walked, until I heard footsteps. I stood still, listening in on the footsteps. There were multiple sets, coming from in front of me. The lights flickered on, and in that split second I saw the skinless corpses lumbering towards me. My heart jumped into my mouth and beat frantically.

"They're not real," I muttered. "They can't hurt me."

"But your brain thinks they're real." The wind chuckled. "And just like in your nightmare, it will feel real when they tear the flesh from your bones."

I remembered the searing pain as their fingers dug into my flesh, tearing and ripping. I remembered how I woke up screaming, drenched in sweat. A drop trickled down my spine.

"What's the matter?" the wind asked. "What happened to that confidence of yours?"

The lights flickered on again, revealing that the shambling corpses had edged closer. Every fibre of my being told me to turn and run, to escape the unthinkable pain that would surely come if I just stood there, but I couldn't move. The footsteps grew louder. Closer. Their lipless mouths let out a chorus of blood-curdling groans. My heart beat faster, pounding against my rib cage. My legs refused to move. The lights flashed on and off. Closer.

The icy wind fluttered around me, chilling me to the bone. "And you thought you weren't afraid of them anymore."

The footsteps drew nearer. I hadn't been afraid of them because Ash was there to protect me. 'Trust me to protect you,' he said. And I did. The footsteps stopped and the temperature around me dropped sharply. I dared to open one eye. The lights flickered, and I saw a giant ice block, rising up to consume the corpses. When it enveloped every last one of them, it shattered, taking the darkness away with it. Even halfway across the country, Ash was still with me. I looked back, noticing the rest of the group stood right behind me.

"I'm okay," I assured them before they could ask any questions, my limbs still trembling.

The wind disappeared again, but I knew it would be back. This little game wasn't over yet, and the thought left me with a twisting knot in my stomach. I decided to pick up the pace, and jogged off deeper into the tunnel. I needed to cover as much ground as possible before the voice returned. There were a couple of surprised gasps behind me, as the others realised what I was doing and came running after me. The breeze did return, slowly at first. It ghosted through the tunnel, picking up speed the further I went, until it became a full-blown gust.

"Are you ready to feel real despair?" it whispered.

"I beat you once, and I can do it again," I said, filled with a new confidence.

"It won't be so easy this time. Your little whore can't save you from this one."

Rage swelled inside of me. "Leave Ash out of this!"

"I'm afraid I can't do that. You see, your whore is the star of this next performance."

"Stop calling him that."

"Why? That is what he is... a whore. How many people has he slept with in the last few months alone? I'm sure even he has lost count. He's probably sleeping with someone else right now, trying to fuck the pain away."

"No. He wouldn't. I believe in him."

The wind cackled around me. "But you left him, remember? Why should he wait around for someone who chose to leave him? Here, why don't I show you?"

I walked on, expecting the darkness to surround me again, but the opposite happened. The light glared at my eyes that had become used to the dark depths. In the distance, I could see someone walking towards me. As my eyes adjusted to the light, I managed to make out the head of blond hair and tanned skin. Ash. I began running to him, but as I got closer, it became clear something was wrong. His eyes burned with a blue flame. I paused, only for a brief moment, and the cold snapped at my feet, rooting me to the spot.

"You," he breathed.

"Ash."

"You left me," he said. I could hear it in his voice. He wasn't just angry. He was hurting, because of me. "You left me, to go running around the country with a fucking vampire."

"I can explain," I said hurriedly.

"I trusted you, Mik. I loved you. And I thought you felt the same way."

My throat closed up on me, making it difficult to breathe. "I do."

"You made me feel human again, for the first time in years, and then you left me. You ripped my fucking heart out and stamped on it. And for what?"

"To save you, and everyone else."

"Save us?" Ash laughed. "By destroying the people who have protected us all our lives? You're not the person I loved anymore. You're no better than those blood-sucking corpses now."

The ice around my feet started to rise, encasing my lower legs. I was starting to lose all feeling in my toes. "Ash, don't do this. Trust me. Please!"

"Trust you? I did that once already, and look where that got me. What was I to you anyway? A way for you to finally get laid? Was that it?"

"No, I don't..." My voice trailed off as the first of the tears filled my eyes.

"Well, you got what you wanted I guess. Have you let the vampires fuck you yet?"

"No. I wouldn't... you were the only one I cared about."

"Yeah, well, you have a funny way of showing it, Mik."

My knees felt weak. I would have collapsed were it not for the ice holding me upright, creeping up to my waist. He was so consumed by the pain and anger that my words couldn't reach him. The familiar chill surrounded me, chuckling in my ear. "Are we having fun yet?"

"I swear, I will kill you for this."

The wind roared, laughing louder. "I'm a part of you," it sang. "This is *your* fear. I'm merely enlightening you."

"No, this isn't my fear. Ash would never–"

"Oh, but it is. Don't you see? You're going to help kill the Silver Dawn. How are you going to explain that one to him?"

"I-I don't know, but I'll find a way. I have to."

"And if you can't?" The words hung in the silence, echoing in my mind. "Well, why don't we find out?"

"Coffin bait, that's all you are," Ash said through gritted teeth. "Do you let them suck your blood while they fuck your brains out?"

Ash walked up to me, grabbing a fistful of clothing. The ice around my legs shattered and he threw me to the ground.

"Does it feel good? Are they that good in bed that you can forget about all the pain you've caused me?"

I didn't bother to pick myself up off the ground, instead choosing to lie there and sob. That he could even think I'd do such a thing, and betray him. His words stung deeper than I could have imagined.

"Well? Answer me!" Ash yelled. I screamed back as his foot connected with my ribs. This wasn't Ash. He wouldn't do this, would he? But the voice was right. How was I going to justify my actions to him?

His foot rolled me onto my back and pressed down, forcing the wind from my lungs. "I'm sorry, but I have to do this." Tears began to roll down his cheeks as he pulled a gun from his waist. I stared down the barrel of his gun, my eyes blinded with tears. "I'm doing this because I love you."

The safety clicked off.

"No!"

Ash's body flew back, as though pushed by some invisible force, and slammed against the tunnel wall. I rolled over onto my hands and knees, looking left and right for something that might have caused it. There was nothing. Ash's body slumped against the wall, blood spattering the side of his head. He wasn't moving.

"Do you see it now?" the voice asked.

"See what?" I screamed. "What the fuck am I supposed to be seeing?"

"Think about it. You want to invade Rachat to remove the Silver Dawn. Ash is a protector of Rachat, of the Silver Dawn." The wind gathered around me, swirling in circles. "What would happen if the two of you met, opposing each other? Will he kill you to protect the city? Would you kill him to save yourself? *THIS* is your true fear."

"No–" I said, choking. "No."

"Yes, yes," the wind chanted. "You're one of the monsters now. Your whore won't take you back. And when it comes down to it, one or both of you will have to die."

My chest heaved. I slammed my fists into the ground, my eyes burning with tears.

"I told you I would make you cry, didn't I?"

"Fuck you," I yelled. The stone beneath me began to crack as my tears fell onto it. Rage and despair consumed me. The wind laughed in my face. I clenched my fists tighter, my screams filling the tunnel. The walls around me cracked. I had no idea what was happening, only that I wanted to lash out. Bits of stone flew off the walls, leaving behind long indentations, like some invisible monster was dragging its claws across them. There was a sharp pain in the back of my head and I was falling forward as the darkness took me.

*****

When I came to I could hear a whirring noise. It felt like we were moving. I opened my eyes and saw that I was on the back of an open-top vehicle, the lights above whizzing by.

"Hey," Nate said. A hand stroked through my hair, my head resting on his lap. I sighed and closed my eyes.

"What happened?"

"You... your ability seems to have grown," Violet said from the opposite seat. "We had to knock you out, for fear that you might destroy the tunnel."

I remembered seeing the tunnel walls cracking. Was that me? "Then the vampire I killed... I didn't imagine it, did I?"

"It's a possibility," Violet replied. "I don't know enough to be sure, but Marcus will know. We will take you to see him as soon as possible."

"What did you see down there?" Daniel asked. "You were talking to something, and then you completely lost it."

"There was a voice. It called itself a part of my subconscious... the manifestation of my fears."

"In all my years, I've never seen someone react like that." Violet sighed. "I'm sorry for making you do that."

"No," I said. "I chose to do it, and I failed."

"Don't feel bad," Sebastian said. "Most people who enter Aldar do so unconscious. Right, Jimmy?"

"Of course," came a voice from the front of the vehicle. "That's why we have this taxi service running along the second half of the tunnel. Saves people having to carry others all the way. The good news is you only have to do it once. If Leigh gives you her consent, you'll never have to face that spell again."

"So what exactly did your subconscious show you?" Nate asked.

"Ash." There was a collective look of worry from the group.

"And?" Nate said.

"I'm sure he'd rather not talk about it," Daniel said. "After all, you still haven't told us what you saw down there."

"True. I'm sorry."

"It's okay," I grumbled, wiping my eyes. I sat up, noticing that we were no longer in the small tunnel where I passed out. We must have been in the main tunnel now, which was much larger. And in the distance there was a small point of light that grew slowly.

"We're here," Violet said. "The city of Aldar."

Chapter 18

The vehicle sped out of the tunnel, the night sky above me dotted with stars. All around me there were stone giants, buildings taller than any I had seen before, reaching up into the inky sky. We drove through the streets on a wide road, and every now and then a similar vehicle would whoosh past in the opposite direction.

"I'll take you to Marcus' residence," said Jimmy. "But it's almost morning. You may have to wait until the evening to see him."

"It's urgent," Violet replied coldly.

I must have fallen asleep for part of the journey. I remember being surrounded by empty, half-destroyed buildings, and then we were in a street of houses and shops, the paths filled with people – vampires I assumed, given the time of day. A few heads turned to gaze at us as we sped past them, but most paid no attention. We crossed a bridge, over a wide river, and I spotted alien structures in the distance. A large, white dome sat on the horizon. A giant wheel was lit up against the night sky. Everything was so different to Rachat. It was so busy, and alive, even at this time of night. I would never have thought such a large city existed anywhere after the plague.

Before I knew it, we were pulling up outside a large house, separated from the rest of the city by a long driveway and surrounding fence. The taxi stopped outside the towering metal gates, and Jimmy leaned over to press a small button on the wall. It buzzed and a voice could be heard coming out of the speaker. "Who is it?"

"Violet's group is back," Jimmy replied. The speaker buzzed again, and the gates swung open. We were dropped off outside the carved, wooden doors, where a middle-aged woman greeted us. She wore a shimmering red blouse, and a black skirt that ended below her knees. Her black hair was tied tight to her head, revealing a set of matching red earrings.

"Welcome back, everyone," she said. Her eyes scanned the group and stopped on me. "I don't believe we have met. My name is Leigh." She extended a hand to me. Was she *the* Leigh that Jimmy mentioned? The one who cast the compulsion spell? I hesitated a moment before taking her hand. She didn't seem much like a powerful witch to me.

"Mikhail," I replied.

"Your accent is not from around here, is it?" Leigh eyed Violet.

"We'll discuss it later," Violet said. "We have information concerning the barriers of Rachat, which I think Marcus will find most interesting."

"I'm sorry, but Marcus won't be seeing anyone else today."

"Do you have any idea how important this information could be?" Violet snapped. Sebastian placed a hand on her shoulder.

"The sun will rise soon, and Marcus must sleep. You know this. Even if I were to disturb him, he would not be of much help. The best you can do is come back this evening after dark, and I will make sure Marcus is free to see you."

Violet gritted her teeth.

"Come on, Dear," Sebastian said, taking hold of her hand. "This war has been fought for decades. Another day will not make a difference."

"Thank you for your understanding. Now, if you'll excuse me I have some things to take care of. I will let Marcus know to expect you when he wakes, and I will need to have a talk with your new friend."

"We'll be back before dark," Violet said, glaring at Leigh, who gave a quick bow and retreated back inside the house.

"Why does she need to talk to me?" I asked.

"Security reasons," Daniel said. "She wants to make sure you're not a danger to the city, and hopefully grant you immunity to the spell on the tunnel."

"Well, looks like we got some time to relax." Nate smiled. "Time for that bath."

"Sebastian and I will be at our place if you need us," Violet said. "Make sure you get some rest before this evening."

"Sure," Daniel said. "What about Mik?"

"He can stay with me," Nate said. "I don't mind."

"Okay, then we'll see you tonight." Sebastian waved, putting his other arm over Violet's shoulder as they walked back down the driveway.

*****

Nate and Daniel led me to their apartment block, which was about twenty minutes from Marcus' residence. They lived in adjacent rooms on the second floor.

"I'm gonna hit the pub after I've cleaned up. You guys wanna join me?" Daniel asked. We declined and went inside, with Nate picking up the pile of mail that had accumulated in his absence. His room was similar to the dormitories in Rachat. He had a double bed, with a table and chair near the window, and a wardrobe in one corner. A door to one side lead to his own toilet and shower.

Nate set his backpack down against the wall and kicked his boots off. He sat on the edge of his bed and flung himself back, stretching his arms out wide and letting out a long sigh.

"Man, it feels good to be back," he said. "No more sleeping on rocks for a while."

I sat quietly on the chair and untied my laces, setting my boots against the wall. My feet ached and throbbed. I winced as I removed my socks, noting how raw the soles of my feet looked. If I were a regular human, I'm sure they would have been covered in blisters.

"Does it hurt?" Nate asked. I nodded. "I've got some stuff that'll help with that." He rummaged through a small plastic box in the bottom of his wardrobe and pulled out a jar of ointment. "Sit down here," he said, patting the end of his bed.

I hobbled over to the bed, my feet brushing against the rough carpet, and sat down where I was instructed. Nate pulled the chair up in front of me. He sat down and lifted my foot onto his lap. He poured some of the ointment onto his hands and began rubbing it in. At first it was cold and stung a little, but soon I was in heaven, his fingers kneading the sore skin. Nate placed my foot back down on the floor, and lifted the other onto his knee. He began working his magic again, and I closed my eyes, letting out a soft moan. My whole body relaxed and I leaned back, resting on my elbows. I hadn't even noticed when Nate stopped and stood up, until I felt his breath on my face. My eyes flew open as his lips pressed against mine. I froze, trying to process what was happening. Nate backed away, almost tripping over the chair.

"I'm sorry," he said hurriedly. "I don't know what came over me." Nate went to the wardrobe, and pulled out a towel and change of clothes. "I'm gonna use the bath down the hall. You can use the shower, and grab whatever clothes you want from the wardrobe. I'm sorry." He left in a hurry, shutting the door behind him.

I flung myself back on the bed, clutching the sides of my head, and let out a frustrated groan. What the fuck was Nate thinking? I thought back to all the times he had gotten close to me, comforting me after I saw Ash again, snuggling closer to me as we slept, holding my hand in the tunnel, and stroking his hand through my hair. He couldn't have feelings for me, could he?

"Fuck." I jumped up off the bed and stormed into the bathroom, slamming the door shut on the way. I switched on the shower, and turned the heat up. The hot water made my skin glow an angry red, which suited my mood just perfectly.

After a while of standing under the shower, I began to feel better. I had been dying for a hot shower ever since I woke up outside of Boursac. I was starting to feel a little dizzy from the heat, so I turned off the water. When I was dry, I went out into the main room. Thankfully, Nate wasn't back yet. I picked out some dark jeans, a t-shirt and hoody from the wardrobe and dressed. I pulled on my boots, and with my hair still damp, I left the room and knocked on Daniel's door.

"Come in," he shouted. I opened the door. His room was identical to Nate's. Daniel was pulling on a red sports jacket over a black tank top. "Hey," he said. "What's up?"

"I changed my mind about going out for drinks."

"Awesome." Daniel grinned. "Now I won't look like a Billy-No-Mates drinking on my own. What about Nate?"

"He said he was too tired," I said, avoiding his gaze.

"Well, let's get going," he said, stuffing a few items into his pockets and grabbing his keys from the table.

*****

We walked down dingy alleys and busy roads, until we arrived at a white building with dark wooden beams, and a sign hanging above the door that read, 'The New Moon'. Inside, the floors were the same dark wood, matching the rafters in the roof. It was mostly deserted, with only a few patrons still left. After all, it hadn't been long since the sun had risen. All of the pubs in Rachat would have been shut long before now, but they didn't have to deal with nocturnal patrons.

Daniel pulled up a stool at the bar and motioned for me to sit next to him. The woman behind the bar smiled at Daniel, and waltzed over to him. Her curly blonde hair bounced as she walked. Her eyes were dark green, and she wore a little too much make-up.

"Hey, Danny. Good to see you back in one piece." She smiled, chewing on a piece of gum. "You having the usual?"

Dawn of Darkness

"Sure." Daniel turned to me and asked, "What are you having?"

"I, ummm... I dunno. I'm not much of a drinker."

"Two of the usual, please."

"Sure thing, Danny," the barmaid said, fetching two small tumblers and placing three ice cubes in each. "So who's your friend?"

"This is Mik. We picked him up during our last assignment. He was exiled from Rachat."

"Oh, you poor thing," she said, filling the glasses. "Here, don't tell the boss but I'll make 'em doubles."

Daniel smiled. "This is Polly," he said. "Greatest bar person in Aldar."

"Oh, stop it you," Polly replied, giggling and swatting Daniel with the hand towel that was draped over her shoulder. She handed us each our glass and took a small plastic card from Daniel, which she swiped into a machine. Daniel pressed some buttons on the machine, before Polly took it back from him and placed it below the counter.

"What's that?" I asked.

"This is how we pay for stuff," Polly said, still chewing. She leaned on the bar, resting on her elbows as she handed Daniel his card back. "Everything's done electronically here. You get paid, your account gets updated with your credits, then when you wanna buy something all it takes is a quick swipe, enter your password and it's done.

No spare change lying around. No lost coins. It seemed like a good system to me. I lifted the drink to my lips. It smelled spicy, though not anywhere near as bad as the rum Hans had given me. It tasted spicy too, and fruity, but it was strong. My lips twitched as I swallowed and shook my head. My throat burned. Polly laughed, and Daniel gave me a quick clap on the shoulder.

"Oi, Pol," a voice echoed across the room. "How long are you gonna keep me waiting?"

"Sorry, Danny. I was just finishing my shift. We'll have to catch up some other time," Polly said, grabbing her jacket from a hook

213

behind the bar. "It was nice meeting you, Mik. If you ever need anything, don't be afraid to head on down here and ask me, you hear?"

I thanked her and she waved goodbye, headings towards a large man who stood in the doorway.

"Keep your pants on, Jack," she shouted to him. "A couple of minutes longer ain't gonna hurt you."

Daniel laughed and shook her head. "Polly's great, isn't she?"

"Yeah," I said. She was a little loud for my tastes, and the constant chewing was irritating, but she seemed friendly enough, even knowing I used to be the enemy until recently. The people of Rachat would never have accepted an outsider.

"You hungry?" Daniel asked. "Because I'm starving."

I couldn't even remember when I last ate. My stomach churned to life, rumbling and groaning.

"I'll take that as a yes then. They do a mean chilli burger here. How's that sound?"

"Sounds great," I replied, my mouth already salivating.

Daniel caught the attention of the barman, who had only arrived a few minutes before, and ordered our food, along with another round of drinks.

"I don't wanna put you out," I said as he paid for me again.

"I think I can spare enough for a meal and some drinks," Daniel said. "It's the least I can do for you. I mean, we're not gonna let you starve, you know?"

"Thanks," I said quietly, finishing off my drink as a new one was placed in front of me.

"So, what happened between you and Nate?" he asked. I looked at him in shock. "I'm a werewolf, remember? I only caught the end of the conversation where Nate was apologising though, and I could smell you were lying to me when you said Nate was too tired to come out."

I sighed. "Nate kissed me."

"Shit," Daniel said, choking on his drink. "Nate's done some pretty stupid stuff since he joined us, but that definitely takes the biscuit."

"I think he likes me... really likes me. He's been trying to get close to me since I saw Ash."

"You noticed that too?" Daniel sighed and shook his head. "Man, I figured he was just excited to have someone like him around. You know, another exile. If I'd known he was gonna pull a stunt like that, I would've knocked some sense into him."

I knocked back some more of my drink. It was Nate who encouraged me to join the resistance, telling me that it was the only way to be with Ash again. Had he said that so I would stay with him? Was he hoping I would forget about Ash? I slammed the glass down on the bar.

"You never can tell about people these days," Daniel said. "I mean, I never would have imagined Nate swung that way."

"Can I sleep in your room?" I asked, remembering that Nate's room only had a double bed. The last thing I wanted was to be sharing a bed with Nate, barely clothed and at this rate, probably a little drunk.

"Sure you can."

It didn't take long for our food to arrive. It looked messy. The chilli burger was a large round bun, with two burgers, separated by melted cheese, and topped with chilli, lettuce, pickles and a thick slice of tomato, complete with a side of fries. I removed the tomato, having never been keen on them, and replaced it with a mound of fries. I squashed the burger down, fearing that it might be too big for my mouth. Some of the chilli leaked out of the sides, making an even bigger mess of the whole thing. I picked up the burger with both hands, holding it over the plate to catch the chilli and lettuce that would inevitably fall out when I sunk my teeth in. I bit down and let out a low moan.

"How is it?" Daniel asked between mouthfuls. I nodded, catching a bit of chilli with my finger that had found its way to the edge of my mouth. Daniel laughed. After over a week of eating only basic foods, it felt good to finally get something filling and greasy inside of me. My stomach roared its approval.

"So, besides the thing with Nate, how are you holding up?" Daniel asked when I had managed to devour the entire burger. I picked at the leftover fries.

"I dunno," I said, washing down the fries with some alcohol. "There's the whole thing with the Silver Dawn and the resistance, Ash, my powers are growing, and then there's that thing I saw in the tunnel. I guess I'm still absorbing it all."

"Do you wanna talk about what you saw? Might help take a load off your shoulders," Daniel said.

I nodded and explained about the skinless corpses from my nightmares, and about how I managed to dispel the illusion. "Then it showed me Ash. He was angry at me for not going back to Rachat with him, and he said some hurtful things. He wanted to kill me, to save me from what I had become. And then I think I killed him, with that new power of mine."

"So you're afraid you guys are enemies now or something?"

"I don't know how I'm going to justify taking down the Silver Dawn to him, but it has to be done."

"Ah, don't worry about that. I'm sure Marcus has a plan to expose them, otherwise, removing them is pointless, right? If we take down their leaders, then people will still believe the teachings, and we'll have accomplished nothing."

"Makes sense," I said. If the citizens of Rachat still believed in what the Silver Dawn taught, then the war would never be over. It wasn't enough to simply free them from the liars. We needed to show them the truth as well.

"You wanna know what I saw when I faced my fears?" Daniel asked. "I saw all my old friends back home, and a load of people I didn't know. I watched them all die because I wasn't strong enough to protect them."

"And did it come true?"

"When Sarah asked to join us, I said no because I kept thinking back to what I saw in the tunnel. I just wanted to protect her, to keep her safe."

"So, that's why you blame yourself? Because you weren't strong enough to save her?"

"Partly, yes. But I think maybe it happened because I was so worried that it might happen. I let the fear get to me. Just don't make the same mistake I did." Daniel downed the rest of his drink and stood. "Come on, let's head back. We'll get you some things on the way so you don't have to keep borrowing from us."

I finished the rest of my drink, screwing up my face. "You don't have to do that," I said, feeling bad that I kept taking from him.

"Like I said, don't worry about it. Besides, we're expecting a big bonus for the information we collected, and I think you've earned a share of it."

*****

We stopped at a couple of shops on the way back to Daniel's room, and picked up some toiletries and a few changes of clothes. I kept it basic, not wanting Daniel to have to spend more money than was absolutely necessary, despite his protests.

I set my things neatly in one corner of his room, and for the first time in over a week, brushed my teeth with a toothbrush that wasn't shared with someone else. When I came out of the bathroom, Daniel was already in bed, taking up the entire left half of it. The blinds were drawn, blocking out most of the sunlight. I sat on the bed and began slowly undressing.

"Hurry up and get in, will you? I'm not gonna jump your bones or anything," Daniel murmured. I laughed. Daniel had an amazing gift for making me feel at ease around him, like it was clear he had no hidden agenda. "I've set the alarm to go off before dark," he said as I climbed under the covers.

"Night," I said.

Daniel laughed and replied, "Morning."

I smiled. It was so nice to sleep in a real bed again, though I couldn't help thinking it was wrong to be sharing a bed with anyone other than Ash. Still, I felt more relaxed than I had since the incident at Boursac and sleep came quickly to me. Ash was still there with me in my dreams, and I was glad.

Chapter 19

I awoke before the alarm went off, snuggling into the arm that was draped over me. It felt so warm and familiar. My eyes shot open when I remembered where I was. The stubble on Daniel's chin scratched against my back as he yawned.

"Is it time to get up?" he grumbled.

"What are you doing?" I asked, shuffling out from under his arm to sit on the edge of the bed.

Daniel rolled onto his back. "Sorry, I probably should have warned you. It's a wolf thing. We like to snuggle while we sleep."

I turned round to glare at him.

"No offence, Mik, but you don't have the right plumbing for me," he said, holding his hands up. "I can't control what I do while I'm asleep."

"Sorry, I guess I'm still a little on edge about the whole thing with Nate," I said, wiping the sleep from my eyes.

"I don't blame you. Do you want me to give him a piece of my mind?"

"Thanks," I replied. "But no."

"You sure? He deserves a good tongue lashing for pulling a stunt like that."

"I think he knows what he did was wrong, and I can't be mad at him for having feelings for me. It's not like we choose these things. I just need to make sure he knows where we stand."

"You're more forgiving than I could ever be," Daniel said, rolling over to look at the clock. "Still half an hour before we have to be up." He lay back down, pulling the covers up over him.

"I'm gonna shower, and then go see if Nate is up. I need to talk with him," I said, standing and heading into the bathroom. I showered in record time and dressed in my new clothes, pulling on a pair of white sneakers that Daniel insisted on buying for me. Then I picked up the clothes I borrowed from Nate and left the room.

I hesitated at Nate's door, my hand hovering for a moment before I knocked on it. Given a choice, I would rather have avoided this talk like the plague. However, I had the feeling I would be seeing a lot of Nate, so I figured it would be best to get it out of the way and try to work things out. There was no reply. Probably still asleep, I thought. I turned to go back to Daniel's room, and spotted Nate at the top of the stairwell. He froze for a second, before continuing towards me.

"I see Daniel took you shopping already," he said, avoiding eye contact as he unlocked his door. Nate strode into the room, unzipping his jacket and throwing it on the back of the chair. "Are you coming in?" he asked. I didn't answer, but walked inside and closed the door. "Just throw them on the pile there," he said when I tried to hand him his clothes. I did as he asked.

"We need to talk."

"Figured you'd say that," he said, slumping down onto his bed. I stayed standing, my arms folded. "Look, I'm sorry. I know how you feel about Ash, and I shouldn't have done what I did."

"Then why did you do it?" I snapped. I had intended on staying calm, but the truth was, I was still angry about the whole thing.

"Because," Nate mumbled, looking away from me. "I was sick of seeing you hurting. I know what you've been going through this last week, because I went through it too. I can relate to your pain. I wanted to try and make it go away. And then I saw you laid there, all relaxed and smiling, and I couldn't help myself."

"Just answer me this. Do you have feelings for me?"

"I dunno." Nate shrugged. "I mean, I've never had feelings for a guy before, so I'm a little confused. I like you, and I guess I feel closer to you because we have that shared history, but I dunno what I'm feeling."

"Okay, then you need to know where we stand. I like you, as a friend, but that's all. I'm not giving up on Ash."

"Does this mean you forgive me?" Nate looked up at me expectantly.

"I guess so."

"Great." Nate smiled. "Let me make it up to you by buying something to eat before we have to meet Marcus."

"What did you have in mind?"

"There's a sandwich shop down the road. Is that okay?"

"Yeah, sure," I replied. Nate grabbed his jacket and I followed him out of the room.

*****

Daniel had managed to drag himself out of bed, and was getting dressed when we returned. We walked over to Marcus' house, eating along the way. Violet and Sebastian were waiting for us outside the gates, and we went up the drive together.

Leigh greeted us at the front door and led us into the lobby. Its white walls were lined with gold-framed portraits, though not surprisingly I couldn't tell you who they were of. Staircases ascended on both sides of the hall, carpeted in red with black handrails, and meeting in the middle, leading to a balcony from which dark, wooden doors led off to the various parts of the mansion. High above us a chandelier hung, illuminating the room with what appeared to be electric candles.

"Marcus will be with you shortly," Leigh said, motioning for us to take a seat on the chairs placed either side of a set of large, double doors. Her eyes landed on me. "Until then, I would like to speak to you. Alone, if that's okay."

I agreed and was led into one of the smaller side rooms. Leigh sat down on a crimson couch with high arms, and patted the cushion next to her.

"Sit," she said, pouring herself a cup of coffee from the china pot that sat on the glass table in front of her. I took a seat on the couch, trying to leave as much room as possible between us. "Would you like a cup?" she asked, and poured one before I could answer.

I took it, not wanting to be rude, and sipped from the small, decorated cup. I had to admit I missed my morning cups of coffee, but this one was too weak and sweet for my liking.

"Why don't you start by telling me a little about yourself?" Leigh suggested, lifting her cup to her mouth.

I responded by telling her of my recent graduation into the Silver Dawn's army, and how I came to suspect something was up after meeting the vampire at Montargis. I described how the General left me unconscious, and how Nate and Daniel discovered me and brought me back to the group. Finally, I told her about the recent growth in my ability, in the hopes that she could enlighten me as to what was happening.

"I, myself, have little experience with Sirens," Leigh confessed. "But you would do well to consult with Marcus about this. He knows much of the vampire bloodlines."

"I will. Thanks."

"Well then, I believe we are done," she said, standing up and brushing down her skirt.

"That's it?"

"What were you expecting? I only needed to know the circumstances under which you came here."

"What about the spell on the tunnel? Aren't you supposed to grant me immunity to it, or something?"

"Already done," Leigh replied. She moved to a small bureau near the door and picked up a small vial for me to see. It was empty. I looked down at the drink in my hands. "Some advice for the future. Don't accept food or drink from unfamiliar witches." She laughed, heading back out in the lobby. I rejoined the group, feeling a little annoyed at Leigh's games. My fists clenched.

"You drank the coffee, didn't you?" Sebastian chuckled.

"Yup." I slouched down in the nearest seat and folded my arms.

"She does that with everyone," he said. "It's like a tradition."

"I never did like witches much," Violet said. "Always meddling with something or other."

Ten minutes later, the double doors opened and Leigh ushered us into the library. At the back of the room sat a short man behind a desk, his hands clasped and his chin resting on them. He wore a simple black shirt, contrasting against the pallor of his skin. His long, golden hair was tied into a loose, off-centre ponytail that rested over his left shoulder and reached down to his waist. Even from a distance I could see he was broad and well-built. His eyes, I noticed, were a deep brown. He couldn't have been much over twenty when he died, I thought. As we approached him, he stood and moved around the desk with such speed that I was unable to follow him. He stopped abruptly in front of me, his face only inches from mine.

"You must be the Siren, Mikhail," he said in a deep voice, looking me up and down – mostly up, given that he was a few inches shorter than I. "I am Marcus." He didn't extend his hand to me, so I kept my hands by my sides.

"Ummm, nice to meet you?" I said, unsure how I should greet an ancient vampire. He gave me a lop-sided smile, and then turned his back to me.

Marcus went back to his desk, walking this time, and sat down. "I understand you have information on the Silver Dawn's barriers," he said. "If so, this may very well mark the turning of the tide in this war. Let's hear what you have."

Violet stepped forward, her hand outstretched with a piece of paper in it. "We found this glyph etched into the pillars," she said, unfolding the drawing and placing it on the desk.

Marcus' eyes widened. He took the paper in both hands, bringing it closer to his face. His fists clenched, crumpling the edges of the paper. "Are you sure this is exactly what it looked like?" he asked.

"Positive," Daniel replied. "The markings around the edge might be a little off. I didn't have a lot of time to memorise it."

"Do you recognise it?" Violet asked.

"Yes, I'm afraid I do. This is Verloren's Seal. It is an extremely ancient magic, meant to ward against all forms of the undead."

"Is there a way past it?" Daniel asked.

"All magic has a counter-magic," Leigh explained. "This particular magic will be hard to break, but I believe I know of a way. It will, however, take some time to prepare."

"And that is where the good news ends." Marcus sighed. "I know of only one creature that could create this seal. One that we have thought extinct for centuries."

"No." Violet gasped. "You can't possibly mean–"

"I'm afraid so," Marcus said. "A pure-blooded vampire."

"Pure-blooded?" I asked. "I've never heard of such a thing."

"Not surprising. Even among the vampires they have remained little more than an old-wives tale. They started with Verloren, or so the legend says. He was the original vampire. Unlike the vampires you know, Verloren was born as a vampire, rather than as a human. As to who his parents were, there is no mention. Some say the mother was possessed when she became pregnant. There are many variations of the story, and it's likely the truth will never be found."

Marcus stood and disappeared in a flash. He returned seconds later with an old, leather-bound tome. The cover was worn and the pages browning. He opened the book on his desk and turned it towards us. We gathered closer to read the page it had been opened on. The word 'Verloren' was printed in large flowing text at the top of the page.

"The stories say that Verloren was able to mate with a human woman to produce vampire children, and in turn they were able to procreate with each other. They became known as the pure-blood vampires."

A wave of disgust hit me, churning in my stomach. I knew vampires saw the world quite differently from us, perhaps because their lives weren't as fleeting as our own, and back then morals may have been vastly different. Still, I couldn't wrap my head around the thought of them participating in incest. It was just wrong.

"No-one knows how much truth there is to the story. In all likelihood, only Verloren himself now knows what really happened, but we do know the pure-bloods were born as vampires, not turned."

"So where do the regular vampires come into the picture?" I asked.

"The pure-bloods discovered they could turn humans. However, they despised those that were once human and kept them as slaves. Until, one day, a slave managed to escape. He found he too could turn humans, and before the pure-bloods knew what was happening, they were surrounded and greatly outnumbered."

Marcus turned the pages of the book, until he reached a picture depicting a massive battle. The figures weren't wielding any weapons that I could see. Rather they were tearing at each other, tooth and nail. Bolts of lightning crashed from the sky into the crowds of vampires, and fires raged.

"The human-vampires, under the command of the former slave, fought against the pure-bloods. Only a few pure-bloods survived, and likewise, most of the other vampires perished too. With the pure-bloods scattered, they eventually became nothing more than a myth."

"And you think the Silver Dawn has managed to capture a pure-blood?" Daniel asked.

"Or the pure-blood is willingly cooperating with them," Marcus replied. "In the end, they have a similar goal. To destroy us human-vampires."

"That's assuming it is a pure-blood," Nate said. "I mean, how sure are you it's a pure-blood doing this? You said it yourself, they became only a myth. So. how can you be sure they even existed at all?"

"I admit, I cannot be entirely sure it is a pure-blood we are dealing with," Marcus said. "But there is one thing I can be sure of, and that is they do exist. I would be sceptical myself, were it not for a chance meeting some five hundred years ago with *him*... Verloren."

"You met Verloren himself?" Violet sputtered.

"Only briefly, but yes, I did. Were I alone that night, I have no doubt I would not be here today."

"How do you know it was him and not some psycho-vamp pretending to be him?" Nate asked.

"Vampires like myself resemble humans because that is what we once were," Marcus said. "Pure-bloods were never entirely human. It is said they may take on the form of a human to deceive their prey, but what appeared to me was Verloren's true form."

"What did it look like?" I asked.

"Has Daniel shown you his half-form yet?"

Daniel shook his head. "He hasn't seen it."

"What's a half-form?"

"It's one of the three forms I can take," Daniel said. "You've seen two of them, this form and my wolf form. The half-form is exactly what it sounds like, a halfway state between the two. Few werewolves are able to achieve it because of the energy and control it takes to maintain it."

"Basically," Violet added, "it looks like a large, furred human with the head of a wolf and clawed hands. Before the plague hit, it was what many people assumed a werewolf to look like."

"Okay, so Verloren looks like a wolf-man?" I asked.

"No, not exactly," Marcus replied. "He looks like *a* half-form, though not that of a wolf, nor any animal I've ever seen. The only word I can think of to describe him is demonic."

"Now you're just talking crazy, old man." Nate laughed. "Demons? Next you'll be telling us you've seen angels and the Easter Bunny."

Marcus rushed forward, appearing in front of Nate with his hand raised. Violet stepped between the two before he could strike.

"I apologise for his rudeness," she said, turning to glare at Nate, who stared defiantly back at her, a smug look on his face. Violet's hand slapped against Nate's cheek, causing him to stumble. He rubbed at his cheek. "Idiot," Violet muttered. "Please continue, Marcus."

Marcus shook his head. "As I was saying, before your rude interruption, Verloren's true form is something that cannot be accurately described, because it is unlike anything of this world. He has long travelled this world, searching for a way to start his family anew, and intent on destroying the human-vampires."

"And now you think the Silver Dawn has him captive, or is working with him?" I asked, testing my understanding.

"Yes, though I think the latter more plausible. Verloren would not be easily captured, or contained for that matter."

"So, what now?" Daniel asked.

"Now that we know the secret of the barriers, we can work on countering its effects. However, this will be no easy task. It will take a week or so to prepare and complete the ritual," said Leigh. "A magic as strong as Verloren's seal will also require some rather unusual components in order to break it."

"We could find them for you," I suggested.

Leigh shook her head. "It would be best if you didn't. Trust me."

"Once the magic is complete, we can begin infiltrating the city. Until then, I will be formulating a plan of attack," Marcus said. "Now, if there's nothing else..."

"What about the blood reports?" I asked.

Marcus raised an eyebrow as Daniel rummaged through his shoulder bag and brought out a stack of files.

"These are the results of blood work performed on the Daeva," Daniel said. Marcus took the top file and flicked through it. "And there are some scrapings from the pillar we found the seal on."

"Take them to the hospital research centre," Marcus said. "I will send word to have them analysed as quickly as possible."

"Sure thing," Daniel replied, stuffing the files back into his bag.

"If that's all, then Leigh will show you out."

Leigh and the others began walking towards the exit. I started to follow, but paused, remembering that I wanted to ask Marcus about my ability. I turned to face him.

"Well?" he said. "If you have something to say, then speak up. I don't have all night."

"I wanted to ask you about my powers," I said.

"Very well, but you will have to make it quick." Marcus sat in his seat and leaned back. "What would you like to know?"

I told Marcus what happened with Cynthia and in the tunnel.

"Interesting," he said, leaning forward and clasping his hands on the desk. "Your powers are progressing like that of a true Siren, though this particular ability is one most Sirens will never acquire."

"What do you mean?" I asked. "You know what's happening to me?"

"One question at a time." Marcus sighed. "Yes, I believe I know what is happening. All Sirens possess the ability to manipulate human emotions. This is the most basic of Siren abilities, and for most Sirens, it will be the only one they ever possess."

"So, some of them gain other abilities?"

"Exactly. Like any of the bloodlines, the more powerful the vampire, the more their abilities develop. In the case of Sirens, they sometimes gain the ability to cause physical damage with their magic."

"You mean like cutting things with my mind?"

"Yes."

"Can you teach me to control it?" I asked. "I can't afford to lose control again."

Marcus shook his head. "No, I cannot. Nor would I have the time even if I were able. I do, however, know we have a Siren in our service who owes me a debt. I will have Leigh contact her for you. I assume you are staying with one of Violet's group for the time being?"

"With Daniel," I replied.

"I shall have her stop by and introduce herself as soon as possible," Marcus said. He jumped up from his chair and walked up to me. With one hand on my back, he guided me towards the doors. "Now, I really must begin preparations. If you'll excuse me..."

"I understand."

Marcus began to close the door, but paused briefly to say, "Oh, and welcome to Aldar. I hope you enjoy your time here, etcetera, and all that nonsense." The doors slammed shut.

I shrugged and wondered what I was supposed to do now. It seemed everyone had left me. I was debating going back into the library to ask Marcus, when a door opened to one side of the lobby. A young man with wavy, brown hair and dark, almost black, eyes scanned the room. His eyes stopped on me and he walked towards me.

"I don't believe we have met before." He smiled, extending a hand to me.

"Mikhail," I said, taking his hand.

"Russell. It is a pleasure to meet you, Mikhail."

The doors behind us opened. "Ah, there you are, Russell," said Leigh. "Marcus wishes to see you immediately."

"I'll be right in," Russell replied. "Mikhail, I have a feeling we'll be seeing each other again. Until then, I bid you a pleasant stay in our city. If you ever need anything, don't be afraid to ask. I would be delighted to help."

"Thanks," I said. He smiled again, this time wide enough to flash his fangs, and then turned to head into the library.

"Nathaniel was waiting for you outside," Leigh said, before following Russell and closing the door behind her.

Sure enough, Nate was sat on the steps outside the front door, his head bowed. He jumped when I touched him on the shoulder.

"Sorry," he said, regaining his breath. "I guess I spaced out for a moment."

We walked back to the apartment block together. Nate said

Daniel was on his way to the hospital to deliver the files, and Violet and Sebastian had gone back home to relax.

"I never did like Marcus," Nate said out of nowhere. "He's just so... I dunno, he gives me the creeps."

"Wolf in sheep's clothing," I said. It was unnerving to think Marcus was many times our age, and yet he looked only a few years older than I did.

"Yeah," Nate agreed. "Do you believe all that stuff he was spouting about pure-bloods?"

"Dunno." I shrugged. It reminded me of being in school, when I had to trust the teachers knew what they were talking about, simply because I didn't know any better. But that didn't necessarily make it true. I only had to remember what the Silver Dawn taught me to realise that fact. "I want to believe him, but–"

"You've been lied to before. You don't wanna make the same mistake again," Nate said. I smiled, because I couldn't have put it better myself. "I feel the same."

When we reached the apartments, Nate used a spare key to open Daniel's room for me. He explained they shared for a while when Nate had arrived in Aldar, until the room next door was vacated.

"Do you have any plans for this evening?" he asked. I told him I was expecting a visit, and Nate offered to wait with me.

"Thanks, but I'm gonna lie down and get some rest," I replied. "I'm not quite as nocturnal as you guys yet."

Nate laughed. "Give it another week or so."

When Nate was gone, I yawned and stretched my arms wide. I kicked off my sneakers and laid down on the bed. Almost as soon as my head hit the pillow I was asleep.

*****

I dreamed of riding giant werewolves through the city, until I was jarred awake by a loud knocking at the door.

"I got it," Daniel said. I rubbed my eyes with the back of my hand and sat up. Daniel answered the door, with only a towel around his waist, his hair and skin still dripping from the shower. A young woman with straight blonde hair and pale skin stood at the door. Well, she looked young, though that probably wasn't the case. She wore a low cut, white dress, patterned with flowers. Only a vampire could wear such a thing in the middle of winter, I thought. Only a vampire.

"I'm Anna," she said. "I'm looking for the Siren, Michaela."

"She's right over there." Daniel pointed at me and burst into laughter as he headed back into the bathroom.

"Mikhail," I corrected her as she walked over to me.

"Right, whatever. Come with me, and don't dawdle. I'd rather this not take any longer than it has to."

I pulled on my sneakers and followed Anna, letting Daniel know I was heading out for a while. Anna led me out into the streets and to a large detached house. The windows of the house were all boarded up or filled in. We went inside and passed several vampires along the way.

"This your new boy toy, Anna?" one of the males asked. "Looks a little young for you."

"Oh, piss off, Carl," she replied. I kept my head down and continued following. When we reached the basement, Anna locked the door behind us. My heart began to race, and I felt the familiar knot in the bottom of my stomach. The lights flickered to life, revealing a large, open room with various pieces of furniture littered around the place.

"You live in here?" I asked. It seemed a little cliché for a vampire to be living in a basement.

"Yes. Are you coming down, or are you gonna stand there all night?"

I cautiously descended the stairs. Something about being locked in a basement with a vampire had me on edge.

"Have a seat." It sounded more like a demand than a request. "Would you like a drink?"

"Do you have anything other than blood?"

Anna responded by throwing a small bottle of pop at me, which I barely caught before it hit me. "I sometimes entertain human companions," she said. "Now, to business. Normally, I would tell you to go fuck yourself, but I owe Marcus a huge debt, and one that I would like to see paid off sooner rather than later. So, do exactly as I say and we can both be on our merry way. Are we clear?"

"Yeah, we're clear," I said. I got the impression Anna wasn't going to warm up to me anytime soon. I unscrewed the top off the fizzy drink and took a sip.

"Good." Anna held out one of her arms. "Show me what you can do."

"You want me to try and cut your arm?"

Anna rolled her eyes. "Yes, what else could I possibly be asking?"

"I've never consciously done it before."

"Just try it, already," Anna said, growling. "I want to see how far you can get without any instruction."

"Okay." I took a deep breath to calm myself.

"Some time tonight would be good," Anna muttered, feigning a yawn.

I focused on her arm, releasing the latch inside of me that held my magic within. The cold wind spilled out, rushing over Anna. As expected, she didn't flinch or even show any sign she could feel it. In fact, she looked a little bored. I concentrated on one small point on her arm and pushed my magic at her. Nothing.

Anna sighed. "Looks like we'll have to start from the beginning, but not tonight. I'm expecting company soon."

"Wait, that's all you dragged me over here for?" I asked.

"No. I brought you here so you know where I am," she replied. "Be back here at dusk tomorrow."

"Fine," I said, not bothering with a goodbye as I walked back up the stairs. I was happy to be getting out of the basement and away from the bitch. I undid the latch on the door, which seemed redundant in a house full of vampires.

"Wait," Anna called out to me. She came up the stairs in a blur, pushing the door shut again. "Before you go, there is one thing I should explain to you about your ability. There are certain *risks* involved with it. Risks that we prefer to keep a secret, you understand?"

I nodded. "What kind of risks? You mean it could harm me?"

"Not you. Your victims. Using your ability repeatedly on the same person in a short time period can sometimes... change them."

"I'm not following."

"When you manipulate a person's emotions, it is only temporary. But if you were to do this for any length of time, or repeatedly in a short time frame, then there is a chance it will become more permanent. Do you understand?"

"I think so," I replied.

"Good, now scram," Anna said, opening the door for me. "If Carl gives you any bother on the way out, tell him to do one. His bark is worse than his bite. Oh, and don't be late tomorrow. We have a lot of work to do."

Without another word, the door slammed shut behind me. I wondered what it was about vampires and slamming doors on people without saying goodbye. After finding the front door without too much trouble, I was left with the task of trying to find my way back to the apartment by memory. I turned right down the road, and wandered for a few minutes, vaguely remembering one of the small buildings we passed.

I thought about what Anna had said, about my ability being able to change people. As far as I knew, I had never repeatedly used my ability on anyone, or for any length of time, except for Ash when he was helping me train. There was a moment of panic when I wondered if I could have subconsciously drawn Ash to me with my ability, but then I remembered that Ash was immune to my ability. He described it as his empathy recognising the emotions weren't his own. With that weight off my chest, I crossed over the road and towards an old run-down building. About ten minutes later, I turned onto a small side road and saw the apartment block at the end, where

Daniel and Nate would hopefully be waiting for me.

I froze. My heart seemed to stop for a split second. Nate. Hadn't I tested my ability on him that night while he slept? It was only for a few seconds at a time, but I had done it several times. What if that was enough? What if I inadvertently changed his feelings for me? The timing seemed right, for it was after that night his behaviour changed, and he began getting physically closer to me. And I had tested the luring song on him earlier that day as well. One word came to mind. Shit!

Chapter 20

The next night, as the sun was setting, I made my way back to Anna's basement. I knew she was going to be mad at me for detracting from my training time, but I needed to know if I had made Nate fall in love with me. And if I had, was there any way to reverse it?

At first, I managed to convince myself I was fretting over nothing, and it was entirely possible Nate was reaching out to me because of our shared past. I kept repeating in my head that he just wanted someone who understood what he had been through, and gotten too caught up in the moment. It happens, right? But then Nate would appear and want to hang out, which was fine, until he started wanting to do everything together.

Of course, it was difficult for me to do much of anything on my own, considering I had no money, and would get lost if I wandered more than a few blocks away. However, it scared me to think of doing everything with Nate, simply because that's how it was with Ash. The last thing I wanted, was to nurture any potential feelings he had for me, not least of all because I didn't want to have to hurt him when I denied his feelings. And at the same time, I didn't want to cut him off completely. I felt bad for him, since it seemed likely I was the cause.

I talked to Daniel about it after returning from Anna's the previous night. He gave me the most incredulous look and tried to dissuade my fears, telling me that Nate was just being impulsive and misunderstanding what he felt towards me. Our talk hadn't helped as much as I thought it might have, but Daniel did bring up some good points. I could tell Nate his feelings were the result of my experiments gone wrong, but as Daniel pointed out, Nate might still believe the feelings were his own. And even if I could get him to believe me, they would still feel real.

I knocked on the chipped, white door of the boarded-up house, and waited for someone to answer, tapping my foot absently. A rather gruff-looking male answered after the third round of knocking.

"Whaddaya want?" he asked, glaring at me.

"I'm here to see Anna." He let me inside and walked off, assuming I knew which way I was going. I found the basement door without too much trouble and knocked on it. "Anna?"

"Door's open," she shouted. I went down into the basement. Anna motioned to a chair at a small wooden table. "Sit, and let's get started."

"I need to ask you something first," I said.

Anna scowled. "Whatever it is, make it quick."

"It's about what you said yesterday, about the risks of my ability."

Anna sighed. "Let me guess. There's some woman out there in love with you, and all you can think is, 'Did I do that?' Am I close?"

"Pretty much," I replied. "What do I do about it?"

"You don't do anything."

"What? How can I do nothing if I'm to blame for making him love me?"

"Him? Well, whatever does it for you, love." Anna laughed.

"It's not funny," I muttered, exasperated.

Anna's expression turned serious, her arms folded across her chest. "There is nothing you can do about it," she said. "For starters, you can never know for sure whether it was your fault or not. And even if you did do it, there is no way to reverse it. Well, you could try forcing the opposite emotion, but that's a potential mine field that usually ends up making matters so much worse."

"So I just carry on as normal, and that's it?"

"Well, look at that. You do have a brain. Now, let's try using that brain for your training, shall we?"

"Whatever," I mumbled, receiving a glare in return. In a way, I was relieved to hear the solution didn't involve poking around in Nate's head some more. I may already have messed it up once, and I'm sure we weren't the first people to encounter the problem of one friend developing feelings for another. So maybe the solution wasn't supernatural at all.

"Okay, so yesterday I tried to have you cut my arm and you failed miserably," said Anna in a flat voice. She certainly didn't mince her words. "Do you know why you failed?"

I shook my head.

"It's rather simple. Your magic needs to be sharp, not blunt. Make sense?"

Again, I shook my head.

"Okay, then watch." Anna picked up a small cardboard box and placed it on the table next to where I sat. "Keep your eyes on the box." I stared at the box, trying not to blink in case I missed anything. I thought I saw the box move, but it was such a tiny amount, I couldn't be sure if I imagined it or not. "That is what you were trying to do," she told me. "Our magic is made for slicing. It is not made for pushing."

"But I've seen it happen twice," I replied. The first time was in the bunker outside Montargis, when the vampire sent Ash flying. And the second was when my ability begun to manifest in the tunnel. Anna raised an eyebrow as I told her about these events.

She sighed. "Do you know nothing about psychic abilities?" she asked. "When two psychic abilities collide, one of two things will happen. They can either mix, or they explode. When the latter happens, the weaker of the two can be sent back to the user with such force that it physically knocks them back."

"I see."

Anna nodded to the box. "Watch again." This time the box tore in several places, like an invisible claw had raked through it. "Imagine it cutting like a blade. Make your magic thin and sharp. Now you try it."

Thin and sharp. It sounded easy. I took a deep breath and let my magic flow over the box. Thin and sharp, I reminded myself. I stared at the box, willing it to be cut. The box stared defiantly back at me, taunting me. I gritted my teeth, focusing everything I had onto the box. Still nothing.

"Okay, give it up before you pop a blood vessel." Anna laughed. "This isn't about force. Straining yourself like an idiot won't achieve anything other than... well, making you look like an idiot."

"Then what should I be doing?"

Anna shrugged. "This isn't an exact science. It's different for everyone. I can guide you to the right path, but you need to find your own way. You need to find the key that works for you. But remember, this is about mind, not body. Stay calm, and focus."

And for the rest of the night, that's exactly what I tried to do – major emphasis on the tried. That damn box was stubborn, refusing to submit to my will. It pissed me off. I wanted so badly to rip the box to shreds, with my bare hands if I had to, because it certainly wasn't working with my mind. By the end of the night, I felt like I had made no progress at all. I hadn't even dented the box, let alone tore into it. If it hadn't been for the fact that I was getting more and more exhausted with each try, I would have continued well into the day too. But I needed to eat and rest, and Anna was starting to feel the pull of the sun. And so, with a heavy sigh, I gave up and headed back to Daniel's room.

*****

Daniel wasn't in, but Nate had given me his spare key. I let myself in and collapsed on the bed. My stomach groaned, but there wasn't anything I could do about it. There was nothing to eat in the room, and I didn't want to intrude on other people's food by raiding the shared kitchen. And without money, I couldn't go out and buy any either.

I decided I would have to go and see if Nate was in. I didn't like leeching off of everyone, especially since they had been so kind to me over the last couple of weeks, but I needed to eat if I wanted to survive long enough to see Ash again, and help rid the world of a great evil. It still hadn't sunk in, that the Silver Dawn might have been conspiring with a pure-blooded vampire all this time. I shook my head. It wouldn't do me any good to start worrying about that kind of stuff. I had more important matters to focus on, like my training, and food. Verloren could wait. There was a knock at the door. I sat up, wondering who it could be, when the door opened.

"Hey," Nate said, popping his head around the door. "I heard you come back. What are you up to?"

"Just starving to death," I said, hoping he would catch the hint.

Nate laughed. "Come on, I know the perfect place."

I jumped up off the bed and Nate took me to a small café. He ordered egg and chips with a coffee.

"What do you want?" he asked. I was still browsing the menu.

"Bacon sandwich," I said, smiling as I remembered how Ash used to cook breakfast for us both. "And a coffee. Extra strong."

We sat at a table near the window, and waited for the food. The woman who had served us brought the coffee to our table. Nate must have torn open at least five packets of sugar and stirred them into his. He was a lot like Ash in that respect. As we waited for the food, an idea popped into my head. Paper should be easier to cut than cardboard, right? Well, that's what I thought. I picked up one of the packets and stared at it. Thin and sharp. My magic swirled around the packet, and then it dissipated.

"What are you doing?" Nate asked.

"Trying to cut the sugar packet with my mind."

"And how's that going for you?"

"I don't have enough energy left," I said.

"No progress then?"

I shook my head. "I don't know what I'm doing wrong, and Anna keeps telling me I have to find my own way of making it work."

"Just give it time. These kinda things aren't meant to be easy," Nate said. "The first step is always the hardest. Isn't that what they always say?"

It was the same when learning to control my ability back in Rachat. The Silver Dawn found me after one of their officers visited the orphanage where I was staying, to give a talk on joining the army. I can't remember what triggered it, but the officer said something that set me off. I didn't realise what was happening at the time, but the now familiar wind flew out from within me, filling everyone in the room with anger.

Fortunately, there weren't many people in the room at the time. Most of the kids managed to escape when the officer snapped. One of the boys, Rick, was beaten to within an inch of his life. I lashed out at the officer, consumed by my anger. My memory gets fuzzy after that. I still remember the sting of my cheeks as the back of his hand hit me. I remember my body screaming in agony. It was two days later when I woke up in the hospital. My body felt numb. The edges of my vision were blurred, and my head swam. I panicked, sending everyone nearby, staff and patients alike, into a fit of terror.

I woke up again later that day, to find a man next to my bed. Brendon, his name was. He was the first of the psychic Daeva to enter the military. Back then he was still a cadet, due to graduate in a couple of months. The doctors kept me sedated to the point where I could barely open my eyes, under orders from General Marsten. Brendon held my hand, telling me everything was all right as they slowly took me off the sedatives. He explained vaguely what happened at the orphanage. Very vaguely. I guess they didn't want me to lash out again by triggering a painful memory. They never did tell me exactly what happened, only that I sustained a couple of broken bones and some severe bruising. To be honest, I wasn't sure if I wanted to know the full truth, if it was bad enough for my brain to block it out. Brendon explained what they thought was happening to me, and helped me control my powers when I was finally discharged.

Turning my ability on and off at will seemed like a difficult task at first, though it proved easy enough once I started to get the hang of it. The real problem, however, was learning to control it once I let it loose. That particular part of my training took weeks, but at least by then I wouldn't have any more unwanted outbursts. Once I figured out the first piece of the puzzle, the rest soon followed. Hopefully it would be the same this time. If I could find that one vital clue – the key to my ability – then I would master it in no time.

"Earth to Mik," Nate said, prodding my shoulder.

"Sorry, I was just thinking."

"Anything you want to share?"

I shook my head. "Not really. Just thinking about when I had to train my first ability. You're right though. The first step is the hardest."

Nate smiled. "I know you can do it."

"Thanks."

Our food arrived, and as always, I lifted the top slice of bread. My heart sunk. The bacon still had its rind on. It wasn't cooked until it was crispy. It wasn't how Ash made it... how I liked it.

"What's wrong?" Nate asked.

"It's not right," I said, describing to him how Ash always made my sandwiches exactly as I liked them.

Nate laughed and took my plate. "You don't get something without asking for it," he said. He proceeded to begin pulling the rind off with his fingers. Then he held his hand over the bacon. His palm began to glow, tiny flames flickering on the surface of his skin. When he returned the plate to me, it was exactly how I wanted it to be. I looked down at the sandwich, reminding me of every little thing

Ash had done for me over the last year. I took a bite, swallowing down the sudden bout of pain that had been rising up.

Nate didn't say anything. He sat and smiled, dipping his chips in the yolk of his egg. I never would have thought something as simple as a sandwich could make me miss Ash so much. If... no, *when* we meet again, I would make sure to let him know how grateful I was for everything.

*****

The next day went much the same as the last. I spent hours staring at that damned box, hoping and praying for something to happen, but it never did.

*****

Day three of my training started with a sudden downpour on the way to Anna's. I huddled under a small balcony on the road opposite Marcus' residence, wishing for it to be over quickly, and reminding myself I needed to obtain a jacket for such weather. Again, I'd have to leech money from someone. After five minutes, the rain wasn't showing any signs of letting up, and I was considering running over to Marcus' when I felt someone at my back.

"I told you we'd meet again," he said. I turned to find Russell with an umbrella, which he held over me. "I saw you from the window, and thought you might need some help. It wouldn't do you any good to go catching a cold now, would it?"

"I was just on my way to Anna's for my training," I said.

"Ah, yes. Marcus told me about your new-found ability. Come, I'll walk with you."

"You don't have to do that."

"I don't mind. I have nothing else to attend to, and our introduction the other day was cut short."

"Well," I started, my arms wrapped tight around me beginning to tremble from the wind and rain. "If you're not doing anything else, I do need to get to Anna's soon. She'll be pissed if I'm late."

Russell laughed as we started walking down the street. "That does sound like Anna. So, how are you finding our fair city?"

"Can't say much for the weather, but the people have been really nice."

"Good old British weather. Some things never change. Still, Aldar has a certain charm to it. You should see it from above."

"Above?"

"On the old London Eye, of course. You've seen the giant wheel along the river, no doubt?" I nodded, remembering the sight of it lit up against the night sky on the day I arrived in Aldar. "If you ride to the top, you can see for miles around. It is quite the sight. Perhaps, you would allow me to show you sometime?"

I stopped and turned to face Russell. "What are you doing?"

"Whatever do you mean?"

"This. Being all nice to me. Offering to show me places. You don't even know me."

He smirked. "Maybe I want the chance to get to know you better."

I felt a sudden tightness in my chest, and the urge to get away from the situation as quickly as possible. "I, ummm... Thanks, for the help, but I think I can make it the rest of the way on my own now." I turned and began walking off once more, the rain beating against my damp clothes and skin.

"Mikhail." A hand caught my wrist. I gritted my teeth and looked over my shoulder. "At least take the umbrella. You need it more than I do." He placed the umbrella in my hand, and then he was gone.

*****

I stormed the rest of the way to Anna's, my head down and hidden beneath the black umbrella. When I got there Anna was waiting at the door. She took me inside and handed me a towel.

"I was beginning to wonder if something had happened to you," she said. I cast my gaze to the stone floor. "Did something happen?"

"No. It's nothing."

"It doesn't look like nothing to me."

I sighed and started to dry my hair. "It's just some vampire that's been showing an interest in me."

"In a blood-sucking kinda way, or something else?"

"Something else... I think. I don't even know."

"Do you know their name?"

"Russell."

"Oh."

"You know him?"

Anna rolled her eyes. "Everybody knows Russell. He is Marcus' progeny, after all. Take my advice and stay clear of him. He is not to be trusted. But enough of that, let's get on with your training."

Anna took the towel from me and brandished a dagger in my face. She held it by the blade, urging me to take hold of it. I grabbed the hilt and examined it. Not even silver, I thought. It was probably for the best that it wasn't silver, for Anna's sake. I'm not saying I hated her, but there were a few times when I felt like I could stab her.

"We're going to try something different today," she said.

"And what am I supposed to do with this?" I asked. "You said it's about mind, not body."

"If you'd give me a chance to explain..." Anna threw her hands into the air. "The blade is to help with your visualisation, since you don't seem to understand what we're trying to achieve here."

"What are we trying to achieve?"

Anna sighed. "Manipulating the shape and nature of your magic. You mentioned that the first time it happened, you were slashing at a vampire's throat with a knife, correct?"

"So you want me to use my magic as an extension of this dagger?"

"Yes!" Anna cheered. "Finally, you've understood something."

I glared at her. "Maybe you just suck at teaching."

She glared back. "I'll suck at more than that if you keep this attitude up. It's not like I wanted to take on this assignment. Now, get to work. I want you to run your magic down the edge of the blade and use it to slash at the box."

I took a few steps back from the table and stretched my arm out towards the box, making sure I couldn't reach it with the dagger. The wind blew outward and I channelled it down my arm, across the sharp edge of the blade. Trying to keep it tamed across such a small area was more difficult than I imagined. It was no wonder I hadn't accomplished anything yet. When I thought I had it under control, I lifted my arm and swung the dagger. And just like before, nothing happened. I grunted in frustration and tried again, and again, and again.

"You're releasing your magic too soon," Anna said. "There's no point in creating a sharp edge if you're going to let it diffuse before it hits the target."

I took a deep breath and repeated the process, focusing on keeping my magic in check. I swung again, and to my surprise a small scratch appeared on the surface of the box.

"Finally," Anna said. "Now we're making some progress."

"It's only a scratch," I said, pouting. It was nothing like what Anna could manage. I wondered how long it might take me to reach that level of skill, if it had taken me over two days of training to manage a tiny scratch.

"Now, get out. I have stuff to do."

"What? You're supposed to be training me!"

"I still have a life." Anna scowled. "Besides, you don't need me to practice. I've given you the tools, and now it's up to you to figure out how best to use them. Take the box if you have to, and practice on keeping that sharp edge until you can do it without thinking. If you can manage that, then try it without the dagger."

"Fine." I sighed and handed the dagger back to Anna.

"Don't you need this?" she asked, raising an eyebrow.

"I've got my own," I replied, picking up the box.

"Well, good luck."

"Whatever," I muttered and headed back up the stairs and outside.

*****

The rain had calmed at least, and I walked back to Daniel's room. Daniel wasn't there so I continued practising in peace and quiet, until Daniel and Nate showed up an hour or so later. They watched curiously as I swung the dagger, its blade whistling through the air.

Nate cheered whenever a scratch appeared on the box.

"You gonna tickle that box to death?" Daniel asked.

"I'm focusing on technique, not power," I said, gritting my teeth.

Daniel and Nate watched a little while longer, until they got bored and went to make some food. I paused my training for a short while to eat with them – steak pie, chips and peas. At this rate, I was going to start putting on weight. I made a mental note that I needed to exercise more than just my mind.

As the night drew on, I reached the point where I had enough control over my magic to attempt it without the dagger. It was much harder than I thought, trying to create that same flow of magic without the blade to guide its path. My first few attempts yielded nothing but frustration, but soon I managed to make a small dent in the outer layer of the cardboard. It wasn't even close to the scratches I could make with the dagger, but at least it was something. I gave up after that, deciding it would be better to go for a jog and clear my mind. Daniel joined me, taking me along the river where we could really stretch our legs. Daniel kept pulling ahead of me. He jogged on the spot, waiting for me to catch up before racing off again, and as we started back, a cold fog began to set in over the city.

That morning, I went to bed exhausted. I was both physically and mentally drained. I didn't even have the energy to complain when Daniel rolled over in his sleep and put an arm over me. To be honest, I didn't mind it. It wasn't anything at all like when Ash cuddled up to me. It was friendly, comforting and warm. There was no awkwardness about it, just two people enjoying a bit of human contact and body heat. I laughed to myself as my eyes closed, because if anyone had tried to snuggle with me a few weeks ago, they would have ended up on the floor.

Chapter 21

"Hey, sleepyhead. Time to wake up," Daniel said, giving my shoulder a quick nudge.

"No," I grunted and rolled over.

"Yes, I'm afraid so."

I ventured to open one eye. Daniel was sitting on the edge of the bed in his boxers, pulling on a pair of socks.

"It's not even starting to get dark," I said.

Daniel stood and went to the window. He opened the blinds, letting the sunlight flood into the room, stabbing at my eyes. I screwed my eyes shut.

"Up. Now!"

"Why?" I moaned.

"We're going over to Violet's, remember?"

I sat up and yawned, using one hand to cover my mouth and the other to shield my eyes from the glaring light. "Why didn't you tell me?"

"I did, didn't I?"

"No."

"Ah, well I meant to. Anyway, it doesn't matter now. Hurry up or we'll be late. You don't wanna be late with Violet, trust me."

With a heavy sigh, I dragged myself out of bed and plodded into the bathroom. I had a nice hot shower, and as always, time seemed to fly by. Daniel was soon banging on the door, urging me to hurry. After drying myself off, I brushed my teeth and exited the bathroom with a towel around my waist.

Daniel had on a pair of blue jeans and a deep green shirt with the sleeves rolled up that brought out the colour of his eyes. I wasn't sure if we were supposed to be dressing up a little – not that I had much choice with my limited wardrobe – so I picked out a pair of black jeans and sweater. When I was dressed, we went next door to make sure Nate was ready. Daniel knocked once.

"Hang on a second," Nate called out.

"It's time to go," Daniel replied, trying the door handle. It was unlocked. We went inside to find Nate hopping about, trying to pull on a pair of jeans. Daniel slapped his face with the palm of his hand, and then shook his head. "Didn't you set an alarm?" he asked.

"I forgot," Nate replied, slipping into a light blue jumper.

With Nate finally dressed, we began our walk to Violet's house. As with the day before, dark grey clouds swelled in the sky, threatening to rain down on us.

"How much farther?" I asked as the first drops began to fall.

"Just over the bridge," Nate said, pointing into the distance. I recognised the bridge from earlier that morning, when Daniel and I went for a run. As we crossed the river, there was a flash of light. Seconds later, a loud rumbling rolled through the air, and the skies opened up in a deluge of giant raindrops. We ran the rest of the way, but it was already too late. Violet's doorbell rang as we huddled under the small porch. Sebastian opened the door. He blinked for a moment, and then laughed hysterically.

"Didn't you think to bring an umbrella?"

"Is something wrong?" Violet asked.

"We're gonna need some towels," Sebastian shouted to her.

"Come on in," he said. "Leave your shoes by the front door and come sit next to the fire to dry off."

"Oh dear," Violet said as she looked at the three of us huddled around the open fire. She handed us each a towel, which we used to dry our hair and faces. "Did you not think to bring an umbrella with you?"

"That's what he said." Daniel laughed, inclining his head towards Sebastian.

It didn't take too long for us to dry off, especially after Nate decided the fire wasn't nearly ablaze enough. Sebastian was in and out of the kitchen, offering us hot drinks and checking on the food. The smell coming from the kitchen drifted through the house, teasing our noses and stomachs.

"Daniel told me you're training with Anna," Violet said. "How's that going?"

"I'm starting to get the hang of it," I said. "But it's much harder than I thought." If there had been a piece of paper or cardboard at hand, I would have demonstrated it for them. Instead, I settled for a brief explanation of what I had learned and was trying to accomplish. I left out the part about what my ability could do to people. Daniel was still the only person I had confided in, and he was sworn to secrecy.

"Sounds complicated," said Sebastian. I often forgot he was an ordinary human, having no supernatural ability other than being able to communicate telepathically with Violet, which I hadn't seen them use all that often. And by that, I mean they usually spoke out loud to each other. Of course, I couldn't be sure how much they kept to themselves.

When the food was ready, we sat down at a circular wooden table. Sebastian and Violet brought in the food – lamb chops with potatoes, carrots and green beans. At last, a real meal. Violet sat down with us. She had a small plastic pouch filled with blood in her hand.

She must have caught me looking because she said, "You can buy them at the supermarket here."

"They even sell werewolf blood," Daniel said. "But it's damn expensive compared to the ordinary stuff."

"Because it's better?" I asked.

"No." Daniel shook his head. "There's not many werewolves around at the moment. Still, making a quick donation is good for earning a few extra credits on the side."

"They come in different flavours too," Violet said enthusiastically. "I prefer B-positive, but it's a little less common than the other types."

In my mind, I imagined a large factory with people on a conveyor belt, heading inside a strange machine that sucked out their blood and packaged it in neat little pouches. I shuddered. Maybe it was more like a tax for living in the city.

When we had finished the meal, we said thanks and decided to wait out the storm.

"Oh, that reminds me," Violet said. She rushed upstairs and appeared seconds later, standing in front of me. "Close your eyes."

I let out a long breath, but did as she asked. I hated surprises, and over the last few weeks I had had more than my fair share of bad ones. There was movement on either side of me, and then a warm weight on my shoulders. I opened my eyes, realising it was a black jacket with a grey fleece inner layer.

"We thought you could do with something to protect you from the rain and cold," Sebastian said.

"You guys shouldn't have," I said, mumbling a little under my breath. Heat rushed to my cheeks as everyone's eyes were on me.

"Please, it's the least we could do for you," Violet said. "And you'll need it if we're to head back to Rachat soon."

My eyes lit up at the mention of going back home.

"Don't get ahead of yourself," Sebastian said. "We may not even be chosen for the assignment."

"Nah, we will," Nate said. The room lit up as a bolt of lightning tore across the sky.

"We have two people who know the city," Violet said. "Marcus would be a fool not to choose us to spearhead the assault."

"I suppose," Sebastian conceded. "But I don't like the idea of going up against this Verloren, or whoever it is."

Thunder clapped in the distance.

"You worry too much, Dear," Violet said, gripping his hand. "How powerful can a single pure-blood be?"

"I'd rather not find out," Sebastian replied.

"We have a nice team," Nate said. "And now Mik's developing a physical ability too. What's the worst that could happen?"

"Don't tempt fate," Daniel said, smacking Nate across the back of the head.

Another bolt of lightning lit up the evening sky. The deep roar followed shortly afterwards Dark was fast approaching, and the storm was showing no signs of letting up. Anna would be waiting for me.

"Do you need to go?" Sebastian asked, catching me staring out of the window and up at the sky.

"Yeah. I just wish it would stop raining first." The wind blew harder, battering the window with a barrage of raindrops.

"That would be a nice ability," Nate said, "being able to control the weather."

Everyone agreed. Unfortunately, we didn't know anyone with that ability, so I would just have to deal with it. At least now I had some protection against the harsh elements, and Violet offered to walk with me, which I was thankful for, especially since she brought an umbrella with her. She didn't bother with a jacket or any warm clothes though. It must be nice being a vampire, not having to worry about such things, I thought. When we reached Anna's place, the door flew open before I could reach it.

"You're late again," Anna growled. She looked up at my escort. "Hello, Violet," she said coldly.

"Anna," Violet replied, her voice carrying not a single trace of emotion. She turned to me and said, "Take care, and I'll see you again soon." She smiled, and then in a flash she was off down the road.

"What's the deal with you and Violet?" I asked as we descended into the basement. I hung my jacket over the back of the chair and sat down.

"Long story," Anna replied, setting another box in front of me. "Now, show me how far you've come."

"We've got all night," I said, prying. "Unless you're gonna kick me out early again."

Anna laughed. "No, we've got all night, but it's clear you haven't spent much time around vampires."

"How come?" I asked, standing to take my position away from the box.

"Because, when a vampire says it's a long story, we're usually talking a few hundred years. It would take several nights to explain the history between myself and Violet."

"Oh. I hadn't thought of that," I said. I decided I wasn't going to get anything out of Anna on that particular topic, so I focused on sending the flow of magic down my arm. With one quick swing of my arm, I managed a tear in the outer layer of the cardboard. A bit of rest seemed to have done me some good.

"Not bad," Anna said. "But swinging your arm will only give away your attack. Part of our strength lays not in the power of our attack, but the fact that it is invisible to those without a psychic ability."

I spent the rest of the night trying to achieve the same result, while keeping my arms by my side. I found it much easier than the first night, though I was back to only scraping the surface of the box, and not even breaking the first layer. The equivalent of a paper cut, Anna called it.

At times the whole thing felt so repetitive I wanted to scream. Still, I was determined to see it through, if only to show that damn box who was in control. Most of all, I remembered I was doing it for everyone in Rachat, to free them from the deceit of the Silver Dawn, and the possible grasp of a pure-blooded vampire. But also, I was doing it for Ash. The last thing I needed was to lose control of my magic. Losing him would be awful enough. Accidentally killing him myself, would be unthinkable.

*****

By the end of our session, I had what I thought was a decent control over my magic without using my arms, but I was reaching the point where I was too drained to continue, and the results were starting to deteriorate. I left Anna's house a couple of hours before sunrise. The storm had passed over, leaving behind only a fine drizzle. When I arrived back at Daniel's room, it was empty, sat in complete darkness. He must have come and gone because there was some food left on the table with a note:

'Made you something to eat for when you get back. Daniel. P.S. The research centre called. They want you to go down there sometime today. I'll explain when I get back if you're still awake.'

I sat down and ate the cheese and salad sandwich, pondering over what the research centre wanted with me. Perhaps, they had found something in the files Daniel had liberated, or maybe they wanted to run some tests on me. Whatever it was, Daniel said he would explain so I pushed it to the back of my mind and went to sleep. I felt strangely alone and cold in the bed. I missed the extra heat and comfort of another person's breathing, even if Daniel did snore from time to time.

*****

When I awoke, I felt the familiar arm draped lazily over me and I pulled it tight against me.

"Can I have my arm back?" Daniel mumbled.

"You're warm," I muttered. Daniel had told me all shape shifters were slightly warmer than humans. "You're like an extra blanket."

"Well, this blanket needs to get up." Daniel laughed. "And so do you."

"What did the research centre want?"

"They want a fresh blood sample to analyse and check against your blood report."

When we were showered and dressed, Daniel led me to the hospital. We checked on Nate on our way out, but there was no answer. The entrance to the research centre was at the back of the large, sterile-white building, sectioned off by two electronically locked doors. A bulky security guard sat the desk outside.

"Mikhail Hart, here to see you about a blood sample," he droned over the telephone. A couple of seconds later he said, "Go on through," and entered a code into the control panel. The doors buzzed and swung inward.

A dark-skinned man greeted us on the other side. He wore a long white jacket, with multiple pens of different colours clipped into his pocket. "Hi, I'm Doctor Reid," he said, shaking our hands. "Please come this way."

Doctor Reid led us through the corridors and to a small lab, where I could see the files spread out along one of the desks. There were two others in the room, wearing the same lab coats, busying themselves reading through the files and various books. I was seated on a small chair while Doctor Reid, whose name I later learned was Adam, explained what was happening.

"The reports mention some kind of anomaly in your blood work," he said. "However, they don't go into any detail on the matter. We want to take a sample so we can examine it for ourselves. Is that okay with you?"

I agreed and rolled up my right sleeve so a tourniquet could be wrapped around my arm. It was tight and uncomfortable, and I could see the vein in my arm start to bulge. Adam poured some alcohol onto a piece of cotton wool and wiped my arm. It felt cold as the alcohol evaporated. I looked away upon seeing the needle, hissing as it pierced my skin and the blood began to flow down the tube into a blood bag. My head began to swim. Blood wasn't usually a problem for me, but this was my blood, and that's a different story altogether. When enough was collected, the tourniquet was released and the needle removed. Adam pressed a small bandage to the spot where the needle had been, asking me to hold it in place and apply a small amount of pressure. He placed the blood bag into a refrigerated storage unit against the far wall.

"There's a number of tests we want to run on it," he said. "Hopefully, we'll be able to decipher these reports properly now."

I tried to stand, but my legs were a little shaky so I had to sit back down. Both Daniel and Adam urged me to sit still and relax until I recovered.

"We've been trying to get in contact with your friend, Nathaniel Summers, as well," Adam said. "If we could get another sample from him to compare with his file too, it would greatly assist us with our research."

"Good luck with that," Daniel said. "He's been out all night, and he's terrified of needles."

I shook my head, wondering if I heard Adam correctly. Why would Nate have a file? Daniel had said the files were from the Academy. Everyone who entered the military had to be examined, both physically and mentally, which meant having a blood test done. But Nate told me he refused to join. When we left the hospital I told Daniel what I was thinking.

"He could have started enrolling, and then pulled out after the tests," he said.

"Maybe, but I don't see why he would have lied about it."

"You'll have to ask him that."

*****

Nate still wasn't back by the time we returned. I went to Anna's, still trying to figure out why Nate would lie about joining the army, but I couldn't come up with any reasonable answers. That night, Anna had a surprise for me.

"This is the last night you'll be seeing me," she said, almost smiling. Whether or not it was because she was pleased with my progress, or happy to finally be rid of me, was debatable. My money was on the latter. "From now on, you need to focus on putting more power behind your magic."

"You think I'll be able to master it tonight?" I asked, surprised. Anna had never shown any faith in my skill.

"No," she said bluntly. "But once I've got you started, you'll be able to practice any time you like, on your own. There'll be nothing left for me to teach you. Well, nothing that I could teach in the time frame Marcus has set."

"Like what?"

"Creating multiple focus points for starters. That alone could take months to master." Anna tore into the box in multiple places simultaneously, just to show off. "Of course, if you have questions, you're free to stop by, as long as I'm not busy."

I nodded.

"So, power. I'm sure you already know this, but your ability is linked to your own emotions. The stronger the emotion you pour into the magic, the stronger the resulting magic will be. However, it's not simply enough to think of something you feel strongly about, because the more powerful the magic, the harder it will be to control. That's why I've had you focus on control until now."

"Makes sense," I said.

"All right, then you're free to leave and practice to your heart's content. I wish I could say it's been a pleasure, but quite frankly, you can be a pain in the backside."

I scowled at her and she laughed. "For what it's worth, thank you."

"Whatever," she muttered. I began walking up the stairs. "If you see Marcus anytime soon, make sure to tell him my debt is settled for having to put up with your sorry ass. And, Mik." I paused at the door. "Good luck."

For a second, I thought I saw Anna smile, but just as quickly, it was gone. I was actually a little saddened that I wouldn't be seeing Anna any more, because I knew there was still more she could teach me, no matter how long it would take. But I had to admit, it would be convenient to practice on my own schedule, not having to worry about conserving my energy for the night.

*****

I began practising as soon as I reached Daniel's room. Anna definitely hadn't been wrong about it being harder to control as I increased the power behind each wave. I would have to increase the power bit by bit. By the time Daniel returned, I had managed a small tear. It wasn't an all-the-way-through tear, but it was an improvement nonetheless.

"You're back early," he said. "Nate's in his room if you wanna go talk to him."

I was in need of a break anyway, so I popped over to Nate's room, intent on confronting him about the inaccuracy of his stories. I hesitated as I reached the door. It sounded like Nate was talking to someone. It wasn't clear what he was saying, but he sounded a little angry. I knocked on the door anyway, and a few seconds later it opened.

"Hi, Mik. Did you need something?" he asked, peering out from behind the door.

"I need to ask you something," I said. Nate's brow furrowed, but he let me in and parked himself on the end of his bed. "You been thinking out loud again?"

"Yeah." Nate looked away from me. "You wanted to ask about my file, right?"

"Daniel told you?"

Nate nodded. "Truth is, I originally said yes to them. I tried to pull out later and... well, you know the rest of the story."

"Then why didn't you say that to begin with?"

"I dunno." Nate sighed. "Maybe I was just ashamed."

"There's nothing to be ashamed about," I said. "Everyone in Rachat has been deceived by them. How were we supposed to know something was up?"

"Yeah, I know. And I shouldn't have lied to you."

"So what made you change your mind about the army?" I asked.

"You remember how I told you about Shannon?"

"Yeah."

"Do you remember her last name?"

I had to think about it for a minute. Normally, I didn't pay much attention to what was happening in the city, but when a Daeva supposedly loses control of their powers, kills a few people, and has to be shot, it's difficult not to hear the stories. I knew it began with an 's'. Sanders? Saunders? Summers? That was it, Shannon Summers. Then the realisation smacked me in the face.

"But that's your–"

"She was my twin sister," Nate said, interrupting me. "We'd known about each other's abilities for a while. After the army found me, I knew it wouldn't be long before they discovered her too. I tried to convince her to join, and she refused. I'm sure you can work out the rest."

A heavy weight sat in my stomach. I felt like an idiot, trying to unravel some big conspiracy when there was a relatively simple explanation. It seemed I had a habit of unearthing painful memories. First Ash, then Daniel, and now Nate too. I really had to try and stop doing that. I could see Nate was hurting, his shoulders slumped and his breath coming in short gasps, so despite my better judgement I sat down next to him and put an arm around him. He didn't cry, but a few tears slid down his cheek. Now I understood why Nate wanted revenge so bad.

Chapter 22

It was almost a month since the incident at Boursac. I spent much of my time focused on training my ability. In the last two days, I had come pretty far, and was now tearing through boxes with ease. There were, however, only a limited number of boxes to use, so I had to find a new practice target. The walls of an abandoned house down the road that was due for demolition served this purpose perfectly. It was a lot tougher than cardboard, but soon I was able to build up enough power, and keep it under control, to leave behind a decent-sized scratch. They weren't very deep dents I was making though, and I knew there was still a lot of room for improvement.

When I wasn't slashing at walls with my mind, I was either exercising the rest of my body, or hanging out with Daniel and Nate. We went back to The New Moon one night, which ended with Nate having to be carried home by Daniel. Amusing as it was to watch, I didn't appreciate the long hug and 'I love you, man,' he gave me. Still, I found it hard to blame him when I kept telling myself it was my fault. And if Anna's advice was anything to go by, all I could do was wait and hope he moved on.

The second night, we went to a movie theatre. We watched an old slasher-horror movie called *'Halloween'*. I jumped out my skin several times, which Violet found hilarious. In my opinion, being a vampire is cheating when it comes to horror films. A few times I started talking to the characters. 'Don't go in there,' I'd tell them, or 'Turn around!' Then someone in the audience would scream, and it would be enough to startle me. In my defence, it was the first horror film I had ever seen, so I was going in completely blind. Of course, the others laughed, probably wondering how it was possible for a trained soldier to scream and jump so much during one film. To be honest, I was wondering the same thing myself.

Daniel, Nate and I were planning on going to the theatre again, but our plans were interrupted when Violet came knocking at the door as we ate.

"We've been summoned," she said. "Meet outside Marcus' residence in half an hour." And just like that, she was gone.

"So much for our plans," Nate muttered.

"Just think how much free time we'll have if we manage to take down the Silver Dawn," Daniel said.

"Just think how much we'll not get paid too," Nate replied.

Daniel grinned. "True. We might have to start pimping you out for some extra credits."

"Very funny." Nate pouted. I stifled a laugh.

*****

After finishing our food, we began the short walk to meet Violet and Sebastian. Leigh came out to greet us, and took us into the library, where Marcus was busy discussing something with Adam. They were hunched over the desk, looking at a pile of papers.

Marcus stood as we approached them. "Thank you for arriving at such short notice," he said. "Doctor Reid was just explaining the results of the analysis on Mikhail's blood." Marcus nodded to Adam.

"Well, as the files described, we found something a little off with the blood sample."

"A little off?" Like what?" I asked.

"To put it simply, we found a large number of abnormal blood cells in the sample we took. If I didn't know any better, I'd say you had been bitten and were becoming a vampire."

"But–?" Nate said, urging him to continue.

"But if that were the case, then the vampiric cells would be attacking the regular blood cells. In your case, that wasn't happening. They just seem to co-exist. Honestly, I've never seen anything quite like it. By all accounts, you should be growing fangs right now."

"So what does this mean?" Daniel asked.

Adam shrugged. "Honestly, I'm not sure. As far as I can tell, the Daeva are humans that have been infected by a vampire, but are somehow immune to it."

"Then I'm a living vampire," I said. But the questions still remained. Why was I immune to it? Why were any of us immune? And more importantly, how were they finding out who was immune and infecting them?

"That's a good way to put it," Adam said.

Nate laughed and slapped me on the back. "Who cares what we are? At the end of the day, we're still us. And that's what matters, right? So don't go getting all mopey, okay?"

"I'm not upset about it," I said. "I just want to know the truth for once."

Marcus coughed. "Moving on." He lifted a tiny velvet bag, tied with a golden rope, and threw it to Violet. "Keep this with you. The magic contained within should allow you to pass through Verloren's seal."

Daniel wrinkled his nose. "Do I wanna know what's in that?"

Leigh smiled. "Probably not. And whatever you do, do *not* open it. Once opened, the magic will be broken."

"Understood," Violet said. She stuffed the pouch into her pocket. "When do we leave?"

"Tomorrow evening," Marcus replied. "We're still in the process of contacting the others who will be accompanying you, and I'll have to bring them up to speed on the issue of the pure-blood"

"How many others?" Violet asked.

"Ten."

"Only ten?" Nate exclaimed. "You wanna take down a city with only fifteen people?"

"We do not mean to destroy the city," said Marcus. "The citizens of Rachat, including their soldiers, are innocents. We merely wish to remove their corrupt leadership."

"And then what?" I asked. "What's to stop someone from assuming power and continuing the war?"

"I realise it will not be easy–"

"Not easy?" I yelled, my fists clenched. "These people believe you guys caused the plague that wiped out most of the planet. They believe if they associate with you, in any way, that it's gonna happen again. So tell me, how do you plan to convince them that the Silver Dawn was wrong?"

"Do not misunderstand my intentions, boy," Marcus growled. "This is about ending a war. We will remove the Silver Dawn and attempt to show the people their lies, but if they will not listen, then there is little we can do for them and they are on their own. We can hardly force them into anything."

"Without leadership, the city will fall into chaos. Without Verloren's magic, they will be left open to attacks from other vampires. You'll be leaving them there to die!"

"And what would you have us do?" Marcus snapped. "The best we can do is hope to convince some of them, and perhaps others will follow. We would be willing to take them into our city, but if they will not accept then we reach an impasse."

"So you'd give up on them?" I felt a hand on my shoulder. I shrugged it off and began to storm out of the library. I stopped halfway to the door. "And to think I actually believed you were the good guys in all this, but all you care about is winning your stupid war," I said, before continuing out of the mansion, slamming the doors on my way out.

I kicked at the gravel outside the porch, feeling the rage swell up inside me. And it wasn't just anger, because I could feel my magic building too. I had to release it somehow before it overflowed and I lost control again. "Fuck!" I shouted, directing all my anger onto a nearby tree, leaving behind a deep scar down the length of the trunk and severing a few twigs.

"Damn, remind me not to get on your bad side," Daniel joked as he stepped out the front door. I might have laughed, but I wasn't in the mood.

"What do you want?"

"I think you're right," he said. "I can't in all good conscience leave those people there to die. So, after this is over, I'll be behind you one hundred percent."

"Thanks," I said. I took some deep breaths to calm myself down. "But what can two people do?"

"Two?" Sebastian said from the doorway. "I think you underestimate us. Violet's kicking up a pretty big shitstorm in there right now."

The edges of my lips crept upwards.

"Any plans?" Daniel asked.

"Exposing the pure-blood seems to be the best option," Sebastian said.

"But that's only the first step," I said. "Even if they renounce the Silver Dawn, there's no guarantee they'll change their beliefs on vampires too. And that's assuming the knowledge of the pure-blood doesn't make them even more afraid of vampires."

"A new leader would have to be appointed quickly to stop the city from going into anarchy," Daniel said. "If we can sway that person, then perhaps they can begin to change the way people think."

"But what would we convince them with?" I asked.

"Evidence of the pure-blood working with the Silver Dawn," said Sebastian. "Maybe the corpse would be enough, though it would be far easier to bespell a few influential people."

"General Marsten," I said. Daniel and Sebastian both looked at me. "He's one of the most powerful people in Rachat, and one of the most well known. I assume he's in on the whole thing since he's been doing the dirty work. If he were to confess in public, then it might be enough to shake the public's faith."

"Kill the pure-blood, compel the Silver Dawn's leadership into a public confession... it could work," Daniel said.

"We should let the others know."

"Already done," Sebastian said. "Marcus seems to be agreeing."

"That's cheating." They laughed and I joined in. It felt so good to laugh that a few tears trickled down my cheeks. I was still pissed off though. Whether or not Marcus was now agreeing, he had been ready to abandon everyone in the city. But I guess that's how vampires are, especially the older ones. Overly practical.

When Violet and Nate emerged from the building, they informed us that Marcus had agreed to the plan, but only under the condition that the vampires kept a low profile during the aftermath, to avoid any suspicion.

"We're meeting at the tunnel entrance at seven, tomorrow evening," Violet said. "It'll take at least an hour to get there, so I want you at my place by half-five at the latest."

"Sure thing, Boss." Daniel gave Violet a quick mock-salute. "You can count on me to get these two sleepyheads up."

Nate and I glared simultaneously at Daniel.

*****

We spent much of the night packing, and searching for extra supplies for me. Daniel had an extra rucksack, and Violet said she had a spare sleeping bag at her place. She brought it over while we finished packing. I made sure to pack my toothbrush and some toothpaste, a spare change of clothes, and a few pairs of underwear and socks. Once the basics were packed, we went to a nearby all-night store to pick up a few extras. We bought energy bars and food supplements mostly, enough to keep us going a little longer between food stops.

Before we went to bed, I double checked I had packed the knife Nate gave me. I moved it from where I originally packed it in the main compartment to the side pocket where I could get to it easier. Having a new ability that could do physical damage was all well and good, but unlike Nate's ability, it wasn't enough to deal lethal damage to a vampire. Still, it might be enough to incapacitate them for a short while, as it had done with Cynthia. With everything ready, we settled down to sleep.

"Scared?" Daniel asked.

"A little. You?"

"We're going up against the big bad this time," he said. "Who knows how many of us will survive?"

"We'll survive."

"How can you sound so sure?"

"Because," I said, my voice barely more than a whisper, "I can't bear to think of the alternative."

Daniel placed a hand on my shoulder, but said nothing. He didn't need to say anything. I felt the uncertainty in his touch that said he wished he could believe everything would be okay. I wondered if he was thinking back to his vision in the tunnel, of watching people around him die. That wouldn't happen. It couldn't. I needed to hang onto that tiny thread of hope because it was all I had. I reached one hand up and placed it on top of Daniel's.

*****

I was the first to wake up that afternoon. I glanced at the clock and noticed I still had an hour or so before I needed to be up. My eyes closed, but sleep evaded me. A sense of unease settled in my stomach. Whether it was the fear of going up against a pure-blood, or excitement at the thought of being able to return home, I wasn't sure. All I knew, was I needed to be up and moving. I went into the bathroom and spent a long while standing under the spray of hot water. It was probably the last shower I was going to get for at least a week, so I savoured it as much as I could, until my blushing skin began to tingle.

It was a little before five-thirty when we arrived at Violet's. There was a taxi waiting outside for us, and Sebastian was loading their backpacks into it. By the time we arrived at the tunnel entrance, there was a large crowd gathering. I spotted Marcus and Leigh at the front. Anna was there too, with two female vampires, and a human male. There was also one group of five I didn't recognise; three males and two females, at least three definite vampires that I could spot. Then there were the lines of onlookers either side of the main group. Hordes of humans, vampires, and even a few werewolves sporting their furs had gathered to see us off.

Every now and then, I felt a drop of water hit me on the nose. The sky was dull and black, the moon peeking out from behind a blanket of thick clouds. Wooden torches and bonfires had been lit either side of the tunnel, swaying in the gentle breeze that made the hairs on the back of my neck stand on end. Anna came up to me as I stood watching the crowds swell. People must have been coming from all over the city to watch.

"I thought I might see you here," she said, smiling. "How is your ability coming along?"

"Great," I replied. " Thanks."

"That's nice to hear, but do you think you'll be up to fighting a pure-blood?"

I turned to the nearest wall and flung my magic at it, leaving a deep scratch, and then another, and one more for good luck. Anna opened her mouth in surprise.

"Rachat is my home. My friends are there. Don't underestimate my desire to save them."

"I will keep that in mind."

"Anna," Violet said. "Shouldn't you be off breaking hearts instead of bothering the poor kid?"

Anna snarled, flashing her fangs.

"Your attention, please," Marcus' voice rang clear above the clatter of the crowd.

"We'll settle this another time," Anna said before going back to her group.

"What's the deal with you two?" I whispered.

"Long story," Violet replied. "Now quiet."

"That's what she said," I muttered and turned my attention to Marcus.

"Those of you who stand before me this night, have been selected to take part in what will hopefully be our final battle against the Silver Dawn." The masses cheered. "But the battle will not be an easy one. We face an enemy that we thought extinct for centuries, and one that will prove a most formidable foe. What we fight for is not only our own survival, but for the hopes and dreams of the future, for a world where we do not have to hide. For centuries, we have hidden in the shadows, alone. And for the last century, we have hidden ourselves away yet again, but no more! We will take this battle to the heart of the enemy, and correct the course of our future!"

The crowd clapped and they yelled. They whistled and they howled. When the commotion started to die down, Marcus spoke once more. "And now I present to you the leader of this brave expedition."

From the sides, I saw Russell heading to stand by Marcus' side. There was more cheering, and Violet let out a long groan. I bit my lower lip and silently cursed the world. Was it too much to ask to not have Russell along for the journey?

"Soon," Russell started. The crowd's cheering came to an abrupt stop. "Soon, we will embark on a journey that will change our future. Some of us may never get to see that future, but know that we will not fail. We will avenge those who have fallen, and those who are still yet to fall. Their deaths will not be in vain. And in the years to come, they will be honoured as heroes who gave their lives in pursuit of a just cause, to rid the world of a great evil that has lurked in the shadows since the beginning of time. For freedom!"

Everyone around us applauded, but not Violet. She shook her head.

"We bid you well," Marcus shouted. "May you all return home victorious."

Russell's eyes scanned the crowd. His gaze stopped on me and he strode towards us.

"Mikhail, there you are. I wanted to apologise if I upset you last time we met. Perhaps, I was a little too forward."

I opened my mouth to say that it was okay, when Violet interjected herself between us.

"Don't you have preparations to take care of?" Violet asked.

"I suppose." Russell glared at Violet, then turned to me and smiled. "I look forward to working with you, Mikhail." Without waiting for a reply, he walked back to Marcus' side.

When he was a safe distance away from us, Violet grabbed hold of my shoulders and turned me to face her. "You are never to be alone with that man. Do you understand?"

"Why?" I asked. Admittedly, Russell came off as a little creepy, but I couldn't understand what might prompt a warning from both Anna and Violet.

"Russell is a sadist, especially to those he takes a liking to, which in this case would be you."

"If he's so bad, then why doesn't Marcus stop him?"

"Marcus is blinded by his love for his son," Sebastian said. "He does not see his true colours. He refuses to."

Marcus and Leigh were leaving to head back into the city, and the fifteen of us heading to Rachat began our march into the tunnel. The vampires sped ahead, leaving only Violet to stay behind with the humans.

"How come Marcus isn't coming?" I asked. "If he's that old, then surely he'd be better off helping defeat Verloren."

"Marcus is old, but as far as vampires go, he's relatively weak," Violet replied.

"But I thought you get stronger with age."

"That is true, but we all reach our limit sooner or later. Marcus' limit happens to be lower than most."

"And Russell?" I asked. One of the humans from Russell's group looked over her shoulder at us for a second. Violet put a hand in front of me, waiting until we dropped back from the main group.

"Russell is more powerful than Marcus. He has Marcus wrapped around his little finger," Violet whispered. "Then again, it is only because of Russell that others do not try to usurp Marcus' position. They fear Russell."

"He calls himself the Prince of Aldar," Daniel said. "Cocky little bastard. Whatever you do, don't go anywhere alone while it's dark. Even if you need to go for a piss, take either myself or Violet with you."

I swallowed hard. "Is he that bad?"

"He's persistent," Violet said. "And he's not above using blackmail and mind games to get what he wants. He tried getting to Nate last year."

"What happened?"

"He almost lost an arm, that's what," Nate said. "I think he learned not to play with fire after that."

"Just stick with us and you'll be fine," Daniel said.

"It would be a real shame if he had an accident, or got killed on this mission," Nate whispered.

"Nate, don't do anything stupid," Violet warned him. "As far as we know, he's not guilty of anything other than being a sadistic jerk-ass."

"And right now, he's in charge," Sebastian added. "Without him, this mission will probably go down the drain. Not to mention the fallout when we return to Aldar."

About halfway through the tunnel, we went through a side door, into the service tunnel. Inside the small passageway, I noted the lights did not flicker on once, and there was no more breeze whispering to me. We took out our flashlights and continued on our way. Nate made sure to point out the place where I had lost control, marked by a frenzy of deep slashes in the walls and floor. I hadn't realised the extent of what my ability had done until then, and it was clear why they had to knock me out. It scared me, that I could lose control again. And what if the next time it happened, someone got hurt because of me? What if, like in my hallucination, it was Ash that got hurt?

I could feel the fear inside of me, the doubt at the back of my mind, and the sudden weakness in my knees. It threatened to consume me. But this wasn't the time to doubt myself. After all, this was why I had trained with Anna, to learn to control my magic. I trained so I could become stronger, for myself, for Ash, and for everyone else in Rachat and Aldar. Failure wasn't an option I had the luxury of.

Chapter 23

The short days worked to our advantage, allowing us to spend most of the night travelling. The vampires, especially those in Russell's group, would get quite annoyed if we stopped for too long while it was still dark. Each night, Russell tried several times to initiate a conversation with me. And each time, I tried to brush him off by sounding as uninterested as possible, hoping he would become bored and find someone else to bother.

On the fourth night, we settled down in some old ruins with enough shelter for the daylight-challenged members of our expedition. There was still a few hours until sunrise, but at the pace we were going, those of us who weren't vampires were beginning to tire, and Russell finally allowed a break for us to recover. I sat with Nate and Daniel around the remains of a small fire that had been used to cook our dinner.

"I can't believe it might finally be over in a couple of nights," Daniel muttered to himself. "Sixteen years since I joined the war effort."

"What will you do when it's over?" I asked.

"Well, there's always more bad vampires to hunt. Maybe I'll try to settle down a bit though."

"We haven't seen many 'bad' vampires," I noted out loud.

"Aldar and Rachat are protected against them," Nate said. "Most of the trouble happens closer to the smaller trading towns and outposts."

"What about you?" Daniel asked. "Rachat may not be safe after all this is over."

"I haven't really thought about it," I admitted. Before I could make any decisions, I had to know what Ash wanted to do. Even though Marcus said the people of Rachat would be permitted to stay in their cities, I wasn't sure how many of them would want to take him up on that offer, either because they wouldn't trust the vampires, or they would refuse to leave their homes.

"Look out, here comes trouble." Daniel groaned. I looked up to see Russell sauntering towards us.

"Daniel, I believe it's your turn to patrol." Russell smiled.

"Violet's already on guard," Daniel said.

"Do not disobey me, Daniel."

"I don't take orders from a stuck-up, conceited–"

"Daniel," Nate interrupted him. "Go. I got this."

"You sure?"

"I can handle a jerk like him." Wisps of smoke rose up from the fallen log we were sitting on. Nate lifted his hand to reveal a charred hand print. Daniel turned and walked away into the darkness, shooting Russell a warning glare as he left.

"And how are you, my little Firecracker?" Russell asked, smiling at Nate.

"Great, until you showed up."

Russell laughed and took another step forward. He paused when the ground in front of his foot erupted, spewing forth a jet of flames. He narrowed his eyes at Nate, who smiled back.

"I only came to talk," Russell said. He sat down on a small rock opposite us. "How are you, Mikhail?"

"I'm okay," I said, looking away from him and taking a sip of water.

"That's good to hear. It must be rough on you, with everything that's happened."

"Would be easier if you left him alone," Nate snapped.

"I mean no harm," Russell said. "I'm merely intrigued by his powers."

"Then go talk to Anna," I said.

"But she is not human," he replied. "You live such a fragile and urgent existence. I cannot help but find myself drawn to that."

"You know what happens when the moth gets drawn to a flame," Nate said. The campfire roared to life for an instant, and then died down. Nate stood and stepped over the log, heading back to the small building where Sebastian was sleeping. "Come on, Mik. We're leaving."

"Sure," I said. I didn't bother looking over my shoulder to see if Russell was following, but I hoped he wasn't. We had just reached the building when I heard my name being called. I glanced over my shoulder.

"You forgot this," Russell said, throwing me the water bottle I had left by the fire. I caught it and went inside without saying a thank you.

We sat and talked quietly in one of the empty rooms, until Violet and Daniel returned. As expected, they were both angry at Russell for trying to separate us, but were also glad to hear nothing had happened. With Violet back, we went to sleep. She watched over us until the sun rose and she was sure Russell could not try anything.

*****

When I opened my eyes, I was alone. It was still dark outside, and moonlight spilled in through the open window. A cold wind danced along my skin, biting and nipping, bringing my attention to the fact that I was naked and uncovered. I sat up, looking around.

"You're awake," a deep voice sounded from behind me. I didn't need to look to know it was Russell. My heart leaped into my mouth, beating violently. Where was Violet? Where was anyone for that matter?

In a flash, Russell was on top of me. Looking down the line of his naked body, I could see him raring to go. His lips pressed to mine, cold and tingling. He forced me onto my back, straddling my waist. His hands ran over my chest, pausing to pinch and rub at my hardened nipples. I threw my head back, gasping.

"You like that?" Russell purred.

"Yes," I breathed. His fingers repeated the movement over and over. Inside my mind, I was screaming at myself for not saying no, and for letting him do this to me. And yet, I couldn't bring myself to say the word.

He crawled back to take hold of me in his hands, working me into an erection. His head lowered, tongue darting out to lick the inside of my thigh. I pushed myself up onto my elbows, staring straight into his smouldering eyes. His fangs extended, he bit down into my thigh, the shooting pain making me cry out.

"What's wrong, Mik?"

I opened my eyes. Everyone was still there. I was covered in sweat and struggling to regain my breath.

"Bad dream?" Violet asked. She was laying to my right, behind Sebastian.

"Yeah, bad dream." The sun was beginning to set, painting the sky in a mix of red and orange. I fumbled absently at my thigh, finding no indication that I had been bitten. "I'm gonna get some air," I said, trying to smile.

"All right, don't go too far," Violet said. "And don't be long. Russell will be up soon."

I nodded and pushed myself to my feet. I found a nice quiet spot on the flat roof of a nearby building, and sat with my back to the crumbling chimney pots, staring off into the distance. My first sex dream. Since that night in Rachat, I thought my first would have been with Ash. But no, of all the people, it had to be Russell. Not Ash, my first real friend and lover. Not Daniel, who I had seen naked, or close to it, more times than I could count in the last couple of weeks, and who had snuggled up to me in bed most nights in Aldar. Not even Nate, who had been a good friend to me since we met, and had seemingly developed feelings for me, even if it was my fault they were there. No, it had to be Russell with his smooth pale chest, and dark smouldering eyes. I slapped myself. Something was wrong with me. Perhaps, everything that had happened in the past month had finally gotten to me, and made me snap. I thought my psyche must have been broken and twisted to even be considering Russell. I didn't move until the sun was almost set. By then Violet was up.

"I was just about to come get you," she said.

"Sorry. I had some thinking to do."

"Anything you wanna share?" Daniel asked. He sat up and wiped at his eyes.

I shook my head. "Personal stuff."

The second the sun was down, Russell was at the door of the building. "Everybody up," he shouted. "You've had your rest." There was a collective groan from most of the building.

Daniel and I waited outside with our things while the others finished repacking and eating breakfast.

"Evening, Mikhail," Russell said, appearing at my side out of nowhere. I jumped, my breath escaping me. Daniel gritted his teeth.

"Evening," I replied, trying to steady my breath and avoiding his eyes. He moved to stand in front of me. He was wearing a tight black tank top that showed off every contour of his upper body, just as I dreamed it. Blood rushed to my cheeks.

"What'd you do to him?" Daniel asked, his lips curled.

"I didn't do anything," Russell said, laughing. "He's reacting to me, that's all."

"Beat it," Daniel growled. Russell obliged, smiling at me before he disappeared in a blur. "Did he do something to you after I went on patrol?"

"No. Nate stopped him."

"Then what the hell, Mik?" Daniel snapped. "Please, tell me you don't have a thing for bad boys."

"What? No!" I exclaimed. "I don't know what's happening. I can't explain it."

"Fuck." Daniel kicked at the dirt beneath his feet. "You sure he didn't do anything?"

"Ask Nate," I said. "He didn't leave me alone for a second."

"Well, this isn't good. We'd better tell Violet."

Violet sighed when she heard the news, and suggested I try and suppress any physical reaction to Russell. The last thing I needed was to give him any encouragement. That was harder said than done. I couldn't say I was physically attracted to him, or at least, not consciously. But whenever he got a little too close, I would remember the dream and blush with embarrassment and anger. Not just anger at Russell, but also at myself for even having dreamed such a thing.

*****

The weather had started out nice, if a little chilly, but soon took a turn for the worse. So much worse, in fact, that we were forced to stop and find shelter only a few hours after we had set off. Fortunately, the landscape was littered with ruined towns, and given the size of our group, we didn't have to worry much about upsetting any small nests of vampires. Not that we ever saw any. Perhaps, they saw us coming and went into hiding.

I said a silent thanks to the snowstorm for giving me the chance to rest my feet some more. They were already beginning to feel a little sore. At least this time I had some decent walking boots, unlike the chunky boots the Silver Dawn issued. I curled up inside my sleeping bag and managed to get a few hours sleep while we waited out the worst of the storm. Daniel was watching over me when I woke up. Outside, I could hear the others talking. The blizzard had started to die down.

My throat felt dry. I pulled my water bottle out of its pouch at the side of my rucksack and screwed off the cap. I was about to lift it to my mouth when it was sent flying across the room. Daniel was stood in front of me, his jaw and fists clenched.

"What was that for?" I snapped.

Daniel didn't reply. He crouched on all fours, sniffing at the floor where the water had spilled out. "I'm gonna rip his damn throat out," he growled.

"Daniel?" Violet asked, peering inside.

"Russell spiked his water," Daniel said, turning to look at me.

"What with?" I asked, my body turning cold. Every hair stood on end.

"His blood. Has he had the chance to drink any of yours?"

"No," I replied. "What does this mean? He can't bond with me unless he drinks my blood, right?"

"Unfortunately," Violet said, pausing. "It's not that simple. Your dream earlier. Was Russell in it?"

"Shit," I mumbled under my breath.

"That's a yes then," Daniel said.

"Will the dreams go away?"

"As long as Russell's blood is in your system, he'll be able to enter your dreams," Violet said. "If he's only added a tiny bit to your water, then it should pass in a couple of days. Until then, you should keep a close eye on anything you eat or drink."

"And if he gets some of my blood before then?"

"Then he'll be able to get inside your head whenever he wants, even while you're awake. You'd feel the need to be close to him too, but it won't come to that."

"Russell likes to keep up appearances. As long as there's other people around, he won't force–" Daniel paused, tilting his head to one side. "You hear that?"

"Dammit. Nate," Violet muttered. Both Daniel and Violet rushed outside. I followed as fast as I could. I caught up to them to see Daniel restraining Nate, who was struggling to break free. Sebastian stood next to them, his arms folded.

"Let me go," Nate screamed. "He fucking deserves it, and you know it."

Violet was close by, pinning Russell to a tree by his throat. I walked up to them, noting the burn marks on the nearby trees.

"If you want him, then you'll have to go through us," Violet said.

Russell laughed. His eyes met mine. "I don't know what you're talking about," he said, wincing as the hand around his throat tightened.

"So you deny spiking his water with your blood so you can mess with his dreams?" Violet asked.

"I can't help it if he dreams about me," Russell replied. He caught hold of Violet's wrist, pulling her hand from him. "You forget your place, Daywalker. I may be younger than you, but I am stronger, and I am your superior."

By now, most of the group had gathered to watch the scene unfold.

"Now," Russell started, glancing over at Nate. "I suggest you get your little rat under control, before I do it for you."

Violet clenched her jaw. "Just remember this, Russell. I am not bound by the sun, like you. If you ever pull a stunt like this again, it will be your last."

"Marcus would have you killed."

"I do not care." Violet's lips twisted upwards as she turned to walk back to Nate and the others. "I would gladly pay the price."

"I'm sorry you had to see that," Russell said. "But I do not deal well with death threats."

"And I don't deal well with people invading my dreams. Stay out of my head, or I'll kill you myself."

Russell moved, disappearing from my vision. There was a cold breath on the side of my neck. "You think you can manage that?" he whispered. "If you would give yourself to me, then I wouldn't have to play these games. I could show you a world you've never imagined, where pleasure and pain go hand-in-hand."

I spun round, pulling the knife from its sheath and pressed it to his chest. "If you like pain so much, then be my guest."

Russell threw his head back, laughing. "Since I like you, I'll make you a deal."

"Name your terms."

"I'll stay out of your dreams, and forgive the death threats made against me."

"And in return?"

Russell smirked. "You let me feed from you."

"Not a chance."

"It's hardly an unreasonable request, Mikhail." Russell shrugged.

"What's to stop me from killing you now?" I asked, pressing the point of the knife harder against his chest. He hissed, the blade breaking the skin, then disappeared again. I turned on my heel, expecting him to be at my back. Nothing. My neck felt cold and wet. Russell's tongue licked at the vein that pulsed faster under its touch.

"What's to stop me from taking your blood?" he whispered. "A little taste, that's all I ask for."

"I know what will happen if you drink my blood," I said. "And I know you won't attack me with everyone watching. I also know that Violet, Nate and Daniel will kill you if you take even one drop."

"But I don't plan on taking anything from you. You're going to give it to me."

"He's not giving you anything," Nate snapped.

"Maybe not now." Russell chuckled. "Think about it, Mikhail. For now, I will honour my end of the bargain, but when I return to Aldar, I will inform Marcus of their threats against me." Russell turned to walk away, then paused. "And just so you know, I shared blood with a human in Aldar before we left. I have already informed him of what has happened. Kill me if you wish, but Marcus will still learn of your misdeeds."

Russell moved to disperse the audience, reassuring them that everything was okay.

"This isn't good," Daniel said.

"I would have been prepared to accept punishment for killing him, but I fear he may implicate the rest of you too," Violet said.

"Mik, you know I would never ask you to do as he says."

"But I have no choice, do I?" No-one dared answer. "How bad will it be?"

"The effect will be temporary. A couple of weeks at the most," Violet said. "He either plans to win you over by then, or find the means to have you share blood again."

"Each time you share, the effects become stronger," Sebastian said. "The first time won't be so bad, but if he can coerce you into sharing again, then you will find it hard to resist him. By the third time, you'll be all but trapped."

"Are you trapped?" I asked.

"I could be, if Violet wished it. The line between companion and servant is a fine one."

"What if he's bluffing about the human in Aldar?" Nate said.

"No," Daniel replied. "Russell is devious enough to have thought this kinda thing through ahead of time. And I wouldn't like to take the risk of calling his bluff."

"Will he keep his word?" I asked.

"You can't seriously be considering his offer," Nate said.

"Will he keep his word?" I repeated.

"I believe he will," Violet said. "As much as I hate to admit it, Russell is not one to go back on his word."

"So I just need to resist him for a few weeks, right?"

Violet and Sebastian nodded.

"Mik, you can't do this," Nate said hurriedly. "Please."

"I don't see what other choice we have," I told him. The thought of sharing blood with Russell revolted me, but I couldn't condemn the others to death if there was a way for me to stop it. And as long as we didn't give Russell the means with which to blackmail us again, the effects would be gone before long. My mind was made up. I turned back towards the camp where everyone would be waiting. A hand caught my wrist.

"Please," Nate whispered. "It won't be as easy as you think."

"It's his choice, Nate," Daniel said. "Besides, if you hadn't attacked Russell, then we might not be in this predicament."

Nate's shoulders slumped as he released his grip on my arm. If there was another way, I would have taken it, but we were out of options. I reached the camp and scanned the area for Russell. He wasn't outside. I found him in one of the small buildings with the luggage. He smiled as I approached him. With one quick stroke I took the knife and sliced it across the palm of my hand. Russell lifted my hand to his face, staring into my eyes as he lowered his mouth to the wound. I hissed when his tongue flicked over my palm, causing his smile to widen. His lips locked over the cut, sucking hard. I gasped and gritted my teeth. His eyes stayed locked on mine, staring down the line of my arm. I pulled my hand away from him, feeling a little light-headed when I saw the blood smeared across his lips, and over my hand. Russell knelt down next to one of the bags. He opened a box with some bandages in, and wrapped a small length around my bleeding hand.

"You won't regret this," he whispered in my ear.

"I already do," I said, storming back outside.

'We'll see about that,' his voice echoed in my mind.

Chapter 24

Having Russell inside my head was annoying, to say the least. Telepathy is an absolute bitch to learn how to control. All those random thoughts flying around inside my brain, and Russell must have heard near enough all of them. He heard everything, from how I was hungry, to my feet hurting, to how I wanted to take my knife and see just how far I could jam it into his skull. He grinned at me when he heard that last one.

And then there were the times when I would think of how close to Rachat we were getting, and I began to feel anxious. The urge to be close to Russell, to have him comfort me, at times like those was overwhelming. My God, it was so tempting. Then he would turn to me and smile, inviting me to join him, and I would be reminded of how much I hated him. The anger helped fight back the feelings of anxiety.

Of course, during all this, Russell would happily contribute to my thoughts, to let me know he was listening. I had no privacy at all, and that annoyed the hell out of me. Still, it could have been worse. Russell was at least sticking to his word and staying out of my dreams. Well, besides one rather strange appearance. That dream was likely my own doing, unless Russell secretly fantasised about being a pirate with a wooden leg. I tried not to think about that particular dream too much, since it refused to be contained by both logic and reason.

I spent the next four days wanting to claw at my skull, to remove the seductive voice that purred and chuckled inside it. Finally, we reached our final camp. Rachat sat proudly on the horizon, surrounded by its high steel walls.

"Gather round, everyone," Russell shouted. "Tomorrow, when the sun sets, our infiltration will begin. I'm going to go over our strategy, and then I recommend you all feed and rest up."

Russell's eyes lingered over me when he mentioned feeding. '*Not a chance*', I thought, glaring at him. He smiled back.

"Our main objective is to find and eliminate the pure-blood, who we believe to be Verloren himself. My group and Violet's group will be focusing on accomplishing this."

"What about us?" Anna shouted.

"We cannot afford any interference. You, and your group, are tasked with crowd control. Lure any humans away that might threaten to interfere. I also want you to try and locate the whereabouts of any high ranking officials who might be privy to the Silver Dawn's secrets. The rest of us will be keeping an eye out for them too. In particular, we have been ordered to capture their General, Philip Marsten, as he will be instrumental in winning over the people of Rachat."

I hoped they would kill General Marsten for what he had done, for everything he had taken away from both myself and Nate.

'*I could help you with that,*' the voice in my head whispered. "Any questions?"

There were none, so Russell began designating the daytime patrols to Daniel, Violet and his own werewolf, Leah. He dismissed everyone, and instructed them to prepare for the battle ahead. I went with Violet and the others to eat. After that, we began to settle down for some sleep.

It was still dark outside, the moon beginning to sink through the velvet sky. I lay in my sleeping bag, thinking about what might happen after the battle. Would Ash take me back? Would he want to stay in Rachat? How many people would even believe the truth?

'You shouldn't think about it so hard,' Russell whispered. *'One, it won't change anything. And two, you're starting to give me a headache.'*

I laughed to myself. At least I wasn't the only one experiencing some discomfort because of our connection. Still, I couldn't shake the feeling of unease and anxiety that washed over me, a hollow pit in the bottom of my stomach preventing me from sleeping.

'Come to me.'

'You wish.'

'Wouldn't you like to discuss the fate of your dear ex-General?' he asked.

'No.' I lied. *'Besides, I don't need to go to you for a conversation.'*

The voice in my head laughed. *'I can hear your thoughts. You cannot lie to me. Come, I only wish to talk. You have my word.'*

I let out a long sigh and sat up. It wasn't like I was going to get to sleep any time soon, and I didn't think he would try anything the day before we invaded Rachat.

"You're going to see him, aren't you?" Violet said, keeping her voice low so as not to wake the others. I nodded and Violet and began to stand.

"Alone," I said. "He won't try anything stupid. Not tonight."

"As you wish," she replied, settling back down. "But if you need help, just yell and I'll be there."

I found Russell sitting outside on a large rock, gazing up at the stars. A cold wind blew, rustling his hair. He looked almost peaceful. Serene. He leaned back onto his elbows and looked over at me, smiling.

"Sit," he said, patting the rock. I sat on the edge, leaving as much distance between us as possible.

"You said you wanted to talk, so start talking." I drummed my fingers against the rock.

"First, you need to relax." Russell took hold of my hand. I tried to pull away, but he held tight. "Shhh. I will not try anything. You have my word on that. But you must try to relax."

I pulled harder against his grip, but it was no use. His eyes stared into mine.

"Relax," he repeated, "and then we will talk."

It didn't seem like I had much choice. I closed my eyes and took a deep breath. A cold wave washed over me, taking my anxiousness with it. The knot in my stomach began to uncoil.

"I bet Violet never told you about this." Russell chuckled. "Just as I can feel your anxiety, I can share some of my calmness with you."

"No, she didn't tell me." I let out a long sigh of relief. "But I still wouldn't have said yes if there was any other way."

Russell released my hand. "Then you understand why I had to do what I did?"

"Because you're a sadistic bastard?"

"Perhaps." Russell laughed. He reached over to trace a finger down the line of my neck. "You know, your blood is intoxicating. Regular human blood can get so boring, but yours, Mikhail, is like a fine wine."

"I'll kill you before I let you feed from me again."

"And I do not doubt your words, but there is still time for me to change your mind. I would so very much like to introduce you to my world."

"Is that what you wanted to see me for?" I asked. "To try and change my mind?"

"Maybe a little." Russell smirked. "But I also want to talk to you about this General, who you so want to kill."

"He took everything from me," I said quietly. "Everything."

"And he should be made to pay. I can help you get your revenge, but I do have one condition. I want to watch while you kill him," he said, as though it were the most natural request in the world.

"What? I-I don't understand."

"Then let me show you." Russell pressed a finger to my forehead. I closed my eyes as images bombarded my mind. I saw myself, stood over a table. General Marsten was strapped down, his skin a twisted pattern of cuts and bruises. In my hand was a blood-stained knife. Russell was watching, excited by my handiwork. He walked up to me, his hands going to my face. He cleaned the blood from my face with his tongue and began to strip me, laying me down in a pool of blood.

I jerked away from his touch. "You're sick," I gasped. "Is that what turns you on?"

He laughed. "Amongst other things."

I didn't dare ask what those other things might be. But then again, what could be worse than a torture fetish? I hoped and prayed I would never learn the answer to that question.

"Do I disgust you that much?" Russell asked.

"You can hear my thoughts. Figure it out for yourself." I wasn't in the mood for soothing vampire egos, not that my answer would have been particularly soothing. And then there were the questions I wanted to ask, such as what Russell was planning on doing to me, and why he chose me. Was he planning to torture me too?

"I wouldn't do *that* to you." Russell smirked. "Unless, you want me to. You're much more valuable to me alive and healthy."

"Then what do you want from me?" I asked, pleading. I was sick of the games.

"I'm looking for something a little different," Russell replied. "For two centuries I was content with my temporary playmates, but it does not hold the same appeal as it once did. I seek something new and more permanent."

My mind flashed back to the images he had shown me. "A partner. You want someone to share your hobby with."

"My hobby," he said, chuckling. "Such an interesting way to put it, but you are right. As for why I chose you... I sensed your hate and distrust of the world. And now, through our blood bond, I can see why." He lifted a hand to my face, brushing against my cheek. "Poor little Mikhail, always alone in the world. Always different. Nobody loved you. You hate them for making you the way you are. They created you, and made you into something not entirely human."

I blushed with anger, feeling the choking heat rush up into my face. He had no right to be delving into my past like that.

"You're angry," Russell started. "But that anger isn't only for me. You're angry at the whole world. You have suffered while they continue their ignorant existence, no wiser of the pain they inflict. Yes, such beautiful anger. They should be made to know the pain they have caused. We could educate them together, you and I, in a duet of pain and pleasure."

"No," I whispered. "I'm not like that. I'm not alone anymore. I have friends now. I have... Ash." But I knew my thoughts betrayed me. That urge for revenge, and the pain of being alone until I met Ash, it was still there, lurking somewhere deep inside me like a coiled serpent. Beneath the determination to bring down the Silver Dawn, there was the underlying anger and lust for revenge. And then there was Ash, the shining light amidst the darkness of my soul. Daniel's words echoed in my mind, reminding me that I couldn't let myself give in to the darkness and become one of the monsters. I wouldn't.

"You cling to the memory of love for this Ashley, but answer me this. What brought the two of you together?"

"Don't you speak of him," I snapped, jumping to my feet. My fists clenched so tight my arms were shaking.

"Pain. Your shared pain drew you to each other. Don't you see? Pain is the true higher power in this world. I want to share that power, the exhilaration, with you."

"Fuck you," I yelled, one hand wrapped tight around the hilt of my knife. I drew it from the sheath, pressing the blade up against his throat, and he let me. He stared right at me and smiled. I pressed the knife harder into him, his lips curling as the skin began to smoke.

"What are you waiting for?"

I felt, rather than saw, someone at my side. "That's enough," Violet said, her hand taking hold of my wrist. "Come on, Mik. He's not worth it."

I nodded, and her hold on my wrist relaxed. I started to pull the knife away, and then drew it down across his chest, leaving behind a deep, crimson tear. Russell gritted his teeth and laughed. "I knew you had it in you," he said, clutching his chest. "That anger. That desire to cause pain. You see, we're not so different."

"Enough," Violet snapped. "You are to stay away from Mik."

"I will do as I please," Russell replied. "And you can do nothing to stop me. I bid you good night, Mikhail. Please, take as long as you need to consider my offer."

"He will do no such thing."

Russell chuckled. "Oh, but the seed is already planted. You cannot stop him from thinking about it any more than you can stop me." Russell disappeared, leaving behind only a small trail of dust kicked up into the air.

"Come on," Violet whispered, leading me back to my sleeping bag. I didn't say anything. I pulled the bag tight around me, my body shivering as though all the heat was sapped from me. Someone shuffled closer behind me, and I felt their hand on my shoulder.

"We'll find a way to free you from that bastard," Nate said. "I promise."

I would have shrugged Nate off, but in that moment I needed to feel the warm, comforting touch of someone who was alive. I closed my eyes. Soon the shivering stopped and sleep dragged me under.

*****

That evening, I was last to awaken. I didn't move until Daniel came to make sure I was awake and handed me something to eat. I looked down at the protein bar in its foil wrapper and didn't feel hungry. Right then, I didn't feel much of anything.

When Russell whispered inside my head, I ignored him as much as I could. When he came to me in person, I turned and walked away. Fortunately, he was too busy with last minute preparations to pursue me. Nate and Daniel tried to cheer me up, but I pushed them away. I only wanted some peace and quiet before the inevitable confrontation that sat defiantly on the horizon.

Before long, we were making our way across the barren plains under the cover of darkness, towards the giant steel walls. Two of the vampires went ahead to incapacitate the patrols that walked back and forth along the ramparts. The Silver Dawn never bothered much with night patrols. They believed they were safe from vampires, and the high walls were more than enough protection against humans. Werewolves might have been the only threat to them, but they were a rare sight near the city. Just in case, they kept a few patrols going.

One-by-one, the beams of light atop the walls went out. I wondered as we approached the walls, looming over us, how we were going to get inside.

'We jump,' came the answer before I could ask out loud. Russell put an arm around my waist, and the next thing I knew, I was rising up into the air, looking down as the people below grew smaller and smaller. My stomach lurched into my mouth, and I fought the urge to kick and scream, feeling that it might be somewhat counter-productive to my survival. Russell wouldn't kill me, but falling at this height would. And then the ground was coming closer, faster and faster. I closed my eyes, gripping onto Russell as tight as I could. Nothing happened. When I opened my eyes, we were on the ground. Russell looked down at me and smirked. I snapped back into myself and pushed away from him, stumbling as my legs felt like jelly. His hand steadied me.

"I'm fine," I growled. The hand retreated, and a second later, Russell was flying back over the wall to pick up the next passenger. "Bastard," I muttered.

"So where do we start?" Violet asked once we were all gathered inside.

"The military base," Russell replied. "We have no idea where the pure-blood might be hiding, but we at least know where the General is likely to be. Maybe he can narrow down the search for us. We'll split up once we get there to cover more ground."

We agreed, and I was left with the task of guiding us to the academy. The streets were deserted, making it easy to navigate without raising suspicion. The vampires held back anyway, following from the shadows so as not to draw any attention to us. I kept my hood up and head down, in case anyone might recognise me. It didn't take long before we were stood outside the familiar white walls. We jumped over again, to my dismay, though at least it was a much smaller jump, and I made sure Violet was the one to carry me over.

"The General's office is upstairs in the main building," I said. "It should be empty by now, but there might be one or two squads still debriefing in the meeting rooms on the ground floor. The officer's living quarters are at the back of the compound, but General Marsten is known for working late."

"Anna, search their living quarters and gather any information from their officers. Violet, I want you to take your group and search the ground floor," Russell said. "But I want Mikhail with my group, to guide us to the General's office."

"Absolutely not," Violet said.

"No, he's right," I said. "They need someone who knows their way around."

"If it will make you feel better, you may choose another of your group to accompany us," Russell proposed. "And I will loan you Andre and Julia to make up your numbers."

"Daniel, you go with them," Violet said.

Daniel nodded and stepped forward, cracking his knuckles. He leaned in close to Russell. "Try anything funny, and you'll be pushing up daisies where you belong."

Russell grinned. "You misjudge me, wolf. This mission takes precedence over my personal plans."

"You'd better hope so," Daniel snarled.

I barged past them, getting sick of the macho confrontation, and began walking to the main building. Daniel followed quickly after me, sticking by my side, with the others in tow. I pointed out a small cluster of huts along the way, and Anna snuck off with her group to investigate. The rest of us entered the main building through the back door and split up into our two groups.

"Lead the way, Mikhail," Russell whispered, gesturing for me to take point. The halls were quiet, as expected. Still, I checked every corner, and we tiptoed down the corridors. Well, *I* tiptoed. The others had a slight supernatural advantage when it came to skulking in the dark.

Once upstairs, we turned right and followed the row of doors, to the one with General Marsten's name engraved on the brass plaque. A slither of light crept out from under the wooden door. I stood to one side, letting Russell and Daniel position themselves to enter first. Russell held up three fingers and began to count down. Two. I took a deep breath. One. Blood rushed through my head. Pounding. Zero. The door burst open. We poured into the room. Empty. An oil lamp was burning. Papers were scattered across the desk. A half-full glass of whiskey sat on a coaster.

"He was here recently," Daniel said, sniffing at the air.

"Looks like he left in a hurry," Russell muttered. "Can you track him?"

Daniel shrugged. "There's a lot of scents in this place."

"Leah, take Erik and Luke," Russell said. "See if you can track the scent."

"Gotcha, Boss." Leah took a deep sniff of the air, and then left the room, heading back towards the stairs. The two males followed behind her.

Daniel was sniffing at the air outside the room. "His scent is all over the place."

"We'll search the whole floor," Russell said. "If he's in this building, we will find him."

We backtracked first, heading to the end of the corridor. The lights were off in the first two rooms, and as expected, they were empty. The light was on in the next room. We burst into the room, and Russell sprinted across to the desk, muffling the surprised cry of a middle-aged man, who almost fell backward in his chair. I closed the door behind us.

"You're not going to scream," Russell said, staring into his eyes. "And you're going to answer my questions honestly. Do you understand?"

The man nodded, and Russell removed his hand. "Who are you?"

"Jack Alestra, finance secretary for the army," he replied, his voice devoid of any emotion. His eyes remained fixed on Russell.

"Good. Do you know where General Philip Marsten is?"

Jack shook his head.

"What do you know about the pure-blood vampires and Verloren?"

Jack's eyes widened. "The what vampires? I just do accounts," he said.

"Calm down, Jack," Russell whispered. Jack relaxed, slumping back in his chair. "You must be tired after a long day at work. Go home. You never saw us."

"I am pretty tired," Jack agreed. He picked up his briefcase from the floor and left the room as he was instructed. His face was blank as he passed me, as though there was no-one home upstairs.

'It's temporary,' Russell said, attempting to dispel my unease. I knew vampires could hypnotise people, but seeing it was a different thing altogether. I couldn't help but be reminded of the guards outside Marmagne, who wore that same vacant expression on their faces because of my own ability. And then there was the nagging voice at the back of my mind, wondering if Russell might resort to doing something similar to me, in order to force my cooperation.

'No,' the voice replied. *'It's more fun if you're a willing participant.'*

The sad thing was I believed him. Not because I thought he was an honest guy, but because I believed he was that sadistic. Taking away someone's free will would be too easy for him. He wanted to watch me suffer, until I finally broke and gave in to my darkness, and to him.

"Come on," Daniel said, nudging me. "There's still more rooms to check." I hadn't realised I was staring at Russell until I had to rip my gaze away from him.

The rest of the rooms were empty too, so we were no closer to finding General Marsten or the pure-blood. We met up with the others on the ground floor. No-one had found any clues.

"It would have to be somewhere with no windows, or underground," Russell said, thinking out loud. "Any ideas?" He looked at myself and Nate. We both shook our heads. "What about the other leaders? There must be more than just this General."

"Salvatore Lavielle," I said. "He's the leader of the Silver Dawn's council. There's five other members, but I don't recall ever having heard their names."

"And where would we find this Salvatore?" Violet asked.

I shrugged. "I've never actually seen him before. Come to think of it, I don't remember anyone ever seeing him. There was a rumour he lives in the church though."

"The church it is then," Russell said.

He split us up into two groups, the first consisting of Violet's group, myself included, and Russell, along with two of his vampires, Erik and Andre. The rest continued the search for General Marsten, while we made our way into the heart of the city. We skulked through the dark alleyways, drawing closer to the church, stopping outside the large, wooden doors. One of them was slightly ajar. The door knob and lock had been broken off.

"Something's not right," Violet said.

"I agree," said Russell. "Erik. Andre. Scout the church grounds. Look for anything suspicious or out of place."

They nodded and disappeared, leaving us to investigate inside. Despite living in Rachat for twenty years, there were only a handful of occasions when I had been to the church. There were a few times I went as a kid, when the old witch, who took over after Mrs. Rousseau, could be bothered to take us anywhere. During my teenage years, I was convinced there was no such thing as a God. I had no business being inside a church.

Both inside and out, the walls were a pure white. The stained-glass windows bathed the large open room in a myriad of colours as the moonlight hit them. Rows upon rows of pews filled the room, facing a raised platform, on which there was a font of holy water, a podium, and a large brass statue of the Virgin Mary behind an altar of candles. The flames flickered in the breeze that followed us in. At the far end of the room was a door. It was open, and like the front doors, its lock was broken off. Nearby, a red curtain lay on the floor that, judging by the rail and hooks above the door, had been used to conceal the passageway from sight.

Daniel sniffed at the air once, then twice. "Where do I know that smell from?" he asked.

"Probably your imagination, you daft mutt," Nate said.

"No, I swear I know that smell."

"Let's go check it out," I said. Violet and Sebastian agreed.

"I'll keep an eye on our friend," Nate said, following Russell to the back rooms. As we climbed the spiral stairs that lay beyond the door, I pulled my dagger from its sheath. There was a banging noise, like the opening and closing of doors.

We stopped at the next floor. The banging was definitely coming from this corridor. I peered out into the hallway and caught sight of a figure in black, working his way down the doors. He was looking for something, peering into each room, and then slamming the door shut. He paused in front of a window, looking out at the sky. The moon illuminated his short, blond hair. My heart stopped. I sheathed the knife and stepped out, walking slowly towards him. Sebastian grabbed my hand, but Violet took hold of his wrist and shook her head.

His head turned upon hearing me approach. I saw his hands go for the gun at his waist. I lowered my hood and his body froze. The lines of his face tightened. I saw the way his eyes sparkled in the moonlight. His smile twisted, like he wasn't sure whether to be happy or sad. He didn't move until I was stood right next to him.

"Mik," he whispered, letting out a ragged breath. "I'm so sorry."

I raised a hand to his face, and he rubbed his cheek against my palm. His cheek was wet. I reached up onto the balls of my feet and pressed my lips to his, but he made no effort to respond.

"I'm sorry," he said again.

"Why?"

"I should have believed you."

I looked him straight in the eye, taking his hands into mine. "I forgive you," I said. The first tear began its descent down my right cheek. "Please—"

My words were cut off by his lips crashing into me. His arms wrapped tight around me, pulling me as close to him as possible. The kiss was sloppy, and it was desperate. Our teeth clashed and our noses rubbed. We both fought for control, trying to devour each other. I had waited for so long to feel this again, and at the back of my mind, I wondered if Russell could feel it too. Would he come rushing up the stairs to stop it?

"I think that's enough for now, boys," Violet said. Ash froze. He looked up to see the others, who moved into the hallway. He pulled me behind him and began reaching for the gun at his waist. I grabbed at his hand. He looked at me, his brows furrowed and lips pressed tight together.

"They're the good guys," I said. His hand twitched in mine, and I could tell he wasn't sure. "You said you should have believed me before. Believe me now, please."

Ash's hand pulled back. He closed his eyes and drew in a sharp breath. "Oh God, Mik. I'm so sorry. I'm such an idiot."

"No," I whispered, holding his head against my shoulder. "You're not an idiot. I probably wouldn't have believed it either."

"No, you don't understand. They took Lucas."

"Is that why you're here?"

Ash nodded against me. He lifted his head to meet my eyes. "After I saw you that day, I couldn't shake the feeling that something was wrong. I wanted to believe you, but I couldn't. I started looking into a few things, and when Lucas caught me, he offered to help out. I was so desperate, I didn't know what to do."

"Did you find anything?"

"I was supposed to meet Lucas yesterday during lunch break. He told me had found something, but he didn't say what. He never showed up. I went to his dorm and the door to his room was wide open. The place was trashed. I thought maybe he'd been broken into, but one of the other guys said they saw the Silver Dawn ambush him and take him away. And it's my fault. I shouldn't have gotten him involved."

"It's not your fault," I said, stroking a hand on the back of his head.

"Yes, it is. I asked him to help. I'm supposed to be in charge of this squad. I'm supposed to look out for you guys. Well, I guess I failed at that. I managed to lose two members in one month."

"I'm sure he knew what he was getting himself into when he chose to help you," Violet said. "You can't place all the blame on yourself."

Ash looked over at Violet. I could see his reluctance in the way he looked at her. Violet may have looked human, but I'm sure he could tell she was undead.

"That's Violet," I said. "She took good care of me. You can trust her."

Ash pulled away from me and walked up to her. For a second, I wasn't sure what he might do. Maybe he blamed her for keeping me away from him, I thought. My fears were dissuaded when he extended a hand to her.

"Thank you, for looking after him," he said, trying to manage a smile.

"And this is Sebastian and Daniel," Violet said, gesturing to them. Ash gave them a quick nod.

"So you think your friend is in here somewhere?" Daniel asked.

Ash nodded. "We know he was dragged in here, but I can't feel him. He could be unconscious, or..." Ash's voice trailed off. "I don't know, something has felt off since I entered this place, and now my empathy is all screwed up."

"Could be *him*," Violet said.

"Okay, my turn," Ash said. He turned to me and placed his hands on my shoulders. "Why did you come back?"

I was dreading this bit. A drop of sweat trickled down my back. How was I supposed to tell him that we wanted to remove the city's leadership? "There's something evil inside the city," I started.

"A pure-blooded vampire," Violet added. She gave a brief overview of what a pure-blood was, and why we believed there was one in Rachat.

"Shit," Ash muttered. "Maybe that's what Lucas found."

"Do you–" I started to say, but my words were cut off by a searing pain inside my head, threatening to burst outward. The others were talking to me, but I couldn't hear them over the ringing that drowned out everything else. I covered my ears, hoping it might muffle the sound, but it did nothing. Amidst the pain and the ringing, I saw a door and a staircase, leading down into some tunnels. Everything was fuzzy, like static. It felt as if something was burning its way through my brain from the inside out. And then there was one last image. Nate stood smiling proudly.

"Russell."

Chapter 25

"What's wrong with him?" Ash yelled. He crouched next to me, a hand placed on my shoulder.

"Russell," I said. The ringing had died down, leaving only a throbbing headache.

"Who's Russell?"

"A vampire who coerced Mik into sharing a blood bond with him," Violet said. "It would appear something bad has happened to him."

"He showed me a basement and some tunnels. Nate's there with him."

"You don't think Nate offed him, do you?" Daniel asked.

I nodded and stood up. "I'm fine," I told Ash, who was watching me worriedly and trying to steady me.

"We need to find this basement," said Violet.

"I'm coming with you," Ash said.

"What about Lucas?" I asked.

"Kat and Brad will find him. I'm not leaving you again. Especially not if you're going to look for this Russell."

"Then let's go," Violet said. "We'll need all the help we can get."

We went downstairs, back into the main room. Erik and Andre were there.

"Look what we found," said Andre. He and Erik pointed to a man, who sat expressionless on one of the pews.

"That's General Marsten," Ash said, surprised.

"He was skulking about in the bushes," Erik said, his eyes wandering over us. "Where's Russell?"

"We're just going to find him," Violet said, not bothering to mention that he might be dead or seriously injured. "Keep an eye on the General until we return."

They nodded and went to stand by the General's side. Daniel led us to one of the back rooms. A bookcase was pulled away from the wall, revealing the door and staircase I had seen in my vision. Daniel covered his nose and wafted the air.

"Yeah, this is definitely the way," he said. "Smells like someone got lit up good."

"That idiot," Violet growled. "He may have signed our death warrants."

Ash looked at me and opened his mouth. I shook my head and mouthed the word 'later'.

The stairs were narrow, leaving only enough room for one person at a time. I went down first, with Ash following close behind. There were no lights on the stairs, and soon we were enveloped by darkness. I pulled out my flashlight and shone it straight ahead. The stairs turned a right angle, and after turning the corner we could see a faint light in the distance. Upon reaching the bottom, we found ourselves in a small room, lined with oil lamps.

We went through several similar rooms, the occasional image appearing to guide us in the right direction. The images were getting fainter each time. Russell probably didn't have much time left. I should have been happy he was in danger of dying, but I couldn't help feel there was something wrong about the whole thing. What if Violet was right, and Nate had sentenced them to death?

Ash stuck close to me, his free hand resting on my shoulder, squeezing gently. His other hand held a firm grip on his gun. I could smell the burning as well now. The smell clung to my nostrils, a mix of burned meat and a metallic, coppery smell. Ash coughed behind me. Despite the smell, we pushed on through a long narrow tunnel. The path started to slope downward into the darkness. At the end of the tunnel was another flicker of light. There was no doubt about it now. Russell was in the next room.

We stopped at the doorway and peered into the room. A blackened body lay to one side. Russell. He didn't move, but I knew he was still there. I could feel a slight pull, an urge to go to him. There was no voice in my head now, and there were no images, just the tiniest of sparks that let me know there was still a part of him in there. Other than the body, the room was empty. Ash and I stepped out. I was about to head for Russell, when a blast of heat slammed into my back, accompanied by a blazing roar and the sound of Violet screaming. The doorway was blocked off by a wall of fire. The large metal door that had been wide open slammed shut. I turned back to the door and tried to pull at it. It showed no signs of moving.

"Violet," I shouted, banging on the door with my fists.

"We're fine," Daniel replied. "The fire caught Violet's arm, but there's no real damage. It'll heal quick."

"The door won't open," I said.

"Stand back," Daniel shouted. We moved away from the door and there was a loud bang, followed by some cursing. "Jesus! Who the hell makes a door out of silver?"

"Someone who wants to keep a vampire or werewolf out," said Violet.

"Or keep something in," I added. "So what now?"

"We'll find a way through," Violet said. "Try and find Nate, but don't do anything stupid."

"Okay. What should I do with Russell?" There was no answer.

"Is he still alive?" Ash asked. "He looks pretty toasted to me."

"Yeah, he's still in there. He probably won't be able to heal that without a lot of blood though."

"What do we do with him?"

"Good question," I mumbled. I wanted to be free of him, but I wasn't sure if I could let him die. How much of that was because of the bond, I wasn't sure.

"You–" Ash started. I looked up to see Nate appear from the other exit, clapping his hands.

"Congratulations," he said. "You've made it through to the final stage of this little game."

"What are you going on about?" I asked.

"You'll find out soon enough." Nate chuckled. He gestured to Russell. "Did you like my present to you, Mik? I promised I would free you from him, didn't I?"

"You didn't do a very good job," Ash said. "He's still alive."

"Oh?" Nate held out his hand. A stream of fire leaped from him to the body, which erupted in flames. The ringing and screeching in my head started again. It felt as though my head would explode. I clutched the sides of my head, doubling over in pain, but just as suddenly, the pain stopped. He was dead. Truly dead this time. "How about now?"

I looked up at Ash in disbelief. He must have known Nate would finish off Russell. And yet, he had taunted Nate into doing it without hesitation.

"I was planning on finishing him off myself," Ash said. "I don't know what happened between the two of you, but I would've killed him to free you."

"But you didn't," Nate said. "I did." He made it sound like a competition.

"Why?" I asked. "There had to be another way. What if he wasn't bluffing? Violet, Daniel and Sebastian might be killed because of this."

"Like I care about them," Nate said, laughing. "They were a means to an end. But you... you're different. We have a special connection, you know?"

Ash's body tensed next to me.

"No, we don't," I said. I took a deep breath and held it, before letting it out. "I didn't want to tell you, but it was my ability that made you develop feelings for me."

"You think I didn't already figure that out? Verloren knows a great deal about the nature of your ability. But the why isn't important anymore. All that matters is that I love you, Mik."

"No," Ash shouted. "I love him."

"You have a funny way of showing it. Do you even know how much pain you've caused him? I was the one who comforted him when he'd lost all hope. I was the one who was there for him."

"That's not fair," Ash said, his fists clenching. "I've been worried sick about him every single day."

"That's enough, Ash," I said, taking hold of his hand. "I know you believed you were doing the right thing, so don't let him taunt you."

"I wouldn't have abandoned you, Mik. I would have believed you. Can't you see that he's not right for you? Don't you remember how much he hurt you? You told me you didn't want to live anymore."

"Is that true?" Ash asked, turning me to face him.

I hung my head. "I thought it was over between us. I couldn't bear the pain, and I just..."

"I'm sorry." His hand cupped my chin, bringing my gaze up to meet him. "I never meant to hurt you like that."

"I know, but we have more important problems right now." I turned back to Nate. "Why are you doing this?"

"Power. Immortality. Cliché, I know. You could have that too, Mik. Verloren would be willing to give you a second life as well. We could spend eternity together. Think of it as a reward for helping us advance our plans."

"I'd never help you," I snapped.

Nate laughed. "But you already have. Why do you think we left you alive? Thanks to you, we now have what we need to crush Aldar."

"How?" I gasped. "And why me? You were already in Aldar!

Why did you need me?" I shouted.

"All in due time," Nate replied.

I shook my head in disbelief. "I trusted you. How could you do this, Nate? What about Shannon? They killed your twin sister, and you're teaming up with them."

Nate burst into laughter. "They didn't kill her. *I* did. I tried getting her to join Verloren in his war against the vampires. We could have made a great team, but the stupid bitch said she was going to expose him. So I killed her. Couldn't have her messing up my plans."

"You sick fuck," Ash yelled. "You killed your own twin?" Ash pointed his gun at Nate. "I didn't wanna have to do this, but I think it's clear you're no longer human."

"No fair, you've got a gun. How about we even the odds? Fire versus ice, winner takes all." Nate's eyes fixated on me when he said 'all'.

Ash smirked. "Fair enough. I don't need a gun to deal with scum like you." He clicked the gun's safety on and handed it to me. "I'll be fine," he said, before I could say anything. "Besides, we'll probably need the bullets for this pure-blood anyway."

"You don't have to fight him alone."

Ash looked at me, his face deadly serious. "If you wanna help, then stand back. I don't want you getting caught in the crossfire."

"No. Let me help. You don't have to do this."

"Yes, I do," Ash replied, smiling. "Male pride and all that. Now stand back."

"Fine," I conceded. "But if you die, I'll never forgive you."

Ash laughed. I went to step back but his hand caught mine and he pulled me into him. Our lips came together. I opened up eagerly as his tongue pressed into me.

"That's right." Nate chuckled. "Say your goodbyes, because you won't get another chance. The next time you see him, he'll be nothing more than a charred husk. And then we can be together, forever."

I pulled back from Ash to scowl at Nate. "I will never love you.

How could I, after everything you've done? I thought you were my friend, and you betrayed me. And if you hurt Ash, I promise I will kill you."

Nate smiled. "You say you made me fall in love with you. I'll just have Verloren do the same to you. It seems only right, don't you think? You forced me to love you, and then you deny my feelings. Do you know how that feels?"

"That was an accident," I yelled. "I'd take it back if I could."

"But you can't. And you should have to pay the consequences, an eye for an eye."

"You first," I said. "For Shannon."

Nate shrugged. "It had to be done. Now, why don't you be a good boy and go stand over there?" He pointed to the doorway behind him. "I'd hate for you to get caught in the blast."

I looked over at Ash and he nodded. As I passed Nate, I paused. "Just tell me one thing. All those times you kept me going, you gave me a reason to fight against the Silver Dawn. Why?"

"To get you to Aldar and back," Nate replied. "That was my job."

Nate took hold of my hand and pulled me towards him. His hand on the back of my head forced our lips together. I struggled against him, pushing my hands against his chest. I could hear Ash screaming. Nate's tongue pushed between my lips. I stopped struggling and reached down inside of me, flinging my magic at him. Nate pulled back, his hand going to his face. A fine line of blood decorated his cheek.

"Worth it," he said, a lop-sided grin stretched across his face.

The taste of his lips turned my stomach and made my blood boil. I jerked back from him and spat on the floor. Looking into his eyes, I could see there was nothing left of the Nate I had known. His eyes were hollow, devoid of anything redeeming.

"See you soon, Mik."

"Not if I can help it," Ash said. Every hair on the back of my neck and arms stood on end. My breath formed a dense mist in front of me. A shudder ran up my entire body. "Mik, go. Now!"

I stepped back towards the doorway, unable to take my eyes from Ash. His chest heaved, fists clenched and shaking. He stared at Nate with such intensity, his hatred seeping out and filling the room. My mouth went dry as I reached the corridor. I had never seen Ash like this before. Nate looked over his shoulder and gave me one last crooked smile as a wall of flames leaped up, forcing me back, stumbling into the corridor. I shielded my eyes from the burning light.

"Ash," I yelled over the roar of flames. There was no reply. Had I made a mistake? Should I have left him to fight Nate alone? A heavy weight in my chest seemed to force the air from me, making it difficult to breathe. I shouldn't have given in to their requests. Fire melts ice. Surely, Ash didn't stand a chance.

"Ash!"

I contemplated charging through the fire, but even a few steps back I could feel the unbearable heat beating against my skin. There was a loud crash, followed by the sound of ice shattering. I was stuck, unable to help, or even see.

'Come to me,' a deep voice rumbled down the corridor. I looked behind me and clicked the safety off the gun. I aimed down the hallway with my right hand, holding the flashlight in my left.

'Come,' the voice said again. I was torn between my curiosity and my worry for Ash. Turning back to the fire, it was clear there was nothing I could do, short of diving through the flames and probably getting myself killed. But if I followed this voice, maybe I would find Verloren. If I could take him out, then there would be no need for Nate and Ash to fight to the death. I could save them both. Even then it sounded like a stupid idea, but it was the only plan I had.

I started cautiously down the corridor, pausing to peer around a corner. At the end was another large room. Torches flickered on the walls. An elderly man sat at the back, on what appeared to be a large throne. His hair was short and grey, thinning on top. He had dark eyes, set amidst a mass of wrinkles and long, bushy eyebrows. In the dim light I saw another body by his side, crouched down on the ground. The flickering light from the torches danced across his naked skin. Ropes bound his wrists and ankles. His body trembled.

"And finally we meet," the old man said. There was no doubt he was the owner of the voice that had called to me.

"Who are you?" I asked, crouching and setting the flashlight on the floor. My hands shook. I steadied my aim with both hands.

"I am known by many names," he replied. "Verloren, Jules, Salvatore. All of these are names you have no doubt heard before." Verloren, I was expecting, but not the other two. My heart began to race. If he were to be believed, then he wasn't working with the Silver Dawn. He *was* the Silver Dawn.

He kneeled by the body at his side, and grabbed a handful of hair, dragging the man to his knees. The man panicked, screaming and thrashing. Verloren leaned in to whisper something and the body went slack. He bent the man's neck back and drew a long nail across his throat. My eyes widened. Verloren's mouth lunged at the wound, blood gushing out. He slurped loudly, sucking the body dry before letting it fall to the floor. I should have shot him there, but I was hesitating. There were so many questions I wanted to ask, questions I might never have another chance to find the answer to.

"Oh, where are my manners?" Verloren turned his blood-smeared face to me. "Did you want some?"

I shook my head, grimacing. "What do you want from me?"

"Straight to business. I like that," he said. "I merely want the coordinates of Aldar from you."

I laughed. "And what makes you think I'd know such a thing? Do I look like some kind of navigation device to you?"

"Actually," Verloren started. He picked up a small device from the arm of his chair and moved to my side in a flash. He tilted my head to one side, running the device along the side of my neck. "You were just the vessel."

The device beeped several times. Verloren let go of me and disappeared. I looked around the room in confusion, until I spotted him attaching the device to a piece of machinery at one side of the room. The lights on the panel and monitor flashed to life.

"Excellent." Verloren chuckled. "You see, last year we discovered a nuclear missile in an old bunker. I planned to use it to wipe out Aldar in one swift strike, but without the coordinates, which you have so graciously provided, the missile was useless."

"Why me?" I screamed. "You already had Nate out there."

"It would have been too risky to have Nathaniel return and have the device implanted," Verloren said. "I'll admit, you weren't exactly first choice, but we couldn't let you continue poking your nose into the origin of your abilities. Two birds with one stone, as they say."

"And where did my ability come from?"

Verloren punched some more buttons on the panel. "I suppose there is no harm in telling you now. After all, you'll be joining me soon enough. Your abilities come from my blood. I had some of it injected into unborn children. You and your friends are the results of those experiments."

"Why?"

"To create my own supernatural army, unbound by the shackles of the sun. Humans are such weak, fragile creatures. I gave you some of my power so you might stand up against those despicable beings that call themselves vampires. Really, you should be thanking me."

"So we're just toys to you? Is that it?"

"Your kind is nothing more than walking blood bags to me," Verloren spat. "We gave your people the gift of immortality in order to serve us. And how were we repaid? By killing most of my family. I watched as my brothers and sisters died in front of my eyes. Were it not for the fact that I need human blood to survive, I would have killed you all with the plague."

"Then the plague was you?"

Verloren cackled. "Yes, that was the first stage of my plan to usher in a new world. You humans were content to welcome the so-called vampires into your society. I had to make you fear them, and so I founded the Silver Dawn and created the false apocalypse."

"How does that help?" I snapped. "What could you possibly gain by wiping out most of the human race?"

"It's simple," Verloren replied. "It was like flicking the reset switch on this pathetic world. And once I wipe out Aldar, I will control what's left of your pitiful race. I can make you fight my war for me. Over time, Rachat will grow, and we will systematically wipe the imposters from the face of the Earth. Then they will slowly forget vampires ever existed, and we can go back to the life we once had, living in secret, able to do as we please."

"But that could take centuries."

"I'm not exactly going anywhere." Verloren laughed. "I have all the–"

He froze, before letting out a shrill cry, unlike anything I ever heard before. There are no words to describe the exact sound. It pulsed and resonated, echoing off the walls. Verloren gasped, clutching at his head. I had heard enough. I aimed the gun at his head and fired three times. Verloren jerked back as the bullets hit him, but he didn't go down. I fired again and again. I hit his head and his chest, over and over, until I was pulling the trigger and nothing happened. I watched in horror as the skin around the wounds began to flow and quiver, not unlike when I had seen Daniel change forms.

His skin began to darken, turning a sickly shade of brown, accompanied by the cracking and popping of bones as Verloren seemed to grow until he towered at least a foot above me. His face grew outward. Two slanted red eyes stared back at me. His mouth opened both horizontally and vertically, filled with row upon row of tiny, sharp fangs. Only two small holes were left where his nose once was. The dark robe he was wearing fell to the ground in tatters. His skin was leathery, almost scaly. Down the length of his arms were glistening barbs, ending in three claws on the back of his hands. His large feet had long, hooked toes. Marcus had been right. Demonic was definitely the right word.

"Your bullets are not enough to kill me," Verloren hissed. His voice retained the high-pitched pulsing quality of his earlier cry.

"Nathaniel is no more, but you and your friend will soon take his place."

I would have let out a sigh, if my knees hadn't been threatening to give way beneath me. If Nate was dead, then Ash had won. Or, at least, that's what I was hoping. Verloren sidestepped into the centre of the room, straightening out his body. The bones in his limbs moved in a way that was completely unnatural, like he had joints in the strangest of places.

"You tremble in my presence. Do you now understand the extent of my power?"

I couldn't move. My legs refused to move. My arms refused to move. Verloren let out a hideous laugh that sent violent shivers down my spine.

"So," Ash's voice came from behind me. "That's a pure-blood." I turned my head. Beads of sweat dripped from Ash's forehead. His chest rose and fell in short, sharp movements. "I can see why you've been in hiding all this time. You're fucking ugly."

"Interesting," Verloren said. "You stand before me in your weakened state and yet you show no fear, but I can feel it inside of you. You are terrified. What can two humans hope to do against an immortal being such as I?"

"You underestimate us," Ash said. He stood next to me, gripping my hand. His touch was like a wave of warmth that washed over me, helping to fight back the paralysing fear.

"No. It would appear I overestimated your intelligence," Verloren growled. He rushed at us, raising a clawed hand. His speed had decreased, I noted, but he was still terribly fast. Before we could react, he swung at Ash, knocking him to one side as if he were nothing more than a rag doll. Ash grunted as his body hit the hard stone floor.

Verloren turned to me. I stepped back and reached for my magic, lashing out at him. The skin on his arm tore, the edges seeming to bubble as the wound knitted itself back together. The edges of his mouth quivered with amusement.

"Did you think such weak magic would work against me?" he asked. "You are a fool."

His hand shot out, pinning me to the wall by my throat. The hinges of his jaw opened, revealing a long, black tongue that traced the line of my neck. I shuddered under its icy touch. He leaned his head forward, and then paused. Verloren let out another shrill cry, coating my face in saliva as the edges of his mouth began to freeze.

"Get your ugly face away from him," Ash yelled.

Verloren let go of my throat, leaving me gasping for air. He smashed at the ice, shattering his own jaw. Ash's eyes widened as we watched the bone reform. Muscle and skin wove itself over the bone in a matter of seconds, until his face was once again complete.

"You will pay for your transgression." He charged at Ash, who managed to dive out of the way, only to be caught by a clawed hand. Verloren gripped at his throat, lifting him up into the air. Ash held onto the scaly arm, encasing it in ice, before bringing a fist up and smashing it to pieces. Verloren screamed and quickly grabbed hold of Ash with his other hand.

"Mik," Ash said, choking.

I unsheathed my knife and ran to Verloren. His other arm was still reforming. I jumped, managing to drive the blade into his skull. Verloren screamed and hissed. He flailed about, trying to shake me while keeping his hold on Ash. He grabbed me with his newly reformed arm and threw me to the floor. The barbs on his arm caught against my shoulder. A burning pain shot through me as they tore into my skin and I landed on my back, the cold stone floor knocking the wind out of me.

I clutched my shoulder as I sat up, my hand coated in warm blood. Ash was attempting to freeze Verloren's arm again. His feet were dangling, flailing wildly. Verloren lifted his free hand up and swung it downward. Ash screamed, the claws tearing down his chest and stomach. I watched in horror as blood arced out from the tips of Verloren's claws. He discarded Ash to one side, and his sharp, red eyes turned to me once more.

I watched Ash struggle to push himself up onto his hands and knees. He collapsed back onto the ground. My throat closed up on me. My heart beat feverishly, drowning out all other noise as the blood raced through my head. It was my fault, I thought. I shouldn't have given in and wandered off on my own. If I hadn't, then Ash wouldn't have come looking for me. I should have waited for Violet and Daniel.

Verloren stepped forward. Tears rolled down my cheeks. "No," I said, the word barely escaping my lips. This couldn't be happening. The pain swelled inside of me, threatening to burst out. I let out a piercing, guttural scream that made even Verloren pause for a moment. All of my pain flew out, slashing at Verloren. He staggered back, laughing. His frozen arm fell to pieces, struggling to reform as my magic hacked at the incomplete bones.

"Your efforts are futile," he said. "In the end, it will all be for naught."

I screamed again, feeling the energy drain from me in one last violent burst. The second of Verloren's arms fell to the floor, disintegrating into a pile of ash. My magic was fading, and his wounds beginning to heal. A deafening roar echoed through the halls, followed by the sound of running footsteps.

A blur of a figure leaped across the room, knocking Verloren onto his back. There was a gut-wrenching cry as something was thrown across the room, landing next to me. I glanced down at it, struggling to regain my breath. Through my watery vision I saw Verloren's tongue, wriggling helplessly on the floor. If I had had the energy, I would have jumped up and away. The thrashing tongue came to a stop, and it went the way of his arm, becoming nothing more than a mound of ash.

Another blur entered the room and stopped in front of me. Violet. She looked down at me, and seeing that I wasn't gravely injured, rushed off to assist the furred humanoid, who was tearing into Verloren. Screams echoed off the walls as claws and teeth dug into him, ripping at his flesh.

I managed to push myself to my feet. The pain in my shoulder was gone, replaced by a tingling numbness. I clutched at it and hobbled over to Ash. He lay face-down in a puddle of blood, groaning and wincing. I helped him roll over onto his back. His stomach was a mess of torn flesh and blood. My heart jumped into my mouth. Blood was still seeping out. I tried to rip the fabric of his top so I could have something to press against the wound, but the material was too tough, and I didn't have the energy left. Sebastian kneeled down next to me. He pulled his thick jumper up and ripped the vest from underneath. He pressed it firmly to Ash's stomach.

"You're gonna be fine," I told him, my tears dripping down onto his face.

Ash shook his head. "It's too late."

"No. You can't leave me, not now."

"Sorry. I guess I'll have to break that promise." Ash's eyelids began to close, his head lolling to one side.

"No, stay awake." I took hold of his head, and his eyes opened ever so slightly.

"Mik, I love you," he said, his voice nothing more than a whisper.

"I love you too," I said. "You can't die. What am I supposed to do without you?"

In the back of my mind I registered that the fighting had stopped. Daniel was crouched down at my side, naked. A hand rested lightly on my back.

"Promise me..." Ash's voice trailed off.

"What?" I asked, leaning in closer.

"Live... for me," he said, his voice getting quieter with every word. His eyes closed again.

"Ash?" I shook his shoulders. "No, stay with me." I couldn't see any more because of the tears. "ASH!" I screamed.

Daniel held me in his arms as I wailed and cried out to Ash. He carried me out of the room, and I struggled against him, wanting to stay at Ash's side. He couldn't be dead. He just couldn't. I cried until my throat was dry and sore, and still the tears kept coming. My eyes stung. I cried until there was nothing left, and exhaustion caught up with me. And then I was asleep, alone once more in the darkness.

Chapter 26

I never did like funerals. Now I hated them even more. There was
only a small gathering at the cemetery; a few friends, his parents and
his brother. The grave was dug close to the ruined church, which was
decorated in all manner of graffiti.

In the days after Verloren's death, the vampires carried out their
plan to have General Marsten, and the other leading officials,
renounce the Silver Dawn, and tell the citizens of Rachat the truth.
The city went into chaos. Hordes of people stormed the church,
burning the insides and vandalising the walls. The mobs went out of
control. General Marsten and Principal Wilkes were among two of
the casualties. Their bodies were defiled and mutilated until they
were unrecognisable. I had sat watching from the top floor of the
academy, overlooking the parade ground as the speech was given. I
saw the looks of anger on the crowd's faces as they rushed the stage.
My only regret is I hadn't been able to join in.

Even now, three days later, things weren't fully under control.
Sergeant Locke, along with several of the other officers, managed to
rally most of the cadets and soldiers after the initial outburst. They

worked day and night, attempting to restore some semblance of order.

As for the missile, well, there were no sightings of anything being fired up into the sky. We assumed Verloren kept it hidden, and it hadn't been ready to launch immediately.

The sun was beginning to set as we carried the coffin and set it down next to the grave, which Brad himself dug earlier that day. It took all my courage to take one final look inside and say goodbye. It looked surreal, as though I was looking at the face of a different person. His skin was ghostly pale and sickly. His hair was straw-like and flat. There was no more sparkle in his eyes. He was gaunt and thin. Katiya burst into tears beside me. I looked up at the orange-tinted sky and wondered where Ash was now. Would he blame me for what happened? I know I did.

Glancing back into the coffin, I felt an overbearing weight pressing down on my shoulders. It was because of me that Ash and the others got involved in all this. It was because of my selfishness, my need to try and convince Ash to leave Rachat, that he and Lucas had tried to uncover the truth. If I had just left, then maybe they wouldn't have been in the church that night. And I wouldn't be standing over the coffin of a dead friend.

Once we had all viewed the body, the family began their eulogies. His Mom recalled a cheeky, brash teenager who was always up to some kind of mischief. She struggled to retain her composure, slowly breaking down as she went on, and eventually ending in a fit of sobs. Her son led her to one side as her husband began his speech. He talked about the time he built a go-kart with his son. He mentioned how proud he was that his eldest had joined the army, and how he regretted initially pushing him away because of his ability. Last was the brother. He talked of his admiration for his older sibling, who always looked out for him, and taught him so much over the years. His voice broke several times as he fought back the tears, but he bravely kept going.

The father was about to close the lid of the coffin when I stepped forward. These people knew nothing of why he died and I couldn't allow that. I addressed his parents directly.

"Your son was a good friend to me," I said. "He died honourably, trying to search for the truth. You should both be very proud of him."

The mother burst into tears. "Thank you," his father whispered.

The coffin was lowered into the ground and we each took a handful of dirt and threw it in, saying our final goodbyes. Brad picked up the shovel and began filling in the hole. The parents thanked him for helping out. "It's the least I could do," he said, wiping at his eyes.

Over in the distance, behind a row of trees, I spotted Violet, Daniel and Sebastian. They were having a funeral of their own, for Nate. I wandered up to them, and they each gave me a long hug. Personally, I couldn't understand why they would choose to give him a funeral. In my eyes, he was nothing but a traitor.

"It's the right thing to do," Daniel said. "We had to give him a proper burial."

"Despite everything, we have still lost a friend," said Violet. Sebastian held her tightly, planting a quick kiss on her forehead.

*****

That night, I lay silently on the bed I had shared with Ash, staring at the ceiling. I wondered what would happen now. Would the people of Rachat choose to move in with the vampires? Would they even accept the vampires, despite learning the truth behind the plague? My mind was made up. I was going back to Aldar with Violet. Rachat held only a few good memories for me, and far more than its share of bad ones. In Aldar, I could start anew.

There was a knock at the door. I didn't answer it. The knocking came again, louder. Still, I didn't move. I sighed and sat up when the knocking threatened to break down the door.

"What do you want?" I snapped as I swung the door open.

A figure in a black cloak stood before me, a hood pulled loosely over his head. He smiled at me, flashing a pearly set of teeth, complete with fangs.

"Ash."

Daniel A. Kaine

COMING WINTER 2012

ORIGIN OF DARKNESS
DAEVA: BOOK TWO

THE PAST ALWAYS CATCHES UP WITH YOU.

ABOUT THE AUTHOR

Daniel Alexander Kaine was born in 1985, in good old rainy England. When he isn't writing, he can often be found curled up with a good book. He enjoys canoeing and bowling, though his skill in both is questionable. Daniel hopes one day to become a werepanther, and invent chocolate that doesn't make you fat.

You can contact him online at: http://danielakaine.com